The Games We Play
Book Two

Little Bird, Big Sky

Copyright © 2022 by Jacquelyn M. Phillips

Cover art by AstonD of 99Designs

A Lady and Her Pen

Jmphillips0009@gmail.com

This is a work of fiction. Names, characters, businesses, places, events and incidents are either the products of the author's imagination or used in a fictitious manner. Any resemblance to actual persons, living or dead, or actual events is purely coincidental.

Printed in the United States of America

ISBN-13: 979-8-9873220-0-0

First Edition

Little Bird, Big Sky

Book Two of the Games We Play Series

Written by Jacquelyn Phillips

For Kelsey
So, maybe it wasn't supposed to be the forever kind of
love. But it was love, initially.

Table Of Contents

Chapter One

"DON'T YOU KNOW you're not supposed to shit where you eat?"

I was sitting in my car in the Sea World employee parking lot, the phone sitting in my lap, my sister's voice booming through the phone's small speaker. "Why is that even a saying? It makes no sense."

"It's a saying because dating someone you work with can leave a *real bad* taste in your mouth. *Especially* if you break up and are forced to work together because the job market is tough right now and searching for a new job sucks." Lucy's voice was angelic and calming to everyone except for me. Whenever I told people my sister's voice reminded me of cat claws digging into a couch, they called me crazy, often commenting that her patients were so lucky to have that voice delivering bad news to them.

"This is different," I argued, checking my foundation one last time in the mirror of my sun visor. I hated my rosy cheeks and always put a little extra layer of foundation on to try to cover them as best as I possibly could. "We're not working in the same restaurant — not even on the same side of the park! And," I continued before she could interrupt me. "We started dating *before* working together. That saying only applies when you start dating *after* you've already been working together."

"You can try to justify it anyway you want, but I hope you're ready to eat next to a big ol' pile of dog crap." Lucy snorted. "I guarantee you it'll take him one week to make some excuse to walk past you just to check up on you and see what you're doing." She paused, probably taking a sip from some fancy cocktail while lounging in her air-conditioned living room on the plush blue couch that somehow had zero stains on it even though they had my toddler niece running around the house. "And what about lunch? Is he gonna want to sit next to you? Won't that take away from you getting to know your coworkers better? Work should be where you escape needing to give your partner love and attention. It's usually a nice break that gives the relationship a chance to *breathe*." I could hear my niece, Hannah, spouting nonsense alongside the television in the background. "When you come running to me because he's accusing you of cheating on him with one of your coworkers because he saw you talking to some hunky whale trainer, you better expect me to slap you in the face with 'I told you so.'"

My stomach flipped over, the protein bar I'd eaten while driving suddenly sitting like cement in my belly. "He'd have every right to accuse me of that," I whispered. "I don't exactly have the greatest track record."

"So you thought you were in love with Lamont. You eventually figured it out."

"That doesn't make it right, Lucy."

She sighed so loudly I had to look over my shoulder to make sure she wasn't actually sitting in the back seat. "Roxanne, you seriously need to get over it. You didn't sleep with him in Vegas. You chose to be loyal to Zach. And the idiot has *no idea* you even laid eyes on another man, let alone have engaged in sexual relations throughout the course of your relationship. It took you a while to figure things out, but you did. Give yourself a little bit of credit."

I closed my sun visor and turned up the air conditioning suddenly worried the sweat on my back was going to stain my shirt. "You're not helping. I'm already nervous as it is." I breathed in deeply through my nose and exhaled through my mouth. "And Zach's not an idiot — except for trusting me."

Hannah's giggles in the background made me smile even though I could practically see my sister rolling her beautiful green eyes through the phone. "You are *so* melodramatic," Lucy said, exasperated. "You *chose* him over Lamont. Don't remain in this relationship as some penance for making a mistake — actually, it wasn't even a mistake. You learned through trial and error and you came to your senses. Be proud of yourself for being able to do that much." She took another sip of whatever fruity drink I suddenly wish I had in my hands to calm my nerves. "And don't get this job because you're hoping it'll mend some fissure torn between you and Zach."

I turned off the car's ignition and opened the driver door, placing my black wedges on the asphalt. "That's not why I want this job," I said placing the phone on the car's roof so I could grab my purse off the passenger seat. "I want this job because I hate what I'm doing now. I don't want to bus tables for ungrateful people anymore and I don't want to be stuck behind a cash register having to push people to try to buy a soda. Zach said the servers here make *phenomenal* tips. And I'll get to see killer whales every day! How cool would that be?"

"I can't believe you *want* to wait tables," Lucy said. "I only did that for a year and I hated it." She bit into something crunchy now – probably some sort of fancy crostini on some ridiculous charcuterie board she made for herself to snack on – continuing to chew as she spoke. "Besides, you're super awkward with strangers.

I think that cash register at least gave you a buffer to separate yourself from the customers just enough to make you feel less awkward. How are you supposed to serve people every day without being able to hide behind a wall? Or a tray?"

I closed my door, slung my purse over my shoulder and turned the phone off speaker before pressing it to my ear. "Well, you hate a lot of things I love so I'm sure this will be a great fit for me." I readjusted the phone, not liking how sweat was beginning to form near my ears. "Besides, working in a restaurant has helped me get out of my comfort zone! I think I'm actually good at making small talk with strangers now. I don't only ask about the weather, which is huge in my opinion."

Lucy chuckled. "Think you could score me some park tickets? Me and Roger would love to take Hannah."

I smiled, thinking of my little niece full of wide-eyed wonderment watching a Sea Lion slide across a stage. "Lucy, I don't even have the job yet."

"You'll get it. It's a serving position. One of those whales in the tank could probably do a better job."

"Thanks for the vote of confidence," I mumbled. "I'll let you know how the interview goes once it's over."

"Before you hang up," she interjected, sounding like she popped an olive or a dried apricot into her mouth. Hannah's high-pitched giggles echoed through my ear drum, causing me to momentarily pull the phone away. "Are you wearing your engagement ring?"

My heart rate increased, the tips of my fingers beginning to tingle. "Of course," I squeaked.

"Well, I think you should take it off," she suggested, almost sounding kind. "Not because I think it's better to pretend to be single for your interview, but because there's something about that ring that makes you a little crazy." She paused, searching for the right words. "You're more *you* when you're not wearing it. It's like it sucks the confidence right out of you and makes you uncomfortable or something. Just – be yourself and I'm sure you'll get the job."

Although it broke my heart to admit it, my sister was right. Most women wanted to show off their engagement ring to everyone – even strangers who knew nothing about your life and could probably care less. I wished I'd never accepted it in the first place. I slid off the small gold band with the tiny diamond my friends and family constantly teased me about and dropped it into my purse, watching it drop to the bottom to mingle with loose change and cat fur.

"Did you just say something encouraging?" I asked playfully, the Human Resources building looming in front of me.

"All I'm saying is that anyone can be a server. You just need to believe in yourself once in a while." She took another bite of something crunchy. "And you better get used to eating next to a big pile of shit because that's what you're about to do daily."

I shook my head. "This will be good for me."

She laughed, again making my stomach twist and turn. "When your relationship with Zach completely falls apart because he catches you flirting with some stud of an animal trainer, I'm gonna be the first to laugh."

#

"MISS VAUGHN," THE Indian man began. His baby blue shirt was in desperate need of ironing, but the color looked nice against his darker skin. "You were born and raised here in San Diego but left for a couple years to attend college at—" He paused, readjusted his rectangular bifocals, and squinted at my application. "Sonoma State University."

I nodded, doing my best to hide how nervous I was. "That's correct, Sir. I wanted to see if Northern California was a good fit for me." My hands were folded in my lap, the urge to bounce my leg up and down gnawing at me.

The man's almost black eyes lingered on my chest just long enough for me to wonder how he managed to land a job in the human resources department. "Why did you come back?"

The conversation I'd just had with Lucy swirled through my mind. *Because I had to run away from the boy I loved to be with the boy who loves me,* I thought. "Well, I want to graduate in four years and with all of the staffing cuts, it wasn't gonna happen in a small school like that," I said instead. When he stared at me silently, I wiped my hands on my thighs and forced myself to continue. "And— well—and I want to get into the Master of Fine Arts program at San Diego State and—I—I thought—well—that meeting the professors may—you know—help."

He raised an eyebrow. "So, you're an artist."

I blushed. "I *want* to be a writer. A poet."

After he leaned back in his chair, he rubbed his fingers over his beardless chin. "That's not something you hear every day." He studied me intently. "That's rather ambitious of you."

I clamped my jaw shut. *Yeah, right,* I silently scoffed. *Why don't you tell my parents that?* Knowing that first impressions are everything, I dressed to impress—

4

not to my mother's standards, but I did my best. I owned one white button-up, which my mother mentioned was too tight around my chest and stomach. To overcompensate, I wore the comfortable, black slacks I currently had for my bussing job—the only pair of black slacks I've ever owned in my life. I thought they were flattering, but my mom felt otherwise, letting me know that if I walked the twelve miles it took to get to Sea World, I might lose enough weight to make my clothes fit. *Not that it matters how you look,* she'd said as I was applying mascara to my lashes. *You're interviewing to be a waitress. I'm sure if you look homeless, they'll hire you.*

I'd ignored her to the best of my ability, spraying my auburn curls with product, applying one more layer of lip-gloss and leaving the house without saying good-bye. I didn't want to give either of my parents the chance to make another observation that would make me even more nervous than I already was. Maybe I wasn't following my family's footsteps—Mom's a Gynecologist, Dad's a Plastic Surgeon, and Lucy's a Gastroenterologist—but a serving job would guarantee me more tips than bussing at a buffet gave me. And the more money I was able to save, the sooner I'd be able to move out of my parents' house and pay back my already obnoxious amount of student debt.

"Ambition is a great attribute to have," the Indian man added, fingering the corner of my one-page resume. "Why don't you tell me why you'd like to work for Sea World?"

"I have friends who work in the park," I answered, lying slightly. *Well, I have one friend who works in the park. One boyfriend. Okay, a fiancé.* "And they mentioned this is an amazing company to work for. So, I wanted to experience firsthand what they were talking about." *I mean, he also talks about how much it sucks, but anything has to be better than what I'm doing now.* "And I love killer whales," I added for good measure.

He smiled, his right front tooth slightly overlapping the left one. He asked me a few more questions regarding *what if* scenarios and how I would handle them. I answered each question with a false confidence—but I remembered Lucy's advice and did my best to be myself, even if it was a little awkward and shy. I took a deep, silent breath. "I think that a friendly smile can go a long way, especially if someone has been dealing with children and crowds all day long." *There you go. Don't crumble beneath the pressure. Keep it cool and confident.* I made eye-contact and flashed what I felt was my best movie star smile, awaiting his response.

"You're exactly what we're looking for at Dine with Shamu," the Indian man said pleasantly, folding his hands together on top of his desk. "You have a wonderful personality and obvious knowledge of the restaurant industry. Your answers today exceeded all expectations." He itched a stiff patch of gelled hair. "Let me file your paperwork so we can prepare your employee profile. Do you have any questions?"

Could you let my parents know that I exceeded your expectations? My cheeks began to hurt, I was smiling so wide. "So—I—I got the job?"

The man chuckled. "Yes. Yes, you did." He held out his hand, which I eagerly shook. "Welcome to the Sea World team, Miss Vaughn."

"Thank you so much," I replied. "I can't wait to start."

When I left the HR building, I inhaled the scent of ocean salt and palm trees, Sea World being located on the backside of Mission Bay. I looked to the left, beyond a black gate next to the security office, and saw employees laughing with one another. My smile widened.

After the Las Vegas trip that had gone from entertaining to embarrassing in sixty seconds flat one month prior, this was exactly what I needed to break me out of my zombie-like trance. Lacie and Jasmine, my two best friends, promised to keep my secret safe—what happens in Vegas, stays in Vegas—and didn't pass judgement, or make me feel like a terrible person, even though I made bad decision after horribly bad decision while in the Nevada heat. Nobody was to find out that I'd kissed my ex-lover, Lamont Carwyn. Nobody was to find out I admitted my love for him in a moment of weakness. Nobody was to find out he broke my heart all over again because he was in a relationship with one of my ex-best friends from Sonoma State. We may not have engaged in coitus, but I had emotionally and physically cheated on my *fiancé*. Before the engagement, when Zachary Cameron and I were long-distance boyfriend and girlfriend, I *had* engaged in that horrendous sexual behavior. Too many times. Far too many times. The entire sophomore year, actually, without my boyfriend ever discovering the truth.

Lamont had been my tall, dark and handsome—a boy I loved for too long, that cliché game of *Cat and Mouse* defining our unofficial relationship. Since I'd ran into him while in Las Vegas, my seemingly never-faltering feelings waivered, my brain finally convincing my heart that Lamont just *wasn't good for me.*

Now, as I made my way toward the employee parking lot, I slid my engagement ring back on my finger, ecstatic to tell my fiancé the good news. He was, after all, the one who discovered the job opening for me. He worked at Sea

World, at a barbeque restaurant called Calypso Bay Smokehouse, and had heard from one of his coworkers that the fine dining restaurant, Dine with Shamu, was hiring. Although Zachary didn't always talk highly about his job and had intended to only be there for one summer, he wound up staying because he didn't want to move back into his father's house, for some reason preferring to live in the small, illegally built, room located behind a furniture shop off of University Avenue.

In a not-too-nice side of town.

The ARCO across the street was always packed because they boasted the cheapest gas prices in San Diego, but there had also been a shooting at the nightclub only a block away six months prior. The last thing I needed was my parents chewing me out for even *thinking* about crossing the street light into that side of town, so they didn't know that Zachary moved out of his dad's house four months ago.

Parked next to my car, I found Zachary leaning against the front door of his dinged up and dented Honda Civic, Aviator glasses framing his sharply angled face. His white t-shirt hugged his body nicely, his softer physique replacing his once muscular one due to poor eating habits and lack of exercise. I sucked in and flexed my own stomach muscles, hating how my belly pushed against the button of my pants. I brushed my bangs behind my ear and lifted my gaze to see my own rosy cheeks reflected in Zachary's sunglasses.

"My, oh, my," he said before emitting a low whistle. "My fiancé is *gorgeous*."

"Oh, hush," I hissed, glancing around to make sure nobody was near enough to overhear us. "You're gonna make me blush and it took me forever to cover up these cheeks."

"Well, I love your rosy cheeks."

This time, I really did blush, flattered. "Thank you, Handsome."

When he smiled his coffee-stained, in-desperate-need-of-braces teeth at me, simultaneously lifting his Aviators so I was exposed to his meadow-frolicking eyes—the ones with golden rays as warm as a San Diego Spring day—the heel of my wedges caught on a rock, causing me to stumble. I fell against my fiancé's chest.

He wrapped his arms around me and chuckled. "Did you just fall for me again or are you just clumsy?"

I shrugged into him. "Maybe a little bit of both?"

He leaned forward and kissed me, hesitantly at first, intensifying the passion when I played with his tongue, pulling his body closer to mine. Maybe it was because of my newfound elation from getting the job, but something inside of me awoke—something that had laid dormant since Zachary's proposal in December. The feeling reminded me of the giddy sensation I had the first time Zachary had visited me in Rohnert Park. I actually *desired* my fiancé, which was strange because I had become used to being intimate with Zachary out of guilt and obligation instead of want and sexual intensity. When I pulled away, I slowly opened my eyes, wanting nothing more than to savor the sensation curling my toes.

"I take it the interview went well?" he breathed, his forehead resting against mine.

I smiled. "I got the job."

He lifted me into the air, twirling me in a circle, again reminding me of our first night together in Rohnert Park. "I knew you'd get it—you're the sweetest little woman in the entire world. They'd be *crazy* not to hire you."

"Thanks for believing in me."

"You know what this means?" He grabbed my hands. "I get to see you outside *and* inside of work."

My sister's warning chimed in my head, but I pushed it away, too excited to care. "You mean we can eat lunch together?"

He nodded. "If we plan it right, we can find a way."

"That sounds like the best part of the job," I whispered, my emotions beginning to overwhelm me.

"Oh, Little Woman," he cooed, kissing my cheeks—the right, then the left. "You've made my day."

Although we hadn't engaged in any coitus in over a month—I'd already overused the "I'm sorry baby, I'm tired" excuse that shouldn't be a problem until *after* marriage—I suddenly found myself eager to climb all over my fiancé.

"I can think of something that might make your day even better."

His eyebrows climbed up his forehead. "Are you saying what I think you're saying?"

I nuzzled against his collarbone. "I know you're supposed to work soon, but maybe we could get together after your shift for some impromptu fun?"

"I like the sound of that." He smirked and smacked my bottom. "You should have job interviews more often."

It was an innocent joke, but I felt my walls quickly surround me, the underlying meaning not lost on me. I pulled away and frowned, all of that passion and desire gone faster than you could say sex. "Is that all I am to you?" I snapped. "Is that all that *really* matters?"

Zachary frowned. "Don't be like that."

I shrugged. "You're the one that said it, not me."

He placed his hand on my butt and squeezed. "Stop being such a brat and give me a kiss. I gotta drive to the other parking lot so I can clock in for work."

The buzzing of uncertainty and annoyance lingered, the want to get away from my fiancé growing. I was glad he had to go to work. It would give me the chance to go home, snuggle up with my cat and find any excuse to ignore his text messages to come over later. But when he smiled at me, I couldn't help but smile back. "I hope you have a good shift. I love you."

He kissed me, my lipstick staining his lips. "I love you more, Little Woman," he replied.

Sometimes, I really wish you didn't, I thought sadly, wrapping my arms around him and hoping my sister was wrong about the two of us working together. So far, it wasn't off to a good start.

#

"ROXY, JUST TAKE the damn prescription," my sister demanded. "Mom takes it. I take it. This world would be a better place if *everyone* took it because then, at least, people would learn how to just *chill* the *fuck* out. Stop being such a drama queen."

I sat in Lucy's office, sandaled feet dangling off the side of the light blue plastic chair. The white paper crinkled beneath my jean shorts, my pale thighs glowing against the florescent lighting. "You're a stomach doctor. I don't think this is *really* under your jurisdiction."

It was noontime and I'd brought my older sister some lunch. I'd driven up to Los Angeles after my final shift as a busser to celebrate the end of a miserable job with my sister and my niece. It was my last weekend off before the beginning of the school semester, and my sister had invited me to stay with her in order to spend time with her and Hannah, especially because Roger, my brother in law, was super busy with surgeries and often went to bed before the sun went down. Lucy enjoyed a glass of red wine before bed, and I figured she was feeling a bit lonely, so I'd accepted the invitation thinking it would at least be nice to escape my parents for a while.

Lucy had asked me to bring her some lunch because she had a cancellation in her schedule and somehow, I was roped into an appointment I hadn't been given a chance to mentally prepare for.

"Thanks for assuming I don't know what I'm doing, little Miss Know It All," my sister replied. "But anxiety in our family runs through the stomach. And *that* is my bread and butter. So, stop doubting me for once in your stupid life."

I shrugged, pretending I didn't struggle with horrific stomachaches because I was constantly overthinking everything. "I know my own body better than you do. I don't need to take the strong stuff—five milligrams of Lexapro is just fine."

"Obviously, it's not." She shook her head, her straightened, blonde hair brushing against her shoulders. She had natural wavy hair that looked salon professional even when she rolled out of bed, but she often straightened it because she felt it looked better. I didn't like it because it made her look like a clone of our mother. "I know you hate listening to me, but this is your *health*. I take my profession very seriously."

"I think a vast majority of my problems have come about *because* I've listened to you."

Her forest green eyes narrowed. "Mom is worried about you."

I snorted. "If she was *really* worried, wouldn't she *do* something about it instead of *gossiping* to you about it?"

"You *always* take what I say the wrong way. Why can't you accept that Mom cares?"

Because she doesn't. I've had to take out student loans for following my own dreams instead of hers. How is that care? When I remained quiet, studying the cartoon diagram of a stomach on the wall, Lucy threw up her hands in defeat.

"Do you *want* to suffer through life alone?"

I began playing with a curl. "Why do you think there's a problem? I already told you, *I'm fine*."

"Oh *really*?" she sneered, crossing her arms over her chest. "Then why do you cry all the time? And why do you always have panic attacks?"

Because I don't want to get married, but I don't know how to tell Zach without hurting his feelings. I began swinging my legs, now focusing on the white tile beneath my feet. *She doesn't need to know. She'll just tell Mom and then she'll rub in my face that she's right.* "School is stressing me out. I graduate in May. I'm applying for grad school and really—"

Lucy, who had reached into her purse producing a brown baggy filled with mini chocolate chip cookies, began mocking me with her free hand as if it were a puppet. "Cry me a river. You're an *English* major. Boo hoo." She popped a cookie into her mouth. "You write *poetry*. Like that's *so difficult*."

I ripped a piece of white paper out from beneath my leg and began to roll it between my palms. "Can you not—"

"Feel free to complain to me when you're in your final year of med school."

I rolled my eyes. "I'm so tired of you and Mom guilting me about being a writer instead of becoming doctors like you. You both like to butt into my business and *usually* you guys make my situation worse. *You* guys make my anxiety ten times worse any time you try to *help*."

"Stop blaming other people for your problems and man up—anxiety is an inner battle." Another bite of cookie, crumbs gathering for a party on her chest. "Just take the Lorazepam when you're having a panic attack. It's not for everyday use."

I stood and began pacing the miniscule square space. "Why do you have such a hard time listening to me? I don't need it."

"I think I know what's best."

I turned and faced her like a bull with its eyes on a matador. "*You* know what's best? My entire life, you've been giving me advice that's come back to bite me in the butt."

"Oh *really*?" She snapped. "Like what?"

"Hmm, let me think," I said, sarcastically. "Like when you told me it's fine for someone to *cheat* on their boyfriend as long as a ring isn't in the picture."

"That's *not* what I said!"

"Yes it is!" My mind whirled back to Sonoma State—when Lamont had a girlfriend and kissed me, and when my boyfriend, now fiancé, Zachary, had no idea I was engaging in intercourse with Lamont frequently because I was in love with him. "You said as long as neither me or Lamont were married, what we were doing was *fine*."

She chuckled. "You just *love* to play the blame game." Lucy turned around and began rifling through her cabinets. "I think I have a sample in here—"

"I don't *want* a sample of anything!" I sat down heavily, the paper crinkling beneath my thighs. "This is what I'm talking about. You do whatever you want without listening to me."

"I *am* listening—for the eight hundredth time, I'm trying to help."

Then maybe find some Viagra for women. "Well, stop. I don't need help."

Lucy continued fiddling through the cabinet, looking at each small box before tossing it back in. "So, you're going to take one pill when you're having a full-blown panic attack. Half of one if you have to drive and function at some normal capacity." She nodded, taking out a small box before shaking it next to her ear. "Just don't drink any alcohol when you take it. May seem like a fun idea—but believe me, it's not."

I crossed my arms over my stomach and held my elbows. "If you were *actually* listening to me, you'd stop trying to push these pills on me. I'm done," I whispered, eyeing the small engagement ring that refused to sparkle in the florescent lighting.

For the first time since I entered her office, she *really* looked at me. "Why don't you tell me what's *actually* bothering you?"

"I—I—just—"

My sister placed her hand on her chin. "I think some sun would do you wonders."

I rolled my eyes.

"No, I'm being serious. You live in San Diego. Aside from the fact that you look like you're from Nebraska, Vitamin D will help your anxiety."

"Okay—I'm done trying."

Lucy washed her hands. "Oh, c'mon. Don't be so sensitive." She dried her hands on three paper towels. "Is this about your upcoming nuptials?"

"They aren't *upcoming*," I said a little too quickly.

Lucy raised an eyebrow. "I think we've found the problem, Quickdraw McGraw."

The chilling sensation began at my fingertips. *I'm okay. I'm okay. I'm okay,* I told myself. The churning in my stomach rose to an uncomfortable pain. *I'm okay. I'm okay. I'm okay.* The ringing in my ears was nearly deafening.

I hated that my panic attacks worked like clockwork—the symptoms were always the same, and my two-word mantra had become the only way to slow them down. Unfortunately, once the latter symptoms began, it was almost impossible to stop the train from derailing. The worst was when my skin would itch as if I were wearing a Christmas sweater knit by my aunt. And as if that sweater was glued to my skin, unable to rip off how uncomfortable I felt.

Lucy took note of my suddenly pale face. "Yup. I knew it." She rifled through her diaper bag sized purse. "None of that school bull crap made sense." She pulled out a water bottle and shoved it into my hands. "Sip this and breathe. Deep breaths in and out. I'm being serious. *Breathe.*"

I nodded, trying to hold back my tears, the water slowly bringing life back into my fingers. *I'm okay, I'm okay, I'm okay.* "It's complicated," I croaked.

Lucy leaned back against the counter. "Try me."

I breathed in and out, my stomach feeling tight, as if I had just finished a round of sit-ups. "I'm not looking for advice."

She shrugged. "You may not want to accept it because you don't like to think your family loves you, but I'm here for you."

"Don't you have other patients you need to help?"

She glanced at the clock on the wall. "You're not leaving until we talk."

I could lie again, or I could tell her the truth and get this suffocating feeling off of my chest. "I don't want to be intimate with Zach anymore," I blurted.

"Did that start when he bought you *that* ring? Because I totally understand."

My shoulders slouched. "*This* is what I'm talking about."

When I stared at my shoes, she cleared her throat. "You know I'm only joking." She paused. "Ish." Another pause. "Well, you should know that's a possible side effect of Lexapro."

"Not wanting to get it on with your fiancé?"

"Not wanting to get it on with anybody," she answered matter-of-factly. "Low libido is definitely a real thing."

I looked at her, surprised. "Really?"

"Well, do you find yourself wanting to do the nasty-nasty with anyone else?"

I thought back to Las Vegas when I didn't want to have sex with Lamont. *And here I thought I didn't want to sleep with him because I learned my lesson.* I sighed. *Nope. Just Western Medicine controlling my body.* "I want to have sex sometimes—but that excited feeling doesn't last very long."

She nodded. "I'm not saying *that's* the problem—maybe you're not attracted to your fiancé anymore—but the pill causing problems may be a possibility."

"Crap," I whispered. "What if I'm not ready for marriage yet?"

"Then why'd you say yes?"

Tears began to flood my eyes. "Because I love him. When the man you love asks you to marry him in the middle of a huge crowd beneath fireworks and fake snow, you say yes."

"Maybe try *not* to think about it." She reached into her diaper bag again, producing a bottle of sparkling water. "You aren't getting married *yet*. Sometimes, engagements last a while. Just pretend you're not wearing the ring and it'll be as if nothing's changed." She smirked. "It's not like it weighs anything anyway."

"Welp," I said, slapping my hands on my thighs. "I think that's my cue to leave."

Lucy laughed. "Take the medicine when you're having a bad day. I swear you won't worry about Zach or school or anything."

I stood and began walking to the door, caught off guard when my sister stopped me and wrapped me in a suffocating hug. "I know it's tough, but maybe you need to let go of what's *really* weighing you down lately." When she let go, she reached into the pocket of her lab coat and scribbled something onto a small notepad. "And I'm not kidding about the prescription. Take it when you're having a panic attack." She paused. "Or find out what's really causing you such bad anxiety and just—get rid of the damn thing."

Even though Zachary came to mind, I refused to let Lucy believe my upcoming nuptials were the source of my stomach pain. In fact, I refused to let myself believe that. "But you're my sister. I can't get rid of you."

"Maybe find some time to get laid," she said handing me the prescription. "You're not as funny as you were when you were getting the D regularly."

My cheeks flushed pink. "I hate you. Do you know that?"

She beamed. "The feeling is mutual, Baby Sis."

#

"HOW'S SEA WORLD?" Luke asked, picking up his menu. "You happier there?"

"*Much* happier," I replied. "I still bus tables, but I'm serving drinks, too. So, I actually make tips!" I paused. "And I'm trying to make friends, which, you know—is outside of my comfort zone."

My male best friend and I sat in a small booth at BJ's, a restaurant located at one of the local malls, Grossmont Center. It was too hot outside, the early September weather reaching record highs, so each of us suggested an activity that required air-conditioning; I said lunch, he said a movie. We decided to make a full date out of it since we hadn't been able to hang out much during the summer. Although school had already begun for me, I didn't mind having a reason not to study, especially when I had the day off of work.

Luke began his first commission-based job as a women's shoe salesman at Bloomingdales—one of those upscale, overly priced retail stores in the heart of Fashion Valley, a mall I could only visit when my mother selected an outfit for me that made others believe I knew the difference between Fendi and Prada. The job was *perfect* for him. He had the fashion sense of an editor at Vogue, while I, on the other hand, was happy wearing sweatpants and t-shirts that I found—and smell checked—on my floor.

The two of us made quite a pair: Luke sporting his Lucky Brand jeans and red button-up that was ironed first thing in the morning, and me in my Target brand sweatpants and my baggy Batman t-shirt that I found crumpled beneath my bed. Although my closet was filled with expensive clothing my mother had purchased, insisting I wear them so I would look like a Vaughn, I refused to wear any of them. I told her the clothes were beautiful but didn't look right on me. She said with a little makeup and the right shoes, the clothes would look fine. I had told her that would be like her buying off-brand cereal and calling it the real thing.

Luke smiled. "Oh, my bad—you *love* your job? Is the world coming to an end? Did I miss the memo?"

"I know, *right*?" I replied. "It's like having a good job has turned me into a whole new person."

"Well, that makes one of us."

I frowned. "Not diggin' the shoe biz?"

He shrugged. "Maybe it's because we haven't been *super* busy, but I thought I'd be swimming in commission by now."

"You got this job three months ago. Give it some time."

"I like to think I'm handsome and charming enough to have quickly developed a reliable clientele."

I chuckled. "You're *gay* and sell *women's* shoes. It's only a matter of time until you're the guy every woman is asking for."

He snorted into his water. "I'm in this business to make money—I don't have *time*."

I giggled, unrolled the black, cloth napkin in front of me and placed it on my lap. "You gays have *zero* patience."

"So, Roxanne, why don't you tell me about the boys from Dine with Shamu?"

"Why? You interested?" I asked, playfully.

"No, not me. But *you* should be."

I glanced at my thighs, avoiding eye-contact, fiddling with the fork and knife on the table. *He's just joking.* I breathed, my face feverish. *There's no reason to panic. No reason to feel guilty.* I sipped my water, the ice burning my teeth. *I'm okay, I'm okay, I'm okay.* "There's a bunch of cute guys, but I'm *not* interested. I have a fiancé, and if you remember, he works—like—three feet away from me."

"Doesn't he work on the other side of the park?" Luke asked.

The waitress interrupted us, asking if we wanted anything other than water. "Could I get a Margarita please?"

The waitress smiled and nodded. "Blended or on the rocks?"

"Blended. No salt."

She asked for my ID while Luke breathed a sigh of relief. "Thank God! I thought I'd be drinking by myself today. Usually drinking at lunch time is frowned upon."

"Never stopped you before," I joked.

Luke smiled at the waitress, who batted her lashes and flushed just slightly. "I'll have a Dirty Martini with three olives, please."

She nodded, being sure to soak in Luke's light mocha skin, five o'clock shadow, dark brown eyes and high cheek bones, before turning around to put our orders in.

Luke crossed his hands in front of him calmly. "You know it's completely harmless to look at beautiful men. You just can't touch."

I sighed, fingering the corner of the napkin on my lap. "There's such a thing as emotional infidelity."

"Let's be real. Looking is the most harmless thing you can do moving forward."

"Can you *not*?" I asked, slapping his hand. "I'm a different person, believe it or not. I'm a good fiancé. Doing all of the things I should've been doing since day one."

"Oh, *right*," he snorted. "Is that why you texted me the other day about running into that good-looking guy from your English class?"

The waitress returned with a pitcher of water, filling Luke's glass to the top while ignoring mine. "Your drinks will be out shortly. Would you like any appetizers?"

"How about the avocado rolls?" I suggested.

She ignored me, still focusing on my best friend.

"How about the avocado rolls?" Luke said, repeating my order.

She nodded and scampered off.

"I would've liked a water refill," I mumbled, my anxiety still simmering in my stomach.

"Tell me just how cute he looked when you saw him." Luke handed me his water glass. "I want to live vicariously through you."

"The last thing I need to do is talk about an old classmate who I used to have a crush on." I drank the water generously. "Can we talk about *anything* else?" I frowned. "How about politics? How sexuality is a spectrum? Are the Kardashians up to anything new?"

"Just because I'm gay doesn't mean I watch the Kardashians." Luke laughed and studied the menu again. "I think it's a good thing Zach's restaurant is on the other side of the park."

I rolled my eyes. "You don't understand what *changing topics* means, do you?"

He smirked at me over the menu.

"He *used* to work on the other side of the park." A droplet of water cascaded down the glass. "It's my fault he doesn't anymore. I encouraged him to apply for a Zoological Assistant position." The waitress dropped off our drinks and avocado rolls, Luke again ignoring her advances. "He has *zero* animal experience," I continued. "So, I didn't think he'd have a chance. But—of course—God hates me, and Zach got it." After taking a sip of the Margarita, I grabbed an avocado roll and took a bite. "He guides people in wetsuits from Dolphin Stadium to the back of Dolphin Point, which is *literally* across the Shamu pool from Dine. He's seen me laughing with a male coworker before and he questioned me about it." I still refused to tell Lucy that she'd been right when we talked on the phone before my interview. I didn't want to give her another reason to say I told you so.

"He is *literally* the most insecure person I know."

I shrugged. "With how bad of a girlfriend I've been, he has every right to be."

"Not really—he doesn't *know* about any of that." Luke sighed, grabbing an avocado roll for himself. "Sweetie, have you put any more thought into *not* marrying him?"

Too much, too often. I stayed silent.

"I only ask because whenever you talk about him lately, you seem a little freaked out."

That's because I am freaked out. But I made him a promise—I said yes—I can't back out. "I know you care about me, but I *really* don't want to talk about him anymore. I feel like he's taken over my entire life and I would just like to spend a couple hours thinking about *anything* but him."

"Well then," he said, before sipping his Martini. "What are you gonna get for lunch?"

"I haven't even looked at the menu yet."

Luke smiled. "How about another cocktail?"

"*One* more. I don't want to fall asleep during the movie."

The waitress returned, flirted with Luke again, and asked if we wanted to order entrees yet. When she walked off, Luke rolled his eyes. "Maybe we should just get snacks at the theatre. I'm tired of this girl eye-fucking me."

"Must be *so hard* to be *so handsome*," I teased.

He finished off his Martini. "It's annoying when straight girls treat you like a piece of meat—I'd rather have a cute guy treat me that way."

I sipped my fruity beverage. "So, speaking of cute guys, have you engaged in any homosexual coitus lately?"

#

"HOW CAN I help you, Miss Vaughn?" Jocelyn Palmer, the professor of my short fiction class, smiled her professionally whitened teeth at me, her dark purple lipstick making me rethink having purple as my favorite color.

I cleared my throat, uncomfortable, nervous and feeling as tall as a mouse. "Do you think I could ask you some questions about the MFA program?"

We were still in the small classroom located in Hepner Hall—an old building in the center of campus that was similar to a maze because of the confusing room numbers—the shades lowered, the only lighting coming from the florescent bulbs on the ceiling. I felt like I was back in my sister's doctor's office all over again. Except this time, I wish I had filled the prescription my sister had given me because my anxiety was through the roof.

My professor nodded curtly, her blonde curls slightly falling in front of her right eye. "Have you given any more thought about pursuing fiction instead of poetry?" The previous year, in Professor Palmer's poetry class, she had accidently found one of my "not meant for anyone to ever read" short stories and forced me to turn in a revised version for my final—threatening to fail me if I did otherwise.

"Yes, I have, Ma'am," I said, still bitter about her not liking my poetry. "I think I have some pages of a potential novel written."

"That's great and all, but I have some bad news for you." She paused, taking note of my fidgeting hands. "And despite what you and my failing students may think, I really *hate* being the bearer of bad news." She paused again, placing her bronzed cheek on her palm. "That's not what you should be focusing on."

My heart deflated, my hands falling to my sides. "But—but—you—the website—I thought—but—a writing sample?"

"For starters, learning how to complete a sentence may help." She glanced at her hot pink watch before gathering together the pens and papers that littered the

18

wooden desk at the front of the classroom. "I have another class to get to. I really don't—"

I nodded, knowing what she was going to say next. "That's okay. I'll just email—"

She shook a pen in my face. "The last thing I need is another email spamming my inbox. How about you sit those sweatpants down and put your note taking to good use?"

I promptly sat in the desk to my left and whipped out a glittery notebook. "Do you think—"

"I think," she said, interrupting me. "You should start writing and stop talking. Yes, the MFA website wants a thirty-page writing sample. No, they *do not* want an excerpt of a novel. You need *two very different* short stories that *really* showcase your writing." She checked her watch again, brushing a strand of curls behind her ear. "The program is on the experimental side of the spectrum—the focus tends to be on socio-political issues."

I scribbled frantically, my handwriting getting worse and worse the quicker she spoke.

"You need *three* glowing—and I mean absolutely *radiant*—letters of recommendation from your professors. Be persistent. Professors are always busy and usually don't have time to help—but don't be annoying because then they won't want to help. Take the GRE. Just don't concern yourself with the math—"

"But don't you *dare* fuck up the writing portion," a deep, male voice concluded from the hallway. Professor Palmer and I looked towards the door.

"Very PC of you, Ezra." Jocelyn scoffed.

The brown skinned, black haired man strolled into the room and sat on the corner of the professor's table. "Make sure you write that down," he said, pointing to my notebook.

"Don't f—um—*mess*—around," I mumbled, the pink ink barely legible beneath my shaking hand. "So, how do I study for it?"

"There's a purple book you need to buy from Barnes and Noble," Professor Palmer said.

"Aren't you running late for a class?" the man asked. "Or are you hoping they'll just give up and leave before you get there?"

Professor Palmer flushed. "If you hadn't so rudely barged in, I'd be on my way already."

"Giving this young woman an unfair advantage, I see."

Professor Palmer smirked. "The program could use some diversity."

"She looks pretty white to me."

"I meant her different writing style—Ezra, do you ever think before you speak?"

I flinched, unsure if she was complimenting or insulting me.

"Now," my professor continued. "Are you done? I'd rather not miss my next class."

The man chuckled. "I'll get out of that beautiful curly hair of yours. I just heard your voice and wanted to see if we're still on for coffee tonight."

"Ezra," Professor Palmer said sternly. "There's this thing in your pocket called a cell phone. Next time, please refrain from this inappropriate behavior and make use of modern technology."

The man smiled, pulling his wavy, shoulder-length hair into a beanie he produced from his back-jean pocket. He reminded me of a prince from a Disney movie, his hair so feathery, I wanted to stuff my pillowcase full of it. "If you'll excuse me, I have students taking a test down the hall. I should probably get back to them and make sure they're not cheating." He paused, hand on his chin, light hazel eyes glancing at the ceiling. "Oh—wait—they can't. They all have different essays."

Professor Palmer shooed him away with her black tipped, glitter topped, and acrylic fingernails. "Go easy on the poor critters. They're only freshman."

He winked. "They gotta learn early." And then he disappeared, his tennis shoes squeaking against the hallway tile.

"He sounds—nice?" I managed, trying not to blush.

Professor Palmer grinned, her hazel eyes gleaming a shade of gold. "That's Ezra Castillo. Mainly teaches graduate classes, but the English Department stupidly gave him an undergraduate Classical Literature class this semester." She twirled a loose curl. "He's nice, but he's a hard ass—especially on his students."

The lingering tension made me smirk. *Oh goodness. Are they—a thing? Does the devil herself have human emotions?* "Is there anything else I should know?"

She placed the pens and papers into a camouflage patterned satchel and sighed. "Lastly, the *single* most important component is the personal statement. Avoid clichés. Stand out. Use your failed pre-med experience to your advantage." She glanced at her watch one final time and swore under her breath. "Don't be afraid to brown nose. Jim Harvey is the granddaddy of the program. I *highly* recommend mentioning how much you'd like to take one of his classes."

"I have a class with him now," I said, feigning excitement. "Film and Literature." *And I hate everything about him and the graphic films he's made us watch so far.* "He's—" I paused, carefully trying out the words in my mind before allowing them to take shape. "An interesting character."

Even though she chortled, Professor Palmer said nothing further on the topic. "I'll email you the letter I wrote when I was applying to programs, so you'll have something to reference—and there's this crazy search engine called Google, which could've probably given you all of these answers. Now, I have to go. If there are any other questions, make sure you ask me at a time that won't put me behind schedule."

"Um—wait—Professor?" I nearly whispered.

Jocelyn Palmer turned around, waiting for me to continue.

I bit my lip. "Is fiction the right path for me? Should I *really* give up on poetry?"

Without responding, she turned on her high heels and left the room. I nodded sadly while I watched her dark blue jeans and bright orange sweater disappear down the hall.

Chapter Two

THE PROFESSOR DRONED on about the potential end of my life, her soothing voice and circular glasses unable to calm the storm swirling in my stomach. The students around me groaned as well, this *required* Shakespeare English class making every English and Comparative Literature major question their decision to pursue writing or teaching.

A black-haired Asian girl raised her hand, fingers trembling. "We have to perform—like—in front of *everyone*?"

Professor Emerson smiled wide and nodded once. "In order to pass this class, you and your groupmates must perform an original rendition of the play assigned. The lines must come directly from the play Shakespeare wrote himself, but you can move them around to fit your plot line." She paused, glancing at each student to make sure all eyes were on her. "And *all of the lines must be memorized.* Failure to do so will result in a failing grade on your final, which will result in some *serious* damage to your overall grade."

More panic rose throughout the classroom like a tsunami, each student turning to one another with widened eyes, silent lips moving one hundred miles per hour.

"Throughout the semester," Professor Emerson continued, her even wider smile indicating that she took some twisted pleasure in her students' terror. "I will provide class time for all of you to work on your performances. You will, however, need to work together outside of our designated class time in order to iron out all of the little details. I know everyone has lives—jobs, significant others, more classes—but group meetings exist in the *real world.* You'll want to make time. Your grade *will* depend on it."

More trembling hands shot into the air, the professor calling on an older gentleman with grey hair and square glasses. I recognized him from my Film and Literature class. He sat in the desk directly behind me and made snide remarks about the professor throughout the entire period. He was obnoxious, but made me laugh when I wanted to cry while sitting through the literature class of my nightmares, complete with R-rated movies and a professor who believed he was God's gift to fiction writing.

"How will we know who our groupmates are and what play we're assigned?" the gentleman asked.

Every horrified face focused on Professor Emerson's long, black hair, wisps of grey breaking through her subtle dye job. "I will email the groups and play options to all of you tonight. Next class period, you'll meet with your group and spend the first ten minutes deciding what play you want and the next ten you'll decide on the theme, who will be playing which character, and how you will begin the process of making your own Shakespeare magic."

I placed my head down on the desk and tried to ignore the acid bubbling against my diaphragm. For the first time since my Anatomy lab sophomore year, I wondered if I'd be able to pass the class. *Why do I have to perform in front of everyone? What does that have to do with writing?*

My hope was that Professor Emerson would assign me to a group that would be composed of competent, confident and collected individuals who had no qualms about making fools of themselves in front of a crowd so that I could hide behind them without being noticed.

I sighed. *I can't take this class. I'm gonna fail.* Another student raised a hand, and even though the professor was speaking, I didn't hear a word she said. *Stupid English major with your stupid core classes and stupid professors who want nothing more than to ruin your life.* I began chewing on the end of my pen. *This is what I get for dropping out of pre-med. As if dealing with my parents constantly reminding me I'm a failure isn't punishment enough.*

"Shakespeare was a playwright," the professor said loudly, trying to keep everyone's attention. "We will respect his genius works of literature and study them in the manner he himself had intended."

What more can we do? You're already having us perform like a bunch of monkeys.

"Instead of writing essays, we will be attending three plays at the Old Globe Theatre in Balboa Park." She handed a red-haired girl sitting at a desk in front of the classroom a piece of notebook paper. "I can't force you to go because the plays take place outside of class time, but I can *strongly encourage* you to attend by assigning a five to ten-page paper analyzing the themes within each play if you decide to forego Balboa Park."

The students around me mumbled beneath their breaths.

"Please sign your name under which plays you will be able to attend."

The red-haired student stared at the sign-in sheet before raising a hand. "Can we bring someone with us?"

Professor Emerson placed her hand on the podium in front of her and began tapping her finger. "I'm sure that won't be a problem. I'll have to talk to the associate at the theatre and see what we can work out." She pointed to the paper still laying untouched on the desk. "Indicate if you're interested in bringing a plus one. It would be nice to share this experience with your loved ones."

Zachary came to mind. *Oh! This could be a great date night. It would be perfect—a romantic night on the town together.* Suddenly, the class requirements didn't seem so bad. Acting out lines that are memorized would be easier than having to create my own lines—which was what I did anytime Zachary and I engaged in coitus. *If I can convince Zach that sex isn't an obligation, then I should be able to convince a bunch of strangers that I'm confident performing Shakespeare. No matter what my parents think, I'm going to prove I made the right decision. I belong here.*

When the sign-in sheet reached me, I signed my name and the number two below each play in purple colored ink. *Maybe this is exactly what I need—what Zach and I need—to spark the fire in our relationship again. A little romance. And, as a bonus, I'll get a better grade for going.*

\#

ONE OF THE obstacles associated with starting fresh at a new school junior year is the inability to recognize familiar faces on campus. Freshman and sophomore year are reserved for that—living in dorm rooms and sharing General Education courses, all afraid of talking to one another, but forced to do so through ice breakers. So, when I arrived at SDSU, terrified and uncertain, nine months prior, it was strange that one face in particular stood out from the crowd.

This young man walked through the door of a second semester undergraduate literature course and sat down at the desk three empty seats ahead of me. His beauty was enchanting, all of the girls unable to listen to the professor's lectures because they were busy doodling his name in their notebooks.

My own hands remained fastened to my desk, my body threatening to melt out of my seat, forming a puddle beneath my feet.

Skinny. Olive skin. Five o' clock shadow. Green eyes verging on teal. A smile that could rip your panties clear in half. Brown hair any girl would be lucky to grasp in passion. A voice only heard in the most intimate of dreams.

My ovaries begged me to go up to him and introduce myself for the sake of procreation and evolution.

My brain told me to stay put and remain unnoticed for the sake of self-preservation and the inability to accept rejection.

But by some strange turn of events, this hunksicle and the two friends he'd been whispering to throughout the class, turned around in their seats and asked me to join their presentation group.

And by some strange miracle, I didn't completely embarrass myself when I spoke. "Yeah, sure." I even added a casual shrug and smile without looking like I was having a seizure.

When he returned the smile before turning to face the front of the class, I took a deep breath and began scribbling doodles in the margins of my notebook. *Me? He wants me to be in his group?* I thought, surprised. Although I knew he only chose me because I was a know-it-all who annoyed the professor every time I raised my hand, I decided to convince myself that he wanted me in his group because he wanted an excuse to talk to me—and maybe because he thought I was cute, too.

From that completely insignificant moment forward, I *knew* I was in trouble.

The boy's name was Matthew, and I *desperately* wanted to be intimate with him—which was beyond strange because, at the time, I believed you had to be in love with someone to experience this sort of sensation. Sitting behind him, day dreaming about his tight t-shirts and running shorts, I let my body feel alive again, subtly squirming in my seat.

That day set the tone for the rest of my first semester junior year: too much school work, too many hours bussing tables, too much drinking, too little enjoyable sex and excruciating sexual frustration. So, to appease the needs associated with my womanhood, I allowed myself to engage in harmless flirtation with my classmate while maintaining a physical distance. Writing it off as a silly crush, it would be in my best interest to *not* overanalyze the fact that he usually went out of his way to be near me. I began to believe I was imagining his advances because there was *no way* someone like him would be interested in someone like me.

But then, something came over me.

I broke my rules.

We exchanged numbers.

I questioned my relationship with Zachary.

The semester ended.

I became engaged to Zachary.

The harmless flirting ceased.

A new semester.

Many more blank faces.

Summer—Lamont—Las Vegas.

A promise to remain loyal in my relationship.

And then came the reception of a single text message that sent me reeling back to that flirty English class. It was one of those late nights where my fiancé was at work and I was locked in my bedroom, snuggled next to my kitten, a romantic comedy playing on my television. I blamed loneliness. No, I didn't ever want to have sex with my fiancé, but when I spent the night at Zachary's place, I did enjoy the comfort I felt when his body was wrapped around me. The truth was, however, there was *much more* than loneliness controlling my actions—Matthew was somebody I couldn't have, and because of that, I ignored my fiancé's two phone calls, too busy flirting with my old classmate to deal with pretending to miss Zachary.

That night, the flirting went farther than it should have, Matthew admitting that he was attracted to me, his words striking a chord deep down, as if we were engaging in foreplay.

He had an excuse—he was intoxicated at a lake house somewhere.

I didn't—I was sober and alone.

Although Matthew and I texted on and off for the remainder of the summer, the flirting faded, my guilt preventing me from responding to any texts that had the slightest hint of provocative language.

I allowed my crush to simmer.

I stopped texting Matthew, afraid that Zachary was onto me, his suspicious glances whenever I checked my phone causing my stomach to flip.

And then fate played a cruel joke on me—just as I was leaving campus, a sexy voice from my past called out to me. I knew who it was before I turned around even though I hadn't seen him face to face in something like a year. When I looked into those teal pools of beauty, my heart pumped so hard, my head began to spin.

Matthew invited me to a house party that he and his roommates were hosting to "start off the semester right."

Hypnotized and willing to do anything he asked me at that moment, I said I'd one hundred percent be there.

And that's how I wound up in my current predicament: searching through my walk-in closet for a conservative, yet sexy, outfit while my future husband sat on the black loveseat in my bedroom, a *Cosmopolitan* magazine open on top of his lap. Sherlock, the kitten I'd adopted from the Humane Society the previous July, lay curled on the armrest, his curious green eyes studying Zachary, his tail swishing side to side over the fuzzy green throw blanket I often snuggled under while doing homework.

"You sure you don't want me to come tonight?" Zachary asked.

I pulled out a purple dress, flipped it one way, then another, and placed it back on the rack. "I'm sorry my love, but I promised Jazz and Lacie we'd have a girls' night out. It's been a while since the three of us have gone out together—just us."

Zachary sighed and turned a page of the magazine, his breathing quiet as he stared at an advertisement consisting of a gorgeous male model—no shirt, skimpy undergarments, tan skin and toned muscles—and a bottle of perfume. It somewhat matched two of the framed posters that hung on the wall over the back of my couch, shirtless actors flexing and tanned and toned, surrounding a collage I had made filled with pictures of Zachary and me at Disneyland, the San Diego Zoo and the Mary-Birch Aquarium.

Zachary turned anther page, glanced at the small muffin top hugging the waistband of his jeans, sucked in his stomach and pulled up the denim until it stretched across his belly button. "Didn't you just go to the movies together?"

I think a dress might be too fancy for a house party. "That was over a month ago." *Maybe something a little less flashy.* "And no offense, but it might be awkward with you there."

He licked his thumb and forefinger before flipping another page. "Awkward?"

I can't ogle over Matt with you there—it would be a little weird. "Yeah— um—well—you know—" I stammered, trying to think of an excuse that wouldn't give me away.

He looked at me. "Since when am I awkward?"

"I don't mean *you*. I meant *us*. We'd be a couple and that'd be awkward with the girls."

He returned his gaze to the magazine, annoyance replacing the worry that had flickered across his eyes. "Oh *please*. Jasmine and Lacie are *basically* a couple."

Now it was my turn to get annoyed. "Stop it. They're my best friends. The three of us—well—we're a trio."

He huffed. "Sure. Keep telling yourself that, Babe."

I didn't respond, instead focusing on the expensive clothing my mother continued to buy me despite my protests. *None of this'll work. It's just not me.*

"With me there," Zachary continued. "You won't be a third wheel."

I moved to my dresser where I kept the casual t-shirts and pants I wore daily. "Does that mean I'm a third wheel when I hang out with you and Omar?"

He glared at me. "You *really* wanna be like that right now?"

"You started it."

"I don't spend every second of the day with him."

If I weren't in the picture, you would. I pulled out a pair of white jeans and tossed them onto my bed. "I hope you know that playing video games on the Internet together counts as *spending time with one another.*"

He turned another page—rougher this time—tearing off the glossy corner. "Are you *trying* to piss me off?"

I closed my eyes, zeroing in on the sound of Sherlock's purring. "I'm trying to explain why spending alone time with the girls is important to me and you're the one being difficult about it."

It was late September. School had *already* taken a toll on my stress threshold, Zachary's constant complaining about his student teaching program weighing me down even further. Although the romantic in me wanted to spend every waking moment beside my fiancé, the realist in me wanted to throw him out of a window without calling an ambulance.

We worked for the same company, in the same theme park.

We studied in the library together, all-nighters stretching into all-dayers.

We spent three out of seven nights together in his small bedroom, where I couldn't sleep because of his snoring.

Yes, we were engaged, but I was beginning to suffocate, the leash Zachary tied around my neck pulling tighter whenever I wanted time to myself.

"I'm not joking," he mumbled.

I took in a deep breath, returning to my closet to find a top to go with the white pants. "These girls are my *only* friends, Zach. I want what I had in Sonoma—girls I can trust to have my back no matter what."

"You spent an entire weekend with them in Vegas."

"That was *months* ago! I need more girl time to keep me sane."

When I turned around, Zachary was pouting. "Why don't you three ditch the party and come to PB with me and Omar? You'll get the best of both worlds. Girl time and boyfriend time."

I rolled my eyes so hard I felt my brain twitch. *Do you ever listen to me? Can you mentally process what I say to you? Or is it too difficult for you to think about anyone other than yourself?*

Omar was Zachary's best friend—they'd been inseparable since high school. They played video games together, went to parties together, drank at bars together, and ate dinner together. Pretty much any time my fiancé wasn't at work, teaching, or hanging out with me, Omar was knocking at the door trying to get Zachary's attention.

I didn't like Omar, I didn't trust Omar, and I would continue to make whatever excuse necessary so I wouldn't have to see Omar. I believed he was bringing down my fiancé in life, but it wasn't my place to say who Zachary could or couldn't be friends with.

"As fun as that may be," I said, pulling a light purple tank top from my closet. "I'm gonna politely decline. You deserve a guys' night. I'm sure Omar will appreciate some alone time with you."

At his silence, I turned around to find that his frown had deepened.

I love you, Zach, but I really need you to leave. The girls are gonna be here soon. I sat down beside him and rested my hand on his cheek, hoping I was hiding my aggravation. "Sweetie, I swear I'll be thinking about you the whole time."

"You can think about me when I'm by your side, too, you know." His voice was soft. Gentle. Kind. His green eyes crinkled around the corners when he smiled, like a seagull had left its prints in the sand.

I inhaled deeply and turned to look at Sherlock. *Why can't he just let me go out with the girls? Do I have to spell it out? Hurt his feelings?*

At first, Zachary's teeth were cute—even though my mother had told me multiple times how distracting they were, I never thought anything about it. However, after dating Zachary for nearly two years and taking copious mental notes of his horrendous hygiene habits, those dandelion crayon colored things protruding from his gums reminded me of fangs that belonged to a troll.

An unbelievably handsome troll, complete with high cheekbones, a French nose, a sharp enough jaw line to cut through a block of cheese, a dimple in his chin, tanned skin, thin lips and a masculine brow line. It saddened me we didn't share the sexual passion that once kept us in the bedroom for days, calling in Chinese take-out and watching an endless array of movies, ditching class or calling out sick to work.

The truth was, as of late, I'd been concocting any and all excuses to keep myself out of his bedroom because I was tired of faking my enjoyment.

But breaking up due to lack of libido seemed a bit unreasonable.

It was just a phase.

A phase where I was terrified of winding up alone.

A phase where I feared hurting Zachary's feelings because I loved him.

I smiled sadly at him. "Zach—"

He grabbed my hand and kissed the ring on my finger. "It's alright. You can go out with the girls. Everyone in the room will know that the most beautiful woman in the world is taken."

The romantic side of me swooned.

The independent woman inside of me cringed.

Taken? I'm not an object to be had. "Honey, please stop worrying. It's *one* night. The girls—and me—we deserve some time alone."

He closed the magazine and threw it on the ground. "Okay, okay, I get it. I'll leave. I know you have to get ready." He paused. "You can stop pushing me away now." When he reached over to pet Sherlock too roughly, the cat dug his claws into the loveseat's fabric to keep from falling off.

This time, I snapped. "Zach, stop it. I've told you a million times—he's a cat. You can't pet him like you would a dog."

When my fiancé dropped his hand, Sherlock fled to the safety of the bathroom that was attached to my bedroom. "What is going on with you? Everything I'm doing lately seems to bother you."

Maybe that's because you are bothering me. How hard is it to pet a cat? "I'm just antsy because the girls are gonna be here soon and I'm not ready."

He nodded, slipping on his flip-flops. "Fine. The last thing I need is for there to be a problem between us. Teaching is stressing me out enough as is."

You're currently causing a problem because you're not letting me get ready. "I know you had a rough week." *But please stop complaining about it. I just need a break for one night.* "I'm sure the students will come around. Me and you are fine." *We have the rest of our lives to tell one another how miserable we are all of the time.* "Remember, this will help you be a better teacher in the long run."

"It's not even the kids. My Master Teacher needs to take the stick out of her ass." He shook his head. "If I got paid, it'd be worth it."

"Think of it as an internship. Plus, you have Sea World on the weekends. I don't think money should be the reason for you to do things because teachers—you know—don't make much money anyway." I paused, realizing I needed to tread carefully. When it came to finances, Zachary was quite defensive, even though he received a large sum of grant money from the government because he and his father were considered "poor."

Unlike me, who hailed from a well-to-do family, led by a mother who refused to pay my tuition because I rejected the medical field, forcing me into an already mind-numbing amount of student loan debt.

"You *know* I'm not doing this for money."

I sighed.

"I *love* teaching," he continued.

"Then you have to push through this," I snapped. "Dreams are never easy to achieve. Once you jump over this hurdle, you'll have your credentials—and then your very own classroom where you can teach however you want."

After he helped me to my feet, he kissed my forehead. "You're right. Sorry for being a dick. Just stressed out. I shouldn't take it out on you."

I refrained from frowning, forcing a smile on my face. *Yes, you should—I deserve it. I'm a terrible fiancé.* "It's okay. We all have bad days."

"If your dad can't pick you up tonight, call me, okay?"

You'll be too busy playing video games. "Have fun with Omar tonight. Crush those Noobs." I wrapped my arms around him and touched my lips to his. "Now get outta here. I have an outfit to coordinate." I kissed him again before gently pushing him away.

"Try not to look too good."

I flushed. "You flatter me."

He smiled and slapped my butt. "Any chance you'll be drunk and frisky later tonight?"

Drunk? Yes. Frisky? Doubt it. "Good-bye, Zach."

"I love you, Little Woman."

"I love you, too," I replied before closing the door, sliding my engagement ring off of my finger.

#

TAKING A LONG look at myself in the mirror, I silently thanked my mother for providing me with nice clothing despite the fact that I usually never wore it. Tonight, it was exactly what I needed to try to impress Matthew without being blatantly obvious about it. Maybe it was strange to pair my off-brand, white jeans with a flowy tank top that was designed by some high-class Italians, but it made me feel pretty. "Hopefully, Matt'll notice me even if I'm not dressed like some hooker."

Just as I was slipping into a pair of small-heeled tan wedges, the doorbell rang, signaling the arrival of my best friends: Jasmine and Lacie. After one last glance in my floor-to-ceiling mirror, I puckered my hot pink lips and fluffed my hair. Then

I frowned. It had been a long time since I cared this much about my appearance. I briefly allowed myself to imagine Lamont's smile before I shook my head. *Don't think about him. Never think about him again.*

"Roxanne! The girls are here!" My mother's voice penetrated my closed door as if it were an open window.

I took the stairs two at a time and smiled when the high-pitched squeals of my girlfriends reached my ears. "I missed you guys!"

Sherlock ran beneath the couch, the clatter of my friends' high heels making his tail puff up like a caterpillar. They walked past the living room and dining area, meeting me by the stairs next to the kitchen.

"We missed you, too, Boo Boo!" Lacie cooed, wrapping me in a hug.

"You are all crazy," my mother said, shaking her head. Her straight, blonde ponytail swished across her thin shoulders. "It's been—what—a *month* since you've seen each other?"

"No! It's been over a month, at *least*," Jasmine replied, making my mother smile.

"Please, don't go overboard tonight," my mother warned. "And be quiet when you get home. Unlike all of you, I've had to work all week."

"Yes, Ma'am," we all said together.

She nodded once more before making her way down the stairs to join my father in the TV room.

"We brought vodka!" Jasmine said a little too enthusiastically.

Both girls were dressed casually. Jasmine's tan, Latina skin brought out her bright, orange tank top, her dark jeans tight against her thick thighs. Her plump lips were painted with fire engine red lipstick, her brown eyes darkened from black eyeliner and grey eye shadow. Lacie, on the other hand, wore a white shirt that hugged her smaller breasts and flared out around her stomach, and a pair of olive-green shorts that stretched across her butt, her athletic thighs on display. Her skin was pale against her green make-up, which brought out the green tint of her hazel eyes. Both wore their black hair straight—Lacie's dyed, Jasmine's natural—hanging freely past their shoulders.

"That's a hard pass from me," I replied. "Some of us adults have to work in the morning."

"You sound like your mother," Jasmine mumbled.

"Well, I'm sorry, but I'm not showing up to work hungover."

Lacie pouted. "But we haven't partied together in forever!"

I shrugged. "You two are more than welcome to go crazy, but I'm still trying to make a good impression at work. Being hungover will ruin that."

"I go in hungover *all* of the time. As long as you make it *look* like you're working, you'll be fine."

I rolled my eyes at Jasmine. "No."

"Party pooper," Lacie whined.

"I'm still drinking!" I argued. "Just not hard liquor. Gonna have a solid beer buzz."

"Fine." Jasmine sighed. "Is Zach coming?"

"By the looks of your naked ring finger, I'm gonna say that's a no," Lacie said before I could respond.

I swallowed hard, my cheeks burning bright red. "We're having a girls' night. I convinced him to leave me alone tonight even though he wasn't happy about it." I paused. "He's hanging out with Omar, so he won't blow up my phone either."

Jasmine and Lacie shared a look that made me nauseous.

"What? What's wrong?" I asked.

Lacie smirked, pulling a fifth of some sort of flavored vodka from a grocery bag. 'We can address the lack of ring later."

"Then what was that look for?"

"Do you worry about Omar and Zach hanging out all the time?"

I walked to the two-door refrigerator and yanked a Stella from the six-pack on the top shelf. "I mean, sometimes I worry that Omar's scumbag attitude is gonna rub off on Zach, but they're best friends. Omar's been in Zach's life longer than I have."

"That's not the kind of rubbing I'd be worried about," Jasmine muttered under her breath.

I narrowed my eyes. "What was that?"

Lacie shrugged. "Those two are a little gay."

"What makes them gay?" I asked, searching through the drawer for a bottle opener.

"Do you watch how they interact?"

If he was gay, he wouldn't bother me about wanting sex all of the time, I thought. "Just because Zach's dad is gay, doesn't mean he is."

"I didn't say anything about his dad," Jasmine said.

"Zach's just *very* comfortable with his sexuality."

Lacie snorted. "Roxy, there's a difference between being comfortable with yourself and talking about your friend's penis."

Jasmine nodded. "The size. The angle. The length. The curvature."

"Oh, c'mon. They're only joking around." I paused, taking a sip of my beer. "And the three of us talk about boobs and periods all the time. You've both peed in front of me. Does that make us gay?"

Lacie laughed, opening the cabinets in search of cups. "I don't know the intimate details of your vajayjay."

"And I don't want to know," Jasmine added.

I sighed. "Zach isn't gay." I took an angry swig of beer. "He wants to do intimate things with me all the time. Does that make me a man?" I didn't want to admit it, but they were beginning to hurt my feelings.

"That's not what we're saying."

"We just don't want you to get hurt," Lacie said, frowning.

"I mean, look at Luke. He didn't know he was gay."

"So—what? I attract gay men?"

They both frowned even deeper. "No—sweetie—we're just trying to say that Zach's relationship with Omar is a strange one."

Yeah, well, Zach said the same thing about you guys. So, maybe everyone needs to stop trying to judge other people's friendships. I sipped my beer again. "My fiancé isn't gay."

They nodded mutely.

"Look, he proposed to me. It's 2012. If he were gay, he'd be welcomed into Hillcrest with open arms. Nobody needs a beard to hide behind these days. If he wanted to be in a relationship with Omar, why waste his time with me?"

Jasmine poured shots for both her and Lacie. "Wait a minute. He proposed to you? That's so *weird* because I don't see an engagement ring on your finger."

I swallowed more beer, the tingling in the tips of my fingers beginning to move down my knuckles. *I'm okay. I'm okay. I'm okay.* "Keep it up and I'm uninviting you to this party tonight."

Jasmine and Lacie made eye-contact before throwing back their shots, refilling the glasses and repeating the motion immediately. I shivered while they followed the last shot with cranberry juice, my throat burning at the mere thought of drinking that stuff.

"How're we getting there anyway?" Lacie asked.

Jasmine nodded. "I didn't bring any money for a taxi."

I rolled my eyes. *Like you'd offer to pay for the ride even if you did have money with you.* "My dad's gonna drive."

They stared at me, mouths agape. "Mr. Vaughn is gonna drive?"

"Yes," I said calmly. "The party is, like, five minutes away. And he's cool sometimes. He doesn't want me to drink and drive, and he said taxis cost an arm and a leg. He was a partier in college, so he gets it." I took another sip of beer. "He knows my mom doesn't approve, so he stays quiet around her."

Lacie nodded. "I could see your dad being crazy in college."

"I bet he was hot," Jasmine added. "He's got that confidence like he slept with a bunch of models."

"Can you *not* talk about my dad like that?" I cringed, finishing the contents of my beer.

"She's not wrong," Lacie said. "He was probably a playboy before your mom came into the picture."

Holding out my hand, I gestured for a shot glass. "If I drink one of these, will you *please* stop talking about my dad like that?"

The girls squealed, nodding excitedly.

"Ladies!" my mother called from downstairs. "What did I say about not getting too crazy?"

Jasmine, Lacie and I giggled quietly, clinking our shot glasses together. The vodka tasted nothing like raspberries, the alcohol burning every surface between the back of my tongue and my stomach. It reminded me of the crazy, black out nights in Sonoma State with my old girl friends, which always made me think of nights next to Lamont.

I closed my eyes and took a deep breath. *Don't go there. You've already thought about him one too many times tonight.*

Lacie reached out and grabbed my hand, running her thumb over my naked ring finger. "Roxy, on a serious note, are you okay? I thought you promised yourself you weren't going to take it off after everything that happened in Vegas?"

"Yeah," Jasmine added. "I thought you two were doing good now."

My forearm glistened after I wiped my lips. *I probably shouldn't have accepted an engagement ring when I'm not ready for marriage.* The girls drank another round of shots, providing me a few more seconds to think before I said anything stupid. *What if you love someone but don't know if you love them enough to spend the rest of your life with them?* "Things have been great," I managed. "He's just—we just—he just—I don't know." In the ensuing silence, I returned to the fridge to grab a second beer. "I'm having a lot of second thoughts and if you're ready to marry someone, shouldn't those thoughts disappear?" More silence as I popped the cap off of another beer bottle. "Forever is a *long* time. I wasn't even committed to Zach three months into our relationship."

"I wouldn't want to marry a gay man, either," Jasmine joked.

"Jazz, she's being serious," Lacie said, shaking her head. "Sweetie, you've changed. You had the chance to have sex with Lamont in Vegas and you didn't."

I frowned. "But we still kissed. And I told him I loved him. Isn't that worse?"

Jasmine shrugged. "This is why I'm single. It's all too complicated."

"Maybe the *idea* of *marriage* is what's ruining things for me. The relationship pre-engagement was fine—things had been looking up."

The girls chuckled.

"I know I'm the problem," I said, sadly. "Even with tonight—I *really* didn't want Zach to come because I have a teensy-weensy crush on the host of the party."

Lacie took another shot. "Is he hot?"

"*Gorgeous,*" I swooned.

Jasmine followed Lacie with one more shot. "Hot or not, he's not the one who's your future husband."

I frowned. "You're *really* a bit much tonight."

Lacie laughed. "I think she's just irritating you so that you'll take another shot."

I politely declined. "Shouldn't have taken the first one, either."

"You sure about that?"

"As much as I *love* being peer pressured, I'm still gonna pass."

"That's alright. I wouldn't wanna be sloppy if I had the chance to fuck a hunk."

I glared at Lacie's smug smile. "That's not why I'm not drinking hard liquor. I told you, I have wo—"

"You can keep telling yourself that," Jasmine interrupted, smirking. "But your bare ring finger says otherwise."

Chapter Three

"YOUR MOTHER HATES that I'm promoting this bad behavior," my dad said, coming to a stop behind another car. "I had to remind her that she's engaged in many forms of bad behavior herself over the years."

The air conditioning coming from the SUV's vents cooled my warm skin. "Let's be real, Dad. She considers anything I do bad behavior. Even the way I breathe isn't good enough for her."

Lacie and Jasmine giggled with one another while taking not-so-flattering selfies in the back seat of my father's car. I turned around and smiled at them, wondering how they were able to remain conscious after consuming an entire bottle of vodka. They may have shared it, but I had to admit I was impressed they were able to climb into the SUV without falling onto the asphalt face first.

"To be fair," my father countered. "You have been giving her some attitude lately."

"To be fair, she raised me that way."

My father shook his head. "You two are more alike than you think."

"Turn left up here," I grunted, not wanting to partake in this conversation. "Mom can think whatever she wants, but at least I'm not an alcoholic."

He smiled. "I wouldn't have agreed to drive if you were."

"I just don't get how this is *bad behavior*," I continued. "I'm over twenty-one. I'm not driving drunk. I'm not doing drugs. I could be out prostituting myself on El Cajon Boulevard to pay for my student loans, you know."

He laughed. "I don't think you're cut out for that line of work. You don't even like wearing a bikini at the beach."

"Have you seen the types of bikinis girls are wearing these days?" I crossed my arms over my chest. "I just – I don't get it. Mom gets upset that I'm at home all of the time, so then I finally go out, and now she's upset about that. No matter what choice I make, she's gonna disagree with me." My dad shook his head but didn't respond, so I pushed harder. "You guys are the ones who drink *all the time*. What's the big deal if I go out for one night?"

"I'm just gonna go out on a limb and say maybe she cares about you and doesn't want to see you get hurt."

I scoffed. "You're terrible at lying."

"I'm not lying."

I shook my head. "You're leaving out one crucial detail."

He readjusted his grip on the steering wheel, a smirk dancing at the corner of his lips. "And maybe she doesn't want you and your friends getting trashed and destroying the house."

"Ding ding ding," I said gesturing wildly. "And that was *your* fault, right?"

My father's cheeks flushed slightly. "Let's just say, there's a reason I don't drink Scotch anymore." He chuckled. "If she didn't love me, your mother would've killed me years ago."

"Mr. Vaughn!" Jasmine shouted as if we were standing across a large room from one another and not sitting directly in front of her. "Can you come to the party with us? You're the *coolest DD ever.* I bet we could find some tequila for you at that gas station right there." She pointed to a gas station as we drove past it.

"Have you *seen* his liquor cabinet?" Lacie asked. "He doesn't drink cheap gas station crap tequila."

"You have a point, Lacie." My father chuckled. "I don't shoot tequila—I sip it. There's a difference between drinking for effect and drinking for taste."

Jasmine wrinkled her nose. "It's all about the buzz! Otherwise, what's the point?"

I shook my head. "You can ignore them."

He chuckled. "Kinda tough to do that when they're yelling in my ear."

"C'mon Mr. Vaughn!" Lacie prodded. "Just come in for one shot."

"I don't want to ruin the party. Besides, I promised Mrs. Vaughn I'd bring home frozen yogurt."

The girls awed, a slight ringing now penetrating my brain. *It's gonna be a long night.*

"That's adorable," Lacie cooed. "Bring her some tacos. Everything is better with tacos." She paused. "Or a cheeseburger!"

"Oh! Can we go to Jack in the Box on the way home?"

"Yeah! *Please*, Mr. Vaughn!"

I turned up the radio and sighed. *I need a beer, pronto.*

"How much have they had to drink?"

I glanced at my dad. "Enough to heal a new outbreak of the Black Plague."

He frowned. "Are they gonna be alright?"

"At the party? They'll fit right in."

"No, not that. At the house—I don't want them throwing up all over the guest room."

I looked over my shoulder and found the girls dancing to the song playing on the radio. "I'm not drinking much, so I'll make sure they don't get to that point." I paused, noticing how flushed their cheeks were. "Or I'll put them to bed with trashcans next to them. Better safe than sorry."

"That doesn't make me feel any better about the situation."

I shrugged. "Jasmine always makes it to the toilet. It's one of her superpowers. Lacie doesn't throw up. But I promise I'll put down some towels under the trashcans if that will ease your concern."

His response was muted when the girls began to sing, their drunken confidence highlighting how low my self-confidence was. Glancing down at the map on my phone, I grew nervous, my stomach doing summersaults against my ribcage.

We were almost there.

Why am I doing this? I fidgeted with my purple, rubber, cellphone cover. *It's not too late to ask Dad to turn around.* I tapped my foot. *Is it too late to tell Zach I'm not ready to get married?* I rubbed my ring finger. *Why did I turn down that extra shot?* "Turn right up here," I said, trying to keep my panic under control. "And then a left at the next light."

"Hey Kiddo, you okay?" Dad inquired. "You're being awfully quiet." He paused. "Not that you're ever as loud as your friends, but you usually join in a little bit. Or you at least make fun of them if nothing else."

I shrugged. "I'm fine. A little nervous."

He switched on his turn signal. "Everything with Zach okay?"

Another shrug. "We got into a little spat earlier, but it'll blow over."

"I know I'm just your dad, and I know nothing, but as someone who is married – maybe he'd be less upset if you'd wear your engagement ring."

I put my hands between my thighs. "He doesn't know I'm not wearing it," I mumbled.

"Oh. I see." He nodded. "You wanna talk about it?"

"No offense, Dad, but I'd rather not. Just please don't mention anything to Mom."

Another curt nod. "Got it."

"Kinda wish I was on their level," I said, gesturing to the girls now singing into imaginary microphones.

"You should be thankful you're not." He stopped in front of the apartment building. His blue eyes were warm, wrinkles forming in smiles on his forehead. "You'll actually remember the party."

That's the problem. I smiled half-heartedly. *I'd probably be better off if I didn't.* "Yeah, you're right."

He patted my leg. "Call me when you wanna be picked up."

I thanked him and exited the BMW SUV. The girls followed, the now four pack in my hand ready to provide me with the confidence necessary to act on my inappropriate feelings.

"You ready to fuck shit up?" Lacie asked.

I sighed. "You talking about my life?"

Jasmine laughed. "I think she meant the party."

"What do we do? I don't know anyone here." I hugged the now four pack against my chest, the two empty slots crinkling against my arm. "Should we knock?"

"Yeah. And then we thank his parents for having us and accept their offer of pink lemonade," Lacie joked.

I glared. "You're not funny."

Jasmine winked. "Follow our lead, Sugar Tits."

Before we could walk through the front door, a group of five obviously underage girls adorned in scantily clad clothing surrounded us, pushing us through the doorway as if we were members of their skank army. The door slammed behind us, removing any fresh air and breathable oxygen from the small apartment crammed with college students of all shapes and sizes. I couldn't help but notice how skinny the younger girls were, their dresses so tight, there was nothing left for the imagination.

Lacie frowned. "This is more crowded than those clubs in Vegas."

"That's because we had a VIP table to sit at," Jasmine replied.

Hip Hop music hurt my ears, the bass and treble shaking the carpet beneath my wedges. Girls giggled in groups while boys bantered with one another. The hallway to my left was dark, but the living room and kitchen to my right were so bright, I wished I'd brought sunglasses.

"Roxy, we are surrounded by *children*," Jasmine whined. "Why didn't you tell me we'd be attending a play date?"

"Who's gonna buy us drinks *here*?"

I laughed. "It's a *house* party. There is booze *everywhere*. Go turn up your charm and show up those sluts."

"But everyone here looks eighteen. They probably couldn't even buy their own booze."

I chuckled. "You know, you two weren't able to go to bars not too long ago."

"Yeah, but—"

I shook a finger at Lacie. "No buts. You've dragged me to a million places against my will and I sucked it up every time. So, you two are gonna stay here. For me."

They frowned. "Fine. Where's your man candy? I wanna see who's worth breaking off your engagement."

"Roxanne?" a masculine voice said from behind. "You *actually* decided to show up and mingle with the commoners?"

Jasmine and Lacie looked over each of my shoulders, their eyebrows raising just enough for me to notice. I turned around to find myself toe-to-toe with the boy who frequented my inappropriate daydreams.

"H—h—hi there, Matthew," I stuttered, hugging the cold beers to my stomach. The music dulled to a hum, my knees shaking, the other partiers disappearing into darkness. *Just pretend you're in class with him again. Keep it professional. He has no idea how you really feel.*

Matthew's bright green eyes smiled at me—a field of unpicked daisies and unkempt grass just waiting for me to frolic through. His tanned skin brought out the blonde streaks hiding in his brown hair, his subtle five-o-clock shadow defined the sharp angle of his chin, and his tight t-shirt left me short of breath. His runner's stomach was, and probably always would be, skinny, toned, and delicious.

Stop ogling, I ordered. *And for the love of God, say something.* "My good Sir," I said in a fake – and awful – accent. "I made sure to leave my crown at home so I could fit in."

He laughed, his hearty baritone creating a giddy sensation in the pit of my stomach. "I'm glad you were able to make it."

Confidence. Ooze confidence. Guys love confident women. I cleared my throat. "I wouldn't miss the chance to drink you under the table."

His eyes focused on the incomplete six-pack in my hands. "I'm sorry, but I'm having a difficult time seeing this as a threat."

I followed his gaze. "Don't let your eyes deceive you."

He shook his head. "Do you have a handle of vodka hiding somewhere in that outfit of yours or something?"

Is he actually flirting with me? I think he is. Okay. I need to flirt back. "A woman's heart is a dark ocean of secrets."

Jasmine coughed, either to warn me to never quote *Titanic* again, or to remind me I wasn't at this party alone.

I tapped my palm against my forehead. "I do believe I left my manners at home as well." I smiled, gesturing toward my girlfriends. "These are my best friends, Jasmine and Lacie."

They exchanged handshakes, the girls scrutinizing him.

"No, no. Where are *my* manners? Your friends here are empty handed. Why don't we fix that?" Matthew placed his palm on the small of my back—thumb roaming two inches up and down my spine—grabbed the now-four-pack from my grasp and guided me through the crowd effortlessly.

A Beer Pong table was set up in the living room, boys and girls shouting at one another about whether or not a trick shot allowed for the removal of three cups instead of two.

I couldn't help but smile at Jasmine and Lacie, both of whom smiled back, heads shaking. Although they knew what I was doing was morally wrong in every way, they had my back—and they obviously saw just how breathtaking Matthew was.

He even offered them drinks.

They were goners.

When the four of us squeezed through the remaining bodies blocking our entry into the kitchen, Matthew introduced us to his three roommates—all of them as equally cute as Matthew in their own way—and gestured to a tray holding neon plastic shot glasses. "Help your beautiful selves. There's plenty more where that came from."

Boys in muscle tanks and board shorts pushed their way into the kitchen, their shoulders bumping Matthew closer to me. His hand brushed against my thigh before he winked and placed my beers on the counter beside me. I swallowed and flushed, staring down at my toes. *I am officially in over my head.*

"You may want to keep an eye on these," Matthew said tapping the beers. "Drunk people are vultures."

I smiled, grabbed a bottle and nodded, a stray curl falling in front of my eye. "Do you know this from personal experience?"

He shrugged. "I may have stolen a few beers back in the day."

"Then maybe you're the one I should keep an eye on."

He smiled, sending my heart into a full sprint. "I hope so."

Breathe, I told myself. *Breathe before you faint.* "Do you have a bottle opener?"

Jasmine and Lacie snorted, averting their eyes when I looked at them. Matthew chuckled, reached into a drawer and handed me a keychain with a bottle opener that appeared to be a souvenir from Las Vegas. I briefly thought about our trip from only a few months prior, which then lead me to think about snuggling up against Lamont, which then made me flush a deep pink. *Will I ever be able to just forget about him?*

"How about those shots?" Matthew suggested, bringing me back to the present.

The girls each grabbed two shots while I wondered how I could decline without looking lame. *Think Roxy, think.* After grabbing my own, I studied the room quickly, spying a small planter box with a dead plant on the counter corner to my left. *Bingo.*

"Let's see if you can actually live up to those wild stories you told me in class." Jasmine and Lacie smirked.

Don't you dare say a thing, I telepathically pleaded, not wanting Matthew to know my drinking escapades had been a bit exaggerated. Although my hands were trembling, I nodded. "Oh, don't worry," I managed to say in a steady voice. "I never disappoint." My sultry tone caught me by surprise. Even Matthew noticed, his eyes flickering with recognition before he placed the cup to his lips.

With a sideways glance to make sure everybody was too involved with their own alcohol consumption—heads tilted back, eyes closed—I dumped the liquid into the planter and grimaced, wiping my mouth with the back of my hand. *I gotta stay away from this kitchen. I won't get away with dumping drinks all night.* Sipping my beer, I wondered how I would manage to impress Matthew for the rest of the evening.

"Chasing with beer? Girl, you really *don't* disappoint."

Jasmine and Lacie looked from Matthew to me, to Matthew, to me again, skepticism plastered on their faces.

Well, that was easier than I thought. I looked at my beer bottle and begged myself not to stutter. "I do what I can to exceed expectations."

Matthew laughed before he excused himself to entertain his other guests, informing us that while we were his favorites, he'd hate to be a negligent host. Lacie and Jasmine each used the opportunity to down another shot, latch onto my arms, and pull me around the kitchen counter to a corner next to the dining room table—probably the only space in the entire apartment not already occupied by sweaty and smelly bodies.

"Since when do you know how to flirt?" Lacie asked.

"I know this might be crazy, but *I am* in a relationship," I replied. "Relationships typically don't come to fruition unless both parties know how to flirt a little bit."

"You've got a point there."

"I just don't know how to come off as smooth all the time."

Lacie laughed. "It's kind of awkward but it works. I say keep going!"

"No, you are being *way* too obvious about it," Jasmine scolded.

"But he *is* eating it up," Lacie noted.

"You really think so?" I asked.

They glanced over their shoulders, watching as Matthew mingled with a group of young girls and his roommates. He made eye-contact, smiled and raised his beer in our direction.

"I thought you didn't want to sleep with him," Jasmine said.

"Want and *can't* are two very different things," I mumbled.

"He is *really* cute, Roxy. Good find."

Jasmine nudged Lacie. "Don't encourage her. She's *engaged.*"

My buzz finally started to hit me, the flirty confidence I initially unleashed while taking too many shots with my former roommates at Sonoma State now filling my spirit. I held up my beer and wiggled my naked ring finger. "I haven't the slightest idea what you're talking about."

Before either of the girls could respond, Matthew slung one of his arms over each of their shoulders, a beer in both hands. "You three heartbreakers down for a game of Flip Cup?"

His cologne filled my nose, my buzz intensifying. I rested my hand on the dining room table, my knees slacking beneath the weight of my desire. *I need to get myself under control.*

"Find yourself a team," Jasmine challenged. "We're undefeated."

I knew she was talking about her and Lacie, but I pushed my shoulders back as if I were a pro at the game, and not someone who had played it maybe a total of two times in my life.

"Oh yeah?" Matthew asked. "According to who?"

"According to every poor bastard who's been stupid enough to talk shit." Lacie grabbed the beer from his left hand and chugged the remainder of it. "Get some cups, Loser." She put the cup on the table and flipped it upside down effortlessly. "Watch the professionals show you how it's done."

#

"BEST FOUR OUT of five," Matthew insisted, wiping his mouth on the inside of his shirtsleeve. "I'll fill the cups this time. You girls have to be cheating."

We laughed— "we" consisting of me, Jasmine, Lacie, a tall blonde with pale skin and freckles, and a short brunette with brown skin and a round stomach.

I glanced down at my empty cup, hoping he wasn't being serious. I purposely filled my own cup because I was intent on *not* filling it up to the top. I was already pink-faced and overly friendly. The beers I'd brought had been consumed, their empty carcasses staring at me from the counter beside me. It didn't seem to matter that my own stash had disappeared because Matthew had somehow produced beers out of thin air in order to fill our cups.

"Girls rule, boys drool!" I shouted, prompting cheers from my teammates and the girls watching. I was yelling above the rest of the noise, no longer feeling timid and shy. My brain felt foggy and the lights in the house shined even brighter. I felt *good.*

Matthew laughed, eyes closed, head thrown back. "Why don't you put your money where your mouth is?"

I scoffed. "That makes *zero* sense."

He stumbled slightly to the right, bumping into one of his teammates. "Let's make it interesting. One final game. Winner takes all."

"Takes all of what?" I asked.

Jasmine nudged me. "Are you flirting?" she whispered.

"I wish I was," I whispered back, most likely not really whispering. "I honestly have no clue what he's talking about."

The television was displaying music lyrics, a mob of inebriated boys and girls attempting to sing into one microphone, their raspy voices still unable to distract me from this godly creature allowing me to bask in his presence.

"He makes me stupid," I whispered to Jasmine. "I really think my brain stops working when he looks at me."

"How did you manage to pass that class you guys were in together?"

I shrugged. "I did a lot of studying outside of class."

"I wanna make a bet," Matthew said, sliding my now-filled-one-third-full-of-beer-red-solo-cup in my direction. "How brave are you?"

You're talking to the wrong girl. "The real question is, how brave are *you?*" I retorted smoothly, Lacie snorting next to Jasmine.

Jasmine snapped her fingers in front of my nose. "Don't let this fool get in your head. I. Do. Not. Lose." She pointed at my crush. "I'm onto you, *Casanova.* You won't get away with your sneaky bullshit around me."

"I have nothing to hide," Matthew flirted, hands up in mock surrender. "Believe me, life is too short to keep such a beautiful feeling hidden from such a beautiful woman."

When I swooned, Jasmine sighed. "Okay, that was sweet but you're seriously just being obnoxious."

"All of you, stop this fuckery," Lacie snapped. "It's game time. Are we gonna play or are you asshats gonna keep stalling?"

I grasped the red plastic cup, foam floating on the beer's surface. My brain and depth perception weren't muddled by hard liquor, but my beer goggles definitely made things more difficult to see. Somehow, this made it easier to flip my cup, the inability to overanalyze giving me the opportunity to play the game with ease.

"I'm sorry," I again whispered to Jasmine, leaning on her shoulder. "He's just *so adorable.*"

"No," she hissed. "Kittens are adorable. He's just trying to distract you so we lose."

"But what if he really likes me?" I asked full of hope, not letting her negativity bring me down from my flirtatious pedestal.

An abnormally tall boy with large biceps and black curly hair took it upon himself to be the official referee. He placed his elongated arm in the air, his deodorant glistening against his armpit hair. "Start drinking when I say, 'go.' Pair up!"

"You're engaged," Jasmine whispered. "You shouldn't care if he likes you or not." She stared at me angrily, her bushy eyebrows furrowed to the bridge of her nose. "If we lose, I'll never forgive you."

"Okay, you seriously have an issue," I replied. "It's a drinking game."

"A drinking game that I've never lost and I'm not starting today."

Each of the team's members tapped their cups together.

The referee waited for a nod from the boys. Then a nod from the girls. "Place your cups on the table and get ready."

I smiled at Matthew, who smiled back.

"Alright then!" the ref shouted. "Three…two…one…go!"

Matthew and I tapped our cups one last time before chugging the warm beer. It was more difficult than usual, the amount of liquid in the cup slowing me down. Once the cup was empty, I placed the bottom half on and half off the edge of the table, gently flicked my wrist, and watched as the cup landed easily on the rim.

"Go Jazzy!" I yelled. "Gogogogo!"

The girls cheered her on, clapping when she finished the beer, shrieking when the cup flipped and landed on the rim. The short, round girl was next in line, beer droplets trickling down her chin while she flipped her cup. The game was close, each player drinking and flipping with ease. Lacie was the final leg of the race. She lifted the cup to her lips, three drops of beer splattering against her cheek, set the cup down and flipped it.

Matthew's roommate flipped at the same time.

Lacie's landed on the rim with a soft thud.

The roommate's danced on the edge before clattering to the side.

The self-appointed referee slammed his Hulk-sized palm on the table before grasping my forearm and hoisting it in the air. "The vaginas are victorious!"

I grimaced; my shoulder nearly pulled out of its socket, the tall boy obviously not aware of his own strength and height. That's when I realized just how many people were watching the game, girls of all shapes and sizes clapping for us as if we were participating in the Olympics.

The boys groaned and growled, Matthew's roommate crumping the flimsy plastic cup with his monkey paw. "This is horse shit!"

"Suck it, boys! We're number one!" Lacie mocked, shaking her shoulders to bounce her breasts left and right.

"It's a real shame you didn't bet me a kiss," Matthew whispered so quietly, I thought I'd imagined it. "You missed your chance."

My skin grew hot as he walked away, immediately surrounding himself with a huddle of half-naked girls, one of whom was in the Army of Skanks that had ushered us into the party with them.

"That son of a bitch thinks I wanna hook up with him."

Lacie raised her eyebrows. "How much have you had to drink? You don't cuss."

"It's not the beer," I lied. "He pissed me off."

Jasmine shrugged. "Well, don't you?"

"That's not the point," I spat. "He's being an arrogant prick. It's like he think he's hot shit." I leaned back against the wall, doing my best to ignore the fact that the room was tilting side to side. "I want him to want me, not for him to want me because I want him."

Lacie lowered her eyebrows. "So," she drawled. "You don't want to hook up with him?"

I frowned. "Have you been listening?"

"Roxy," Jasmine said hesitantly. "What exactly do you want to do?"

I glanced beyond the kitchen and the living room, over the guests' heads and through the hallway. I don't know if it was the beer or if it was my damaged pride, but I wanted nothing more than for Matthew to admit his attraction to me. "Let's go straight into the lion's den."

The girls looked at one another.

I nodded. "It's time to check out his bedroom."

#

AFTER MY FATHER wished us goodnight and disappeared downstairs, I filled three glasses of water and encouraged the girls to drink it while they ate their Jack in the Box burgers. Not wanting to throw up immediately, I made myself a piece of toast coated with peanut butter and jelly and took a bite, my stomach churning slightly.

"I envy your ability to eat that," I said, watching as half a tomato slice fell onto the counter.

"I envy your skinny ass," Jasmine said through a mouthful of bread.

"Yeah, right. Skinny," I mumbled, the toast tasting like sand on my tongue. I sucked in my stomach and flexed my muscles, hoping the flowy top hid my belly. I downed my first glass of water and refilled it, sipping the cool liquid to calm my nerves. Although I was able to smile and laugh with the girls, deep down, I felt like burying myself alive in a deep, deep hole.

"Your dad is the best," Lacie cooed, crumpling up the brown paper that had covered the hamburger. "Well—second best. Cheeseburgers are the best."

"Yeah, he can be cool sometimes."

Lacie yawned, her bare feet sounding like a stampede in the early morning quiet. "Let's go to bed, Jazz. Love you, Slutbag." She blew me a kiss.

"Please, for the love of God, do not puke on the carpet," I whispered loudly.

Jasmine grabbed the empty bottle of vodka they had finished before the party. "This is my cuddle buddy for the night."

I cringed. "My mother is a doctor. She'll know how to make your death look like an accident."

"Goodnight, Bitch. Thanks for tonight. It actually wound up being fun."

They disappeared around the corner.

Sherlock meowed at me, his green eyes asking me if I liked to get myself in trouble. "Don't you judge me. Those girls are my friends." The door slammed, making me wince. "My soon to be *dead* friends."

Sherlock meowed again, his forehead pressing against my shin. He padded his small feet down the dark gray stairs, his fur blending in with my father's expensive, plush carpet in the dim lighting. I followed his lead. My legs easily made it down the stairs having memorized the twenty steps it took to reach the landing on the bottom floor because I'd lived in the same house for twenty-two years—minus the two years I lived in Rohnert Park as a resident in the dorms at Sonoma State University. I tiptoed down the hallway, careful to shut my door with no more than a click because my parents' master bedroom was only a few feet away at the end of the hall.

When I switched on the light, my eyes fell directly upon the black fuzzy box resting on top of my coffee table. I burped, acid burning the back of my throat as my eyes moistened. *What's wrong with me?* I turned right into the connecting bathroom, Sherlock's meows bouncing off the walls. *Why can't I stop crying? Like seriously. Why can't I get a grip?* I kneeled and placed my cheek on the porcelain seat. *I don't deserve Zach. I don't deserve a boyfriend at all.*

The night hadn't ended like I imagined it would.

Matthew had caught Jasmine, Lacie and I sneaking into his room, an adorable smile plastered on his drunken face. "Ladies!" he said, spreading his arms wide. "Welcome to the Thunder Dome!"

His room was pretty standard for boys living together: an imaginary line drawn down the middle with two beds, two desks, two lamps and two dressers on either side of the room. Matthew's twin bed was on the left, covered with a red comforter and grey pillows where I imagined Matthew and I could engage in heart-felt pillow talk.

I had no idea how exhilarated one could feel just by *looking* at a bed.

"Yes," Matthew whispered when he noticed where I was staring. "That is where the magic is made."

Although I knew he was kidding, the wink he threw in my direction made me wish I wasn't in a relationship.

"What's with all the Mardi Gras beads?" Lacie asked.

Matthew shrugged. "Doesn't everybody have them?"

"I don't," Jasmine said. "How many girls did you flash for these?"

"I never flash and tell."

While the three of them laughed with one another, I sat on the floor by Matthew's bed, my head weighing as much as my backpack on the busiest day of school. My brain was telling me to go home and go to bed, but the beer I drank was convincing me that I had a chance to be intimate with someone like Matthew. *I need to find a way to get us alone. The girls will understand.* Unfortunately, two of Matthew's friends pushed open the door, each with a thirty pack of Coors Light in hand. I sighed and leaned my head against the bed, eyes closed. *I'm such an idiot. Why am I here? Why do I not care about cheating on my fiancé? I need to stop acting this way.* I folded my hands in my lap. *This isn't Lamont. At least you were in love with him—Matt is nothing but eye candy.* I glanced at the beers now in the hands of my friends. *Maybe I should just drink another beer to make everything disappear completely.*

And then something amazing happened.

An open beer was held out in front of my face. "Your best friends seem interested in my best friends." He looked over at Jasmine and Lacie, who were giggling about God knows what. "Or at least interested in the beers they have. I thought we could sit back and watch the catastrophe unfold."

I raised my sight to meet Matthew's snow-melting eyes. I shivered. "Maybe they'll live happily ever after."

He laughed before sitting cross-legged beside me. "Always the eternal optimist."

We watched as the girls sipped from their cans, the boys inching closer and closer. "I just love my friends."

He snorted. "I may be drunk, but even I can see those girls are more interested in those beers than they are in those boys."

I shrugged and took a sip of the beer he had handed to me. "Beers don't play games. Boys do."

"Clearly, you've never woken up next to the porcelain throne wanting to die."

I chuckled. "That's not *really* a game because you bring that upon yourself." I paused and took another sip. "But boys? You can *always* guarantee they'll end up breaking your heart."

He raised an eyebrow. "For someone who's usually so optimistic about things, that's a bit cynical, don'tcha think?"

I both loved and hated how close he was sitting by me. I wondered if he could hear my brain and heart arguing with one another. *He obviously isn't interested. Who cares? I'm the one who shouldn't be interested. I'm engaged. But I want him to want me. Ugh. I'm too drunk.* "I'm not being cynical—it's realistic. I've never had a beer let me down before. But a boy?" I took another sip as I thought about Lamont and the way he broke my heart over and over again. "They only want *one* thing." I shook my head. "And it's not love. Even if it's wrapped up in a pretty bow that may seem like love, it's really just sex in disguise."

He leaned closer to me, his cologne brushing against my nose with so much force, it almost fell off my face. "Sounds like you've been hanging out with the wrong guys. We're not all bad." Somehow, he shifted even closer. "Hey—I'm sorry I haven't been able to talk too much. I'm not trying to make excuses, but I'm the host, so I gotta entertain everyone. Wish it could just be you." We looked at the boys in the backwards neon hats and cut-off t-shirts who were trying way too hard to kiss my friends. "How was summer? Ready to graduate?"

We fell into comfortable conversation, both of us sipping on our beers, my guilt loosening its grip, slipping beneath the drunken haze fogging my judgement. I told him about my new job at Sea World, about the Vegas trip minus Lamont, and about being required to act in front of a crowd in my Shakespeare class. I even mentioned my plans for graduate school, and how I needed to take the GRE without having adequate time to study for it. He told me about his lack of job, his ridiculous class schedule filled with a million different sciences, and a week on vacation in Yosemite with his mom, dad, and sister.

"I'm *really* glad you're here. I missed seeing you," he said huskily.

This was it. This was the moment. I leaned forward, lowered my eyelids and licked my lips. All of the nights spent together working on school projects, nights texting one another until after midnight about Literature, days cracking jokes in class—all that friend-zoning leading to this moment.

"Dude! Matt!" My head snapped to the side, eyes filled with fire. There was one of Matthew's roommates, hair akimbo, something stained on his cargo shorts, motioning for Matthew to stand up. "Yo! It's our turn to play Pong, Man. Why're you hiding here? We have a tournament to win."

And before I even had a chance to react, Matthew followed his roommate without looking back.

Beyond frustrated and embarrassed that a drinking game was more important to Matthew than spending quality time with me, I decided to pull the girls away from the boys and encourage them to leave the party. I texted my father on a blurry phone screen and attempted to get the attention of Lacie and Jasmine. Unfortunately, they were sloppy drunk and more interested in the boys who didn't even come close to passing my beer goggle inspection.

"Ladies," I tried again. "It's getting late. Let's get outta here."

The boys protested, turning their scrawny backs toward me. Angry, I shoved them to the side, grabbing my friends' arms and yanking them into the bathroom, slamming the door to give us privacy.

"Roxy, what're you doing?" Lacie asked. "Those boys are giving us beer!"

Jasmine blinked as she examined the white tile and wooden counters. "There's been a *perfectly clean* bathroom in here *the whole time,* and I was forced to wait in that long ass line for that nasty hole in the wall?"

I sighed. "Those boys aren't attractive. They're *actually* unattractive." I caught sight of my reflection in the mirror, my cheeks burning red from the lingering embarrassment, my hair beginning to frizz, my eyes bloodshot from the booze. *Who am I to judge? I'm not looking too hot, either.* "You know—they're not up to your standards."

"Standards?" Lacie asked.

"Those don't matter when they have *free beer.*"

"Yeah, I get that." I crossed my arms over my chest, wishing I could be free like them—not tied down by love and guilt. *Yeah, that sounds great,* the voice in my head said sarcastically. *And then you can be alone forever.* "You'll thank me when you wake up sober tomorrow."

"They can't be ugly. They're *so tall,*" Jasmine emphasized.

"What does that have to do with their looks?"

"Roxy, they have *beer,*" Lacie repeated.

I took a deep breath, wishing I had another drink. *Maybe I could just leave them here and they can find their own way home.* "You guys, I wanna leave."

"But Roxy," Jasmine swooned. "They're so *tall.*"

"What about Matt? Where did he go?" Lacie asked.

He left me the first chance he got. "I don't care. I'm tired and want to go to bed." *I don't want to have my feelings hurt again.* "If we leave now, I'll convince my dad to stop at Jack in the Box."

The girls looked at one another and nodded. "Let's get the fuck outta here."

When I opened the door, planning to lead the girls through the massive crowd without losing them to another boy offering them free booze, I felt the familiar tingle begin to prick my fingertips, the cold knob fogging beneath my clammy touch.

There, sitting on the bed, was Matthew. And he wasn't alone. A plain-looking redhead in a plain-looking dress with a plainly obvious smirk plastered on her freckled face was in the process of finding her way beneath his covers.

He smiled at me, surprised. "I thought you'd already left."

"Oh, sorry," I muttered, my stomach falling to the floor. *He thought I left already. He couldn't care less if I was here.* "We're leaving now." Knowing my friends would say something to embarrass me, I tried to usher them out of the room quickly.

Matthew stopped me at the door frame, his grasp firm on my elbow. "Hey— what's going on?"

"I didn't realize that your Beer Pong game was taking place in that girl's mouth."

His grin was infuriating. "I found someone else to play for me." He paused. "And when I came back, you were gone."

Jasmine glared. "You're a prick."

Ignoring her, Matthew leaned close to me. "Are you okay?" he asked softly.

No, I'm not. I swallowed back the beer returning up my throat. *I'm a huge idiot.* "Just ready to go home."

He frowned while the girl still sitting on the bed scooted closer to his pillow. "But it's still so early! We have plenty of booze to go around."

"Yeah—well—I've got work in the morning."

"You're so responsible," he said, sounding somewhat disappointed. "You sure I can't convince you to stay?"

Not with that girl smirking at me like that. I shook my head, part of me still wondering if he really did have feelings for me. *What if that girl is just a friend and she's taking things the wrong way?* "I really wish I could, but I'm still new and need to impress the boss."

He smiled beautifully. "Like you could ever disappoint anyone." He opened his arms wide. "Thanks for coming. It was great to see you—as always." When he leaned in, I closed my eyes and puckered my lips, finally feeling that he and I were on the same page.

However, when he didn't return the gesture, I opened my eyes and found him staring at me with a mixture of confusion and repulsion. "What're you doing?" he snapped.

My cheeks felt like fire.

"You have a boyfriend—I don't—wow—I can*not* believe you think I'm that much of a scum bag."

My heart raced. "Oh—no—I—you—our texts—"

He shook his head and took two steps back. "I would've never pinned you as a cheater."

I blinked, swirling back to Sonoma State when I begged Lamont to stop asking me about Zachary. When I seriously considered ending my relationship so I could be intimate with Lamont guilt free. When I realized I wasn't pretty enough because he'd rather be with my best friend, not me.

Jasmine and Lacie yelled at Matthew, calling him names made more colorful by their obscene language. My phone vibrated in my pocket signaling the arrival of my father, the tears threatening to smear my eye-make-up kept at bay by a sudden wave of relief crashing over me.

I could finally escape the apartment and go home.

Now, I sat on the grey tile of my bathroom floor, head resting on the cool toilet seat. I didn't think I'd be sick, but my stomach hurt so badly, I was afraid to go anywhere else. "Why am I like this?"

Sherlock rubbed against my curled-up legs, providing me with a brief sense of comfort, before inspecting his empty food dish and meowing.

I squeezed my eyes shut and took a deep breath. "It hurts so bad," I whined. "Why does it hurt so bad?" *Because you're a cheater. You deserve the pain. And then some.* My stomach churned uncomfortably.

Sherlock meowed again.

I frowned. "It's your job to comfort me. You're doing the opposite."

His big green eyes focused on me, his black tail whipping like a slithering garden snake.

"Can't you see I'm in the middle of something right now?" I grabbed a sheet of toilet paper to dab at the tears and mucus running down my face.

He meowed, softer this time, once again rubbing his short fur against my thigh.

My teeth began to clatter, the tile feeling like a pile of snow beneath the rising temperature of my skin. I sobbed. "My life is falling apart—I've done this to myself."

Sherlock stood on his hind legs and gently pawed at my cheek before touching his forehead against my skin.

"I know I need to call him," I croaked, shifting my body so I was now laying on the bathmat surrounding the bottom of my toilet. "I need to tell him everything. Lamont. Matthew. Our failing relationship. That stupid ring." I inhaled. "I want to be happy." Then exhaled. "*Us* to be happy." I reached out and stroked Sherlock's back. "Can things go back to how they were? Before he proposed? Before Lamont?"

Sherlock began to purr.

"Maybe I can try to fix it." I took my phone out of my pocket and dialed my fiancé's number. "Hey there, Babe," I managed in a semi-steady voice, now focusing on the sound of Sherlock licking his mid-section, my eyes closed. "I know you're sleeping but I wanted to let you know I'm home safe. I hope you had fun with Omar." I paused, the silence of the voicemail piercing my eardrums. "I had a pretty good time with the girls." My mouth was growing dry. *Just tell him the truth. If he loves you, he'll find it in his heart to forgive you.* I hiccupped. *If I tell him the truth, he won't love me anymore. I'll be all alone.* "I love you, Zach. Goodnight."

When I clicked the "end" button, I opened my eyes and found Sherlock's face invading my personal space.

"Stop looking at me like that. I know I'm an idiot. I know going to the party was a huge mistake." I rolled over and stared up at the white ceiling. "I don't get why this is so hard. I love him—I don't want to break up with him. I just—marriage? Am I *ready* for that?"

After staring at the bathroom fan for fifteen minutes, I pushed myself off the ground and began shedding my clothes as I walked toward my dresser.

"Who else could love someone like me?" I pulled an overly large white t-shirt over my messy curls. "Anxiety. Panic attacks. Trust issues. English major. Family disappointment. Fat." I started crying again. "And apparently, my tear ducts are broken."

Sherlock stood in the bathroom's doorframe, tail still twitching, eyes curious.

"Zach probably wishes I was the person he met in high school." I walked past the cat, the red bathmat fuzzy beneath my heels. I turned on the water faucet, filled the glass I'd forgotten to take upstairs the night before, swished and spit out the taste of cheap beer still clinging to my teeth.

After Sherlock meowed again, I reached under the sink, grabbed a plastic container and unscrewed the lid.

"Eat your heart out, you selfish little kitty," I said lovingly, dumping out a small pile of treats.

He ate greedily, his ears turning to the right and left, his whiskers moving with every chew. I zoned in on his tiny shoulder blades, the way his paws tucked under his belly, the almost nonexistent white furs at the end of his tail—somehow these small details were able to ground me, my stomach muscles beginning to loosen. I rested my palms on the grey tiled sink, closed my eyes and bit down on the inside of my cheek, willing myself not to cry anymore.

"Time for bed, Sherlock. Please join me when you're ready. I don't want to be alone tonight."

Chapter Four

I PLACED THE two black napkins rolled around one knife, one spoon and two forks on the tan table, the server map indicating that this party of four also needed a booster seat. My carefully eye-lined eyelids felt as heavy as a textbook due to crying myself to sleep the night prior, but I somehow had managed to evade a gnarly hangover, only a slight headache resting behind my forehead. *I'm never going out again.*

"How's the Dine lookin' this morning?" Dominick asked.

I looked up and smiled at my coworker. "Front row. Should give the five of us five tables each."

Still considered *the new girl* of Dine with Shamu, I remained professional—well, shy—so that my coworkers and managers viewed me as a hard worker, and not just a silly writer with her head in the clouds. I'd been serving at the restaurant for two months now, but only on weekends because I went to school throughout the week, so I always felt a little unsettled at the beginning of every shift, afraid that my awkwardness would ruin my guests' experience.

"Awesome," Dominick said, smiling, his straight, white teeth shining against his dark, Filipino skin. "What some help?"

"Sure. Thanks," I replied politely.

Even though I didn't have a crush on him, I couldn't help but appreciate how good-looking Dominick was. He often spoke about his gym routine, making it a point to get a two-hour workout in his schedule every day, and eating enough protein to feed the killer whales for a week. I frequently admired the way his white button-up tightened around his muscles when he lifted a tray full of dirty dishes, my own strength faltering by the end of the second Dine. To top it off, he was one of the individuals at Sea World to welcome me to the crew, introducing himself with zero hesitation, showing me some serving tricks he'd picked up over the years and offering to help me whenever needed.

"I'll take care of East County," he said, grabbing a container of silverware rolls. "Let me know if you need more and I can get 'em from the back."

East County was Dine with Shamu's slang for the right side of the dining area, which happened to be farthest from the kitchen—much like how many San Diegans believed East County was at the farthest end of San Diego County.

The restaurant was arranged in a horseshoe shape around one half of the killer whale pool. It was an outdoor dining area, which should've been rather obvious because killer whales couldn't feasibly be located *inside* of a building, but somehow, that was not common knowledge to our guests. Sure, there were wooden awnings covering the tables and cheap, plastic chairs, but the sun had a mind of its own—*how dare it shine on four tables when the rest of the tables sat in the shade.*

In the middle of San Diego summer, it's hot. The problem was that guests believed I had the power to control the heat. Or find an umbrella to cover their table. Both equally impossible. I often found myself holding my tongue whenever a guest complained about the heat when they were wearing a tank top and shorts—they didn't have to wear the itchy, white, long-sleeves of an Oxford button-up, high-waisted black pants suffocating everything located from the belly-button down, and an ankle length apron further incubating the legs, producing sweat in places I didn't know could perspire.

It wasn't my job to remind guests they were sitting in an area with a nice breeze, sipping on seven glasses of Coke or eight refilled, unsweetened iced teas—extra lemon, real sugar, please—eating salads and steaks while I beckoned to the calls of six or more tables.

I did, however, have to remind my guests they were sitting in a twenty-four-hour splash zone. There was at least one ten-thousand-pound whale swimming in the pool at any given time, and while I often joked that *it'll cool you down from the sun*, guests found it difficult to comprehend this concept.

The thing was, despite the uniform and the guests, I *loved* my job. I loved being outside. I loved watching the whales interact with one another. I loved conversing with the trainers about the types of animals they had worked with before. I loved the guests that didn't treat me like a servant and more often than not, left me a generous tip on the table once they got up to leave.

And I *adored* my coworkers.

Sea World was my place of escape from the real world, and I could count on my coworkers to make me smile even when I didn't think my facial muscles could do that ever again.

"Hey, Roxy?" Dominick now stood beside me, small patches of moisture clinging to the edges of his black hair. "I was wondering if you wanted to come out with some of us next Friday. It's my birthday and we're going to Phil's. Then laser tagging."

I groaned a little on the inside. *I just promised myself I was never going out again.* "I don't think I've met Phil yet."

His laughter was kind. "No, no. I meant Phil's Barbeque. It's a restaurant."

"Oh," I chuckled, embarrassed. "Clearly, I've never been. Sounds fun, though!"

He nodded. "It's always packed. We're gonna get there around six, but we probably won't get in until seven thirty. You have a million options on the menu—best BBQ I've ever had. Worth the wait."

I smiled. "Sounds amazing. I can meet up after work."

"Feel free to invite your boyfriend," he added before walking through the push doors leading to the kitchen.

I frowned. Since Zachary and I often lunched together, his schedule somehow coordinating with mine, I had to introduce him to my coworkers as to avoid any awkward interactions. Part of me was embarrassed to admit that Zachary was my fiancé, and if he sat with me and my coworkers, they would know he was more than a boyfriend. So, I chose to sit with him and his coworkers, whom already knew all of the details of our engagement. Being in the food service industry, I got away with not wearing my engagement ring because I told Zachary I was too afraid to lose it from washing my hands a million times a shift. Therefore, I was able to keep him as just a boyfriend during business hours and have him return to being my fiancé upon arriving home.

Having Zachary eat lunch with me wasn't all bad, though. I would vent freely about irate Dine guests while he shared stories about people who insisted they would fit in a medium wetsuit when it was clear to everyone else in the room that they wore an extra-large. We never displayed any public affection, afraid that we'd get in trouble for so much as accidentally brushing against one another's arms. It was refreshing—no pressure to be intimate, no nagging conscience telling me to hold my fiancé's hand, no pouting from Zachary because I wasn't in the mood to be romantic. We were able to be *individuals* instead of a package deal, and I cherished those moments especially when Zachary and I lay in bed, me staring at the ceiling fan, tracing my finger repeatedly around the small diamond ring, my fiancé snoring by my side.

I picked a piece of black fur off my white shirt and made my way over to Dine with Shamu's front desk, joining the other servers to pick numbers out of a bowl so we could gather our serving stations, the hostess preparing to open the gate fifteen minutes before ten o' clock so that the guests could be seated and tended to while the trainers prepared their microphones.

I wondered if answering the same questions over and over again bothered them—like who is Shamu, why are they black and white, or what's the deal with the dorsal fin tilting over—or if they actually enjoyed educating the guests who eagerly raised their hands when a trainer walked by.

"Thanks for including me," I whispered to Dominick, *really* feeling like a part of the crew. "I have to be honest though—I get a *little* competitive when a score is involved."

He grinned. "So, you any good then?"

I shrugged. "Intense is a more accurate word."

He smiled again, writing his table numbers on a blank sheet of scrap paper. "I want you on my team."

"You talking about Friday?" Ricardo asked, now glancing at the map.

Dominick nodded. "Roxy *actually* agreed to go."

I flushed when Ricardo slow clapped. "It's about damn time. It only took us asking you to come out eight hundred times." He put on his apron. "You'll have fun. We're fun people. A fucking blast, actually."

You haven't asked me to hang out that many times, have you? "And you're *so humble* about it."

Ricardo laughed, the sound releasing some of the tension from my chest. "Who knew? This girl's got jokes."

Every female worker at Dine with Shamu had a crush on Ricardo—age, color, race, marital status, none of that mattered. They all loved him. He had black spiked hair, lighter olive skin, dark brown eyes filled with an appreciation for life, and a smile that made every girl go out of their way to talk to him. He had a knack for deflating tension and negativity with his humor, and a charm so dazzling, it blinded all those who were lucky enough to experience it.

I swooned, my cheeks flushing pink. *He thinks I'm funny. Okay. I promise I'll never go out again after this one time.* "Sometimes, I guess."

"Good call inviting her," he said, elbowing Dominick. "She's gonna fit in perfectly."

#

"ROXY, COULD YOU fill the water classes? Roger and Lucy are almost here," my mother said, her lotion-smooth hands covered in orange and yellow oven mitts.

62

The kitchen was *always* decorated according to the holiday season, my father forced to dig through the overly stocked hallway closet whenever my mother decided it was time for a change. The greatest part was, we lived in San Diego, so these "seasons" my mother embraced didn't actually exist.

"I'm excited to see baby Hannah," my mother continued, her light brown eyes glistening. "Lucy said she can already differentiate shapes. She's gonna be as smart as her mama. And grandmama."

I rolled my eyes. *Another prodigy. Great.* "Pretty sure I was able to read at her age."

My mother chortled. "Yeah. Sure."

Not that you'd remember anything about my childhood. "Do you want ice in the water?"

"Honey, please cover the steak," she told my father, ignoring me.

"No ice then," I muttered, searching through the high cabinet shelves for a ceramic water pitcher.

"It's gonna get cold." Not only was she ignoring me, she was also ignoring the fact that my father was ignoring her because football was on the television. "*Honey,*" she growled, the potatoes steaming hot on the aluminum tray she placed too heavily on the stove. "*The steak. Please.*"

Although an almost inaudible sigh escaped my father's lips, he nodded, his crystal colored eyes never leaving the pigskin soaring across the field, his feet stepping with a zombie-like enthusiasm on the tile floor.

My mother shook her head and walked over to the sink to drain the green beans. "And once you're done with the waters, Roxanne, could you *please* get the salt and pepper shakers? Also, butter and sour cream."

I sure hope I get a tip after all this, I thought sarcastically. I placed the water jug on the middle of the table. "Anything else, Master?"

"What did you just say?" my mother asked, the tips of her ears turning pink.

"How about we all get along tonight?" my father asked. The game was now on commercial break. "We're going to have a wonderful dinner together. Hannah is an absolute delight."

I smiled at him. "Is your team winning or something?"

He smiled back. "By two touchdowns."

My mother took a deep breath and exhaled, the steam rising from the potatoes swaying away from her. "They'll be here any minute."

I reached into the pantry and grabbed the pumpkin and squash shaped salt and pepper shakers. "You seem to forget that Lucy grew up in this house. She knows our family isn't perfect."

"Honey," my mother addressed my father, choosing to not acknowledge my presence any further. "Did you remember to dust, sweep, vacuum and mop? I don't want Hannah to get sick from whatever Roxanne is dragging in from Sea World."

"It'll be good for her immune system," I murmured, searching the fridge for non-fat sour cream and salt-free butter.

My father snorted, covering it with a cough when my mother glared at him, hands on her hour-glass hips. "Yes, I did it when I came home from work. And yes," he continued when my mom opened her mouth. "I already changed out of my germ-infested shoes when I did it." He ran a hand through his gray hair, which had begun to thin as of late. "She's going to be fine."

The doorbell rang before the front door opened, signaling the arrival of the favorite daughter. "Guess who's here?" Lucy sang, her angelic voice filling my stomach with dread.

The glow that touched my mother's high cheekbones made me want to dump the sour cream all over her silky, hair-sprayed, flawlessly styled, straight blonde hair.

"Satan? Is it really you?" I called out over the clacking of Lucy's and Mother's expensive heels on the tile.

"Hardy-har, you gremlin," Lucy replied, unravelling the hot pink scarf curled around her neck even though it was warm enough to wear short sleeves outside.

I grimaced when she and my mother kissed one another's lip corners as if they were once college roommates and not mother and daughter. It even bothered me that my father was so invested in welcoming the Lovelace clan that he *turned off* the television despite the crazy score—something he never did when I tried talking to him. He and Roger shook hands and hugged like the two handsome, plastic surgeon peas in a pod they were.

"Oh, don't worry about me. I'm your nameless server. This is a twenty-four-hour splash zone. Please be aware that everything is included with your dinner, except for gratuity and alcohol." I placed the butter and sour cream on the dinner table and waved awkwardly when Roger and Lucy finally made eye-contact with me. "Why, *hello there* lovely people. Where's the munchkin at?"

Roger turned and pushed the stroller toward me, Hannah's kind, green eyes melting away the layer of hate that encased my heart whenever surrounded by my family.

"Hi there, you chubby chipmunk," I cooed, placing my hands beneath the baby's armpits and lifting her to my face, rubbing my nose against hers. "You are quite the sight for sore eyes." I smiled when she giggled, flashing those bubble gum gums in my direction. "At least *you* appreciate me even though I refuse to join the medical field."

"Roxanne, get the wine ready," my mother said, taking off her apron. She adjusted her orange blouse, the material stretching across her breasts. "There's red and white. Grab two of each. Lucy, you're not still breast feeding, are you?" She snatched the glorious creature from me, shooing me to the refrigerator.

"Nope," Lucy said. "I've been pumping. I don't have time to have a kid on my boob twenty-four seven. She's already twelve months old."

One year old. She's a year old. You don't have to be one of those people who talk about age in months. I frowned, wishing that I were at work so I could at least make money for being treated like a slave. "Gotta love *family* dinners," I muttered, grabbing two bottles of Chardonnay chilling on the refrigerator's top shelf.

"Why didn't you tell me sooner?" Mother whined. "I would've had your dad make margaritas."

Because nothing says causal family dinner like tequila when a baby is present. I smiled and winked at Hannah when I placed the white wine on the two marble coasters Roger purchased for my mother last Christmas. Hannah giggled. *At least there's a member of the family that doesn't completely hate me.* I turned away to retrieve the other bottles. The red wine was located in a special cabinet above the sink, which allowed bottles to remain stocked on their sides.

"What blend did you want?" I asked.

"I'm sure whatever is just fine," Lucy said. "But please, at least grab one Cab."

Then whatever is not fine. I rolled my eyes.

"Make sure you grab a dessert wine for the movie we rented," Mother said.

"Thank you, but we honestly can't be up that late. We have Hannah."

"That's nonsense. Roxanne would be happy to watch her —"

"No, she doesn't have to do that. I'm driving to the hotel anyway, so I wasn't planning on drinking—maybe just one glass."

An uncomfortable silence grew above the snapping together of high chair safety buckles.

"Hotel?" my father asked.

Lucy glanced at Roger, who scuffed the toe of his brown dress shoes against the tile, before shrugging. "Yes. A beautiful suite at the Hyatt on Mission Bay."

"We thought it would be nice for our weekend vacation," Roger added hesitantly, his thin face blushing red.

"You have a room here," my mother asserted. "Here. In your *home.*"

Lucy shook her head. "No. This is *your* home. Our home is in L.A."

My eyes widened. *Did she just—oh my.*

"Mrs. Vaughn," Roger said. "We always appreciate your gracious hospitality. We just—we have Hannah and we don't want to imp—"

"Impose?" My mother's voice grew shrill. "Lucy, I *never* get to see you anymore. I thought you were planning on staying the weekend here?"

"Yes. Here. *In San Diego.* Roxanne was generous enough to get us Sea World tickets. We think Hannah is going to love it."

I remained quiet. *Don't bring me into this. For the first time ever, I'm not the one who messed up.*

My dad stepped away from Roger and placed a comforting arm around my mother's shoulders. "You're never an imposition. You're our daughter. Your mother and I were looking forward to spending time with you—all of you— especially our granddaughter."

Lucy smiled. "You guys, we're gonna be in town *all* weekend. We plan on spending ample time with you. We just thought—"

"We have *plenty* of room here. We even purchased a new crib for Hannah."

Roger sighed. "You're both so generous—"

"Lucy," my mother interrupted. "Why on *earth* would you get a hotel room? You have a *beautiful* room here. You've *never* stayed in a hotel when you've come to visit."

I grinned. *Well, well, well. It appears that the child who sits at the right hand of the mother has fallen from greatness.* Slowly making my way over to the counter where the food was sitting, I absorbed every word that left their mouths. *This is much better than reality TV.*

"Can we not be like this?" Lucy asked, beginning to uncork one of the Chardonnay bottles. "I've been looking forward to this dinner all week. Please don't ruin it."

My mother's petite ears flushed red at the tips, her lips tightened into a tight line—one that always preceded an argument. "I'm just trying to unders—"

"Mother," Lucy warned, her wine filling a little too close to the rim of the glass. "Stop."

"Stop? Stop what? Stop wanting to spend time with my daughter?"

I cringed.

"No. I'm asking you to stop freaking out. I want to spend time with my husband and daughter—we haven't had a lot of time together as a family lately."

Hannah swirled her finger in a drop of white wine that splashed on the table in front of her, toes curling and uncurling beneath a pair of princess socks.

"Roger?" My father turned to his son-in-law. "Is everything okay? Are you two having problems? Why aren't you spending time together at home?"

He shook his head. "We've actually never been better. Work has just been bus—"

"Is my house not good enough for you?" Mother was nearing hysteria, the creamy coloration of her chest just above her orange blouse beginning to flush purple. "Are *we* not *good* enough for *you*?"

"That's not it at all, Mrs. Vaughn—"

"I wasn't speaking to *you*, Roger!" my mother roared.

I picked a green bean out of a serving dish and popped it into my mouth.

"Don't you *dare* talk to my husband that way!" Lucy gestured wildly, her wine spilling over the rim and onto the rug my mother purchased to prevent the wooden table from scratching the tile.

"This is *my* house and I can talk to *my* guests any damn well way I please. Not that you care about *my* house—not *your* house, as you made so clear—even though I raised you in it."

"Mother, you're being ridiculous! I never once said I didn't want to spend time with you. You're freaking out over *nothing*."

"You think *I'm* being ridiculous?" She grabbed one of the plates from the table—white with dark green trim around the perimeter—and smashed it to the ground. "I'm freaking out because *I don't even know my daughter anymore!*"

Silence ensued, followed by small sniffles and quivering lips from my little niece. *Oh no. Nonono. Don't need a meltdown.* Preparing for a war I never thought would take place between my mother and my older sister, I swallowed a fourth green bean and unclipped the baby from her seat.

"What the *hell* is *wrong* with you?" Lucy shouted.

"You made me do this!" Mother replied.

I smiled at Hannah. "Yes, that's your crazy grandmother. Let's hope you don't inherit any of her irrational genetics," I whispered in a goo-goo voice, trying to distract her from the chaos now echoing off the professionally decorated beige walls. "This must be one of the side effects of empty nest syndrome." I paused. "Except I'm still at home."

Even though my mother and Lucy did not approve of Sherlock being around the baby, I didn't have a choice at the moment. The cat was locked in my room whenever company was present, and I didn't want him to get in the middle of the battle upstairs. I closed the bedroom door behind me, placed Hannah gently on the carpet and collected three plush animals from the top of my comforter to keep the child entertained. Sherlock glanced curiously at the little girl, ears twitching back and forth.

"Play nice, Kitty," I warned, his tail swishing like a worm beside his curled up hind legs.

I turned on my plasma screen television to an episode of *Sex and the City*, needing some background noise to prevent Hannah from realizing that her mother was screaming directly above us. Although the baby studied the colored screen with wide eyes, Carrie and Mr. Big having sex in thirty-two-inch High Definition, I did not change the channel.

"As pleasant as the TV makes it seem, sex isn't always that great." I shook my head, now thinking about Lamont. "Maybe if you're with the right person. That one special person." I groaned. *That's your infant niece. This is not an appropriate conversation. And these are not appropriate thoughts.*

Hannah's little peach of a hand stroked the yellow puppy that resembled my old dog, Molly, and her pink cheeks lit up with satisfaction.

"It's a real shame the rest of our family believes I'm gonna taint you with my writing like it's some sort of terminal disease."

She continued to pet the stuffed dog, squealing with delight.

"You'll be a wonderful doctor, I'm sure. Carry on the Vaughn family legacy with pride."

The dog fell to the side, Hannah trying to pull it up to her chest.

"Maybe you'll be a veterinarian. That's still a doctor." I paused. "Just don't forget about your loser aunt when you make it big, okay?"

Sherlock hopped off the full-sized bed and studied Hannah, two pairs of green eyes refusing to break eye-contact.

"Or you could rebel against them and be who *you* want to be. Forget about them."

Hannah reached out a chubby little arm and grasped Sherlock's tail with her fingers. I held my breath, afraid that the cat would react and scratch her, the Siamese side of him lashing out. Instead, Sherlock turned around and rubbed his head against her skin. Exhaling, I collapsed on the ground and smiled. "I gotta tell Zach about this."

I reached into my pocket and pulled out my cellphone, noticing I already had a text message. Only, it wasn't from my fiancé. It was from a number that was unknown to my phone, but forever etched into my brain. It wasn't much of a text— a simple "Hi." But it was from someone I hadn't spoken to in months. Someone who resided in my brain far too often. Someone who's ears must've been burning because I was just talking about him to my niece.

Lamont.

I dropped the phone as if it were a hot potato. *What does he want?*

Both Hannah and Sherlock were looking at me now, their curious stares making me self-conscious. "Don't judge me," I hissed. "You don't know what he put me through—neither of you were there."

The phone vibrated again.

I swallowed.

Glancing down, I saw Zachary texted me asking how dinner was going.

"It's just like sophomore year all over again."

I shook my head and picked up the phone, making it a point to delete Lamont's text so I wouldn't be tempted to respond. *That ship has sailed too many times.* I did, however, take a picture of Hannah and Sherlock and send it to Zachary, accompanied by a short paragraph explaining what happened with my mother. And then I followed up with a text that I actually meant: *I wish you were here.*

I put my phone back in my pocket and watched the television, trying my best to ignore the tingling sensation beginning in my toes. *What did Lamont want? His girlfriend must've broken up with him or something.* I sighed. "It doesn't matter. He doesn't matter."

I reeled back to Vegas—to the moment Lamont told me he loved me just to try to get into my pants. *Don't go there. He's not worth it.*

Hannah pet Sherlock softly, which made me smile again. "How about we play a game, Little One?"

I don't know how much time passed before a loud knock interrupted the barking noises I was making behind the stuffed dog, which was making my niece giggle uncontrollably. I appreciated that her innocence could distract me from the fact that I wanted to text Lamont back—I wanted to know about his relationship status. I wanted to know why he texted me. I wanted to know what made him think of me.

Lucy entered the room, her black eyeliner smeared beneath her lower lashes. "Mom wants you to know that dinner is ready." She noticed Sherlock rub against Hannah's back and sighed. "You know I don't like her being near that cat."

I hoped she wouldn't notice the fact that the four girlfriends on the television screen were discussing blowjobs, even if some of their words has been replaced to be appropriate for cable television. "It's a cat," I replied.

She crossed her arms over her chest. "I'm aware. A cat that shits in a box and is covered head to toe in waste particles. And a cat that you refuse to get declawed, which could result in serious infection if he scratched my baby."

I scoffed. "You let Hannah play with Mom. At least Sherlock won't throw plates at people."

"Mom didn't throw it at anyone," she spat. "She's not crazy."

"Lucy, she shattered a plate because you're not spending the night. Sherlock hasn't stopped purring since he laid eyes on Hannah."

"Mom's had a stressful week," she said. "Teenagers with STDs. Unwanted pregnancies. Women suffering from early menopause." She paused. "Don't you ever ask Mom about her day?"

I shook my head. "She never asks about mine."

"You really need to grow up."

I rolled my eyes. "Why aren't you guys staying here anyway?"

"Don't tell Mom and Dad, but we're trying to have another baby." For just a moment, I thought I saw sadness in her eyes, but she blinked it away. "We haven't had any luck."

"You know Mom and Dad would be thrilled." I frowned. *Is something more going on? Are you and Roger actually having problems?*

"Yeah, but Hannah was conceived so easily. It was like the first time we'd fucked without any birth control."

I cringed and pointed at her child. "Can you not talk like that?"

She sat on the loveseat and shrugged. "Well, anyway, this time around has been tough. If Mom knew, she'd try to get involved—hormones and specialists and all that crap. And then having sex with my husband wouldn't be fun anymore."

I ran my palms over the carpet. "Please, spare me the details. I don't want a visual."

She angled herself toward the floor-to-ceiling mirror on my closet, pulled some lipstick out of her pant pocket and reapplied. "Having sex in Mom's and Dad's house is weird."

I chuckled. "You used to do it all the time."

She capped her lipstick. "Yeah, but once you move out, that shit is weird."

"Why didn't you just let Mom and Dad know you hadn't planned on staying? Maybe they wouldn't have freaked out so much if they hadn't been caught off guard." I stood and brushed the fur off my pants.

She shrugged. "I didn't want to hurt anyone's feelings—it was stupid—I should've given Mom notice so she could've gotten it out of her system. I didn't think she'd freak out the way she did, though."

Holding my tongue, I lifted my niece, kissed her cheek and handed her over to my sister. *You shouldn't be having another baby if you're condoning Mom's irrational behavior.* "You know, I won't give the child my rebel spirit just by being near her."

"I wouldn't call you a *rebel.* I would call you an idiot."

"Seriously," I sighed. "You let me babysit her in L.A. but whenever Mom is around, you act like she's gonna catch something from me."

She glared. "As I said before, dinner is ready." She stood, brushed off her child's velvet, black, green and purple dress, and walked past me. "If you could keep your attitude in check for one night, I think we could all have a nice evening together."

"I wasn't—"

Lucy turned on her heels and left the room, closing the door behind her.

I looked at Sherlock, who I could've sworn shrugged at me. "No matter what I do, I'm in the wrong. I quit, Sherlock. I quit."

#

AFTER WAITING IN line for thirty minutes, ordering a chicken sandwich with a side of French Fries and awkwardly sitting in a metal chair placed at the middle of a table set for thirty, I found myself having a fantastic time.

Initially, I was nervous, regretting not inviting Zachary because I didn't have someone to lean on in the event that I grew uncomfortable. I had walked up to the line wrapped around the restaurant, timidly approaching my coworkers' familiar faces. Not knowing the appropriate way to greet everyone outside of work, I smiled and waved before shoving my hands into my jean pockets. I listened as everyone talked about their lives to one another, reminding me that they'd all been working together for at least a year. I stared at the tops of my black and white Converse, rocking from my heels to my toes, questioning what had prompted me to agree come to this soiree in the first place.

Now, I was glad I told Zachary this was a "work thing" strictly for Dine with Shamu employees. Instead of worrying about his social awkwardness and making it even worse by trying to answer questions for him, I was able to crawl out of my shell far enough to interact honestly with my coworkers and get to know who they were outside of their uniforms.

Cassandra, one of the coworkers who was closer to my age than the others, sat across the table from me, her long, dirty-blonde hair hanging straight past her breasts. We had spoken a few times when running food together, but not about anything personal or consisting of any depth.

That changed at the dinner table.

I learned that she was in a long-distance relationship with a long-term boyfriend. I learned she was also a student at SDSU, studying Hotel and Restaurant Management. I learned she went to the gym on campus every day because she lived around the corner, and that she usually watched Jeopardy while she pushed herself through a one-hour workout on the elliptical. I also learned that she dreamed of owning her own restaurant chain one day because being a manager wasn't good enough.

I was quite surprised to find out that Cassandra and I had a lot in common. A family that expected too much. An older sister considered an angel among women. Far-fetched dreams. A crazy work ethic. A long-term relationship she didn't seem too excited about.

The more we spoke, the more I wanted to become friends with her. I even believed she wanted the same—her big, brown eyes were attentive when I spoke, and her pink lips smiled often, a smudge of barbeque sauce refusing to leave its perch on the corner of her mouth.

Even Jennifer, who was shy and quiet at work—often only speaking when spoken to—was animated and engaged in the conversation, asking questions and relating answers to her own life experiences. She'd become one of my better friends in the short time I'd been at Sea World. As a Kitchen Lead, it was her responsibility to teach everyone how to work in the kitchen and to keep employees working instead of gossiping with one another over coffee. She'd showed me the ways of Dine with Shamu in the beginning, and the more time we spent together, the more we opened up about things not involved in typical small talk. She was two years younger than me, studying film at one of the junior colleges in San Diego, and aspiring to work in Hollywood as a director. Although young, she supported her mom and dad with her minimum-wage pay, putting her own dreams on hold to make sure her family could survive if she ever decided to leave.

Unlike me, who'd basically inhaled my chicken sandwich and French fries, stuffed to the point where it hurt to breathe, Jennifer ate like a mouse, each bite of her steak cut into teeny-tiny squares. The way she was able to get equal parts bread, meat and sauce was fascinating. "I always eat like this," she informed me when I asked her, half-jokingly, how she had the patience to eat her food that way. "I hate being messy. And I just like food." And then she laughed.

"No wonder you're so skinny," Cassandra said. "I wish I could do that. I always eat like a hyena."

I held up my Bud Light. "I hear ya, Sister."

We laughed, Jennifer's cheeks darkening to a shade nearly purple. "No, it sucks. People are always waiting on me."

"You all done yet?" A drunk Dominick interrupted, squatting down behind my and Jennifer's seats. "We've got laser tagging to do."

Jennifer gestured to him. "This is exactly what I'm talking about."

Dominick smiled, a small speck of pepper stuck on his canine tooth. "I've had enough lunches with you to know that you eat like a sloth."

"Mouse," Jennifer corrected. "Sloths have that ugly thing to worry about." When Dominick laughed, Jennifer slapped his shoulder. "Why're you in such a rush anyway? You know you're gonna lose."

"Unlike most who get sloppy when drunk, my senses get heightened. It's like I become Spider Man."

Cassandra shook her head. "You didn't get bitten by a radioactive spider."

Jennifer poked Dominick's cheek. "Your cheeks are bright red. That's a dead giveaway you've had too much to drink."

Dominick frowned at me. "Pfft. Drunk, Schmunk. You have faith in me, don't you?"

I smiled. "I think I have a surprise for you that will help everyone's morale."

He squeezed my shoulder and stood. "A surprise? I knew there was something special about you."

Glancing down at my lap, I blushed. "I don't think you're ready for it."

He scoffed. "Once the sloth finishes her food, we're heading out. Now, I gotta mingle—I can't believe everyone from work *actually* showed up. It *never* happens." He paused. "Where's Zach? I remembered to invite him, right?"

I shrugged. "Yeah—but—uh—he's busy tonight. Stressed about lesson plans and student teaching." *But probably doing nothing about it. I'm sure he's engaging in virtual foreplay with Omar in some stupid computer game.* "He was bummed he couldn't make it."

Dominick wiped his forehead, which was moistened. "I totally understand. Just wanted to make sure I invited him—I know you two come as a pair."

I swallowed the tart taste in my mouth and forced a smile. "Two peas in a pod."

When he disappeared to the other side of the table, Jennifer studied her food while Cassandra studied me. "What's the big surprise?"

I sipped on some water, allowing an ice cube to rest on my tongue. "Nothing crazy—kinda goofy—embarrassing really."

"Embarrassing?" Jennifer asked.

I swished the ice cube from one cheek to the other. "Yeah, but sometimes being goofy can be fun. Especially if at least one other person wants to do it with you."

Cassandra shook her head. "Do we *all* have to participate?"

"Only if you're lucky enough to end up on my team." And I downed the rest of my beer in the hope of drowning out any remaining nervousness. I was ready to show my coworkers the real way to play laser tag.

#

WHEN I STEPPED out of the car, Dominick took one look at me and started slow clapping, causing the other Dine with Shamu employees to turn in my direction.

I should've ordered another beer. I smiled, trying my best to mask my anxiousness. "You all ready to lose?" This was a side of me my coworkers hadn't seen—the girl that embraced her inner twelve-year-old because it made her happy to be carefree every once in a while. And because I was a Vaughn, I didn't know how to half-ass anything, so I went *all out.*

Ricardo laughed and raised his hand for a high five. "That. Is. Epic."

Dominic lifted his right eyebrow. "If you're gonna do something like that, you better've brought some for everybody."

Their excitement made me giddy. "Well, not for *everybody*." I reached into my pocket and pulled out two tubes of face paint—one black and one white. "Only teammates."

"You're crazy," Ricardo said. "I love it!"

Although I was slightly embarrassed, seeing all of my coworkers nodding their approval instilled a sense of confidence I wanted to have when around these people. While in the car, I'd done a minor wardrobe adjustment to prepare for laser tag. I'd pulled my curls into a high ponytail, constructed a headband out of an American flag bandana, reapplied my Superman red lipstick and used four cotton swabs to carefully paint two black and white lines beneath my eyes.

When I saw Dominick eye my bandana, I pulled another from my back-jean pocket. "Don't worry, Birthday Boy. I knew you'd want to be on my team, so I got you one, too."

His smile was so bright, I wondered if he'd gotten his teeth whitened right before dinner. "You're the *best!*" He tied the bandana around his head and stood patiently as I painted lines beneath his eyes to match mine. My other coworkers talked excitedly around me, my heart thrumming against my chest nervously; they, too, wanted face paint, taking the paint tubes from me once Dominick's design was done.

"Team Blue!" he shouted, pulling me into a hug. "This is awesome. I knew you were more than that quiet girl at work. Thanks for coming out—I think you really helped pump everyone up for this."

I smiled, a pressure I didn't notice lifting off my shoulders as I watched other members of the Blue Team draw on one another's faces, laughing the whole time. "I wasn't kidding when I told you I'm competitive. I take this stuff seriously."

Dominick patted my back. "We'll see how good you do out there."

When he walked away to go mingle with our coworkers, Cassandra nudged my side. "Dang girl. You're not who I thought you were."

I flushed. "I—um—is that a bad thing?"

She shrugged. "You're just so quiet at work. I would've never guessed you had something like this hidden up your sleeve."

"Well, work isn't really a place where face painting is appropriate."

Jennifer, who had two hearts now painted on her cheeks, joined us. "Roxy, this is amazing! *Such* a great idea."

Although it wasn't a big deal, hearing the compliments of my coworkers and seeing their laughter made me feel more appreciated than I'd felt in far too long.

Unlike at my last job, where none of my coworkers cared to learn about my life outside of bussing tables, my Dine with Shamu team had invited me to join a second family. They believed I was good enough to be included.

I had officially become one of them.

"C'mon, Roxy! Blue Team's gotta show Red Team who's boss!" Dominick shouted, gesturing for me to follow.

I smiled and nodded, Cassandra and Jennifer walking beside me. Nothing felt forced. Nothing felt fake. It was exactly the kind of night I needed to escape from the stress of my engagement and the pressures put on me by my family. *All of this feels right. I belong with these people. I finally have a family that accepts who I am. Who likes me for me.* And the happiness I experienced from this realization was like nothing I'd ever felt before.

#

I WALKED INTO the kitchen, the industrial strength fly fan above the door providing me with some relief from the early October heat wave. The large, stainless steel dishwasher was loudly cleaning the white and blue plates, the clank of ceramic still hurting my ears despite the hundreds of hours I'd already put in at Dine with Shamu.

Non-slip shoes splashed through small puddles of water and crushed crumbs of food gathered variously over the red-tiled floor, food runners delivering pans of chicken, potatoes and steamed vegetables—only a few of the many items we offered on the buffet line—in and out of the buffet room, sneaking a small tidbit into their mouths here and there before the leftovers were scraped into a green-waste bin.

I placed my black, circular tray on the stainless-steel table we called "the server table" and began scraping food off of the guests' plates into a double bagged trashcan.

One of the older female servers entered the kitchen, a big smile on her slightly wrinkled face. "Roxanne, you need to go outside. Now."

I raised an eyebrow. "I just asked my tables if they needed anything. I know eight needs a Coke. What did I miss?"

She shook her head, her black, wavy ponytail dancing against her shoulder blades. "There's a cute boy out there. He looks about your age."

This happened frequently whenever I worked. The older women at Dine believed they had the power of an enchanted matchmaker, always attempting to pawn me off on some unsuspecting customer who merely wanted more lemon wedges for his iced tea.

They were worse than my mother.

"I'm in a relationship," I reminded her. "Why bother?"

"There's no harm in looking, is there?"

Although she winked at me, I shook my head. *Why does everyone encourage me to be a terrible fiancé?* "I'm only going back out there because the little girl at table eight wants her Coke." *But I mean, if I see him, I see him. Can't avoid him if he's by my section.*

I walked through the double doors and smiled at the guests who cheered for whales jumping out of the water, their heavy bodies producing a loud and large splash at the far end of the pool. When I turned to pass the buffet room, I froze. Apparently, my coworker wasn't the only one who noticed this boy.

A circle of men and women surrounded two individuals standing by the buffet room windows. The first one, the young man my coworker mentioned, had the face of a fifteen-year-old—blemishes and soft features—and hair the color of a salt and pepper mixture: gray like a man in his eighties with hints of his youth standing tall like blackened tree trunks after a forest fire. Even his eyes were grey, the color of the ocean anticipating a storm. Everything about him appeared elongated: long face, long nose, long torso, long legs, long arms. Sure, he was cute, but he seemed *much* younger than me, his bright smile reminding me of an adolescent trying beer for the first time.

The other individual—an older gentleman—talked excitedly to the guests, a *very strong* English accent making it difficult for me to catch what he was saying. Where the young man was long, this man was round: round face, round nose, round ears, round belly. A brown, leather safari hat with a dark brown and white feather sticking out covered his hair, black, thick-rimmed glasses magnifying his olive-green eyes, and a white mustache hugging the skin between his nose and pale, upper lip.

I didn't understand why such a large crowd surrounded them. *Are they movie stars or something? I've never seen them in anything before.* And then I realized the men weren't what these people were interested in. They were all staring at what was perched on the thick, leather glove that adorned the older gentleman's left hand.

A large bird with a sharp, yellow beak, curious black eyes, dark brown feathers and yellow feet attached to deadly, black talons. Around the bird's ankles were small leather straps, one of which had a jingle bell attached. I smiled briefly, wondering if this was how these men kept track of this wild animal when it was flying free. I moved my eyes back up to the bird's face, knowing it was impolite to stare, but unable to look away. The creature was *beyond* magnificent. I'd never seen anything like it before—at least, not in person outside of an enclosure. I wanted to push past the crowd, walk up to the two handlers and ask a million questions about the predator.

"Hey, Roxy. You there?" Dominick waved his hand in front of my face, breaking me free of my trance.

The high-pitched whistle that the trainers blew when the whales performed the correct behavior touched my ears, followed by applause from guests sitting at their tables.

I blinked, blushed and chuckled slightly. "Yeah—thanks—my bad. I got— uh—a little—erm—distracted."

He gestured toward the supervisor's desk, where two of our bosses stood at a computer helping guests with merchandise purchased from the small rack displayed beside the cash register. "Doesn't bother me, but the supervisors won't like it."

"I appreciate you looking out for me."

He nodded as I briskly walked to table eight to give the little girl her drink. Once I checked on the other tables to make sure my guests were happy while the whales and trainers continued to put on a show, I made my way back to the kitchen for an extra napkin and a bowl of sugar packets.

Unfortunately, the older woman ambushed me again. "So, did you see him?" She nudged the left side of my ribcage.

"The boy?" I responded. "Did *you* see the bird?"

Ricardo, who had been filling more glasses with ice and soda, nudged the right side of my ribcage. "Why don't you ask him about it? The perfect excuse to have a conversation."

I laughed, shaking my head. "Don't be ridiculous. The best-looking thing about that boy is the bird his safari-hatted coworker is holding."

The woman whistled. "You're tough to impress."

"Maybe you should ask him if you can hold his bird," Ricardo teased before picking up his tray and walking outside.

Shrugging, I prepped the tip trays I was going to place on my tables once the whale interaction was finished, ignoring the prickly feeling on the back of my neck. "The man I'm in a relationship with works in *very close* proximity. Holding a stranger's bird would *probably* upset him." I'd made the decision to be the good fiancé Zachary deserved after the whole Matthew fiasco, and that included only speaking to any member of the opposite sex in a professional manner. Especially when my coworkers, like the older woman who was still smirking at my back, suggested I make the moves on every guest with a penis. "Now, if you'll excuse me," I continued, grabbing a black napkin, a bowl of sugar packets, and two straws. "I have guests to attend to."

For the rest of the Dine, I did nothing but work. I bussed plates from tables, refilled drinks and handed out tip trays with peppermints on top. I waved good-bye to guests as they stood to leave and threw away any wrappers before the wind blew them to the ground. I did everything in my power to avoid the men and their bird, my attention remaining on the tips of my shoes whenever I passed them.

So, when the safari-hatted man called out, "Excuse me, Miss," I nearly dropped the stack of nine plates piled on top of my tray.

"Y-yes?" I stuttered, fingers gripping the side of my tray so hard, my knuckles whitened.

The man smiled. "I didn't mean to startle you."

It took me a minute to decode his thick accent, his kind demeanor softening the stiff muscles in my shoulders. I tried to keep my eyes focused on his leathery face even though the bird was much more beautiful to look at. "That's alright. I was just—in the zone—trying not to—you know—drop plates and stuff."

"I'm sure carrying plates takes great skill and focus." When he laughed, I laughed, too, enjoying how personable this man was. He was friendly in ways that many Sea World employees outside of Dine with Shamu weren't. Most of the time, different restaurants and different department staff members ignored one another, searching out the uniforms of fellow coworkers to avoid feeling like a fish out of water.

I readjusted the grip on my tray, resting the back of it against my diaphragm.

"I'm just screwing with you. Could you grab me a Diet Coke on your way out? It's hotter than Satan's ass-crack today."

I snorted. "No problem. Just give me one second." I tried to step forward, but he continued talking.

"Beautiful. I'm Ronnie—that kid over there?" He nodded to the young man with the salt and pepper hair, who was obviously flirting with three uninterested female guests simply trying to enjoy their cheesecake. "That's my son, Peter."

I nodded and smiled, my left arm beginning to shake beneath the weight of the plates. "I'm Roxanne. Let me grab that Diet Coke before my arm gives out."

"Right. My apologies, Miss Roxy." He gestured to the kitchen. "And thanks in advance for that Pop."

"But really quick, what kind of bird is that?" I asked.

He grinned and lifted the bird higher, an air of confidence washing over him, pulling me along with the tide. "This is a female Harris' Hawk. Her name is Munyeca. She's a killer."

Chapter Five

SHERLOCK CROUCHED DOWN to the carpet, his butt shaking in the air as he prepared to pounce.

"Please don't mock me like that. It's rude."

The little black cat ignored me, launching himself into the pile of crumpled papers collected in the middle of the room. I cringed when I heard one of the papers rip and tear in his mouth.

"I know they're not great, but you don't have to rub it in."

Zachary chuckled. "It's a cat—crumpling that paper turns your beautiful poetry into a toy." He leaned over and kissed my cheek.

I sighed. "If it's so *beautiful*, why is Professor Palmer so adamant about me pursuing fiction instead?"

"You should do what *you* want to do, Roxy. If you want to write poetry instead of fiction, then do it. It's your life, not hers."

We were sitting on the loveseat in my room, the small, wooden coffee table supporting Zachary's socked feet, while his thighs supported my bare feet, my back resting against the loveseat's armrest. There were dirty clothes scattered across the floor, stacked schoolbooks next to the bathroom doorway, and brand-new cat toys on the cat tree, which Sherlock ignored while he continued to destroy my poetry.

This was how my weeknights unfolded. Zachary would come over to my house and read for pleasure while I slaved over my schoolwork. We spent every one of our free minutes together, and even though I could find him irksome, I was comfortable with our routine. He pretended to listen when I complained, and I pretended not to hate the fact that he would ignore any and all advice I offered when he complained. We were like that old married couple current married couples were afraid of becoming.

And we weren't even married yet.

"But she's a professional. If she thinks I have a better chance at writing fiction, why should I think otherwise?"

Zachary's grassy eyes wilted slightly beneath a lush forest of eyelashes. He was tired, his bitten down fingernails fiddling with the pages of *The Jungle Book*. I'd already tried to question him about the lesson plan he was supposed to prepare to use in his class the next day, but he'd huffed, running his hands through his fluffy, brown hair, which was streaked blonde from the sun. He'd just finished complaining about his Master Teacher—a woman who did nothing but criticize Zachary whenever he taught, always putting him down and discouraging him from following his passion for teaching history to high school students—and apparently, me questioning his work ethic only made the situation worse.

"You have to do what makes you happy. Otherwise, what's the point?"

I stared at him blankly. "Oh, I don't know. Maybe—just maybe—being able to live in a house that *isn't* a cardboard box in an alleyway."

He snorted. "If everyone had that mentality, we teachers would just give up."

We teachers? You're avoiding doing a lesson plan. You're not a teacher. I bit my tongue, afraid that if I said anything, I'd hurt his feelings. Instead, I looked back down at the notebook sitting in my lap.

"What're you working on now?" he asked.

I leaned my head back and stared at the ceiling. "My application. Dr. Palmer is having me write short stories in her class instead of essays so that I have material to turn in. She's gonna critique them for me and let me know if I have a chance of *actually* getting into the program."

He leaned over and kissed my cheek again, his hand resting on my knee. "You're meant to be a writer—poetry, fiction, it doesn't matter. Just let the words come to you instead of trying to force it. You'll do great." He shifted slightly, reaching his hand to my chin to face him. He pushed his lips against mine, forcing his tongue into my mouth, his zipper rising and pressing against my calf. "You're meant to get into the program."

At least try to pretend you mean what you're saying and not just trying to get into my pants. I rolled my eyes, holding back a groan—and not the good kind. *I really don't have time for this.* Breaking off the kiss, I placed my palm on his muscular chest and pushed him back. "Sure. Yeah. If I pass the GRE."

He sighed, obviously frustrated with my lack of desire. "Then why don't you stop complaining and start studying?"

I wrinkled my nose. "Thanks for the groundbreaking advice."

"You've been non-stop complaining about the test lately. Do something about it and you won't have to complain anymore."

Oh really? Maybe you should take your own advice Mr. Complain About Student Teaching But Never Actually Complete A Lesson Plan or Teach The Kids Anything. "You wanna go down to Barnes and Noble and buy the freakin' book for me then? Because it's something—like—fifty bucks, which I can't afford."

He opened the book in his lap and shrugged me off as if my problems didn't matter. "I think I'm a little busier than you."

I slammed my notebook on the carpet. "Oh *really*? Do you *actually* believe that?"

He shrugged again. "I teach. I make lesson plans. I have class to attend. I work on weekends."

"Lesson plans? *What* lesson plans? You make half-assed Powerpoints and *complain* about the fact that your Master Teacher doesn't like you and then do *nothing* to fix it. Class? What *class*? You attend a seminar everything Thursday—and *that's it*! *One class*! And work? You put people in wetsuits and lead them to a dolphin pool. *Boo freakin' hoo.* You have to walk all of *five minutes*. You don't do *anything* that would be considered *real work*! You brag to me about how you and your coworkers mess around for half of your shift." I could see his neck reddening with anger, but I didn't care. "Maybe if you *actually* listened to your teacher's advice instead of reading those stupid novels that have *nothing* to do with the curriculum, then she wouldn't be chewing you out all of the time."

After a moment's hesitation, he huffed and slammed his book shut, the abrupt noise startling Sherlock so much that he ran under the bed, no longer wanting to frolic through my failure. "I'm going home," Zachary said, voice wavering slightly.

I grabbed his hand when he moved to stand, suddenly overcome with guilt. "I'm sorry. You made me mad." I paused, still feeling him pulling away. "Why don't we talk about—uh—well—um—your birthday?"

He sat down heavily, the back of the loveseat tapping against the wall. "So, you can yell at me for that, too? It's *my birthday*. I should be allowed to do what I want."

I glanced at him. *Why do I feel bad? He deserves to go home for being such a jerk.* "I *still think* the theme is extremely *inappropriate* for someone who has a fiancé."

He rubbed his eyes. "Roxanne, it's *just* a toga party. The boys are throwing it for me. It's not the end of the world."

The "boys" were the individuals in the fraternity Zachary had been kicked out of, but with whom he kept in contact via social media.

"Maybe if we didn't have to argue about whether or not you should wear something *beneath* the toga, then I wouldn't see it as a big deal."

"You're *really* gonna bring that up *again*?"

I crossed my arms over my chest. "Oh, I'm sorry. I didn't realize it was okay to showcase your genitalia while you're *engaged.*"

"Roxanne, it's a *toga* party. Do you think the Greeks *really* wore something beneath their togas?"

My patience was now as thin as a strand of hair. "So, that's it then? You want the attention."

He frowned. "No. I'm not trying to flaunt anything. But historically—"

"Oh, shut up," I spat, my cheeks burning. "*This isn't ancient Greece.* You want *all* of the attention on your penis. That's all you ever want."

"I don't get you." He glared. "I told you I'd wear basketball shorts if that'll make you comfortable, but that *still* didn't make you happy!"

"That's the problem—*you don't understand.*" I rolled my shoulders. "Someone who *actually* wants to get married would *understand* how inappropriate it would be to have your penis on display. How would you feel if I wore a toga with nothing beneath it?"

"I want you to wear a toga. You said no."

"*That's not the point!*" I threw my hands in the air. "Zachary, you're not even in that fraternity anymore. It's time for you to let it go and *grow up.* Maybe— just maybe—this is why your Master Teacher criticizes you *all of the time.* Because you don't ever listen!"

"See? This is why I can't talk to you. You're being a—"

"*Me?*" I stood, needing to put space between us. "You're the one being a total A-hole!"

He stood, too, shoving his feet into his sandals. He collected his book, wallet, keys and cell phone from the coffee table before turning to look at me. "Maybe if *you* stopped being so *negative* all of the time, people could stand being around you."

I flinched, eyes stinging.

He huffed. "See? There you go again—with the fucking crying. No wonder your parents hate talking to you. And no wonder Jasmine and Lacie only hang out with you when booze is involved. You're fucking impossible to be around."

I sat back on my bed. "Get out. Now."

"Too bad I was *already* leaving."

Refusing to fall prey to the hurt that washed through me when he slammed the door, I stared at the framed pictures of us that cluttered my bookshelf. *I don't deserve this. He's being a child.* Sherlock walked over and rubbed against my legs, trying to comfort me. I swatted at a stray tear and wiped my nose on my arm. *But he has a point. I need to stop crying. I don't understand what my problem is.* Sherlock blinked and sat, staring at me, head tilted slightly to the left. "Sometimes, I really hate him."

The cat meowed and hopped into my lap.

"He's driving me *insane*. What self-respecting, engaged, twenty-three-year-old throws a *toga party* for his twenty-fourth birthday? And he wants to be *naked*. Like he doesn't already get enough attention as is."

As I scratched behind his ears, Sherlock's body began to vibrate, his purrs soothing my frustration. *Maybe all things really do come to an end.* "But he's my best friend, and I don't want to lose that."

Sherlock's claws kneaded against my shorts, their points scratching my skin.

"I can't do this. I need to write."

Unfortunately, I could focus on nothing but my dysfunctional relationship and the fear that prevented me from getting out for the rest of the night.

#

"HAVE ANY FUN plans tonight?" Jennifer asked when I was preparing the servers' beverage station Saturday morning.

I smiled half-heartedly and shrugged, more than dreading my plans. "I'm sure *most* people would *love* to attend a yoga party. I'm just *not* that person."

Jennifer nodded her understanding. "If you don't like toga parties, why go?"

I pushed the "brew" button on the coffee machine. "I don't have a choice. It's for Zach's stupid birthday party at this stupid house on Frat Row—a fraternity he *isn't a part of anymore*."

Fraternity Row was located behind the San Diego State University campus. A row of fraternity houses all built next to one another, the ground littered with trash, beer cans and vodka bottles, mice gathering to munch on whatever remnants of pizza and ramen noodles they could find. That much testosterone in such a little space was the perfect setup for little-to-no hygiene, mistreatment of women and unnecessary outbursts of Fight-Club-esque violence. Zachary had told me stories of how dirty each house was because he'd lived there once upon a time—like when he gave me an STD as I was leaving Northern California because he had shared a towel with one of his housemates. Why *anyone* would want to attend a party in such disgusting circumstances was beyond me.

"Are you wearing a toga?"

85

I chuckled. "Absolutely not. Zach and I have been fighting about this for weeks. For some reason, he doesn't get how having his penis out for everyone to see is completely inappropriate."

"Maybe he's trying to pretend he's not growing up," she suggested. Her mocha colored hands were busy placing chocolate Shamu shaped cookies on white plates, a shadow cast over her round face from the black Dine with Shamu baseball cap that kept her gorgeous, thick, Latina hair out of the food. "Like, maybe he's in denial? Or maybe he misses his single life? Didn't you say you've been having problems?"

I fiddled with the bright pink bow that held back my curls. *What if she's right? What if I'm not the only one having second thoughts about the engagement?* "But he proposed to me—shouldn't that mean he's ready to *not* be single?"

She nodded. "That's what I think—but—you said yes—shouldn't that mean the same thing?"

Yeah, it should. Yet, neither of us is doing anything about it. "It's complicated. Why is it so complicated?"

"Maybe the party'll be fun?"

I snorted. "And maybe my boyfriend won't act like a drunk idiot."

After pulling on a pair of disposable gloves, she began tossing together a Cesar salad in a large, silver bowl. "Are you going alone?"

I finished organizing three different types of sugar packets into small, blue bowls. "No, thankfully. I'm going with two of my girlfriends and my gay friend, Luke." I opened the fridge to make sure there was enough creamer and orange juice for the breakfast seating. "I wouldn't go if they weren't. I'm not great at fraternizing with strangers. You have anything fun planned for the night?"

"I'm not going to a toga party, that's for sure."

Our laughter was interrupted by one of our supervisors, William. The restaurant would be opening in five minutes, which meant the servers needed to be summoned to draw numbers for sections.

"Servers!" he hollered, capturing the attention of the five servers present. "The sooner we open, the sooner everyone can get seated, the sooner we can clean and get ready for the next one."

We herded out the kitchen's double doors, following William's plaid shirt like cows following a rancher with a wheelbarrow full of hay. William was my favorite supervisor at Dine with Shamu. He was approachable, yet strict when it came to getting work done. Friendly, and borderline flirty, William was quite the charmer, but he was happily married to his teeny-tiny blonde wife who worked on the event team at Sea World. He was also quite handsome: brown eyes, brown hair always styled, freckles on the bridge of his nose and a smile that was so kind, he could convince any distraught guest they were having the time of their lives.

William was the kind of man I believed Zachary was going to be—had a steady job, owned a condo, wanted children and always bragging about how happy he was in his relationship—until he'd decided a toga party was how he wanted to celebrate his first night of being twenty-four. *Does four years really make that big of a difference? Am I crazy to believe he should be growing up and not down?*

When all the servers surrounded the front desk, William lifted the small, white bowl holding five bottle caps with five different numbers on them. "Discover your destiny," he joked, each server eagerly awaiting their chance to pick their section. "At least we're busy enough for all of you to serve today."

I drew section one and looked at the map of tables. I was going to be tending to the far-left end of the Dine with Shamu horseshoe, tables one through six requiring my service. Once everyone was through the entrance and seated, the real work began. Running back and forth past the buffet room, football maneuvering around small children and hungry parents; the rush of it all distracted me from my other surroundings, including two falconers standing by the empty large tables nearest the buffet table, beneath the blue, wooden awning.

In fact, I didn't notice them until the whale interaction began—fifteen minutes after the regularly scheduled ten-thirty breakfast—and after my guests were happy with their drink levels, their plates overfilled with pancakes, eggs and bacon. It was a surprisingly cool morning, my sleeves buttoned down at my wrists instead of rolled up to my elbows. This was what I enjoyed most about San Diego's autumn: cool mornings before scorching afternoons.

After giving table five a refill of orange juice, I headed back toward the kitchen, my eyes drawn to the pool by the tail flukes of the male, ten-thousand-pound whale splashing water over the other side of the pool. That's when I saw Ronnie—his leather safari hat with the gray and black feather—busily talking to a man I didn't recognize. Ronnie's arms were free to gesture wildly, the other man holding the big, brown, beautiful bird atop his left, gloved hand. Noticing both men attempting to keep warm in their Sea World issued black jackets, I decided to ask if I could help warm them up.

"Hey Ronnie," I greeted him, smiling. "Are you gentlemen interested in a cup of coffee? It's unusually chilly this morning."

The man I didn't know was hiding behind dark sunglasses even though the thick marine layer had yet to burn off. He wore a black baseball cap, black pants and black shoes along with his black jacket. *Maybe not the friendliest individual.* At the sound of my voice, he stepped back, almost as if he didn't believe someone was talking to him.

Ronnie nodded enthusiastically. "That would be beautiful." His chapped lips cracked into a smile. "Almost as beautiful as you."

I shook my head, brushing off his verging on creepy charm. "No need for flattery." I turned my attention to the other man. "How about you?"

Again, he appeared surprised that I spoke to him. "Thank you. That'd be great." He may have mumbled but there was something sweet about his voice. Made me think of caramel dipped apple slices on a summer day.

"Cream? Sugar?"

Ronnie winked. "Looks *and* great service. No wonder they hired you."

Blushing, I rushed into the back to pour two cups of coffee, the kitchen buzzing with gossip and clanking pans, the smell of potatoes and French Toast making my stomach grumble. The coffee was hot, the ceramic cups burning my fingers slightly.

"Looks like those bird boys have taken a liking to you." Dominick pushed a glass against the tab beneath the ice slot on the soda machine.

I scoffed. "This is like—*maybe*—the third time I've interacted with them."

He raised his eyebrows, Diet Coke overflowing from the glass. "You only work three days a week. I work five and they haven't spoken one word to me."

"They don't have time to chat. They have to take care of the entire park by themselves. Corporate has them on a tight schedule."

He chuckled. "And yet, you know so much about them."

I flushed. "No—I—you know—I'm just making assumptions."

"No judgement," he teased. "But I'm pretty sure they've only been here for maybe two weeks. And you aren't the most talkative person. So, I think it's safe to say they like you and you like them."

I grabbed a white bowl and placed three sugars and five creamers inside. "There's nothing stopping you from walking up to them and asking questions if you're *really* interested in what they do." I searched for two small spoons and pointed the rounded side at him. "I'm just in server mode. They looked cold—and tired. They work crazy hours and I thought coffee might help them."

"Do they?" He smiled. "And how do you know their schedule?"

Picking up my tray, I turned my curls and pink bow to him. "Because I'm friendly. You should try it sometime."

"They may get the wrong idea if I smile at them like you do."

"*Oh please*," I scoffed. "Ronnie is old enough to be my *father*."

"Yeah, but *his son* isn't."

His sarcasm made me snort, his laughter trailing me all the way to the falconers. I wasn't flirting with them intentionally, but I did get some satisfaction from their attention. Ronnie and his son were so nice to me, both often walking over to my section with the hawk to scare away pigeons, answering any and all questions that popped into my head and holding conversations with me that distracted me from wiping down my tables and sweeping the floor.

I remained transfixed on the bird multiple times throughout the breakfast, lunch and dinner sessions whenever the falconers were present—there was just something about the winged creature that was fascinating.

"Thanks, Gorgeous," Ronnie said when I picked the cups off of my try and placed them on the table. "Coffee is just what I need."

The other man glanced at the bowl of cream and sugar. "Thanks, but how am I supposed to stir it?"

I produced both teaspoons and placed them beside the cups, a snarky grin on my face. "I'm not a rookie."

He gave me a closed lip smile, brownish-red eyebrows rising above his sunglasses.

I nodded toward the Harris' Hawk. "Who do you have working today?"

Ronnie tore open a creamer and poured it into his coffee. "Ruby. Smaller than—and not as fast as—Munyeca. She needed to rest today, though."

"He fed her too much food yesterday and she refused to fly to the glove this morning."

I smirked. "That's how I usually feel after lunch break."

Ronnie shook his head. "Don't listen to John. *I'm the boss*—he just pretends to know more than I do."

Before Jonathan, the other falconer, could respond, I placed my tray between my arm and my hip. "As much as I'd love to listen to the two of you bicker, I have to get back to my tables. Don't wanna miss out on any tips."

Ronnie smiled. "My good looks and conversation aren't enough of a tip for you?"

Jonathan stirred his coffee, shaking his head side to the side ever so slightly. "I would run away now. He's nothing but a dirty old man."

"It was nice meeting you, John," I said, inching toward my tables.

"What's wrong with appreciating a beautiful smile?" Ronnie asked.

"Maybe if you focused on pigeons, I wouldn't have to worry about them attacking my guests," I chided playfully over my shoulder.

"The contract is for Gulls, not pigeons," Jonathan replied, matter-of-factly.

Dominick walked by just then, grinning at me.

I shook my head. *Maybe I should take my own advice and focus on my job instead of the falconers.*

#

JASMINE, LACIE, LUKE and I hopped out of my father's BMW and closed the door behind us, our bodies happily buzzing from our pre-gaming session back at my parents' house. My mother was out with some friends from her office and my father had turned up the sound on the television, so my friends and I were able to listen to loud music and guzzle mixed drinks in the kitchen without my mother complaining from the couch downstairs. Before we left, we poured some extra booze into four water bottles and tightened the caps, hiding them from my dad so he wouldn't lecture us about why we're not allowed to have open containers in the car.

I stared at the beige, decrepit building, my stomach swirling and twirling like a carnival ride. *What am I doing here?*

"Let me know when you're ready to come home," my dad shouted, window rolled down, college students chuckling into their hands as they walked by. "Try to text me before two. I don't want to wake your mother, especially after she's been drinking."

More laughter and snide remarks came from the individuals milling around Fraternity Row in search of their own party.

I blushed. "Thanks, Dad. I'll do my best."

When he drove off, waving as he rolled up the window, I sighed. *I need to remember to thank him tonight. He's been really cool lately.*

"Your dad is so fucking cool," Jasmine said, watching the car turn left at the stoplight.

Okay, maybe we have been hanging out too much. She legit just read my mind, I thought, smirking.

"*Seriously* though," Lacie said, fluffing out the hair touching her shoulders. "I can't believe he doesn't care when we get *hammered*."

"We've been over this before," I mumbled.

"He probably wants to get some time away from your mother," Luke teased.

I rolled my eyes. "They both were partiers when they were our age." I paused. "They're *still* partiers, actually. And my dad *loves* my mom. Don't ask me why."

"Some guys like crazy women."

We stopped in front of a white young man with a poorly grown mustache and a black suit with a purple tie standing in front of a black, iron gate, his hands tucked beneath his armpits. Short and scrawny, his "tough guy" persona wasn't exactly working.

I smiled politely. "We're here for the party."

He glanced at me and frowned. "It's a toga party."

Though Zachary begged me thousands of times to dress in a toga, I *refused* to succumb to such juvenile behavior. I also wasn't confident enough to waltz around hundreds of people in nothing but a sheet being held up by a piece of rope. So, instead, I asked my friends to support my decision and convinced them to dress in *regular* party attire.

I'd found a flattering plum colored tube-top dress—tight around the breasts, loose around the midsection—and a black belt with a bow adorning my diaphragm, giving some shape to my body, especially because I was sucking in my stomach to appear skinnier than I actually was. My zebra-print high heels helped accentuate my legs, but I still felt self-conscious watching itty-bitty, teeny-tiny girls everywhere around me.

"Those girls could *really* use a sandwich," Luke murmured.

"Or an entire fucking pizza," Lacie added, making Jasmine giggle.

"I am *aware* it's a toga party," I said to the Frat Boy, frustrated. "My fiancé— who just so happens to be the birthday boy—knows I'm not wearing a toga. He and I discussed our opposing views on the whole 'toga' thing at length."

He shook his head. "Right. Sure."

"Where the fuck is *your* toga?" Jasmine asked.

I held my hand in front of her, afraid she might attack him. "Look, his name is Zachary Cameron. He's in there right now."

"I don't care."

Lacie stepped forward. "What's your fucking problem?"

"How about this?" I asked. "Why don't you turn around, walk up those stairs and ask for the soon-to-be-married birthday boy?"

He laughed. "Kinda fucked up for someone who's engaged to come to a toga party."

"*That's* what I told *him*," I spat. "But this is what *he* wanted."

"You're not making any sense."

Before I started screaming at the horrible mustache, the girls pulled me to the side, rubbing my arms. "This guy is a total fuck head," Jasmine said.

"Just call Zach," Lacie suggested. "He'll let us in."

"This just—like—*of course* this would happen tonight," I whined. "I should've *never* come. I've had bad feelings about it *all* week."

Jasmine frowned, patting the top of my hand. "Oh, Roxy, don't say that. That jerk doesn't know who we are. Zach'll let us in."

I watched as the creepy mustache allowed a group of sorority-looking girls in torn apart sheets enter through the gate. "*Are you fucking kidding me?*"

"Okay, she's swearing," Luke said. "Maybe we should go somewhere else to get cocktails or something. There's gotta be a bar close by."

"Am I not *fucking* pretty enough?" I yelled. "If they don't consent, that makes you a *rapist*!"

The young man refused to make eye-contact, his brows furrowing to the bridge of his nose.

Lacie placed a hand on my cheek when she noticed my eyes watering. "Don't let him get to you like that."

I sighed. "Can we please go home?"

Jasmine glanced at the bouncer before returning her gaze to me. "Sweetie, we're already here. Seriously, *call Zach*! He'll let us in."

Ignoring my better judgement, I pulled my phone from the side of my strapless bra and dialed Zachary's phone number, my water bottle full of liquor resting beneath my armpit.

Three phone calls and three angry voicemails later, still no answer.

"I can't do this." My buzz intensified into an emotional panic. "I'm calling Dad."

Lacie shook her head. "Maybe he just doesn't want to be rude. Like—maybe he's with friends or something."

"Or *maybe* he's purposely ignoring my calls because I *don't* belong here."

Jasmine turned to the mustache man. "Could you *please* let us in?"

He snorted. "I already told you. This is a *toga* party. You *obviously* weren't invited."

"Listen," Lacie snapped. "Her fiancé isn't answering his phone."

"And that concerns me *how*?"

"Because he's the fucking *birthday boy*!"

He shrugged. "That's what you keep saying, but why should I believe you? You're not even in togas!"

"You know, a toga party seems a *little* gay, don'tcha think? A bunch of naked guys in sheets—sounds like a normal Saturday night in Hillcrest."

I glared at Luke. "You are *not* helping right now."

He shrugged. "I'm just saying—it's suspicious."

I glared harder. "Now is *not* the time to speak from experience."

"Speaking of gay," Lacie said, snapping her fingers. "What about Zach's buddy? Isn't he supposed to be here?"

I sighed. "For the love of all that is holy, could we not start that again?"

"Why don't you call him instead?"

"Because he's the *last* person I wanna see right now."

Jasmine frowned. "But if Zach isn't answering his phone, then Omar is our only hope."

Why? Why does it have to come to this? "Well, what—um—what if he's not here?"

Luke laughed. "*Yeah, right.* Those two are *always* together."

"What is *wrong* with all of you?"

"Oh, man," Jasmine said. "I was just thinking—they're together. In togas. And Zach isn't answering his phone."

Lacie snickered. "Now *that* sounds suspicious to me."

"I hate all of you." Scrolling through my phone, I found Omar's number and clicked it. "My fiancé is *not* gay."

"You're right. Maybe he just exudes homosexuality for no reason."

I turned my back on Luke and tried to use my fake enthusiastic voice when Omar answered—the same voice I used with my guests at Sea World. "Hey—uh—friend! I'm standing outside and the guy at the gate won't let me in."

"Are you wearing a toga?" Omar asked.

I pursed my lips. "No."

"Well, it's a toga party."

I closed my eyes. "I am *well aware* that this is a toga party."

The bouncer straightened his tie. "Who comes to a toga party not wearing a toga?"

"Where the *fuck* is your toga then?" Jasmine repeated, having not received an answer the first time.

"I need to keep out assholes like you."

Luckily, before our poorly mustached blockade and my entourage could engage in a screaming match, the black gate swung open. Out walked a dark-skinned Persian boy with black, Brillo-pad hair and a smile so devious, it would've been asked in for questioning if it were within a fifty-mile radius of a murder scene.

"Hi Omar!" I waved, trying to push past the young man in the suit.

He turned to my fiancé's best friend. "You know these people?"

Omar nodded. "I wish I didn't."

I frowned. "Thanks, Douchebag."

"This is Zach's fiancé."

The bouncer raised his eyebrows. "The birthday boy? He's engaged?"

I balled my fists, the plastic water bottle now crinkling in my grasp. "That's what I told you—like—a *million* times!" I stomped my heel, wanting to throw a temper tantrum.

Omar nodded again, ignoring me. "He is. I don't know why. He can do way better than her."

Before I began screaming, Lacie grabbed my arm and led me up the stairs, Luke and Jasmine following behind. "That guy's a fucking tool. Let's go find Zach and have some fun."

Right. Fun. Why didn't I go home when I got the chance?

#

"HOW ABOUT I get you ladies—not *you*, Roxanne—something to drink?" Omar asked, walking backwards in front of us.

I glared, unscrewed my water bottle and took a long swig of my cocktail. "We're good. Don't wanna get drugged tonight."

Omar chuckled. "Your stupidity is adorable."

College boys and girls talked with one another, bodies bouncing lightly to the beat of electric dance music, the walls closing in from the loud bass, my jaw trembling from the speakers in every corner. Flashing lights and fog machines polluted the courtyard, too many sweaty bodies rubbing against one another in front of a poorly constructed stage with a DJ table on top.

Lacie snorted. "It's guys like you that ruin the party for everyone else."

Omar bowed. "And it's girls like you that make a man wish he were gay."

"Is that so?" Luke asked. "Because that would explain *so much* about you."

Omar turned his back on us, inebriated sorority girls resembling the waves in the story of Moses, his sleazy vibes pungent like the scent of a dead skunk.

"Now that he's gone, can we go find Zach?" I asked, frustrated.

While my eyes scanned the crowd, I couldn't help but notice that we were the only ones not wearing togas. I took another large gulp of my drink, trying to drown the uncomfortable sensation coming alive in my stomach as my peers stared judgmentally.

Lacie swigged from her plastic bottle. "Why don't you ask Zach's boyfriend where he is?"

My shoulders slumped. "If anyone brings that up again, I'm leaving."

Jasmine tapped my water bottle. "Oh, lighten up! You know we're just giving you a hard time."

"Well, stop. You're all making me feel worse about being here."

"We're gonna have fun," Luke said. "You just need to drink more."

"I'll have fun when I find my fiancé."

Omar sidled up to my side, his voice reminding me of a threatening hiss. "I know where he is."

"Why the *fuck* didn't you say something earlier?"

"Oh, my, my—*very* ladylike language." Omar smiled, his face disappearing around his Cheshire Cat teeth. "Why would I tell you? He's having so much more fun *without* you."

Luke grabbed Omar's shoulder, stopping him in his tracks. "Stop playing these fucking mind games. Can't you see how upset she is? You know she *never* cusses."

"Boo fucking hoo. She wouldn't even wear a toga for him on his *birthday.* Everyone would be happier if she left before he saw her."

I blinked repeatedly, trying to prevent tears from falling. "Let's just go."

"Stop being such a prick," Lacie warned Omar. "You're on *real* thin ice."

"Tell us where he is *right now,*" Jasmine demanded.

He shook his head. "Find him yourself. I have *pretty* girls to entertain. You're wasting my time." Omar slithered off towards a group of five unsuspecting, under-age looking girls.

"They don't have dicks!" Luke yelled after him. "You better bring a strap on!"

I stared at my pink toenails and fidgeted with the hem of my dress. "Why did he say that? Do you think—Zach—did he—does he not want me here?"

Lacie rubbed my arm. "Don't listen to that rat. I'm sure Zach is wondering where you are. Omar is jealous that Zach would rather spend time with you and not him."

"If that's true, then why did Omar answer his phone? Zach didn't, and he knew I was on my way here—I texted him when we left the house."

Luke shrugged. "He's wearing a toga. I don't think sheets have pockets."

"He's *supposed* to be wearing basketball shorts underneath—*those* have pockets."

We made our way up a staircase lit up with blue and red Christmas lights, the steps covered in sticky puddles and black stains. As we turned right into an open door leading into what appeared to be a dorm room kitchen, I dropped my plastic bottle to the floor, the lid popping off, vodka and lemonade spilling out like the guts of fresh roadkill. There, sitting on the tile, taking pictures on the phone he didn't answer, was my fiancé.

He was surrounded by girls who were wearing outfits that Greeks and Romans would be ashamed to call togas. His face was so red, one might believe he was sunburned instead of verging on blacking out. His legs were crossed and beneath that white sheet, there was no sign of basketball shorts. The girls had their hands all over him—on his cheeks, his shoulders, his chest, his stomach, his thighs—and he was *basking* in their whore-ish attention. Their bodies were glistening with glitter, their perfectly shaped figures tempting him to cheat on me right in front of my face. *Omar was right.* His happiness radiated throughout the circumference of the living room, more and more half naked girls pushing past me to wish my fiancé a happy birthday.

I cringed when two girls kissed him on either side of his face, camera phones flashing, crimson lipstick branded on his skin.

"Oh, shit," Luke breathed. "So this is what a Roman bath house looks like."

"My God," I choked, placing my palms on my nauseous stomach. "Oh. My. God."

The girls resembled Greek goddesses—glowing tan skin, flawlessly straight hair, eyes that sparkled like the glitter on their lids. I glanced down at my dress, at the belt hiding the fat around my ribs, my "flattering" dress now showing off the pooch I'd acquired over the last couple of months. I wrapped my arms around my chest, struggling to keep the panic at bay. *He wants girls who look like that. Prettier.*

Skinnier. Taller. Sluttier. He doesn't want to marry someone like me. My fingers tingled. My nausea rose to an uncomfortable level. My muscles tightened. *I can't do this here—not in front of everyone.*

"Luke, we need to get Roxy away from this. Now," Jasmine ordered. She put her arm around me and tried to turn me away from my fiancé. "Lacie. *Help.*"

The girls grabbed my elbows and yanked my body around, Luke standing behind me, his hands pushing firmly on my shoulder blades. "It's okay, Honey." Lacie cooed. "We'll get you another drink. No use crying over spilt vodka."

I looked over my shoulder and made eye-contact with my future husband, who stared blankly past me as if we hadn't been dating for almost three years. As if he hadn't confessed his eternal love for me. As if he hadn't asked me to be his wife.

"He doesn't know who I am," I croaked.

Lacie inched closer. "What do you mean?"

I shook my head. "We made eye-contact and he looked right through me. He didn't even recognize me."

Lacie patted my forearm. "He's just drunk."

Jasmine tightened her grip on my arm. "He wouldn't recognize himself if he looked in a mirror at this point."

"He's—he's—" I swallowed. "He's happier without me." *Omar was right.*

And even though I'd been secretly questioning our relationship for quite some time, seeing him so elated without me—seeing him happier than he's been in months by my side—hurt me more than I thought possible.

And there, at a fraternity house reeking of booze and marijuana, I discovered exactly how it would feel to lose Zachary Cameron.

How it would feel to be completely *alone.*

I began to cry.

Jasmine heard my sobs and placed both of her palms on my cheeks. "Oh, no. No, no, no. You are *not* going to cry."

Her eyes were huge, her nose only inches from mine. I cried harder. "I knew this was a mistake."

Jasmine began wiping tears away with her chubby thumbs. "Don't say that. We can still have a good time."

I closed my eyes and tried to steady my breathing. "I should've stayed home. Zach doesn't want me here. He wants to fuck one of those stupid sluts."

"You're *way* more beautiful than any of them," Luke said.

"Yeah fucking right," I mumbled.

Lacie snatched an unopened beer can from a short, blonde boy draped in a sheet covered in pink roses. "He can go fuck himself. There are a million guys here who are hotter than him. Let's find you someone better."

"But he *knew* I was gonna be here. He *invited* me. He told me he *wanted* me here. Why? To watch him cheat on me?"

Jasmine frowned. "He's an ass. I mean, you saw how drunk he was—are you sure his eyes were even open?"

I took a deep breath. "He saw me, eyes open, and *didn't recognize me*. He's my fiancé and he—he—" I started to cry again. "I want to go home. You guys can stay but I—I—I just—I can't do this."

Luke snorted. "Oh, stop crying. This is a blessing in disguise. Now, you have a reason to break up with him without feeling bad."

Lacie slapped his chest. "Now is not the time, Luke. Jesus—how much have you had to drink? You've been very opinionated all night, and not in a good way."

He chugged his hundred-proof vodka, which had a single splash of orange juice mixed in. "I may be a *little* drunk. But I'd tell Roxy the truth either way because she *deserves* to know it."

"Well, keep your mouth shut and put yourself to good use," Jasmine snapped. "Find Roxy a guy with a big dick—one that can easily be seen through his toga. That'll make Zach jealous."

I shook my head, looking at the Bud Light Lacie had placed in my hand. "I should've worn a toga. He's getting back at me for asking him to wear basketball shorts—and for me refusing to wear a toga."

"That's horse shit."

I handed the beer back to Lacie. "His phone was in his hand. He was intentionally ignoring me. It's his birthday—Omar made a good point—why didn't I just wear a stupid toga for him?"

"Do you *hear* yourself right now?" Jasmine yelled. "No offense, but you sound pathetic. He's the one who fucked up, so stop blaming yourself."

I glanced down at my feet wondering if I could leave the party without them noticing. "I gotta use the bathroom. Fix my makeup and stuff."

The girls nodded. "Want our help?"

I shook my head again. "No, thank you. Why don't you all look for that bulge you were talking about earlier? I'll come find you when I'm done, and we can find some more drinks."

Making my way past drunk college kids proved more difficult than I thought. There were empty bottles and cans lining the cement, girls stumbling in all directions, boys grabbing at my hair and my dress—when I finally made it to the bathroom line, I took a deep breath, brushed my bangs out of my face and closed my eyes. *Keep it together. Just breathe. Once I get to the bathroom, I can call Dad and get outta here.*

The line was about five girls deep, the only bathroom I could find located in the back of the labyrinth I somehow had managed to navigate without getting trampled.

I pulled out my phone and opened a new text message, inputting the sequence of numbers I was ashamed to have memorized. I began typing: *Hey there, Stranger. Long time no talk.* I pushed send and exhaled, not realizing I had been holding my breath. "If Zach doesn't care, why should I?" I whispered.

"And I thought I was the only one here who knows wearing a toga was stupid," a male voice mumbled beside me.

Startled, I turned to the right and saw a young man leaning against the wall, his left foot propped up on the stucco behind him, his arms hugging his chest, a lit cigarette dangling from his lips. The shadows made it difficult to see his face, but I took note of his baggy, black jeans, his grey hoodie and his grey and black San Diego baseball cap tilted just slightly.

Feeling awkward, I shoved my phone back to the side of my bra, covered my stomach with my arms and grabbed my elbows. "You talking to me?"

He chuckled, the cigarette bouncing slightly. "No, I'm talking to the other girl not wearing a toga."

His voice was smooth, like a shot of Don Julio on a cold night. I found myself wanting to indulge in it, listening to the small twang that slipped between his syllables.

I looked around. "I don't see anybody else."

"Guess that means I'm talking to you."

Blushing, I fidgeted with the hem of my dress. "You mean, you're not a fan of all the slutty toga outfits?"

I ignored the glares from the girls beside me and smiled when the young man snorted. "My girlfriend made one of the sluttier styles. She's in the bathroom probably trying to find a way to make it shorter."

I sighed into my hands, shaking my head. "I'm *really* bad at talking to people. I didn't mean—I'm sure she's—togas aren't—I give up." I blushed even harder. "I'm done talking now."

He flicked his cigarette butt to the ground and emerged from the shadows, a friendly smile chipping away at the anxiety settling in my stomach. "No, don't worry 'bout it. She's a ho. And she's mad at me for not wearing one." He shoved his hands into the hoody's pockets. "Dressing up isn't really my thing. But if she's gonna slut it up, I'm not gonna argue." From what I could see, he was missing a tooth—the one right behind his canine—and he had grey stains near his gums that resembled the cigarette ashes smoldering on the ground behind him. "What's your excuse?"

His brown eyes welcomed me to engage in the conversation. "Dressing up is one hundred and ten percent my thing, but I think toga parties are a *joke*." More glares and angry whispers from the girls in front of me. "Worst part is, my boyfriend is the birthday boy. He, too, is mad at me for not dressing up."

He laughed. "It's a little embarrassing for your *boyfriend* to be mad at you for not dressing up."

I pursed my lips and nodded. "Tell me about it."

"If it means anything, you look way hotter than the girls I've seen in togas."

I smiled my first genuine smile since I stepped out of my father's car. "I wish my boyfriend felt the same. He didn't even recognize me when he saw me—he was too busy swimming in a sea of tits and ass."

"To be fair, it's tough to say no when it's being thrown in your face." He paused and glanced toward the bathroom. "Don't tell my girl I said that. She'd take it the wrong way and get mad at me."

I would too, I thought.

He now leaned against the wall beside me, the line still not moving, girls taking selfies and using one another's bodies as a crutch to remain standing. The boy's face was round with cheeks that were prepped to store acorns this winter. Even his sweatshirt couldn't hide the spherical shape of the belly sagging over his jeans.

"To be honest," I began. "I think I'm gonna leave. Toga or not, I don't belong here."

"Hey, whoa, don't leave me here. Then I'll be 'that guy' who didn't wear a toga. At least with you here, you're 'that girl.'"

Shyly glancing over at him once more, I extended my free hand, the other still fiddling with my dress. "My name is Roxanne, but everyone calls me Roxy." *Thank God it's dark*, I thought, hoping my eyes weren't too puffy or my makeup too smeared.

He shook my hand eagerly. "I'm Leonard—Leo. You here alone? Cuz *obviously* your boyfriend doesn't count."

"I'm pathetic, but not pathetic enough to come to a party alone. I brought my best friends with me. You'll be pleased to hear that they also aren't wearing togas."

Another smile, accompanied by a sparkle in those dark, dark eyes. "Then it should be easy to find you out there."

"Did your girlfriend drag you here?"

"Nah—the opposite. My brother's the DJ. I'm here to support his dream and shit."

Before I could respond, an extremely twiggy girl latched onto Leonard's elbow and planted a kiss on his cheek. Her hair was bleach blonde on top but dark brown on the bottom, her face thin and nose long. She was pretty, but the scowl on her face wasn't.

"I'm ready to dance now, my love," she said possessively, her voice resembling the growl of a dog that spotted the mailman.

"We'll see you out there, Roxy," Leonard said before following his poorly togaed girlfriend, her lace underwear and bra showing through the draping, lavender sheet.

When I turned around to make sure nobody had taken my place in line—somehow, it had disappeared, my assumption being that all five girls were in the bathroom together—a pair of hands grabbed my waist. Shocked, I slapped away the hands and whipped around, wondering if there was any way I could run.

Unfortunately, it wasn't a stranger.

I was now face to face with the boy who asked for my hand in marriage but didn't recognize who I was only moments earlier. Zachary Cameron.

Chapter Six

"BABY! YOU'RE HERE! I've been looking *everywhere* for you!" Zachary yelled, drool running down the corner of his mouth.

Anger burned my cheeks and curled the tips of my hair. "Are you *serious* right now?"

Stumbling to the side, Zachary again grabbed my waist.

Again, I slapped his hands away. "Don't you fucking touch me."

Zachary frowned, his drooping eyelids hiding those grassy green meadows I now wanted to light on fire. "What's going on? Omar said you got here not too long—"

"Shut up," I snapped, hands balled into fists at my sides. "Don't play *stupid* with me. I *saw* you."

"I don't know what you're talking about."

His confusion made me even angrier. "In the kitchen. Surrounded by all of those skinny, slutty girls." I paused. "Actually, *smothered* is a better description."

"Baby," he whispered, grabbing my waist so hard, I winced. "I think you're mistaken."

I pushed his hands away once again, stepping back from my fiancé. "And I think you're an asshole."

This time, he winced. "What's going on? Why didn't you call me?"

I remembered seeing the phone in his hand, the girls pushing their breasts against his face to fit in the screen of the camera. "I did!" I yelled, storming past him. *Get away from him. Run away before he makes you cry again.* Just as I was about to escape around the corner and into the courtyard, Zachary grabbed a hold of my wrist.

"Can you hold on?" he pleaded.

"What?" I spat, turning to face him. "What do you want from me?"

"Talk to me," he begged. "You're not making any sense."

That's because you're a drunk prick. Lipstick smears still lingered on his cheeks and forehead. "Do you know what it's like to walk up to your birthday party and not have the doorman let you in because he doesn't believe that the birthday boy is engaged?" My voice grew louder. "Or to have your fiancé's best friend tell you that your fiancé is *purposely* not answering his phone because he's *too busy*?"

My voice was verging on shrill. "But in reality, he's *too busy* thinking about who he's gonna fuck tonight because every girl here is a fucking whore."

Zachary glared at me. "Keep your voice down. How dare you talk to me like that?"

"Talk to you *how?* Telling you the truth for *once?*"

"I didn't ignore your call—I don't have service here. And those girls you saw? They're old friends of mine. You should've said hi—I would've introduced you."

"Forgive me for not walking right into the beginnings of an orgy."

"Roxanne, why didn't you call me?"

I stared at him. *Are you even listening? We just talked about this!* A beer can skittered across the cement, spraying backwash all over the ground and walls, a staggering couple feeling their way around us in search of a dark place to hook up. "Give me your phone."

After a moment of hesitation, he lifted his toga, reached into his basketball shorts and produced his cell phone.

I raised an eyebrow. *You didn't have those on earlier. Did you put them on because Omar warned you that I was here?* I entered the password and flipped the screen so that his drunk eyes squinted at the backlight. "See all those missed calls? And those texts? And those voicemails?"

He nodded.

"*They're from me.*" I gritted my teeth together to keep from screaming. "Unless there's another Roxanne I should be concerned about?"

Zachary pulled me close, my palms now resting against his half-bare, half-togaed chest. My anger softened like butter left on the counter for too long. "I'm sorry. I didn't see any of those." He was slurring, his words tripping over one another. "We must've been taking a picture." He paused. "Maybe I get bad service here." Another pause. "Roxy, I would've answered if you called."

I sighed, defeated. *I'm talking to a wall. A big, stupid, drunk wall.* "But you didn't, Zach. You were too busy with those other girls."

His eyes watered. "They mean *nothing* to me."

The sincerity in his voice loosened the tight knots in my shoulders.

"You're the one I want to be with," he continued. "You and *only* you. My *beautiful* fiancé."

Despite knowing better, I wrapped my arms around him and pressed my lips against his. *I want to believe you.* He placed his palms on my back and pulled me into him. *But I don't believe you.* My stomach twisted uncomfortably. *I don't want to ruin your birthday. I just need to let it go for tonight and we can deal with it later.* "And you're the man I want to be with," I whispered, hoping to convince myself that it was true.

Zachary smiled against my lips, his hands wandering straight to the material around my butt. "How about we dance and makeup?"

I licked the whiskey residue from my mouth, hating myself for being so weak willed. "That sounds like a wonderful idea."

He grabbed my hand and led me back to the courtyard, straight to where I'd left Luke, Lacie and Jasmine. The girls hugged me as if I'd been missing for years. In reality, I'd only been away for maybe forty-five minutes.

"What took so long?"

"Where'd you go?"

"What is *he* doing here?"

"Why is *he* holding your hand?"

"Are you okay?"

I let go of Zachary's hand, grabbed the drink Jasmine was holding and gulped it down, gasping when the liquid burned my throat. *No. Nothing is okay. Everything is wrong. I just can't deal with it right now.* "We talked. All is well."

Lacie pulled me close and lowered her voice so Zachary couldn't hear. "What's going on? He didn't even *recognize* you. How can you let that go?"

I took a deep breath and leaned into her ear. "It's his birthday. We'll talk about it another time—when we're both sober."

Lacie shook her head. "*Please* be careful. He doesn't deserve you."

Although I knew ignoring the problem would only make it worse, the last thing I wanted to do was admit that Zachary wanted to be with someone who wasn't me. I followed him into the mob of boys and girls in the middle of the courtyard and lost myself to the beat of the music, the need to keep my relationship afloat at an all-time high, my self-confidence plummeting to an all-time low.

#

WHEN I OPENED my eyes, my heart beating to the DJ's remixes, I reached my arms into the sky and smiled, all of my concerns disappearing beneath the beers and shots I was handed because I was standing next to the birthday boy. The dance floor had become something out of an erotica novel, the boys and girls trying to have sex through their togas, a variety of liquids splashing beneath everybody's feet.

It was one of those rare moments where I felt wild and free—*happy* even—despite being at a party I didn't want to attend.

Until three girls I recognized from the kitchen incident came over, shoved me to the side and began grinding against my fiancé. I waited for him to react—to inform them he was *in a relationship with me and loved me* and then take me in his arms and kiss me—but instead, he laughed and continued to pump his fist in the air.

Luke came up next to me with one hand holding a vodka bottle, the other holding an orange soda bottle. "What's he doing?"

I sniffled, my meltdown teetering on a cliff of sanity. "Being a terrible fiancé." I paused. "And I feel like I can't be mad because of my behavior with Lamont. It's like I deserve this or something."

"Why do you do that to yourself?"

"Maybe because I *am* a horrible fiancé. This is what I do. I self-sabotage everything. I even texted Lamont because I was mad, and I'm upset because the asshole hasn't responded yet."

He shook his head. "Why do you text *him* out of *all* people? Don't you have *anybody* else you can trunk text *without* completely turning your world upside down?"

Shrugging, I held my hand out toward the vodka. I was too drunk and emotionally drained to even question when he'd gotten it or who he'd gotten it from. "Self-destructive behavior? Karma? Guilt?"

When I swigged the vodka, trying not to gag, Luke handed me a bottle of orange soda. "Stop doing that to yourself. You didn't bang Lamont in front of him. What he's doing is ten times worse."

I cringed, the orange soda bubbles tickling my teeth. "Your logic makes *zero* sense."

"Lamont is *hundreds* of miles away. He lives in the past. So, you texted him—no big deal. You're not sending him nudes and then telling Zach about it."

"Yeah, but I still—"

He took the bottles from me and gestured toward Zachary, who was surrounded by his groupies. Orange soda spilled over Luke's fingers and onto the ground. "No. You need to stand up for yourself. Texting Lamont all night won't help anything. Go over there and do something about this."

"You're right. I can do this."

Luke kissed the top of my head. "Go show him who's a bad ass bitch."

After smiling up at my best friend and taking a deep breath, I stormed past those three girls, grabbed Zachary's chin and forced him to look at me. "Earth to Zach! You do know I'm standing right here, don't you?"

I heard Luke shout "You go girl" behind me, despite the music pumping throughout the cement buildings.

Zachary's temples were damp, his sweat glands purging his body of the Wild Turkey Whiskey he'd been drinking all night long. "Well—yeah. How else would you be holding my face?"

"Then what the fuck are you doing?" I didn't feel like myself—the alcohol had changed something inside of me. I was filled with strength and courage. And *a lot* of pent up rage.

He squinted at me. "What're you talking about?"

"I'm just curious—do you *really* want me to be your wife? Or do you want to be a single frat boy who can fuck anything with legs?"

His eyes were glossy, wandering everywhere except my face. He even giggled when a girl with a blonde bob touched his lack of hairy chest with her three-inch long acrylic fingernails.

I grabbed his chin again, pulling his attention back to me. "Zachary! You son of a bitch. I'm trying to *talk* to you!"

He finally looked into my eyes and frowned. "Why the fuck are you acting like this?"

"Me? You're the one being a drunk piece of shit!"

I was screaming at him and hadn't realized it. The throng of dancers around us had turned to face us, their whispers mingling with the musical lyrics swirling around me. I felt a million eyes on me, judging me for being "that girl"—the one who can't handle her alcohol, the one who cries over the smallest inconvenience, the one who causes a scene and embarrasses herself in front of a crowd of strangers. Zachary pushed his moistened, brown hair out of his eyes, his bushy eyebrows appearing to slide down his face. Maybe the alcohol was hitting me harder than I thought it would, or maybe I was just beyond angry, but Zachary's handsome face was morphing into the Frankenstein Monster.

"Why did you even invite me?" I asked. "If you wanted to fuck one of these dirty skanks, why have me in the way?"

Jasmine, Lacie and Luke circled Zachary and me, trying to prevent onlookers from getting involved.

"Why do you keep *saying that*?" Zachary yelled.

"Because you're *all over* anything showing their tits around here! It's like you don't even know I'm standing right in fucking front of you! I'm sorry I'm not a fucking whore and refused to wear a toga. I. Am. *Done*."

He placed his hands on my shoulders, his thumbs pressing roughly into my collarbone. "Stop cussing at me. You're embarrassing me in front of *everyone*."

"Obviously, they're more important to you than I am."

Giggling girls mocked me, raising their voices to a shrill pitch in order to incite laughter from the boys around them.

Zachary's face and neck darkened to a blood red color. "Stop it. *Now*."

"No. *You* stop." I shoved Zachary's hands away, stumbling slightly. "I'm leaving." I knew I was slurring and my vision had grown a bit fuzzy, but I didn't care. "Go fuck yourself, Zachary Cameron." Luke steadied me with his slender hands. "I don't want to see you ever again."

"You tell him," Jasmine said.

Lacie latched onto my elbow, preventing me from storming away. "Let's just calm down and get you some water."

"Why don't you find me a fucking fiancé that has the decency to cheat on me behind my back, not in front of my fucking face."

Luke grabbed my other elbow. "Roxy, you shouldn't do this here."

"I'm *tired* of holding back. I should've done this *a long time ago*." I pulled the gold diamond ring from my finger and dropped it on the cement. Then, I stepped on it. My friends gasped, Zachary flinching as if I'd slapped him. "Maybe *you* should wear a ring and see how it feels to be someone's property. Like you're some kind of fucking show cow. You've broken my heart, Zachary Cameron. I hope you're fucking happy."

"Honey," Luke whispered. "Let's call your dad and get outta here."

Not caring about the fact that everyone was still staring, pointing and shouting in an attempt to further escalate the drama, I shoved past Zachary and walked toward the hallway where I found the bathroom earlier. I didn't look over my shoulder, didn't listen to the laughter following me, didn't even breathe, afraid that one more emotion would push my anger over the edge and I would crumble into an uncontrollable meltdown. *Don't you dare cry, Roxanne. You did the right thing. He's an asshole. Zach could've been a gentleman and cheated behind my back like a decent human being.* Jasmine's and Lacie's high heels were clacking on the ground behind me, their otherwise silent presence providing me with a smidge of comfort. *At least they love me for the hot mess that I am.* The line for the bathroom wrapped around the hallway corner, girls missing large portions of their togas chatting about how they wanted to have sex with Brad or Chad or Thad, only pausing in between their drunken monologues to swig from a plastic vodka bottle or can of Diet Coke. I continued forward in an attempt to escape the chaos, looking for an unoccupied bedroom where I could hide.

Unfortunately, everyone else had decided that the rooms should be used to continue the party in ways even HBO would find inappropriate.

Boys did lines of cocaine off coffee tables stacked high with pornographic magazines.

Girls took tequila shots from strangers that had pill bottles hiding in their pockets.

Boys and girls no longer sported togas. They now preferred to spread out on bed sheets, boxes of condoms opened and waiting on top of the nightstand.

I only stopped at one of the occupied rooms when a vaguely familiar voice shouted my name. There, smiling at me as if I were a lost puppy and not someone on the verge of a serious panic attack, was Leonard. "Well, look who it is. I hope your night's improved, Miss Roxanne." His twang echoed throughout the room.

I'd never been happier to see a complete stranger in my life. "Afraid not. It's gotten worse. Much worse."

"You know him?" Lacie asked, stepping through the door frame.

I shook my head. "Nope. Not really."

Jasmine looked over Lacie's shoulder, took note of Leonard's appearance and crossed her arms. "Then how does he know your name?"

The vacant desk chair resting beside Leonard's plaid recliner called out to me, my feet beginning to hurt in my heels. I stepped over piles of dirty clothes and textbooks that lined the floor like landmines and happily sank into the chair.

"I promise I'm not so bad," Leonard said winking at the girls, an unlit cigarette dangling between his lips. "Don't let the baggy clothes and diamond earrings fool you."

Lacie edged further into the room, gazing around at the Bob Marley posters and marijuana paraphernalia. "Is this your room?"

Leonard snorted. "Do I look like a pussy ass frat bitch to you?"

"Well, your name *is* Leonard," I teased.

Jasmine raised an eyebrow. "If you don't know him, how do you know his name?"

"Leonard? Your name is *Leonard*?" Lacie asked, surprised.

"I swear I don't know him," I said, smirking.

Leonard smiled with his ash-stained teeth. "Obviously, my parents had higher hopes for me. I go by Leo. Suits me more."

His girlfriend was sprawled out on the full-sized bed, her toga carefully aligned so her rear end wasn't exposed for all to see, her hair sticking in matted clumps against her forehead. She was breathing heavily, drool pooling near her lipstick-smeared chin.

Jasmine frowned. "If this isn't your kind of thing, then what're you doing here?"

"My brother is the DJ and I'm here to support him." He gestured his thumb at his girlfriend. "I'm *still* here against my will." After looking my friends up and down, he chuckled. "You don't exactly fit the sorority slut profile. What're you doing here?"

"We were forced," my girlfriends both replied pointing at me, giggling with one another.

"They're lying," I said, sticking my tongue out. "I'm the one who didn't want to come."

"Is she gonna be okay?" Jasmine asked, nodding toward Leonard's girlfriend.

Leonard nodded, chuckling. "She's aight. This ain't her first rodeo, if you know what I'm sayin'. She just wanted a nap—lets me get a break from the douche mob out there."

"Why don't you be a gentleman and take her home?"

"Do I look like a gentleman?"

Lacie laughed. "She seems perfectly fine."

The girlfriend twitched, snorted and began breathing heavily again.

"Besides," Leonard continued. "Have you ever tried to carry a dead-weight body before?"

Jasmine looked at the girlfriend and gestured at her skinny body. "What does she weigh? *Maybe* ten pounds?" She paused and smirked at Leonard. "Can you not handle that?"

Leonard pulled the cigarette out of his mouth and stored it behind his ear. "Why would I want to leave when I'm surrounded by *such* friendly people?"

"These are the friends I mentioned earlier," I said, twirling the desk chair first to the right, then to the left. Focusing on the smashed remains of a spider on the ceiling helped keep my spinning world at bay. "That's Jasmine and that's Lacie. Don't let their attitudes fool you—they can be quite pleasant." I then realized one of my friends was missing. "Where's Luke?"

"Pretty sure he's doing damage control out there," Jasmine said.

Lacie took a pillow off the bed and tossed it at me playfully, her aim about five inches too far to my right. "Speaking of which, do you wanna talk about what the fuck just happened with Zach?"

I scowled. "*Why* would I wanna talk about that?"

"Maybe because you caused a *huge* scene and Luke stayed behind to make sure your fiancé didn't follow you."

I looked back up to the ceiling. "Nope. I've got nothing to talk about."

"Maybe you should *seriously* reconsider marrying Zach. I know you don't want to talk about it and I know it freaks you out, but the two of you don't seem ready for this kind of commitment. Most of the time, you can't even commit to wearing the ring."

My phone vibrated, reminding me of the text message I'd sent to Lamont earlier. *Don't look at it. Don't even think about it. You're having enough problems as it is.* "It's a piece of crap ring, anyway. You two have said so yourselves."

Leonard raised an eyebrow. "Trouble in paradise?"

I refused to make eye-contact.

He snickered and pulled a bottle of vodka seemingly out of thin air. "You want some of this?"

I smiled and nodded. "You are my angel. How did you know vodka is my favorite?"

"Lucky guess." He handed it to me before placing his index finger in front of his lips. "Don't tell my girlfriend. Technically, it's hers."

I threw back the booze and cringed, the straight vodka burning a hole straight through my throat. "She already doesn't like me. I've got nothing to lose."

Leonard reached for the bottle and winked at me when I handed it back. "Drinking her vodka probably isn't the best way to break the ice."

Jasmine sat on the ratty, gray comforter, careful not to touch Leonard's girlfriend. "Roxy, how do you two know so much about one another? You obviously know him—why are you denying it?"

I shrugged. "I *don't* know him. We met briefly earlier. Unfortunately, his girlfriend pulled him away before I could ask for his credit card and social security numbers."

She laughed. "Thanks for the clarification, bitch."

"That's one thing this sham of an engagement is missing. Clarification."

"Well, well, well. The canary has sung." Omar's voice curled around my spine like a boa constrictor preparing to eat its dinner. "Think you could repeat it again so I can share it with Zach? I'm sure he'd like to know you think your engagement is nothing but a lie. Maybe now he'll believe me when I tell him your entire relationship is a fucking joke."

"Just because you want to stick your dick in every hole in Zach's body doesn't mean you can talk to Roxy like that," Lacie spat, her gold eyeliner glinting as she glared at him.

Omar flushed, lips pressed into a straight line. "I'm his *best friend.* It's my job to let him know that his girlfriend doesn't love him."

"Oh *please*," Jasmine sighed loudly. "Just because you want to fuck him— you have *no idea* what love is."

"Zach deserves to know that Roxanne is nothing but a two-faced, callous bitch."

I sniffled, feeling sick. "Don't worry, I'm leaving. You can have him all to yourself." *I can't cry in front of him. I can't let him win.* Breathing in deeply, I turned away and wiped my nose. *He's just being a jerk.*

Leonard stood from his chair, crossing the room in four large steps, his meaty hands pinning Omar to the doorframe. "Who the fuck are you? Get the fuck out before I cut your tongue out of your mouth."

Omar began shaking like a cat doused in water. "Are you who Roxy is fucking behind Zach's back?"

Leonard reached into his back pocket and produced a switchblade. "If you don't get out now, you'll never find out."

Omar hurried out, his toga snagging and ripping on the door handle.

Leonard placed the knife back into his pocket and casually strolled back to his recliner. "Sorry you ladies had to see that. Something about his ugly face made me snap. Roxanne, you alright?"

I nodded mutely. *No. I don't think I'll be alright ever again.* "Thanks for having my back."

"We need to keep this guy around," Jasmine said, her big brown eyes wide.

Leonard smirked. "I doubt you could afford my services."

I fidgeted with the hem of my dress, feeling uneasy. Leonard patted my forearm. "But I'd do it again for you."

Lacie leaned against the wall, her back crinkling an unframed poster of neon plants. "Roxy, you need explain what the hell is going on. Two seconds before you lost your shit, you told me everything was okay. What happened?"

"You keep mentioning a ring," Leonard interrupted. "I don't see anything on your finger."

"Even if she was wearing it, you wouldn't see it."

I rolled my eyes at Jasmine before turning to Leonard. "Yes, I'm engaged. I threw it on the floor."

"Fuck." He cringed. "Shit must be serious. What'd he do?"

"He's a piece of shit," a forlorn voice nearly whispered from the open door, floating through my ears like a ghost through the wind.

I slowly spun the chair toward Zachary, my jaw tightening, hands squeezing the plastic armrest. "Of course, that little rat had to run and tell you where to find me."

Leonard whistled. "This must be the fiancé."

Zachary gazed blankly at him. "Who are you?"

"Nobody you need to know."

Lacie and Jasmine exchanged looks before gesturing at Leonard to leave the room with them. With one last glance at his slumbering girlfriend, Leonard mouthed that he'd be outside if I needed him and narrowed his eyes at Zachary's back as he closed the door.

Zachary sighed, eyes bloodshot and puffy. "Who was that, Roxy?"

"What's it to you?"

"You're my fiancé. I should know."

"Oh! *Now* I'm your fiancé? How *convenient* for you." I shook my head, turning the back of the chair toward him. "Go away. I don't want to talk to you."

"Roxy, *please*," he breathed. "We need to talk."

"*Really*?" I spun the chair to face him again. "What do we need to talk about? The fact that you're the world's worst fiancé or the fact that this engagement is nothing but a lie?"

He hesitated before sitting beside Leonard's now-curled-into-a-ball girlfriend. "You don't mean that."

I glared. "You wanna tell me how I feel now?"

"I know things have been weird with us lately, but I mean it when I say I wanted to spend every moment of tonight with you—and *only* you."

"Zach, you're talking out of your ass. You've spent the *entire* night ogling and touching other women. *The entire night.* I may be drunk, but I'm not *stupid*."

His moistened mouth was working at his fingertips, his swiss cheese colored teeth gnawing at what was left of his nails.

"If you want to cheat on me, *go for it*. At least be a gentleman about it and do it behind my back." *Just get it over with so we can be even.*

"Roxy, I don't want to ch—"

I held up my ringless hand, not wanting to hear anymore slurred lines. "Stop lying. Stop it right now. You can't lie to me when I've watched *everything* unfold with my own *two eyes*."

Leonard's girlfriend twitched slightly, snoring.

"If you'd let me talk—"

"No!" I yelled. "I'm done. When we were dancing, your eyes were focused on *everything* but me. When I tried to kiss you, I missed because you were rubbernecking some brunette that waved at you. You ignored my calls because you were *too busy* taking pictures with *half naked* women. What could you *possibly* have to say?"

His shoulders slumped forward. "Roxanne, I'm *sorry*. From the bottom of my heart—*I am so sorry*. I didn't mean—I would never—it's just—" he paused, fiddling with his toga. "I—I—I wore basketball shorts like you asked." He lifted the bottom of his toga to prove a point.

After all that, that's what you decided to say? "Yeah. Great. Thanks." I took a deep breath. "I saw them earlier—I also saw that you *weren't* wearing them when you were surrounded by half naked women. You only put them on because Omar told you I was here."

He half smiled. "But I *did* put them on! Proof that I have a fiancé."

I didn't think it was possible to get any angrier. Turns out, it was possible. "*Proof*? Basketball shorts? What on God's green earth does that mean? That isn't a chastity belt—we've had sex *multiple* times while you were wearing basketball shorts. How is *anything* you're saying supposed to make me feel better?"

He stood and took two steps toward me before I glared, forcing him three steps back. "I don't know how to say this without pissing you off, but I'm gonna say it anyway." He took a deep breath. "*Every single girl* at this party has been giving me more attention in the last few hours than you've even *considered* giving me the past few months."

I inhaled as if he'd shoved me in the chest. "Is *that* what you want? Attention from some slutty sorority girls?"

"Don't you get it?" He shook his head. " I want *your* attention, but you *refuse* to give it to me."

"What is it with you *needing* attention? Why do you need reassurance to feel good about yourself? Why can't you just *believe* I love you without me having to screw you all of the time?"

"Because I need it!" He was panting hard, as if he'd just finished a marathon. "I *need* my girlfriend to want me. Physically."

I hated that he had the ability to make me feel guilty only seconds after he made me uncontrollably angry. "Oh *really*? When was the last time you called me beautiful when I was wearing sweatpants?"

No answer.

"The last time you kissed me *just* to kiss me? Without some sexual ulterior motive?"

No answer.

"Or the last time you tried to finish me off before finishing yourself?"

A frown.

"You don't want me. You just want some sex doll." I curled a loose strand of hair around my finger. "Your hand can do the same thing—and then you wouldn't have to deal with my *nagging* or my *crying* anymore."

He sat back down, silently, rubbing the tops of his thighs with his palms.

"Zach, seriously. What are we doing?"

His eyes moistened. "Do you still want to get married?"

This was the moment for me to tell him the truth. *We're rushing into something that's already failing. If we can't survive an engagement together, how are we gonna survive a marriage?* I opened my mouth to answer him but froze when I caught a glimpse of my small, diamond ring glistening in the gap between his curled thumb and forefinger. My heart softened. "Do you honestly believe we're ready to get married?"

"I know I want to spend the rest of my life with you."

"How can you say that after everything that's happened?"

"I think," he whispered. "You're the one who doesn't want to spend forever with me."

Tell him how you're feeling. Tell him he's right—you're not ready. Tell him you're freaking out and need to slow things down. The longer it took me to respond, the deeper his frown lines grew. "Zachary," I whispered. Glancing up at the squashed spider again, I shook my head. "This isn't a conversation we should be having right now. We've both been drinking—alcohol does crazy things to the brain, you know?" *And I don't want to say something I'm gonna regret.* I reached out and patted his knee. "Tensions are high. We've been fighting a lot. Tonight is not the right time to do this." *I can't tell you I'm not ready to get married on your birthday.* "My friends are waiting for me." *And I'm tired of fighting.* I placed my hands in my lap. "It's your birthday and you deserve to have a good time. Omar was right. I ruined everything tonight. I'm just gonna go."

When I stood to leave, Zachary's arms wrapped around me with an unexpected intensity—an embrace that was reminiscent of the warmth we once shared in our past. As he let go, he played with my hands and slid the engagement ring back on my finger. "It's dirty, but I don't want you—or me—to lose it." Part of me cringed, but the other part smiled. "Stay with me tonight," he whispered.

I leaned into his exposed collarbone. "You can stay at my place. My dad'll let you sleep in the guest room."

"No. Come to my place." He rested his hand on my butt and pulled me closer. "I can drive."

His sudden erection told me what he *really* wanted, which brought back my anger. "You can *not* drive. If you *really* want to have sex, you can sneak into my room when my dad goes to bed."

"What do you mean I can't drive? I'm fine." He swayed side to side without moving his feet. "We should go to my place. We don't have to sneak anywhere."

"I'm not leaving my friends here and my dad is their ride home. And no—" I said when he opened his mouth. "You will *not* be their ride. I refuse to let you drive like this."

His eyelids drooped even further. "This is just another excuse for you not to have sex with me, isn't it? After *everything* we talked about?"

I took a step back, balling my fists at my sides to refrain from scratching his eyes out. "Is that *all* you fucking care about?"

Now his eyes opened. "What did you just say to me?"

"You fucking heard me. Getting fucked is all you fucking care about! And all I'm doing is trying to make sure you don't die in a fucking ditch somewhere."

He scoffed. "Clearly, you've drank too much tonight. I don't appreciate you talking to me like that."

"And I don't appreciate you being an asshole."

"You're being a drama queen."

"And you're being an idiot! You can't drive home, Zach. You'll kill yourself—or worse—someone else."

He glared. "Maybe if you learned to trust me—"

"Oh, *shut up!*" I snapped. "This isn't about trust. This is about me making sure you live long enough to see your next birthday."

Leonard's girlfriend awoke dazed and confused, her bloodshot eyes searching for her boyfriend. "Who are you?"

"This is about you doing everything in your power to not have sex with me," Zachary said, ignoring her.

"You're impossible!" I yelled, throwing my hands up. "Do *whatever* you want! Drive home! Be a fucking idiot! Why don't you take one of those sluts home with you since that's all you fucking care about?"

Leonard's girlfriend stood. "Where's my boyfriend?"

I silently pointed to the door.

She looked at me, confused, before stumbling out of the room.

Zachary was breathing heavily. "Is that *really* how you feel?"

"You're *refusing* to listen," I hissed. "All I want is for you to get home in one piece! I even offered to have you stay *with* me."

He shook his head. "Yeah, *sure*. All you want is to go home without me."

I give up. He wants to hear what he wants to hear. "I'm leaving. I'm done. Text me when you get home, if you want. Have fun with those sluts. Happy fucking birthday, Zach."

Chapter Seven

LAYING IN BED a few hours later, I couldn't help but wonder how the decisions we make daily ultimately impact what happens in the future. I stared at my phone, text messages lighting up the screen. I should've felt guilty texting the boy that was toxic for my relationship with Zachary, but instead, I felt regret for leaving Sonoma State in order to make the relationship with Zachary work. Had I stayed in Sonoma, I wouldn't be lying in bed crying because my boyfriend could be dead in a car on fire in a ditch somewhere. Or worse: sleeping with one of those beautiful girls from the party. Had I stayed in Sonoma, I wouldn't be texting the boy who broke my heart—I would be cuddling next to his tall, lanky body, his soft snores luring me into a comfortable sleep. Had I stayed in Sonoma, I wouldn't be engaged to a boy who needed constant reassurance to believe I loved him.

I placed the phone face down on the pillow next to Sherlock, who was sleeping soundly beside me. "If you loved him, would you be texting Lamont just to prove a point? Get over yourself, Roxy. You don't know anything about relationships, and you've been in the same one for almost three years."

Sherlock stretched and groaned before curling into a smaller ball.

"But Lamont is home on a Friday night. All alone. He's not pretending not to be engaged so some random whore can blow him on his birthday." I shook my head and turned over to stare through the darkness at the ceiling. "What's wrong with me? Why am I like this?"

Closing my eyes, I promised myself I wouldn't do this again. I wouldn't text Lamont when I was mad at Zachary. I wouldn't question if I made the wrong choice coming back to San Diego instead of staying up north. I wouldn't hope that Zachary would cheat on me so I'd have a legitimate reason to end the engagement without sounding insane.

I circled my arms around Sherlock and inhaled the scent of his fur. "I hope we both it make it out of this without completely resenting one another." I felt my fingers begin to tingle. *We might already be past the point of no return.* "What're we gonna do?"

\#

"OH YEAH, BABY," I moaned. "Oh yeah. That's the spot." Zachary's body was weighing me down, the sound of our slapping stomachs providing percussion for the guitar solo drifting through the laptop's speaker.

When my fiancé kissed my neck, I rolled my eyes. *I don't have time for this tonight. I'm too tired.*

We were in Zachary's hot and stuffy bedroom, a pincher bug crawling up the poorly painted wall beside my hip. The mattress was bouncing against the wall behind my head, the wooden headboard still propped up next to the dresser, Zachary too lazy to finish building his furniture after living in the same room for nearly a year. I stared at the white fan on the ceiling that was moving in slow motion, Zachary's quick movements making me wonder how women on TV so easily achieve orgasm.

A nice bruise was beginning to form on the inside of my thigh.

"*Oh, yes,*" I whispered fiercely. "You're so—" I ran through a list of adjectives in my head, unable to come up with anything creative. "Hard." His thrusting picked up the pace, his actions now resembling a dog humping the leg of its owner. I closed my eyes and clenched my jaw. "Oh, I'm so close," I lied. *Close to losing my mind. Maybe I can practice my lines since I have nothing better to do.* "Keep going."

"Wait, wait," Zachary panted, sweat glistening on his three chest hairs. "Why don't we switch it up?"

When he rolled onto his back, I let out a sigh, hoping that he took it as something sexual and not something impatient. *Why bother? You don't actually care about how this ends for me.* I wanted to tell him that I needed to get home so I could practice for my Shakespeare performance, but the desperate excitement in his eyes made me bite my tongue. *He won't last much longer anyway. I can leave after this.* I climbed over him and kissed his lips. "Great idea, Babe," I whispered, my mouth moving to his jaw and neck, my tongue moistening his tan skin. *Try to think positively*, I thought. *This will be a great opportunity to work out. No gym membership needed. That's it, Roxy. Silver linings.* I smiled at myself. Zachary mistook this as encouragement, his hands reaching up to grasp my breasts. *Oh! And I have ice cream at home! Now, that's something I can really look forward to.* I shifted my lower half so Zachary and I connected, his satisfied grunt convincing me he had zero idea how uninterested I really was. *Okay, now let's get this ab workout started.* I began moving my hips back and forth. *Man, this burns. I should really go to the gym.* I breathed heavily, my heart beating too fast. *This is pathetic. How am I this out of shape?*

"Roxanne," he moaned, eyes shut, tongue moistening his chapped lips. "You feel *so good.* How are you *doing this?*"

I sighed. *Drama Queen calm down. It hasn't been that long since we've had sex.* Shifting my legs slightly, I leaned over and kissed Zachary to keep him quiet. *I need to focus on my abs—you're distracting me.* With another quick adjustment, I took note of the sudden surge of pleasure rushing between my legs. *Wait a minute. Oh. Okay, this feels good.* I smiled, continuing to move my hips at a steady pace, the pleasure building. *Here we go. Yes. Yes!*

Just as I was settling into the rhythmic motions my body yearned for, Zachary took it upon himself to begin thrusting, and even though I pushed down on his shoulders in an attempt to stop him from moving, he wound up flipping me over onto my stomach, ruining any chance I had of achieving climax.

While my fiancé grunted, I exhaled. *Well, might as well practice my lines. Get a jump start on the work I gotta do at home.*

It was Wednesday night—and the first time we'd seen one another since Zachary's toga party. Although he'd called and left multiple apologies on my voicemail the next day, it took me forty-eight hours to call him back. I was hesitant to listen to what he had to say, but we did agree to meet at his place on Wednesday to talk out our problems over a romantic dinner. I thought this meant we'd go somewhere like PF Changs, have a couple glasses of wine, figure out why we've been disagreeing so much lately, and then go back to his house where we would cuddle and do our school work.

Instead, we engaged in make-up sex, which would likely be followed by cheap, and fattening, Chinese takeout from our usual MSG infested restaurant just up the street on El Cajon Boulevard. We never addressed our problems. I had mentioned the weather, he briefly asked about class, and then he'd desperately taken off my clothes.

It was probably the worst thing to do in an attempt to mend the relationship overall, but it was the best thing in his mind for the moment.

When Zachary grabbed my hips, I winced. *Okay, don't think about the bruise. Think about Shakespeare. For fear less day should look their shames upon—*

"God, you're so hot." The words hissed through the gaps of his crooked teeth. He turned me over so that I was now sitting on top of him, facing his feet. "Ride my cock."

Instantaneously, my fake interest in having sex with him faltered, any and all sexual energy in my body evaporating out of the room.

As a lover of the English language, it was rare to find a word that made me want to vomit. But the way Zachary used the word "cock" left me feeling itchy, like my skin was made of a poorly knitted wool sweater. My fiancé *loved* to talk dirty—in particular, whenever we had sex because he liked to be reassured that he was big and hard and hot. These descriptors tumbled out of my mouth not meaning anything anymore, my goal to get Zachary so fired up, I could quickly roll out of bed, and continue my school work.

Tonight, I wasn't in the mood to pretend to enjoy sex with Zachary because I was already pretending everything in our relationship was fine. *How now Stranger! Wither—Wither—shoot. That doesn't sound right. I don't think it's supposed to be Stranger—*Zachary grabbed my hair in his fist and yanked, pulling back my neck a little too roughly. "Ow, Babe!" I said, slapping his hand away. "Don't yank at me like you yank on yourself. That *really* hurt."

He tugged once more before completely letting go. "Sorry, Baby. You just feel *so good.*"

My neck was pounding, and tears touched the corner of my eyes. *This needs to end. I can't do this anymore.*

"How's it feel for you?" he breathed.

"So good," I lied, arching my back to match his movements. *How now Spirit, wither wonder thee.* I smiled. *Okay, Spirit sounds right. Thee isn't right, though. Ugh. I wish I could look at the script.* "So, so good." I needed him to finish. I needed to get home so I could rehearse because my group would be practicing together in two weeks' time. *I think it's you. Wither wander you.*

"Are you close?" Zachary asked.

To memorizing my lines? I would be if we actually did what we're supposed to be doing tonight. "Oh, yeah," I lied again. "Super close."

"Fuck. You've got me so close. So fucking close."

Great. Let's finish this already. My thighs are beginning to chafe.

"Keep doing what you're doing."

I placed my hands on his knees and looked at the ring on my finger. *Everything about us is a lie. Why can't we talk about our problems? Why do we keep pretending everything is okay?* "Oh, yeah Baby."

"Oh, Roxy!" Zachary thrusted. "I love you!"

I sighed. *Do you really? Or are you lying about that, too?*

#

"HOW'S THE SPAGHETTI?" Father asked me over dinner the following evening.

"Why? Did you poison it?" I teased.

He laughed, shaking his head. "Considering the fact that I'm also eating the *same* spaghetti, I find your question flawed. If I wanted to kill everyone at this table, I would've made myself a different batch."

My mom sighed, which made me grin. "He used ground turkey meat instead of ground beef," she said.

"Your mother would like us to consume less red meat throughout the week. I've been trying to find comparable alternatives."

I took another bite. "I honestly can't tell the difference."

"What about you girls?" my dad asked Jasmine and Lacie, who both sat across from me at the dining room table.

Jasmine nodded enthusiastically. "Your cooking is awesome, as always, Mr. Vaughn."

"Yeah," Lacie chimed in. "My mom won't even cook, so this beats Stouffers."

My father laughed. "Well, aren't you too kind."

"I think the zucchini and bell peppers you added to the sauce were a nice touch. It helps balance the acidity in the tomatoes—and they add a yummy crunch." I bit a red bell pepper in half. "Food Network really penetrates your brain after you binge watch cooking shows instead of sleeping."

He smiled smugly at my mother. "I told you it was a good idea."

"Oh please," my mother scoffed, her veggies pushed to the side of her plate. "Just because Roxanne gives her stamp of approval doesn't mean it's a good idea. She's an *English* major. Her opinion isn't exactly what I would consider *credible*."

I glanced at my friends, who were now studying their plates as if they would be receiving a quiz on what they ate after dinner.

"So," Father said, a little too cheerfully. "How's school going for you two?" He picked up his wine glass and took a generous sip before swirling some noodles around his fork. "Are you enjoying any of your classes?"

I breathed a small sigh of relief. *Solid topic change. Keep all attention away from me. Nicely done, Dad.*

Lacie dabbed her lips with the green cloth napkin my mom used to match the green stripe on the trim of the dinner plates. "It's awful. I have *two* classes at eight in the morning where attendance is *mandatory*. I've already missed two."

I glared at her. *What have I told you about being honest with my parents? Especially about school.*

My mother shook her head, disappointed. "If you're struggling to wake up for a class you probably don't even need to shower for, how're you gonna be able to keep a *real* job in the adult world?"

Seemingly unfazed, Lacie took a large gulp of her ice water. "I don't graduate for another year, so I've decided not to worry about it."

I placed my palm over my eyes. *You're gonna make my mom judge me for my choice of friends on top of everything else.*

My father fiddled with his place mat, which had a wide-eyed cat inside of a Jack-O-Lantern smiling up at him. "How about you, Jasmine? Are you planning on graduating this spring?"

"I wish," Jasmine replied. "I partied a lot freshman year and changed my major a few times, so, I'm a little behind schedule."

"You still party a lot," Lacie mumbled, Jasmine elbowing her.

Holding back the urge to kick both of them beneath the table, I squished a cherry tomato with my fork.

"So, neither of you are graduating in four years?"

Lacie shrugged, blissfully oblivious of my mother's judgmental tone. "With the economy the way it is, it's better for me to stay in school anyway. Do you know how difficult it is to find a job right now?"

For the love of God, Lacie. Are you doing this on purpose?

"And what kind of job are you looking for?"

Don't say it. Please, Lacie. Just lie, I pleaded, telepathically.

"Psychology," Lacie stated confidently.

I groaned into my pasta. "How about those Chargers, Dad?"

"Psychology," Mother repeated slowly, her delicate hand swirling her wine glass. "Isn't that one of those majors you pick when you don't have greater aspirations? Much like being an English major."

"Honey," my father said sharply. "Lacie is not your daughter. Maybe that should be your final glass of wine."

My mother frowned. "I apologize, Sweetie. I meant no offense."

My fork clattered on the side of my plate. *Of course, you meant offense, Mom. How else is she supposed to take it?* I stared at my friend, waiting for her to fight back.

"No offense taken, Mrs. V." Lacie smiled. "I know I want to help people, but you're totally right. I have no idea what I'm doing."

"At least she admits it," Mother said, looking at me over her wine glass.

"Admits *what*?" I challenged.

"Admits that she has *no idea* what she's doing."

I gritted my teeth. "I *want* to be a writer, Mom. Without a shadow of a doubt."

My mom glanced up at my dad, who narrowed his eyes and shook his head. She took a large sip of her wine before resting her forearms on the table. "I'm not referring to your writing. Although I do not agree with you, I know that's what you want to do."

At first, I was caught by surprise, already planning my snarky response in my head, not at all prepared for her to agree with me. "Wait, what?" My stomach swirled my dinner around uncomfortably. "Then what were you referring to?"

"I was talking about your engagement to a fag."

"Here we go," my father muttered, reaching for the bottle of wine to refill his glass.

Lacie and Jasmine paused for two seconds before laughing so hard, small tears formed in the corners of their eyes.

"Mrs. V!" Jasmine shouted at an unnecessary decibel. "We've been saying the *same thing*."

I sipped my water, my stomach now tumbling my spaghetti like clothes in a washing machine. "Please, *please* don't start with this again."

"You mean to tell me your *best friends* have brought this to your attention and you're somehow *still* in a relationship with a queer?"

My father placed his napkin on his plate and pushed his chair away from the table. "This is where I take my leave."

"Can I go with you?" I asked, dread filling the remains of my stomach, my appetite vanishing.

He shrugged sympathetically before grabbing his wine glass and making his way downstairs into his man cave.

I glared at my friends.

"We *just* had this conversation," Lacie continued. "At Zach's birthday party, actually. He takes *every* chance to take his clothes off."

"That doesn't make him *gay*," I argued.

"It does when he wants to do it at a *frat party*."

"Why are you *doing* this?" I hissed at my friends, feeling a sense of betrayal I hadn't felt since Tiffany started talking to Lamont behind my back.

"We're worried about you, Roxanne."

I slowly turned to face my mother. "Since when have you felt anything but *hatred* toward me?"

She sighed. "Marriage is serious. The last thing I want is for you to come home one day and find your husband in bed with some big, hulking black man with diamonds the size of apples in his ear lobes."

"Mom," I said, placing my elbow on the table to show her my ring finger. "I'm already engaged. Don'tcha think it's a little late to have cold feet?"

"Engagements can be broken without all of the nasty paperwork. You are too *young* to have a divorce on your record. You already gave up on trying to have a *real* profession, *and* you've given up on trying to fit into your jeans. You're running out of the qualifications men are looking for in a potential lover."

"I don't know about all that, but me and Jazz don't want you to get hurt," Lacie said, taking note of my reddening cheeks.

"That's what I don't get," I said, exasperated. "Look at my track record. *I'm* the one who's gonna end up hurting *him*."

The silence that followed made my chest constrict. *It's true. They believe it, too.*

"Roxy," my mother whispered, clearing her throat. "Your father and I are quite concerned about you getting married at such a young age. Zach's father is homosexual. His mother *found* her *husband* in *bed* with his *best friend*—and that was after they'd been married for twelve years. We don't *ever* want you to endure the same thing."

"He's been my *best friend* for the past few years. Don't you think homosexuality would've come into one of our conversations by now?"

"*Best friends*? Do you braid each other's hair and share gossip?"

The more she spoke, the more offended I grew. "Mother, I've had *enough*," I snapped. "He's my fiancé. I would know if he was gay." The doorbell sounded, saving me from having to defend my relationship any further. "Zach is here. Can you all *please* drop this conversation completely?"

"Zach is here?" my mother asked, surprised.

"Yes, that's what I said." I threw my napkin on top of my plate. "You know he always comes over at this time so we can do homework."

"But your girlfriends are here. Why didn't you cancel?"

"Because I have homework to do. Jasmine and Lacie are more than welcome to join."

"We're kind of in the middle of talking," Lacie said, voice low.

"*Talking?*" The doorbell sounded again. "You're *insulting* me and my fiancé! It's like you're all obsessed with him. All you do is talk about him being gay. You're a bunch of wolves who cried homosexual." I pushed my chair back. "I've asked *all* of you to stop a *million* times, but you refuse to respect me. I'm over it."

Jasmine frowned. "We were kind of hoping you'd come out with us tonight."

"I have school in the morning and homework to do." *I'd rather fail a class than go out with you two tonight.* "So, I'm sorry. Can't tonight."

Both girls nodded solemnly, my mother finishing her wine before apologizing to the girls for my behavior.

Later that night, after my mother and father fell asleep, and after Jasmine and Lacie left to go out drinking in Pacific Beach, I initiated sex with Zachary—the first time I'd *actually* wanted to be intimate with him in longer than I cared to admit— to prove to myself that my fiancé wasn't gay. But as he laid his head on my chest afterwards, my eyes scanning the pages of a book I had a quiz on the following day, my mind refused to stop overthinking and overanalyzing everything my mom and friends said at dinner.

All I could see when I closed my eyes was Zachary bending over Omar's trembling body, the two of them cuddling afterward and whispering video game lingo to one another. Although the mere idea of Zachary cheating on me made me light headed, I reflected on my own infidelity and realized I deserved to get hurt like that.

I set my book down and stared up at the ceiling. *What if he is gay? What does that say about me?* Taking in three deep breaths, I forced myself to not think about Sonoma State and the fact that moving back to San Diego for Zachary was a *horrible* mistake.

#

"THIS IS GONNA be amazing," I whispered to Zachary, who sipped from a Styrofoam cup filled with black coffee. "I can't wait to see the actors bring the story to life."

He nodded. "I'm gonna do my best to understand the plot."

Only five minutes earlier, Professor Emerson shouted out to all students milling around the Old Globe Theatre that *King Lear* was going to begin shortly. We finished purchasing snacks and beverages from the concession stand before showing our tickets to the Old Globe employees, who proceeded to direct us to our seats.

"I thought you read the play?" I asked as he sat down.

He snorted. "You only read it because it was a requirement for your class. Why would I read it?"

"Because you *told* me you read it when I asked you last night. You lied to me. Why would you lie about something like that?"

Although we were whispering, those sitting around us began to shift uncomfortably.

"I don't have time to read something not related to my studies." He shrugged, oblivious to my frustration.

Oh? But you can read The Jungle Book *instead of making lesson plans?* "You could've told me you didn't read it instead of lying straight to my face." I paused, taking a deep breath. *If he lied about that, what else has he been lying about?* "I asked you to read it so we could enjoy this together."

"They're setting it in a modern style dictatorship, not in Shakespearean time. I'll listen and be fine."

They're still gonna use the original lines from the play, Jerk. I opened a bag of skittles and shoved a handful into my mouth to keep quiet. *Don't cause a scene. Your classmates are here.* "Yeah, because you're *so good* at listening," I mumbled.

Luckily, the orchestra struck up the opening music, drowning out my attitude.

Zachary smiled at me and kissed me on the cheek. "This is gonna be great. Thanks for inviting me, Little Woman."

I swallowed my Skittles, hating that guilt and irritation were waging a full world war in my stomach. I had invited him because I thought it would be a fun date idea – but now, I wished I hadn't. I hated that he lied to me about little things, and I hated how oblivious he was to my frustrations. *Maybe it's not that he's* clueless, I thought. *Maybe he really just doesn't give a crap about how you feel.*

To the outsider looking in, it should be easy to end a relationship void of passion, bursting at the seams with arguments and differing opinions. But for us, it was terrifying—maybe we weren't *in love* anymore, but we *were* best friends. And losing your rock? The one person who was there for you through the hardest of times?

We would be alone.

I would be alone.

I began to sweat, my fingertips tingling. *I'd be alone with my anxiety.* I fiddled with the Skittles bag, my chest suddenly heavy, my lungs fighting for steady breaths. *So, he doesn't really listen to me. What husband does? It's not a big deal.*

Taking note of my discomfort, Zachary grabbed my hand and squeezed. "You alright, Little Woman?"

His concern lifted the anxiety just as suddenly as it hit me. *Maybe he doesn't care about the little things, but he cares about me.* I nodded, inhaling through my nose, breathing out of my mouth.

"I love you, Roxanne."

My heart thumped against my chest just once. "I love you, too."

Even though I meant it, I didn't mean it the way he thought I did.

Chapter Eight

"WHY DOES IT feel like we haven't seen one another in forever?" I asked Luke over breakfast the following weekend.

He added four sugars to his coffee before sighing. "Because your life has become nothing but Zach this and Zach that. Doesn't matter that the last time we hung out, you threw your engagement ring on the ground and stepped on it. Doesn't matter that your fiancé was basically cheating on you in front of your face. All that matters is that you get to feel less guilty about Lamont by allowing him to continue to torment you."

"Wow. Skipping any and all pleasantries before I even get a chance to drink anything." I frowned over the menu, feeling as if he'd just shoved me in the chest. "Did I do something to you? You're not Mr. Perfect when it comes to your dysfunctional relationships."

We were seated at a metal table that had a plastic vase with a fake rose as a centerpiece. The restaurant was busy, the only seating available in the sun on the patio. College students with black circles beneath their eyes and makeup from the night prior smeared on their cheeks sat at the neighboring tables, attacking breakfast burritos with an aggression similar to the Sea Gulls trying to take food out of guests' hands at Sea World.

"Yeah – you did do something. I'm one of your best friends and you've been avoiding me like the plague because you're so consumed with your toxic engagement. It's like one day you hate Zach and the next day, you're swooning over him. I've never seen you act like this before."

"First of all, that party was last weekend, so I haven't been *avoiding* you. I had a busy week." Torn between pancakes and or an omelet, I placed the menu on the table, feeling defensive. "Second of all, when was the last time you were in a real relationship and not just some casual hook up? You have *no idea* what I'm going through right now."

He sipped his coffee calmly. "I'm not going to make this about me because this is about you. I'm aware of my relationship history. I know it's not pretty. The thing is – I know you've been burned in the past and I know you've been with Zachary for a while now, but you're getting *obsessive* of him. And not in your typical 'clingy girlfriend' kind of way. I'm just trying to figure out if you're staying with him to punish yourself because you loved Lamont or if you're grasping onto this relationship with any and all of your remaining strength because you think you'll be alone for the rest of you life."

I began to feel a headache setting up camp between my eyes, my chest growing tighter and tighter. "This is a lot to unpack before noon." I rubbed my eyes. "No offense, but you're being extremely judgmental for someone who jumps from bed to bed in order to avoid any sort of real intimacy and commitment."

"Don't attack me because you know I'm right and you're afraid to admit that I just hit the nail on the head."

The waitress returned with my mimosa and asked us if we needed a few more minutes for food. Wanting to prevent Luke from tearing me apart any further, I told the waitress I wanted the pancakes with whipped cream and strawberries while Luke ordered Huevos Rancheros and a Bloody Mary.

"Coffee *and* booze?"

He stuck his tongue out. "Who's being judgmental now?"

Sipping the mimosa, I shrugged. "No judgement. Merely making an observation."

"Look, I'm not here to lecture you, but Jazz texted me the other night about how you bailed on them, and it got me thinking more about your behavior. You don't even respond to my text messages anymore."

I rolled my eyes, wishing I'd ignored his text about meeting up together to gossip. "Oh please. You're just going to jump to conclusions without even talking to me first?"

"What do you think I'm doing right now?"

I sipped my mimosa. "You're attacking me." He didn't respond, patiently waiting for me to continue. "Look, Luke, there were no *plans* that night with Lacie and Jasmine. Yes, they came over for dinner, but I had zero intention of going out that night. It was the middle of the week and I had homework to do."

"No, you didn't," he argued as the waitress dropped off his Bloody Mary. "Zach came over and interrupted everything."

I took another sip of my mimosa, wishing I could crawl back into bed. Lacie and Jasmine hadn't spoken to me since that night, and although I felt somewhat guilty about it, I was also mad that they would assume I would go out with them without them even asking me if I wanted to. "Yeah, Zach did come over. *To do homework*. Like we do *every* night together. Jasmine and Lacie go out to party instead of studying. I don't do that. And don't just sit there looking at me like you don't know that. I've never been the type to go partying when I have homework to do."

He shook some pepper into his drink and stirred it with a celery stick. "This isn't about your insane work ethic. This is about the fact that your fiancé, a guy you're not even sure you still love, has taken over every single aspect of your life. I get you having to do homework – that's who you are. But does he have to be sitting next to you watching you study?"

My stomach began to hurt—guilt replacing hunger pains. *I don't need this right now. I have enough on my plate.* "I know it's hard for you to understand, but I do love Zach. I'm not trying to obsess over him – we just have our routine. And him coming over during the week to do our homework together is part of it."

He held his hands up, surrendering. "I don't want to fight with you and I can tell I'm making you feel bad. I'll stop – I just needed to talk to you because it sucks to see you hurting like you were at his party. You have the *saddest* upset face." I snorted as he smirked. "Seriously, just be aware of the messages you're sending us. You know, your *best friends.*"

I thought back to my four best girlfriends from Sonoma State and how our relationships fell apart because I chose Zachary. How being in a relationship with him and running away from Lamont had become more important than the once unbreakable bonds I thought I had formed with them. I then thought about how much it hurt to lose them, feeling the pinching in my stomach all over again. "I'm not doing it on purpose." I paused, taking another sip of my drink. "To be honest, and please don't go running to them, but Jasmine and Lacie have been upsetting me lately. I probably wouldn't have gone out with them anyway – Zach or no Zach. Homework or no homework. They're talking trash about me in front of my parents, they're dissing my boyfriend, and they don't seem to understand the importance of hard work when it comes to my parents and how they're making themselves look bad, which in turn, makes it look like I don't know how to choose the right friends."

He nodded, chuckling. "I went to high school with those girls. Believe me— they can be a bit much, and I'm *fully* aware of that. I just know they do have your best interests in mind. They just have to wade past their own selfish wants and needs first."

The waitress delivered our food before tending to the other tables like a butterfly pollinating a field of flowers. Although the food smelled phenomenal, my mouth turned dry at the thought of eating. I sipped my mimosa instead. "Do you think Zach is my soul mate?" I blurted.

Luke chewed and swallowed, carefully thinking through his words before speaking. "You're talking to the wrong guy. *Soul mate* isn't in my vocabulary." He took a big gulp of his Bloody Mary and patted his lips with his napkin. "But I will say, no matter who the guy is, nobody is worth losing your best friends. Because when that guy breaks up with you, your friends are gonna be there to pick up the pieces and help get your life back together."

I lathered my pancakes in syrup and began cutting them with my fork. "Can we talk about *anything* else? You've succeeded in making me feel like the worst human being in the world and it's not even noon yet."

He smiled. "Fine. Enough about your drama. I have news."

"Thank goodness. I'd like to get my appetite back."

"Remember that guy with the bulge from the party?"

I cut into the pancakes, straining my memory. "*Remember* is too strong of a term. I recall you *pointing out* some guy with a bulge."

His smiled widened. "Turns out, he too, is a fan of bulges."

After swallowing a bite, I placed my fork down. "So, are you saying that he prefers the company of men?"

Luke shrugged. "I told you toga parties are gay."

I swallowed the sweet pancake and shook my head. "I hate you, sometimes."

He winked. "Don't lie to yourself, Roxanne. That's no way to talk to your soul mate."

#

ZACHARY AND I studied our costumes in my bedroom's floor-to-ceiling closet mirror.

"You look beautiful, Domina," he grunted in a poorly executed Roman accent, bowing from the waist. "I'm going to *ravage* you."

Knowing he was attempting to embrace his character's role, I decided to play along, creating my own awful accent. "Get on your knees and please me, Gladiator."

I flushed when his knees hit the carpet, his hands latching onto my butt. "Yes, Domina." He kissed the sweet spot between my legs, the silky material of my dress leaving little to the imagination.

This year, it was my fiancé's turn to choose our costume theme. Zachary chose the characters Spartacus and Domina from the X-rated Starz TV show, *Spartacus*. It wasn't a show I enjoyed—overexaggerated violence and excessive

134

amounts of blood made me uncomfortable. However, I did have to admit that once you watched a couple of episodes, the storyline was addictive. It told the tale of gladiators and their roles in entertaining the wealthy Romans, tying in slave-with-superior sexual relationships and family drama that put the Kardashians to shame. Throw in two or three penises and a handful of boobs every five to ten minutes, and that created a show perfect for the guy who told me millions of times that he strove to look like the warriors from the movie, *300*.

Zachary wanted to be the main character, Spartacus, which meant I would be Domina—the Roman queen who loved Spartacus but pretended to only use him to fulfill her sexual desires. The woman who played Domina was a *beautiful* actress, clothed in a sexy red gown that hugged all of her curves, and her tan skin appearing even darker against the abundance of gold jewelry she wore every episode.

I began to giggle and kissed the top of Zachary's head. Maybe it was his excitement, but a sort of giddiness washed over me. "You are *quite* the gladiator, Zachary." I bent over to kiss his lips. "You look just like Spartacus. Definitely nailed the costume."

He pulled me down to the carpet so that I was laying on top of him. "You're *way* hotter than the real Domina."

I rolled my eyes. "You're crazy."

He smiled. "I'm serious! I would *love* to ravage you right now."

This was one of those rare days I cherished—Zachary and I hadn't fought, not once. Instead, we'd been lovey-dovey, joking with one another and sharing genuine smiles. I couldn't remember the last time things felt so right between us.

"You're totally lying, but you're sweet."

He kissed me, his hands absently twirling the curls hanging down my back. "You're so bad at taking compliments."

Not wanting to ruin the moment, I refrained from telling him that his belt was digging uncomfortably into my lower stomach. I tried shifting slightly, only to make it hurt worse. "Well, you look amazing. Just like Spartacus himself."

"How about we do something to celebrate how good we look?" He flashed his most flirtatious smile at me. "How about it, Domina? Let me make you feel things you've never felt before."

I raised an eyebrow. *We've been dating forever. There's nothing you haven't made me feel already.* "Are you still in character or are you being serious?"

He shrugged. "A little bit of both."

Time to ruin the moment. "We spent a lot of money on these," I said. *And yet, somehow, you've managed to get a costume more revealing than mine.* "How about we don't take them off just yet?" The pain from the belt was beginning to become unbearable, but I didn't want him to think I was uninterested. Even though I really didn't want to have sex.

"Who said we have to take them off?" Zachary asked, his hand moving up and down my back.

I placed my palm on his stomach, taking note of the muscles I hadn't noticed the last time I touched him. "Have you been working out?"

Not only was it the perfect subject change, but it also made my fiancé smile like a child in an ice cream parlor. Apparently, he had been—every morning for the last three weeks. Two hours. Treadmill and weights. *How did I not know this? And how did I not notice sooner?* I wondered. He might not have the same definition those chiseled hunks on TV had, but he looked great. *Has it really been that long since we've had sex?*

"Why didn't you tell me you were working out? I would've gone with you and hopped on the elliptical or something. I'm gonna look like a whale next to you."

Zachary snorted. "Domina is a curvy woman. You look *just* like a Roman queen."

Is that supposed to be a compliment? Statues of Roman women have eight hundred rolls. My self-consciousness sky-rocketed to a whole new level. *Maybe he wants me to be fat so all of the attention will be on him.* I held in a sigh. *How much attention does he really need? Like his lack of costume won't already give him enough.*

According to Zachary, who dedicated way too many hours of extensive research on the matter, and who decided it was necessary to purchase overly-priced—albeit authentic—costume pieces on a website selling old television show attire, the *traditional* gladiator garb consisted of very little *actual* clothing.

The Cingulum—or the belt—was made of thick leather and wrapped around the lower stomach, bearing a strong resemblance to the belts given to wrestling champions, minus the jewels and the gold. The Galerus, which was *typically* made of medal, was leather for Zachary's costume—it reminded me of the tail feathers on the hawks at Sea World. It ran from his wrist to his shoulder, a large, leather strap around his chest keeping the costume piece from slipping. The Subligaria— which I called a diaper, only to have Zachary angrily correct me—barely covered his man parts and showed off the dimples beneath his buttocks. Lastly, there were the sandals. Leather straps wrapping around his muscular and tan calves with a rubber base beneath his feet.

Now wondering if Zachary could feel my flab pushing against his stomach, I rolled off him and lay on my back, rubbing where the belt had been attempting to impale me. After glancing down at his spread open legs, I took a deep breath and focused on the ceiling. "You're probably gonna hate me, but I have a naggy request for you."

He shifted onto his side, resting his elbow on the carpet, his hand against my cheek. "What's up, my Queen?"

Time to ruin the whole day. "I hate to be such a prude, but could you *please* wear something beneath that diaper? Your—um—package is coming unwrapped."

He narrowed his eyes. "I already told you. It's a *subligaria,* not a *diaper.*"

I didn't take my eyes off the ceiling. "Whatever. Could you please wear something beneath your *subligaria?*"

"Gladiators didn't wear underwear."

It was my turn to narrow my eyes at him. "And *you're* not *actually* fighting to the death in a coliseum. You *will* wear underwear, or I will *not* be wearing my engagement ring."

His face fell. "I was only kidding. Of course, I'm gonna wear underwear." He paused. "Could you maybe have a little faith in me? Just once?"

I don't know how. You're too good at letting me down. "I just—I don't want everyone ogling you like that. You're my fiancé."

Zachary raised his left eyebrow, a smirk creeping onto his face. "Is someone a little *jealous?*"

I slapped his shoulder. "Not *jealous*—just—I dunno—*protective.*"

He scooted closer, his hand resting on my diaphragm. "You're the only girl I want looking at me."

The conversation between my mom, Lacie and Jasmine came to mind, suddenly making me uncomfortable. *But what about guys? Do you want them looking at you?* I flexed my stomach muscles, and turned my back on my boyfriend, no longer wanting him to touch me. *Why am I like this? Why do I let what they say get to me?* Frowning, I studied myself in the mirror.

Unlike Zachary, I was covered up; the only skin exposed being my arms, neck, face and part of my right leg. Domina was a classy Roman queen, exuding sex through her confident demeanor, rather than completely exposing herself. I'd managed to pull together an outfit that resembled Domina's royal wardrobe by doing my own extensive research via online shopping.

Victoria's Secret had a red, satin, full-length lingerie gown that showed off way too much cleavage and had a slit running from my ankle to right beneath my lady parts. The problem was that my boobs were *nowhere near* big enough to match the real Domina's, so I also purchased a red push-up bra that was lacy and extremely feminine, but most importantly, pushed my breasts up two sizes, making my back hurt just from the thought of how big they were.

Secondly, so people wouldn't think I was trying to be Jessica Rabbit if I wasn't standing beside my gladiator fiancé, I searched Amazon for costume jewelry that was similar the gold jewelry Domina wore in the show. Not caring how fake it looked, but more concerned about how cheap it would be for my bank account, I found a necklace that jingled whenever I walked, matching earrings, two arm bands that looked like snakes, and a crown that looked like a bunch of leaves sewn together.

And then there was my favorite part of the costume—the shoes. A pair of black, four-inch high wedges with gold-trimmed bottoms. I'd spent half of my paycheck on them, but as I gazed down at my red-painted toenails, I decided that walking on high-heeled clouds was more than worth the expense.

"You are the *finest* Roman Queen I have ever laid eyes on," he continued. "Get that ass over here and let me take advantage of you."

"You'll wrinkle my dress," I teased.

"Like I give a damn about that."

Maybe it was his husky voice or the way he looked over my shoulder through the mirror, but when his hand cupped my breast, my body reacted. I pushed my butt into his crotch and giggled. "Consider that your invitation to get me out of this dress," I purred.

"Can we leave our costumes on? I need to practice how I'm gonna flex tomorrow night."

My lady erection fell hard and fast. *You have got to be kidding.* I stood up and moved over to the loveseat, needing space. Sherlock meowed at me. "You know what?" I shook my head. "Never mind."

He sat up and frowned, confusion filling his pupils. "What? We spent a lot of money on these consumes. I really want the chance to win it back in the contest."

"Zach, it's a *costume* contest. Not some orgy peep show meant for you to try to get more attention than you already do."

This year, instead of attending a Halloween party Downtown or at a friend's house, Zachary decided we should go to the huge—and mainly gay—event hosted in Hillcrest every year. The city would block all traffic on Normal Street, create a perimeter out of chain link fences and erect a giant stage where costume contest participants would flaunt their stuff in an attempt to win a five-thousand-dollar cash prize.

Zachary said he chose the event because of the contest's grand prize.

As I looked at him now, I wondered if my friends and my mother were right. *Am I just blind? Is he really using me to hide his secret?*

When I agreed to this event initially, I didn't think anything of it. Absorbed in school and work, I didn't ask any questions—Zachary had found a fun thing to do where we could dance and participate in a contest to potentially win some money. Sounded great to me. Thinking back, I wished I had paid more attention so I could've suggested an alternative without seeming as if I was afraid my fiancé was potentially a gay man. I also wished I had asked what night the event was taking place—unfortunately, it fell on the Saturday before Halloween, which happened to be my birthday. A dinner would've been nice, but Zachary chose Nightmare on Normal Street instead.

"I don't think you understand how the gay community works."

Oh, and you do?

"They want a show," he continued. "We have to do *something* that's gonna *really* make us stand out."

I patted the cushion beside me, inviting Sherlock to come closer. I needed to busy my hands by petting the cat, otherwise I was going to strangle Zachary.

"Then why don't you just whip out your genitalia while you're on stage?" My voice was *dripping* with sarcasm.

He didn't seem to catch it. "You really think that'll work?"

I glared at him. "Get the hell out of my room."

"What?"

The conversation from dinner with my mom and my friends jumped to the forefront of my mind, anger and fear dancing a fierce tango, building tension behind my eyes that was sure to become a trophy-winning headache. "You *really* need to learn how to use your brain before you speak."

He furrowed his eyebrows. "Roxanne, I was *joking*. I would never do that. I—I don't want to hurt you."

My fiancé is gay. My fingertips began to tingle. *He doesn't really love me.* My ears began to ring. *This is all a mask.* My stomach began to churn. *Why are we doing this anymore? It's all just a lie, isn't it?*

"Roxanne?" The concern in his voice brought me back to my bedroom. "Are you okay?"

I closed my eyes and took a few deep breaths, trying to ignore how light headed I felt. "Yes, I'm fine." *Get out of your head. You and Zach have a normal relationship. Don't let anyone else try to alter that.* "I—I just—I didn't feel so hot for a second."

He kneeled in front of me and grabbed my hands. "I feel like something is stressing you out. Is it me? You should know I'm kidding about this kind of stuff."

But you're not kidding. You told me you needed the attention. That my attention isn't good enough for you. I shrugged. "Maybe I'm just extra sensitive because my birthday is coming up."

Zachary smiled. "Oh, yeah—being twenty-two is *so terrible.*"

I playfully slapped his arm. "Okay, now you really have to go. I've got work and you've got papers to grade."

He nodded and began placing his clothes in his tote bag. "Good point. I can't wait to see how many students actually passed this time."

When he shoved his shoes into his bag and zipped it up, I stood and grabbed his wrist. "Why are you putting your clothes away?"

"Look at me," he said, gesturing to himself. "I look great. I don't want to change yet."

"My parents are upstairs."

"So?"

I let him go, afraid I'd squeeze his hand off. "What do you mean, 'so'? They don't know about these costumes yet and I'd like to warn them before they see you."

He pouted. "Oh, c'mon. Your parents love me. They won't care."

My dad is going to have a stroke. "No. Change."

"But—but—I spent all this money—"

I ground my teeth together, grabbed his tote and dumped all of his clothes on the ground. "Get. Changed. Now."

#

SHERLOCK LAY ACROSS my neck, his ten-pound body choking me, waking me from a deep sleep. I grabbed a hold of his midsection and lifted him off, gasping for breath, and dropped him to the floor despite his protests. The black alarm clock on my nightstand read 6:38AM—a full two hours and twenty-two minutes before it was set to ring.

I glared at the cat, who was now meowing at me persistently, requesting breakfast. "Go away," I snarled at him, turning my back. "We've talked about this. My neck is not your bed."

The meows stopped, but his little paws were now walking over me, my comforter stretching taut where he stepped. When I reopened my hazel eyes, I found his green ones studying me, his charcoal colored nose only centimeters from mine, his purrs growing louder when he realized he had captured my attention.

I sighed. "You just tried to murder me, and it's my birthday. Can't you just let me sleep for a few more hours?"

Sherlock dropped his tail and scooted even closer, his whiskers now tickling my cheeks.

I closed my eyes and began to breathe heavier, hoping to trick him into believing I was asleep.

He responded by stepping on my face, pressing his weight on me until it hurt.

"What on *earth* is wrong with you this morning?" I grumbled, shoving him off and onto his side.

He meowed, aggressively this time, swishing his tail across my sheets.

Time to switch up my tactics. I grabbed him and hugged his furry body against my chest, squeezing harder each time he tried to escape. Only when his meows resembled an ambulance did I let him go, afraid I'd pushed him to the point of scratching me.

I smiled when he jumped off the bed and disappeared into the bathroom, his claws aiming to destroy the scratching post. *"Finally.* Now, I can sleep."

But after tossing and turning for thirty minutes, I threw back my covers and swung my feet over the edge of the bed. Sherlock was sitting there, smiling smugly at me. "You're a real jerk, sometimes."

He meowed, turned his back and ran into the bathroom, meowing louder once he reached his empty food dish.

"I'm not rewarding you for being a brat," I told him, walking into the bathroom to shed my pajamas and take a shower. "You're not eating until I say so."

Having heard my shower turn on, my mother—who never slept past five because of her Monday through Friday work schedule—took it as an invitation to enter my room without knocking. She proceeded straight into the bathroom.

"Happy Birthday, Roxanne!"

I gasped and attempted to cover myself, sucking in my stomach, wishing my shower door wasn't glass. "*Mom*," I warned. "Do you *mind*?"

She waved her hand absently at me and gazed at herself in the mirror. "Nothing I haven't seen before." She began pulling at the skin of her face, probably wondering if she should research plastic surgeons that didn't know her husband. My father refused to do work on her because he believed plastic surgery would hinder her beauty. "Why're you up so early? I figured you'd sleep in today."

I leaned back against the cold tile, wondering if the cascading water was hiding my naked body in the slightest. *Why are you small talking with me? Especially when I'm in the nude?* "Sherlock tried to kill me when I was sleeping and I couldn't fall back asleep."

Although she was so engrossed in her reflection, she probably forgot I was in the shower, I couldn't help but feel extremely embarrassed. *Maybe if I just open my mouth long enough, I could drown myself.*

"Cats—didn't I tell you they're not to be trusted? And they make me itch." She sat on the closed toilet seat and stared at the flowers painted on her toenails. "Did you decide what you wanted to do today?"

Okay, but seriously, is this happening right now? "Mom, I don't mean to be rude, but could we have this conversation in like—I dunno—twenty minutes? I don't want the water to get cold."

She nodded absently and apologized—another thing my mother never did, especially to me. "I'll go wake your father and have him get started on your breakfast. If Zach is awake, invite him, too. We'll make extra."

When she left the bathroom, I stared at Sherlock, who hadn't moved from where he sat beside his food dish. "Did I just imagine that? You saw it, too, right?" He meowed and began to purr, rubbing his cheek against the bowl. "I wonder what's going on with her?"

I got the answer directly after I told my mother that Zachary and I were going to Sea World to celebrate my birthday. I was biting into a piece of bacon at the kitchen bar top, Zachary sitting in the chair beside me, my dad on my left, and my mother on Zachary's right.

"Have you heard from your sister lately?"

I chewed slowly, the news anchor on the television droning on about the chance of rain within the next few days. *Oh, c'mon. It's my birthday. Can we keep pretending you like me and aren't overcompensating because you're not talking to Lucy?* "What did the prodigy child do now?" I swallowed and took another bite.

My dad shook his head. "Sherlock has a higher ranking in this house than she does."

I laughed, bacon bits flying out of my mouth. "Well, happy birthday to me!"

"Honey," my mother warned my dad. "Lucy hasn't done anything *wrong*. She's just not—being her usual self."

"And," I drawled. "That's a bad thing?"

My parents didn't laugh, but I did notice Zachary stifle a chuckle.

"Lucy hasn't spoken to us since the dinner party," my father told me.

I don't blame her. Mom smashed a plate on the floor while throwing a temper tantrum.

"She hasn't returned any of my calls or texts," my mother added. "I apologized for everything and she told me it was okay, but clearly it's not because she's avoiding us." She paused. "I think it's Roger."

Or it's because you're a nut job and you shattered a plate. "You think *what* is Roger?"

My mom lowered her voice as if afraid Roger, who lived in Los Angeles, would overhear us. "I think he's the reason she's being so distant. Did you hear how he spoke to us that night? He's *never* been disrespectful like that. Something is going on."

Yeah, he's all pent up because Lucy wants to have another baby. "To be fair, you were screaming at his wife." I cut into a pancake with the side of my fork. "He was standing up for her."

"His explanation just didn't make sense," my mom continued, not listening to me. "What're they trying to hide?"

The fact that they're doing the dirty. "I think you're looking into it too much. Lucy is an adult—she has a kid—she'll get in touch when she's free."

"Hannah is my granddaughter. I want to see her, too."

Then maybe use paper plates at dinner next time. "Roger and Lucy just need to get over that whole thing." *And get over themselves.* "Mom, stop overanalyzing it all. Roger's an arrogant jerk, but he likes you guys. Give it time."

My mom sighed. "Did you want to go shopping today?"

I'd sooner die. "Zach and I are going to Sea World, remember? Wanna see what it's like without being in uniform."

"What time are you coming home?" Dad asked. "That way, I can have dinner ready before you go to that party."

"Probably around five. The event doesn't start until eight."

"Wait until you see my costume," Zachary said excitedly.

I forced myself to smile. *Please, for the love of all that is holy, do not bring up that you'll be in a diaper tonight.*

"I saw Roxanne's," Mom said. "It's a very pretty dress."

"What's your cos—"

"*Spartacus*," Zachary interrupted, deepening his voice. "The mighty gladiator!"

I telepathically asked my dad to not say a word. He made eye contact with me, his blue eyes lighting up with held back laughter, but stayed quiet. Not wanting the conversation to get awkward, I pushed my plate away and excused myself. "Thank you for breakfast, but I gotta get ready now. Don't wanna get too bloated."

Zachary nodded. "*Especially* me. Just wait until you see my costume."

"You already mentioned that," I mumbled, running down the stairs, my dad's silent laughter ringing through my ears.

#

THE SHAMU SHOW finale was adorable: three whales heaving their massive bodies onto the center stage, tail fins erect, posing like the superstars they were. Zachary and I clapped and cheered along with the rest of the spectators, standing to escape the madness of leaving the stadium—two exits, twenty-five thousand people.

"Those poor trainers. I wonder if they actually enjoy dancing on stage like that," I said, some woman pushing me to the side as she tried to corral her five children.

Zachary shook his head. "Dolphin trainers make fun of them."

After another person shoved me, nearly knocking me into a small child on my right, I grabbed Zachary's hand and climbed up two rows of bleachers. "I'm not dealing with this crowd right now. Let's just wait it out."

He kissed my cheek. "More time for me to spend next to the most beautiful woman in the world."

It was one in the afternoon and I was happily buzzed from the two lime flavored beers I'd drank so far. I rested my cheek on Zachary's shoulder. "Why do they make fun of them?"

"Because the trainers don't get in the water with the whales anymore."

The trainers were pouring buckets of fish into the whales' mouths. "That's not *their* fault. If that accident hadn't happened in Florida, they'd still be getting into that pool with the most dangerous animal in the world."

Zachary shrugged. "I think being *any* kind of trainer would be awesome. You know how cool it'd be to tell people you're a trainer at Sea World?"

Frowning, I let go of his hand and pretended I needed to scratch my leg. "That's not why they do it. They love the animals."

"Yeah, I love animals, too, but think about it. Dolphin Trainer on you resume. I'd be the guy who stars as the prince in the dolphin show, obviously."

I rolled my eyes behind my sunglasses. "Why would they hire you? You have *zero* animal experience."

"Because I'm good looking and know how to swim."

Why is he like this? I need another beer. "This may come as a surprise to you, but those aren't the requirements they want for *training wild animals.*"

"I'd love to be a zookeeper for elephants. Imagine me working with those giant wrinkly cute critters."

"What about *teaching*? I thought *that* was your dream job?"

He began biting his nails. "I dunno. After how things have been going this semester, I don't think teaching is a good fit for me."

Before I could respond, a frantic flock of pigeons flew by my face, startling me. As I covered my head to avoid being pooped on, I heard a familiar accented voice shout my name. "Miss Roxanne! You can't hide that curly hair from me, even out of uniform!"

When I turned around and smiled, Zachary followed my gaze. "Ronnie! Where've you been all day?"

The round-bellied man with the round face and the safari hat with the feather sticking out began climbing down the bleachers, his huge brown and black boots sending echoes throughout the stadium. "I've been teaching these knuckle-heads how to do the job properly," he teased, gesturing his thumb toward the audio room where two men stood talking to one another on the roof.

One of them was Jonathan, the shorter man who didn't speak much but had accepted a cup of coffee from me a few weeks prior. The other, I didn't recognize. He had short, blonde hair—a sharp part toward the left side of his head—with waves resembling low tide gelled to the right. He wore black-rimmed, square glasses that rested on his chubby cheeks, his white skin flushed pink from sun exposure.

"Pfft," I scoffed. "I haven't seen you around Dine lately. You're clearly avoiding me."

Ronnie smiled wider, shaking the stainless-steel bench as he sat beside me. "Lassy, I'd do *anything* to accidentally on purpose run into you."

Zachary placed his hand on my thigh, a gesture that took me by surprise—not because my fiancé was the jealous type, but because I'd forgotten he was sitting beside me. "I'm Zach. Her fiancé."

I tried not to cringe, not liking his territorial tone. Not that I wanted to keep my relationship a secret. I just hadn't found the right time to bring it up to my falconer friends. *Why didn't we leave with the crowd? Why did I have to be stupid and wait?* "M—my—my bad. Didn't mean to be rude. This is Z—Zach. Zach, this is Ronnie." *Why am I being so weird? I have nothing to hide.*

Ronnie slapped his knee and chuckled, which made me blush. "No need to get protective, Lad. I'm old enough to be her dad." He laughed again. "I doubted she'd be into that kind of thing anyway."

Zachary didn't laugh.

Although I was wearing my engagement ring, it was hidden between my crossed legs, digging into the skin beneath my thighs.

"Besides, I figured she was already spoken for. She's fuckin' beautiful."

I shook my head, Zachary's grip tightening on my leg. "You flatter me."

"I know she is," he responded, leaning into me.

"Those boys, however," Ronnie said, gesturing again at the two men, who were moving away from one another; planning on flying the hawk to Jonathan's arm, I assumed. "They don't know, and they probably wouldn't care. They're used to preying on beautiful things."

I giggled nervously, my leg beginning to hurt from my fiancé's grip. "Why are there three of you here? Is the bird population really that out of control?"

He nodded. "That's why we haven't been at Dine. The seagulls are bastards—and this Halloween bullshit makes it worse because kids drop their fucking candy and their parents don't give a shit." He scooted closer, whispering loudly enough for Zachary to hear beside me. "Technically, the contract only allows for one bird. So, we have one bird in the park at a time. The rest are in my trailer in the East parking lot."

Sensing Zachary's discomfort and taking note of the loud speaker informing guests that Shamu Stadium was now closed, I stood and opened my arms. "You have to get back to work and we have to get outta here before Park Ops yells at us."

"What're they gonna do?" he asked, returning the hug. "Hit you with their brooms?"

"They're vicious," I joked, stepping down two steps to distance myself from Ronnie and the two men now at opposite ends of the stadium. "They might throw a half-eaten hotdog at me."

Ronnie shook my fiancé's hand and nodded at me. "It was great to meet ya, Lad. You are quite lucky to have her in yer life."

As Zachary and I exited the stadium, now heading in the direction of the Sea Lion and Otter Show, my buzz disappeared, replaced by a guilt I didn't fully understand. I wanted another beer so I didn't have to think about it.

"I didn't know you were such good friends with the bird guys," Zachary said with a suspicious tone that put me on the defensive. "I've never heard you bring them up—like—ever."

First of all, they're falconers, not bird guys. "That's because I'm not good friends with them." *Second of all, unlike you, they're actual animal trainers who know what they're doing.* I tried distancing myself from him, focusing on the Spooktacular Halloween decorations of different marine mammals holding candy corn or lollipops.

Zachary didn't get the hint. He took a hold of my hand, pulling me closer. "He recognized you from the top of the stadium. You totally lit up when you saw him. You have inside jokes." He paused, allowing my guilt to deepen. "Sounds pretty fucking friendly to me."

The smiling plastic seal with the half-eaten chocolate bar in its flipper and a witch's hat tilted on its head frowned at me suddenly. I blinked, only to find it smiling again. "I'm friendly with everybody at work. It's called having good customer service."

"Why didn't he know we're engaged?"

I sighed. "I don't want to lose my ring at work. I wash my hands a lot and I'm worried it'll go down the drain."

He began swirling his thumb over the back of my hand. "I get that, but how did it not come up? You obviously talk to them a lot."

Because that's the last thing I want to talk about. "It's funny, actually. There's this thing called *working* that I have to do when I'm at *work*. Unlike *you*, who stands around chit-chatting for most of the day because you have no *real* work to do."

He winced, dropping my hand. "I'm not trying to start a fight. I was just wond—"

"I could *really* use another beer right now, couldn't you?"

Realizing I didn't want to broach the topic any further, Zachary nodded and followed behind, his head hanging lower than usual.

I took a deep breath and stopped, turning to stare into the green beauties I no longer wanted to wake up to every morning. "Why can't we get along anymore? Like—is it possible for us to stop fighting about—I dunno—everything?"

Zachary shrugged. "I'm tired of fighting. We used to be best friends—thick as thieves. What happened?"

We sat on a bench that was bathed in sunlight, my armpits beginning to moisten. "Do you want the honest answer?"

"I've *always* wanted honest answers from you." His eyes were pleading, his hands fiddling with his jeans.

Tapping my thumbs together, elbows resting on my knees, I wondered if I should be open with him. I feared he would end up hating me. *Of course, this has to happen on my birthday.* "Should we really get into all this right now?"

His silent stare made me breathe in through my nose and out of my mouth.

I slid the engagement ring on and off my finger. *How can I tell him the truth without being the worst person on the face of the planet?* "Well, if I'm being honest, things began going downhill after you proposed."

He looked away. "So, does that mean you don't love me?"

Not like I used to. "No—I do love you. But something about this ring put serious pressure on this relationship. On me." My hands felt clammy. "I'm not ready to be engaged. I'm sorry I said yes. Not because I don't want to be with you—because I do—but because I should've been honest from the beginning. I'm not ready to get married."

"Why?" he croaked. "Why do you feel this way?"

"I just—" I sniffled, not knowing if I was tearing up because I was hurting his feelings or because I was finally lifting a huge weight off my chest. "I don't have the best answer. Something isn't *feeling* right. I thought I wanted this, but our future marriage is already breaking us apart. Doesn't that mean something?"

"But we're in love—"

"Zach," I interrupted, grabbing both his hands. "I need you to look at me and tell me that you're honestly happy."

Those beautiful green eyes faded to grey, the corners glistening with tears, which made me cry harder. "I can't. I've been miserable."

I wiped at my face, not wanting to draw attention to us. "Then why didn't you say anything?"

He looked at his shoes. "Why didn't you?"

I brushed my forearm across my nose, focusing on the slime now making my arm hairs glisten. "Because I didn't want you to hate me."

"Roxanne, Little Woman," he breathed. "I could *never* hate you. I'm upset you weren't honest with me, but I don't *hate* you for it."

"Technically," I said, half-smiling beneath my tears. "You'd be a hypocrite if you did hate me because you weren't honest with me, either."

"How about we make a deal?"

I licked my chapped lips, the sun beginning to burn my face. "What kind of deal?"

Although he wasn't exactly smiling, he gently slid the engagement ring off my finger and held his open palm in front of us. "Until we're both one-hundred percent ready to spend forever with one another, this ring will remain in its box— out of sight, out of mind."

"Are you sure you don't hate me?"

He closed his fingers around the ring. "Just don't hide your feelings from me again, okay?"

But how do I tell you I don't know if I'll ever want to get married? That I'm not sure if you're the one? I thought back to my conversation with Luke. *What if you're not my soul mate?* I nodded. "Okay."

I felt as if he was squeezing his heart instead of the ring, making sure that any and all true emotions were seeping through his fingers, splattering against the hot cement. "You promise?"

I noticed the three falconers walking with one another in the distance and tried to ignore the way my stomach flipped. "I promise," I said, with all of the false confidence I could muster.

Chapter Nine

THIS WAS A first for me: watching while men openly flirted with and unabashedly touched my boyfriend even though I was standing beside him holding his hand. Sure, there'd been times when we were at a Downtown nightclub and drunk guys made moves on me as Zachary awkwardly stood beside me doing nothing to stop it. And yes, I'd been present when women targeted Zachary if he appeared alone, his toga party being the extreme version of that scenario.

But being witness to homosexual men making my boyfriend blush and giggle was not something I was at all prepared for.

After Zachary and I agreed the engagement was more problematic than it was beneficial, a *huge* weight had been lifted from my shoulders. Even Zachary was walking with his shoulders back and head held high, which I hadn't seen in quite some time. While at Sea World, we enjoyed a couple more beers, held hands as we walked across the park and kissed for cheesy photos whenever approached by one of the park's photographers. It felt as if the engagement had never taken place, and with the added pressure gone, he and I meshed once again.

My concerns about our relationship only resurfaced as we were leaving, looking around the parking lot for Zachary's car.

"Why don't we just go home?" I asked, resting my cheek on his shoulder. "I'm exhausted. We could cuddle and watch a movie." I was confident we'd both be on the same page now that we'd had such a wonderful afternoon with one another. "Maybe a lil' something after the movie." I reached down and grabbed his butt, smiling up at him.

His frown fell to the asphalt. "But what about Normal Street?"

I shrugged. "Who cares? As long as we're together, I'm a happy girlfriend."

His frown, somehow, fell deeper. "But we bought our costumes—I spent all that money—the contest."

"We can still wear them on Halloween."

Now, he began to pout, his mood changing drastically. "Roxanne, we made plans," he barked. "We're going."

I pulled away, wanting to push him to the ground. "Fine," I snapped back. "It's my birthday, but *whatever*. Let's do what *you* want to do instead. All that matters is what *you* want to do – my birthday doesn't matter."

He ignored me, opening his car door and sliding in. I almost didn't get in thinking I should call my dad to come pick me up because the *last* thing I wanted to do was sit in a confined space with him.

I told myself I was *not* going to the party.

And yet, here I was at the Normal Street event, surrounded by men exposing skin and women covering up every inch of their bodies. Glancing at Zachary, and then at myself, a sad realization hit me. *We fit in—he looks gay and I look like a lesbian.* I drank whatever vodka and juice mixture an extremely flamboyant bartender made for me, until only ice cubes banged against my lips.

I needed another drink immediately.

Once we'd returned to my parents' house, the last thing I wanted to do was get into costume. I'd locked Zachary out of my room and told him I needed to take a power nap if we were *really* going to the party. Instead of taking note of my disappointment, he told me he was going to do the same, and happily made his way upstairs to the guest room.

That was, surprisingly, one of the most refreshing thirty-minute naps I'd ever taken.

After getting dressed, hair spraying my curls and applying my make-up, I'd looked in the mirror feeling pleased with the final product—confident, even, that I did look like a proper Domina. *Not bad as long as I can suck in my stomach in all night.* I knew it was a good costume when my mom told me I looked beautiful. I couldn't even remember the last time she'd said that without blatant sarcasm.

It wasn't until Zachary emerged from the back bedroom in his costume that I, again, questioned why I was even putting up with this nonsense. My dad was *not* pleased with Zachary's lack of clothing, his laughter from our earlier breakfast having morphed into a seething disappointment—in Zachary's choice of costume or in my choice of boyfriend, I wasn't sure.

I had yet to explain to my parents that the engagement was off, but my mother somehow knew something was amiss. Not only did she keep her mouth shut when she saw my naked ring finger, but she also *hugged* me and patted my back, whispering words of caution before we left the house. "Be careful tonight. I don't think you know what you're getting yourself into."

And even though I wanted to brush it off as I climbed into Zachary's beat up and faded, gold Honda, I knew she was right.

"Aren't you stoked?" He glanced in the rearview mirror, turning his face side to side, lifting one eyebrow, then the next. "How good do I look? Great, huh?"

My phone vibrated beneath my armpit, my bra the only piece of clothing able to hold my ID, money and cell phone. As Zachary continued to ramble on, not waiting for me to answer, I pulled my phone out and read a *Happy Birthday, Roxanne* text message that made me quite giddy.

Thank you, Lamont, I typed, trying to keep the screen tilted away from my boyfriend.

"Do you think I should've worn less eyeliner? More? Does it make my eyes pop? I think it gives me a more gladiator look."

He continued to ask questions, only to answer them as if I wasn't present. I didn't mind though—I was too exhausted to give him the reassurance he was seeking and would've said something that hurt his feelings.

Doing anything fun tonight? Lamont asked.

I glanced at the annoying piece of work in the driver's seat and rolled my eyes. *I wish,* I replied. *Being taken to a party against my will.*

"So, I've been meaning to ask you something," Zachary said, nervously. "But now that I think about it, since we're not engaged anymore, maybe it won't be a big deal."

I crossed my ankles and calmly faced him, even though his tone and my buzzing phone had me sitting on edge. "Think you could ask the question without that ominous preface?"

He turned the radio all the way down and cleared his throat. "I've been thinking about how we're gonna win the costume contest and I think we'll have a better chance at first place if we don't mention we're in a relationship."

My phone vibrated again. I raised an eyebrow, resisting the urge to see what Lamont said, trying my best not to let Zachary anger me. "Care to elaborate?"

"The gays won't want heterosexuals to win."

The spaghetti dinner from hell came to mind, alarms sounding off like ambulance sirens in my head. "So," I paused, not liking where this was going. "You want us to pretend we're gay?"

He shook his head. "Nobody will believe that. I want you to pretend I'm your gay cousin."

Taking a deep, steadying breath, I clicked on Lamont's text messages, no longer caring if Zachary saw who I was texting.

Want me to come save you?

We could do a movie night at my place?

My heart tumbled over and over again, my thoughts spinning like a tornado. *My ex-lover is flirting with me and my ex-fiancé wants to be gay. I need to drink immediately.* I put the phone beneath my thighs without responding to Lamont knowing that if I *did* reply, I'd ditch Zachary and drive myself the eight hours it took to get to Rohnert Park. "Zach, did you smoke something or are you clinically insane?"

Taking note of my tone, he frowned. "Why're you mad? I thought you wanted to win this contest, too."

I want a boyfriend who wants me. I want to go home and cuddle with my not gay boyfriend. I glanced at my thighs, imagining what my birthday would've been like if I'd made a different choice sophomore year. *No, Roxanne. Don't go there. Stay out of the past.* "I didn't even want to come," I mumbled. "Why can't we win because our costumes are phenomenal? Isn't that the point of a *costume* contest?"

He snorted. "This is the *gay community.* Things don't work like that."

Even though we were on the freeway, my fingers itched to pull on the door handle. "And since when did *you* become such an *expert* on the ways of the gays?"

He winced, my voice too loud for the small confines of the car. "My dad went to the event last year. He told me the contestants who won had some sort of sexual routine planned out."

"Can you stop talking to me until I've consumed enough alcohol to make my liver stop functioning?" I pinched the bridge of my nose. "This whole conversation—you *wanting* to be gay—it's making me sick." *Just take me home. You'll have more fun without me holding you back.*

"Why do you say it like that? I don't *want* to be gay. In order to win, I need to *pretend* I'm gay."

The night only got worse.

"Hey there, Gladiator," a feminine male voice slurred behind me. I turned around to find Zachary's face a dark shade of pink, a beanpole of a man rubbing his hands up and down Zachary's stomach. "Where's your sword?"

We were waiting in line at a makeshift bar that was beneath a black tarp littered with glow-in-the-dark stars, the bartenders wearing silver spandex shorts and glitter on their chests. I turned back to the line in front of me, Zachary's apparent pleasure filling my stomach with a sickening sensation. *I need another drink. Pronto.* The world was already spinning, the speakers next to the bar hurting my ears, but I needed *more* booze—I wanted to forget everything that already happened, knowing the rest of the night would continue to spiral downward at an alarming rate.

When we first entered through an opening in the chain-link fencing that indicated where the perimeters of the event were located, we had to show our IDs to a tall, black man in a very tight police costume, who smiled and complimented our outfits before asking my boyfriend if he was single. I would've been uncomfortable, but Zachary merely laughed, putting his arm around me before leading me to one of the tarp setups where people were getting drinks. It was reassuring to know that Zachary wanted to show he was straight, apparently having forgotten he wanted to be my gay cousin earlier.

Unfortunately, as the night pulsed forward, the "harmless" flirting became aggressive, more and more people refusing to believe we were in a relationship because Zachary was "too good looking" to be straight. I began to question if it was actually because someone as good looking as him was in a relationship with someone who looked like me.

Two hours or so into the event, my anger reached a level that made my chest hurt. Zachary *clearly* had consumed *more* than enough alcohol and was *glowing* from all the attention the gay party attendees were giving him. And as the smiles got wider and the advances more sexual, I drank and drank and drank, not once admitting to my boyfriend that his behavior was making me question his sexual orientation.

Why are we still together? Why can't we just let each other go? "It's in his pants," I replied to the man with a pixie haircut, dyed bright green; the man who had asked my boyfriend about the location of his sword. I grabbed his hand off of my boyfriend and tapped his wrist. "And it was in me earlier."

The man grimaced, huffed and turned away, swishing his hips as he stalked his next prey item.

Zachary laughed, his stomach jiggling just slightly, the beers he'd consumed making his attempted six pack disappear. "Looks like someone's *jealous*."

Biting my tongue, I turned back to face the bar, the white tips of the bartender's hair shining bright in the backlight. "What can I get ya', Beautiful?"

I smiled. "Something fruity and strong."

He winked, his fake eyelashes so long, I wondered how he was able to keep his eyelids open. "Those are my favorite kind."

For the first time that night, I sincerely laughed. "Unfortunately, mine too, apparently."

He looked behind me at my boyfriend and raised a drawn-on eyebrow. "Does he want anything?"

"Probably your dick."

The bartender threw back his head in laughter, which made me feel the tiniest bit better.

"What did you just say about me?"

I glared at my boyfriend and crossed my arms. "Why does it matter?"

The strobe lights from the giant stage in the middle of the venue bounced off Zachary's flushed face, beads of sweat setting up camp on his forehead. "Because I wanna know."

I rolled my eyes. "Are you *really* enjoying this?"

His head lolled to one side. "Well, yeah. Where have you been? Can't you see how much everybody loves me?"

The bartender returned with a large shot glass and a plastic cup complete with a sugar rim, orange wheel, lime wedge and cherry. He pointed to the shot. "You're gonna want to drink that one, pronto." He then pointed to the cocktail. "A little citrus vodka, peach schnapps, grapefruit juice and pineapple juice. Topped with a little bit of orange liqueur." He looked at my boyfriend again. "They're both on the house, Sweetie. Take your time with the cocktail." He leaned over the table to whisper to me, "It'll help you forget all of that nonsense happening next to you, Little Miss Bradshaw."

Blushing, I thanked him graciously. "You really think I look like her?"

"Your hair is darker." He pouted his maroon lip-lined lips. "But you've got that vibe and that beauty going for you."

Why is it that everyone knows what to say except my stupid boyfriend? I threw back the shot and smiled, surprised. "Wow. That was delicious."

He winked again. "Fruity and strong."

I reached into my bra and grabbed a twenty, dropping it in the tip jar. "You one-hundred percent just made my birthday special. Thank you so much."

I barely had time to grab the cocktail when Zachary latched onto my arm and pulled me away from the bar. "What's going on with you tonight?" he asked.

"I'm just wondering if I should be worried."

"About what?"

"About how much you're enjoying the flirting and the compliments and the—*touching*."

His eyebrows formed a frown on his forehead. "What the hell are you trying to say?"

"Well, you were happy we ended our engagement so we could be *cousins* instead of in a *relationship*. You wanted to be *here* rather than in bed with me. You're blushing like a school girl at a football game." I took a deep breath. "Is *this* what you want? The attention of other men?"

The surprise and confusion on his face quickly twisted his handsome features into the definition of offended. "Are you calling me *gay*?"

Do you need me to spell it out for you? I shrugged. "Why don't you tell me what I should think?"

And then the offense melted away into hurt—the kind of hurt you see when you call your dog a bad boy. "How could you even say that to me?"

After your actions tonight, how could I not? "Why don't you put yourself in my shoes?"

"I have been in your shoes!"

Men and women in vibrant and multi-colored costumes, a drink in each hand, curiosity brightening their hazy eyes, now surrounded us. It reminded me of the toga party, only this time, Zachary was yelling at me and the spectators had every intention of watching the drama unfold as if watching a soap opera.

"Girl, those shoes are the bees knees," a man in a Cher costume said. "I'll take 'em if you wanna get rid of them."

"Fuck that girl," a man dressed in a skin-tight Mario costume shouted. "*Actually*, why don't you fuck me, instead?"

"What do you *mean* you've been in my shoes?" I asked, incredulous.

He gestured around him. "You're just mad because *you're* not the one getting *all* the attention. *Everywhere* we go, as soon as I leave your side, boys *flock* to you—and I *know* you fucking *love it*. I can't even trust you at work. Those fucking bird bozos are *all over you*!"

"At least they respect you enough to *not* do it in front of you!" I gestured wildly, my vodka cocktail splashing all over my arm. "These people act like I don't exist and you're going along with it!" I could feel myself slurring, the last two drinks skewing any of my remaining judgement, but it didn't slow me down. "And I don't act like some love-struck *idiot* when someone pays me a compliment. *Especially* if another woman compliments me." I put the cocktail to my lips and titled my head back, the vodka and fruit juice mixture sliding down my throat.

Two men—one dressed as Cruella and the other as a Dalmatian—suddenly stood between us, pushing Zachary and I apart. "If you two don't stop, security is gonna shut the party down. Shut the fuck up!"

"*Oh please*," I yelled over the music, the laughter and the chaos. "You bitches are *way more obnoxious*. Get over yourselves."

Cruella put one arm around Zachary's shoulder, and one hand on Zachary's lower belly. "You don't need that bitch. You can have me and my bitches. We won't give you any trouble."

I shook my head and glanced at my heels, my anger quickly morphing into defeat. *Screw this. I give up. They can have him. If this is what he really wants, why should I get in the way?*

"Who're you calling a bitch?" Zachary asked, shrugging off Cruella. "That's my girlfriend and she's the sweetest little woman in the whole world."

I looked up at him. *Wh—what did he say?*

Cruella snorted. "It's a *real* shame you think so. *Clearly*, you prefer things *rough.*"

As the men walked away, Zachary reached out and gently grabbed my elbow, the melted ice from my drink sloshing over the plastic cup onto my fingers. The cup slipped from my hands and crashed onto the asphalt, cold liquid splashing over my exposed toes. "I'm sorry, Little Woman. I just got caught up in everything."

Emotionally fatigued and beyond intoxicated, I stepped toward him, my heels splashing in the remnants of my drink. "Really?"

He kissed my temple. "I love you, Roxy. I don't know what's going on lately, but you seem to keep forgetting that."

My eyes stung from the cool air, tears threatening to make *another* unwanted appearance. *Because you make it seem like you want nothing to do with me.* Vulnerable, drunk and insecure, I leaned into my boyfriend's bare side. *If you really loved me, I wouldn't need to question it, would I?* The eyes of the remaining individuals around us continued to mentally undress my ex-fiancé. I choked back a sob. "Can we get another drink?"

Zachary nodded. "We gotta hurry, though. The contest is about to start, and we still haven't choreographed something sexy."

I thought back to the conversation in my room, where he actually considered revealing his penis because he thought that would guarantee us a victory. *If he weren't gay, would he have truly considered that as an option? If you really love someone, wouldn't you want to keep that stuff for yourself and your loved one only?*

Stretching out my neck, I looked beyond all of the bare skin, fake hair and glitter, searching for the nearest makeshift bar. "What did you have in mind?" I asked, feigning interest, truly afraid of what his answer was going to be.

"Something sexy," he said, maneuvering the two of us around two short women—one dressed as Tonto, the other dressed as the Lone Ranger—who both complimented how beautiful my curly hair was. I smiled at them, but before I could thank them, Zachary continued to talk. "Something that involves lifting up your leg." He pulled me in tight, his breath fondling my earlobe, his hand rubbing up and down the outside of my thigh. "Because you have *phenomenal* legs. The lesbians will dig it."

Okay, seriously? What is happening right now? I quickened my pace toward the tent where booze was being served, pushing past a line of individuals who were too busy ogling my boyfriend to notice me cutting ahead of them. "How about we don't hypersexualize ourselves?"

Zachary asked the bartender for two shots of pineapple flavored vodka and a cup of Sprite so I could chase it down. I didn't mention that after my last drink, my taste buds had gone rogue, so a chaser didn't matter. "Do you want to win or not?"

I don't even want to be here. When the bartender placed the shots on the plastic table top, I grabbed mine quickly and threw it back without thinking twice. *Why would I care if we win or lose?* "I just want to go home, honestly," I said after gulping down some Sprite. "I'm not exactly comfortable here."

Zachary shifted me away from the bar and made me move my feet toward the elongated stage-runway-thing that was lit up with green and purple lights. A man with two leaves covering his junk and a rubber snake draped across his shoulder bit his lips after looking at my boyfriend in a way I never had. "What're you doing later?" the man purred.

Apparently, Zachary didn't hear him because he continued to shove the two of us through the crowd toward a line where a man dressed in extravagant drag— big, black permed hair, maroon red dress, white foundation and a drawn-on beauty mark—was writing down costume names in order to announce them during the contest.

"What do you mean you're not comfortable here?" Zachary asked.

Isn't it obvious? I don't have a dick, but I don't like vagina. "I'm tired. And my mom baked me a cake. Doesn't cuddling in front of the fire sound nice?" Knowing I had to keep his interest somehow, I leaned into his ear and sucked on his lobe. "I'm *really* drunk. You can take advantage of me."

"You know what else sounds nice? The five-thousand-dollar grand prize." He pulled away from me. "We can cozy up after we win."

I sighed, swallowing back the drunken tears that were raining on my ego.

Two men, one dressed as Caesar and one dressed as Brutus, gathered in line behind Zachary and me, their togas resembling those of the sorority girls at Zachary's party. "Oh my, Zeus!" one of them exclaimed. "Look at those buns! They are a gift from the gods!"

Zachary turned around, giggled and blushed. "Stop it," he gushed.

I grit my teeth.

"I simply must get a squeeze!" the other said, reaching out his hand and cupping Zachary's butt.

My boyfriend jumped slightly, giving one half-assed attempt to brush the man's hand away, his face as red as my dress.

I balled my hands into fists. "That's it—no more. I'm fucking done, Zachary Cameron. You can take this relationship and shove it up your ass!"

Ignoring Zachary's feeble attempt to stop me, I pushed past two women dressed as zoo animals and curtains of glitter floating through the air like pollen. The exit was right in front of me, two police officers—real or costumed, I had no idea—standing with their arms crossed just in front of the chain-linked fence. I only stopped when Zachary grabbed my elbow so forcefully, I nearly sprained my ankle turning around.

"Roxanne, what the *hell* is going on?"

Everything I'd drank throughout the night was heightening my emotions, kindling the wildfire of my thoughts and feelings. "I'm done. It's *my* fucking birthday and I don't want to be here anymore. I'm going home."

"But why?"

"*Seriously?*" I gestured at his costume and then twirled in a circle to point at our surroundings. "*Because of you!* You're loving the attention in a *repulsive* manner. I have *never* acted like you are right now—*never.*"

He glared. "Oh *great.* This again."

"Yes, *this* again. I am *not* going to be your beard, Zach. If you want this kind of attention, just admit it! We can go our separate ways and call it a fucking day."

"Stop accusing me of being gay!"

I stomped my heel, bracing myself for the heavyweight shouting match we'd been avoiding. "Then stop acting like it! You want to be treated like a heterosexual? Then put some fucking clothes on and stop asking for attention from other men!"

"Stop fucking cussing at me!"

I looked away from him.

Zachary took a long, deep breath, the leather strap on his chest rising and falling. "Roxanne, tell me the truth. Do you *really* think I'm gay?"

"Here I am—I've been here, beside you, all night long—and you've been acting like I don't exist. I am a *woman* and I need a *man* who wants to be with me. We *just* had this conversation at your birthday party, and this is the *last* time I'm going to have it."

"Is this why you ended the engagement?" he spat. "Because you're done with me? This is just a hop, skip and a jump from you breaking up with me."

I glanced around at the event, everyone drinking and laughing and having a great time. The costume contest had already begun, cheers and claps coming from those standing around the stage-runway-thing. "I should've stayed home. It was a *huge* mistake to come here."

"Was it also a *mistake* to start dating me?"

His question took me by surprise. "What?" *Yes. It was a mistake.* "What does that have to do with anything?" *We've been together for three years now. It's a little late to have buyer's remorse. Although, Lamont is texting me. It's very tempting to just run away.*

"Do you want to break up with me?" He enunciated each word slowly, his eyes glazed over from the beer and vodka he'd been drinking all night long.

I shook my head. *No. It wasn't a mistake. Being with Lamont would've been a mistake.* "No, I don't. But I can't be in a relationship with someone who is *always* gonna be looking at someone else or wanting something more."

He closed the gap between us, reaching out for my hand.

I watched it happen in slow motion, my pulse beating with the music around us. *What're we doing?*

When I didn't make a move toward his hand, he lowered his arm until it dangled limply at his side. "Roxanne, I love you. I promise, you're the only one I want."

"You're lying." I swiped away a tear, my eyeliner staining my fingertips. "If my attention isn't good enough now, it'll never be good enough. I spend *every* free moment with you. I'm in a fight with my best friends because of you. I may not ogle you *all the time*, but I've tried being a better girlfriend to you." I covered my face, now sobbing into my hands. "But it doesn't matter. Nothing I do has ever been good enough. You don't believe I'm good enough."

Without warning, Zachary wrapped me in an embrace that was meant to be comforting but reminded me of a patient being forced into a strait jacket. "You are *more* than enough, Roxanne."

"Then why do you need so much attention from everyone else?"

"I'm sorry, I just do."

"Then you don't need me," I cried into his bare shoulder.

He squeezed me tight, his belt digging into my pelvis. "Please don't leave me."

When I looked at him, I realized that he was crying, his eyes red and puffy. Even though I knew what should be done, I didn't know how to do it. *How do I end this without hurting him? Without hurting me?* I sighed, hating how the night had turned around for the worst. *Happy fucking birthday to me.*

"Please, Roxanne."

I nodded, realizing that my fear of winding up alone had officially trapped me in a relationship that should've ended before it began. "Don't worry, Zach. I'm not going anywhere."

#

"HOW'RE YOU TWO still together?" Jasmine asked the following Taco Tuesday over Margaritas at the Mexican restaurant near my parents' house. "It's obvious more now than ever how gay he is."

Frowning, I sipped my second mixed drink, already feeling the effects of the first. "Well, I was strong enough to break off the engagement, so you should be proud of me."

"Sure, that's a step in the right direction, but you're still an item," Jasmine said. "I don't want to see you get hurt. Mainly, I don't want you to go to jail for murdering him when you catch him with some other guy's dick in his mouth."

I winced. "That's a little harsh."

"If you didn't want the truth, why did you ask us to come out with you tonight?" Lacie asked.

I need you to pull me out of this. I'm sinking in quick sand and I need you to throw me a branch. "I just need to vent, I guess," I said, instead. "I'm beginning to think that maybe he has a point."

Both girls cocked their heads to the side, their matching bangs falling slightly over their eyes.

I took another generous sip of my margarita. "He kept telling me I was upset because, for once, I wasn't the one getting attention. And it made me think—I dunno—maybe he's right."

Lacie shook her head. "How do you *always* end up doing this to yourself?"

"Hear me out." I scooped a solid helping of salsa onto a chip and shoved it into my mouth. "Whenever we go out lately, I don't get any attention. Matt pretty much ignored me at his house. That guy at Zach's party wouldn't let me in because I didn't fit his kind of pretty." I paused, grimacing at the memory. "It's just—like—even Zach has been so focused on himself lately, I feel invisible."

Jasmine frowned. "But doesn't he want to have sex all the time?"

I shivered, afraid to admit another hurtful realization. "But it's not like we're making love or enjoying one another's company." I took another large sip of my drink, savoring my buzz. "It's more like he's pretending he's in a porno or something—like his nasty talk is supposed to get me going. It grosses me out."

Lacie snorted into her drink. "You mean you don't like a little encouragement?"

I rolled my eyes, licking salt off the glass' rim. "The way he does it is a total turn off."

"Sleeping with a gay guy would turn me off, too."

"Says the girl who tried to make out with a gay in a closet," Lacie joked.

Jasmine glared at her. "I didn't know Luke was gay at the time!"

The waiter stopped by to refill our bowl of chips, also placing three more ceramic dishes full of salsa in front of us.

"How shallow would that be of me, though?" I asked, salting the chips. "I can't break up with him because I'm not sexually attracted to him. Relationships are so much more than physical."

"Yeah, but you're kind of being a hypocrite. You're upset that you're not getting the physical attention you want from Zach, but you won't end the relationship even though you're not giving him the same physical attention."

I finished chewing a chip and frowned at Lacie. "I still give him physical attention. I hug and kiss him and tell him how handsome he is."

Jasmine nodded. "But do you mean it? Because if you're doing it out of habit, it's fake."

"You're basically lying to him."

I gulped down the last of my cocktail, loving that the waiter brought me another before I had to ask.

"Your relationship isn't exactly *healthy*," Jasmine added. "It's like—this margarita." She took a long sip and smacked her lips together. "Although delicious at first, if I drank these all day, every day, that would make me an alcoholic."

I stared, not following.

Lacie laughed. "She's trying to say that you two are too dependent on one another—like alcoholics with booze."

"Like I said, it's all fun and games until you can't get out of bed in the morning without a shot of vodka."

"We'll deal with your problems later," Lacie waved Jasmine off, reaching across the table for my hand. "When was the *last* time you spent a night doing what *you* wanted to do *without* him?"

I grabbed a chip, broke it in half and dipped the smaller piece in the salsa. "Matt's birthday party." I chewed, my stomach in knots. "And look how well that turned out."

Jasmine snorted.

"I hope you just got lime up your nose."

"Okay, that's not the best example," Lacie agreed. "But you *should* be doing more of that!"

"You didn't even get to do what *you* wanted to do on *your* birthday. What kind of bullshit is that?"

Lacie shook her head. "Maybe you should slow down. We're in a family establishment and your voice carries."

Jasmine put her hand over her mouth, embarrassed. "I'm sorry, but I just really get into it when we're talking about Roxy. She deserves *so much better* than that asshole."

"Zach isn't all bad," I argued. "Just lately—he doesn't seem to be using his brain."

"I'm not saying he's a *bad guy*," Lacie emphasized. "I'm just saying you need to start being selfish and start thinking about *yourself* instead of him."

I took the straw out of my drink and held the glass to my lips, needing a larger gulp. "So, you want me to be like you guys?"

Lacie smiled. "Exactly!"

"You need to think about what you want," Jasmine repeated. "Stop thinking about what everyone else wants. Sometimes, you need to be selfish. Otherwise, you'll never be happy."

I smiled. "I've missed you guys. I'm so glad you were both free tonight."

"Well, who's fault is that?"

Lacie smacked Jasmine's shoulder. "You don't need to be a bitch. Don't mind her, Roxy. She's only acting out because we've missed you, too."

I held up my hands in surrender. "No, she's right. It's my fault. I've been so scared about my relationship with Zach that the rest of my life is—well—disappearing."

"You have straight A's," Jasmine said. "We know you've been busy with school. We may not be the greatest friends all the time, but we're not *that* bad."

"Speaking of school," I muttered. "I have to tell you what happened last night."

The previous night was a designated rehearsal for me and my "play-mates" to work on our lines and cues for our Shakespeare class performance. Unlike other groups that still hadn't memorized any lines, our group had already gotten together on several occasions to fine-tune our plot, costumes and props in order to make the entire play authentic and entertaining. We had to make our fellow students—and Professor Emerson—believe they were watching a *real* Shakespearian play, and my over-achiever-Type-A personality wouldn't settle for anything less. With only two weeks left until the big day, we were all determined to make our performance *perfect*. Two groups had already performed, setting the standard very high, and the eight of us wanted to put the other students to shame.

We were to perform our rendition of *A Midsummer Nights' Dream*, where Oberon owns a dive bar run by his fairies in the middle of the woods. His right-hand man, Puck, places date-rape drugs in the drinks of four unsuspecting guests—thus beginning the tragic love square that the story highlights—and Titania makes love to a donkey to the soft vocals of Marvin Gaye. I believed that Shakespeare himself would've been impressed with the final product.

The rehearsal had gone better than anticipated. The woman playing Titania brought two bottles of wine—the setting *was* in a bar, and it was *crucial* to get into character—to ease some of the pressure, the man playing Demetrius brought new scripts with all updated stage, light and sound directions, the girl playing Hermia—a Theatre and English double major that nobody liked because she believed she was more talented than the rest of us—had to leave rehearsal early for another class project, and the girl playing Helena brought homemade brownies to get us through the rehearsal. Zachary had attended to record each practice performance so we could watch ourselves in order to fix any issues or make any improvements before we made complete fools out of ourselves in front of the entire class.

Two and a half hours into practice, and after our second run-through proved to be our worst performance yet—everyone was flubbing their lines and laughing at the jokes—I decided to call an intermission, needing something to eat before I ripped someone's head off. My "play-mates" said they needed to go over one more scene before breaking, which didn't include me, so I gratefully sat in the desk beside Zachary. The problem was, once they started rehearsing, I realized I couldn't leave, their lack of focus making me nervous.

I looked over at my boyfriend and smiled. I lowered my voice and asked Zachary if he wouldn't mind crossing the street to get me something from Pita Pit— a small franchise we visited together at least once a week. He grinned and nodded as I told him *exactly* what I wanted on my pita. When he got up from his seat, he kissed my cheek and handed me his half-eaten brownie, so I could munch on it while I waited for his return. My "play-mates" nailed their lines and executed their punch lines so flawlessly, I couldn't stop laughing. Once the scene ended, we all poured some wine and plugged the video camera's cord into my laptop so we could go over the scenes we'd practiced thus far. My "play-mates" visited the vending machine in the hallway, pulled pre-made lunches out of their backpacks and chugged water bottles, yet as time ticked by, my boyfriend was still nowhere to be found.

"Are you getting to the part where Zach fucks up?" Lacie interrupted. "Because it kinda sounds like shameless self-promotion to me. I'm not gonna go watch your fucking play no matter how good you make it sound."

I snorted into my drink, definitely feeling the tequila surging through my blood. "Patience is a virtue."

Jasmine polished off her margarita and smiled. "We love you, but we *really* don't care about your play. Get to the good shit."

I continued the story from the moment Zachary walked into the classroom forty-five minutes later than he should have. Hungry and light-headed from lack of food and two glasses of Merlot, I asked my group if they could rehearse the next scene without me, and I sat at a desk in the far corner of the classroom so I wouldn't disturb them.

"Zach, what took you so long?" I hissed, unwrapping my pita.

"There was a line and I had to figure out what to order for you."

"I told you what I wanted – were they out of some things?" After taking a large bite of the pita, I forced myself to chew and swallow, wondering if I'd just eaten paste. "What. The Heck. Is. This?"

Zachary frowned. "Um—a pita?"

Feeling suddenly nauseous, I took the end of the pita and began unravelling the wrap. "Okay – I'm a little confused. You said you had to figure out what to order for me, but I told you *exactly* what I wanted before you left." I turned to glare at him. "To be honest, I shouldn't even have to tell you what I want because we go there *all the time* and I always order the *same exact thing*." I took a deep breath, looked at the mangled pita and struggled to keep my voice down. "I know they weren't out of everything I normally order. What did you get me?"

Glancing at his still wrapped pita, he scoffed at me, gesturing toward the desk angrily. "Like you know exactly what I—"

"Turkey," I interrupted. "On colder days, you like to add fresh bacon. Spinach. Tomatoes. Olives. Mushrooms and jack cheese on the grill. Hummus when you're in the mood, and you *always* get mayo. I think you've *maybe* gotten Feta cheese once because you were feeling adventurous after studying for three hours, but you didn't really like it—and on rare occasion, you'll get pickles if it strikes your fancy that day."

Flabbergasted, Zachary stuttered. "H—How do—do you—"

"I pay attention," I spat, grimacing at the horrible mixture of ingredients staring at me. "And *clearly*, you don't! We've been together for how many years and you don't know what I like—or don't like, apparently. You got me *uncooked* mushrooms and black olives. I *hate* black olives. Who eats uncooked mushrooms willingly? And *what is this*? Sriracha? Seriously? When have I *ever* eaten hot sauce? I want you to name *one time* right now."

He shook his head, mumbling to himself.

"Don't you *dare* call me ungrateful," I growled. "It's not my fault *you* messed it up. I told you *exactly* what I wanted, and you didn't care to listen. You *literally* gave me the opposite of what I asked for."

"At least I went and got it for you."

"Oh, *great*. You want a gold star? I should've just told everyone I needed a break and gotten it myself."

He frowned. "Look, I'm so—"

"No." I held up my hand, not wanting to hear another word. "I'm tired of hearing you apologize. You wouldn't have to apologize if you took your head out of your ass and actually listened to me."

"Do you want my pita?"

I wrapped up the mess of a pita on my desk and slammed it next to Zachary's dinner. Lettuce, hot sauce and mushrooms spilled out onto the desk like road kill guts. "No. I don't like what you get. I want you to go home and leave me alone for a while. I'll have my dad pick me up. We're done here."

He opened his mouth to say something, but I left the classroom to scope out my options in the vending machine, my stomach needing something to soak up the wine, and my brain needing something salty to counter my anger.

Lacie and Jasmine gawked at me, the waiter dropping off more salsa and a few glasses of water, clearing off our empty glasses wordlessly.

I nodded. "We've been dating for *almost three years* and he doesn't know what I like. I know *everything* about that asshole. Likes. Dislikes. Sometimes in the mood even though he usually doesn't like. He got me *everything* I specifically *didn't ask for.*" I blinked and rolled my shoulders, definitely feeling drunk, but thinking I could have one more without going overboard. "I don't even know how that happens. Like—he must have messed it up on purpose. That's the only explanation. There wasn't a single thing on that pita I liked. He even messed up the cheese. How does cheddar translate to goat?"

Lacie chuckled. "Do you need another drink?"

I shrugged. "Fuck it. Why don't we have one more?"

The girls looked at one another, eyebrows raised. "Not that I'm arguing with getting another drink, but maybe you should slow down." Jasmine pointed at the plastic cup sitting in front of me. "Drink some of that water first."

"My once upon a time fiancé is gay and can't even order me the kind of food I like. I think I deserve something better than water."

Jasmine turned around and waved at the waiter. "Could we get another round, please?"

"So, a messed-up sandwich-thing was the final straw, huh?" Lacie whistled. "Not the gay ass grabbing. A Greek sandwich wrap."

Jasmine nodded. "The sausage fest should've definitely pissed you off more, but the pita sounds frustrating."

"*Almost three fucking years,*" I emphasized, ignoring them. "And he doesn't know that I *hate* mushrooms and *really hate* black olives. Have you *ever* seen me eat hot sauce? Not even salsa – but hot sauce." The waiter dropped off the drinks and smiled, wondering if we wanted anything else. Before the girls could refuse, I asked if I could please order a bean, cheese and rice burrito, knowing that I needed something with substance before finishing the last drink. "Three fucking years," I repeated sadly, pulling the margarita closer to me.

"Even I know you hate black olives. *All* olives, actually. No dirty martinis for you!" Jasmine said.

I sighed, twirling a curl around my finger to prevent myself from grabbing another chip. "Me and Zach are *officially* on a break. Not just the engagement, but the whole shebang."

The girls gasped.

"I told him one week of no calls, texts, Facebook, nothing. I even told him to avoid me if he saw me in the library. Or anywhere on campus. You guys were right—we're suffocating one another. And if we want to keep this relationship together, we have to do something. And I just needed a break from it all."

Lacie smirked. "One week probably won't stop him from being gay."

I frowned. "You know, sometimes you say things that really help, but most of the time, you say sucky things like that."

"Ignore her," Jasmine said as Lacie giggled into her straw. "Do you honestly believe a break will solve your problems? Will it make him learn how to order food that you won't hate?" She paused. "Will it make him want less attention from— uh—other people?"

Where's my burrito? I need to eat. I can't think straight. "Every relationship has problems. You two are chronically single—you wouldn't understand."

"Bean, cheese and rice burrito?" the food runner, who had long, straight, blonde hair pulled into a tight bun asked, interrupting us.

I smiled and tapped the table, beyond excited. "Maybe it's not much," I continued when she walked away. "But it's a step in the right direction."

"Maybe this is a sign you're not meant to be together."

"Yeah," Lacie agreed. "Because you don't have a penis."

I took a giant bite of my burrito and swallowed it down with a gulp of margarita, the girls laughing until they were pink in the cheeks. *But if we're not meant to be together, then why did he come back into my life like this? Has this relationship been a waste of time?* I took another bite of the burrito. *Was it a test that I failed? Should I have picked Sonoma State? Lamont? Have I just made mistake after mistake?* I cut another bite out of the burrito, swallowing a fork-full of beans and rice. *What am I supposed to do, now?*

Chapter Ten

ONE OF THE main reasons I decided to get out of the medical field was because I grew faint, and often sick, at the sight of blood, guts or broken bones. Fainting in front of Lamont my sophomore year and vomiting into the trashcan outside of my Anatomy class almost every session proved that following my family's occupational prowess simply wasn't for me. I figured being an English major would guarantee me a life of zero blood, zero needles, zero broken bones, and zero reasons to run to the nearest waste receptacle.

I did not expect to come face to face with all of my worst nightmares, all of which had been reincarnated in the form of one man: Jim Harvey.

The only reason I enrolled in his Film and Literature class was because I'd come across his name as one of the Fiction professors for the MFA program, and I thought getting the opportunity to impress him would help my chances of getting accepted into the program myself.

The first day of class, I sat in a front row seat, eager. When he walked into the classroom, I immediately imagined him to be what the son of Billy Crystal and Christopher Walken would look and sound like: extremely suntanned and leathery skin, an elongated oval face, fluffy gray hair with streaks of white, and a beard-mustache combination that was combed neatly around his small, pink lips. I immediately noticed he possessed a weird tick, which wound up distracting me during his many confounding and self-centered monologues. He would lift his sleeve around the wrinkled skin of his bicep, even if the shirt sleeve hadn't slipped, so the hem of the sleeve would grow tighter and tighter around his arm. This little quirk kept me from taking notes or focusing on anything of importance in his later lectures.

That first day of his class, I had pulled out a notebook, totally preparing myself to be the teacher's pet, my eyes set on the prize of becoming SDSU's next published writer.

I left that class with my bones shaking and my stomach clenched like a piece of wrinkled up notebook paper.

It wasn't the fact that he conducted half of the class period without any lights on at nine o'clock at night, or the fact that he spoke in a manner so arrogant, I was afraid to raise my hand for fear of being mocked. It was the fact he assured us all he *hated* violence, yet, the assigned films on the syllabus were loaded with blood and gore and *detailed violent imagery.* I ran my eyes over the list of movies we were going to watch—*Trainspotting, Charles Manson Superstar* and *The Devil's Rejects* to name a few—and highly considered dropping the class along with any hope of joining the MFA program.

The only reason I pushed through my fears and remained enrolled in Film and Literature was because my mom and dad gave me some advice after that initial class that stuck with me: *You can't just give up anytime you feel anxious. Stop letting it control you. Fight through it and you'll come out that much stronger.* Half-way into the semester, I'd been able to fight off my anxiety in class no matter how terribly violent or pornographic the film was. My jaw would hurt from clenching my teeth and my stomach would ache from my tensed muscles, but I made it through each class more confident than I'd been when I first walked in. Unfortunately, panic attacks weren't as easy to control when you weren't taking your *prescribed* anxiety medicine. Zachary had urged me to stop taking it because he'd done some "research" and the article said it "wasn't good" for my body and was "the reason why" I didn't enjoy sex anymore, one of the many possible symptoms of the medicine being a "low libido" for women. I'd wanted to tell him I didn't want to have sex anymore because I was unhappy, but quitting my medicine and suffering through panic attacks would be easier than admitting to my boyfriend – or to myself – that our relationship might be beyond mending.

Two weeks into going cold turkey and I could feel my body humming, my heart racing, my stomach churning, any and all happy feelings being sucked from my body as if a vacuum had touched my soul.

Having given up my front seat for one near the back and against the wall—Jim Harvey tended to spit when he spoke and stared at you without asking anything if you sat in the front, and after he told me flat out I was wrong when I attempted to answer a question, I decided the front row was not ideal for me—I squinted at the notebook on my desk, the only light illuminating the short story in front of me coming from the movie being projected on the screen. I had attempted to watch the movie because Ewan McGregor was the main actor in *Trainspotting* and I loved his performance in *Moulin Rouge,* but quickly had to leave the room and escape to the nearest bathroom to wet my face and take a few steadying breaths. When I returned to my desk, I pulled out a notebook and stared at the lined page, distracting myself from the fact that Ewan McGregor's character was injecting heroin straight into his vein.

I thought about the Lorazepam—the strong medicine my sister had given me in the beginning of the semester for extreme panic attacks only—sitting in my nightstand at home and wondered if it would be considered a lie if I took it when I got home and "forgot" to tell Zachary about it.

And then I wondered why it was even his business. It was *my* body after all, not his. *And you're on a break*, my mind taunted. *He doesn't need to find out, especially when you're not together.*

And then the idea hit me: a short story about a fairy tale world where drugs replaced currency. A banana would cost a joint and a cow would cost a kilo of cocaine. Although I would have to dedicate vast amounts of time to research because I knew nothing about drugs, I figured setting up the characters and their contribution to the story would distract me from the anxiety slowly creeping up each individual vertebrae of my spine.

I picked up my pen and began to write. *Once upon a time, there was a princess named Snow White. Although one may believe she was given that name for her porcelain skin, she was actually known as the one you went to if you sought out the highest quality cocaine in all the land.* I smiled as the ideas flowed, my pen scribbling across the paper with a flourish. I was so absorbed in my make-believe, illegal substance filled world that I didn't notice the movie had ended, my eyes adjusting once the lights turned on.

"Roxy."

My head snapped up at the professor's deep and raspy voice. *Shoot. He caught me not paying attention.*

Only, another girl in class began to speak. She, too, had auburn curly hair and pale skin, but she had light blue eyes and a very defined jaw. The grey-haired man with round glasses who sat behind me snickered—he played Oberon in my Shakespeare group for our other class—and leaned forward to whisper, "Almost the end of this semester, and he *still* confuses you guys."

I shrugged as if it didn't bother me, but deep down, it hurt my feelings. Professor Palmer would be disappointed to hear I was doing a terrible job impressing Jim Harvey. My dream of being accepted into the MFA program was flying further and further out the window.

"We don't look that much alike, do we?" *For one, she's prettier than me.*

Oberon shook his head. "I think Harvey can't see through his tinted glasses."

"Maybe I'm just invisible."

"Sometimes, walking in the shadows is a good thing."

I sighed. "And sometimes, you scream because you're being attacked by a bear and nobody hears a thing."

"If you wanna be heard so bad, why don't you go up there after class and tell him he's mistaking you two?"

"It's not like he's calling me Karen. He's just calling *her* Roxy."

"Just say something. I'm sure the other girl doesn't like being mistaken, either."

Afraid Jim Harvey would eventually notice me talking, and afraid to create an even worse image of myself, I returned my attention to my notebook, debating whether or not I should do as Oberon said and clear up who is who. *You're a Vaughn. Stand up for yourself—for once.*

So, when class ended, I pulled up my big girl panties, marched straight up to Jim Harvey and slapped on my customer service smile. Even though my fingers had gone numb and sweat was building up on the back of my neck, I stood up straight, not wanting him to smell my fear.

"Excuse me, Professor?" I asked, timidly.

He turned to me slowly, his dark grey hair shining white beneath the classroom's prison-like lighting. He didn't say one word, but a single nod and a sideways grin encouraged me to continue.

"I don't want to be rude, but I think you're confusing me and the other girl with the curly hair."

He lifted his right hand to his veiny left bicep and began fingering his shirt sleeve.

I swallowed. *Just keep going. Don't let him scare you.* "You see, I'm Roxy. That girl and I both have curly hair, so I totally understand the confusion, but her name is Karen. I just—I—I thought—you might like to know. I don't know why— well—why she hasn't said anything or why she answers you. The thing is – her name is – she's Karen. I'm Roxy."

His eyebrows disappeared behind his lightly tinted sunglasses. "No. I didn't confuse you. You're mistaken."

That caught me off guard. I forced myself to continue. "Um—you called her Roxy. Um—I'm—I'm Roxy. She's Karen."

"No. I know who you are." He shook his head. "And I know who she is. I don't confuse my students."

He really believes he can do no wrong. "Oh—uh—my mistake. I just—you— okay. Have a good night, Professor." Readjusting the straps of my backpack, I left the classroom feeling like an idiot. *Well, that's the last time I ever stand up for myself.*

#

WHEN I FIRST saw a piece of paper fluttering beneath my windshield wiper in one of SDSU's many parking structures, I panicked, quickly walking to my car to see what I could've possibly done wrong. Upon closer inspection, I realized it wasn't a parking ticket, but rather a piece of notebook paper with terrible handwriting on it. I recognized the chicken scratch immediately and leaned my back against the car's driver side door as I read a love note composed by my ex-fiancé.

He referred to a more innocent time of our lives: the summer before junior year of high school and the summer before Zachary was to be a freshman in college. We had dug a giant hole in the sand at La Jolla Shores and sat together in the pit watching the waves, my hand resting on his chest, and how when I placed my palm on his skin, his body buzzed as if he'd had a couple of beers. He then wrote about the first time he visited me in Rohnert Park and how I wobbled into the middle of the street in too high of high heels and too many alcoholic beverages wreaking havoc on my liver.

The next time I found a note the following day after Jim Harvey's class, my heart felt all a flutter. At this point, Zachary and I had been on a break for six days without any communication what-so-ever. In this note, he mentioned how seeing my naked body for the first time in years completely took his breath away, my body so grown up and developed compared to who I was in high school. He still wondered if that entire night had been a dream—before that night, he had honestly believed he'd never hold me again.

The following day after work, I found yet another note. He confessed that not seeing me this last week hurt more than when we lived on separate halves of the state because now, it felt as if half of his heart had been ripped out. He told me how much he loved me and apologized for being such a terrible boyfriend lately. He didn't want to lose me and planned on doing whatever he could to prove that to me.

Especially avoiding the attention of others because the only attention he *really* cared about was mine.

The next note was found by my dad on the welcome mat at our front door, attached to a Snickers candy bar. Still in my pajamas, I wondered when Zachary had found the time to stop by because he was scheduled to work the morning shift at Dolphin Point. This time, the note simply said, "Cramps suck." I'd smiled to myself as I opened the candy bar and snuggled on the couch in the TV room with Sherlock.

Although Zachary and I had needed some space from one another, I woke up on the ninth day of our break and realized how much I really missed him. Doing my homework alone on the couch felt strange. Sitting in the library without him procrastinating by playing video games left me glancing at the empty seat beside me, hoping he would magically appear.

Reading all of Zachary's letters and notes reminded me of all the wonderful moments we shared together before our relationship travelled further and further south. My heart, which had grown hard with cynicism, now softened with hope; a hope that convinced me our love still existed. It had simply been hiding beneath the pressure of an engagement neither of us was mature enough to handle.

Each note proved we still shared something special: a sincere and romantic relationship between two young twenty-something-year-olds worth working through the kinks.

I stared at the phone on my nightstand and wondered if this break had gone on long enough.

When Zachary answered the phone, my heart swelled with love. "Little Woman," he cooed. "I've missed you."

#

I WIPED MY profusely sweaty palms on my pink, purple, green and yellow polka-dotted tights, my fingers leaving moistened trails on the thin material.

"Maybe they won't notice if I don't show up," I said, tapping my thumbs against my thighs. "Or I can just fail. As long as I pass the written final, I can get a C in the class."

"Oh, knock it off," Zachary said, grabbing my hand, providing me with a reassuring squeeze. "You've been working your butt off. You're gonna knock it out of the park."

It was nearly ten o' clock, which meant my Shakespeare class would begin in twenty minutes, which meant I was twenty minutes away from forgetting all of my lines and fainting in front of the entire class. I swallowed the miniscule amount of saliva coating my mouth, took a deep breath and wiped my free hand on my tights again. "I really don't think I can do this. I'm gonna make a fool out of myself."

"But your character is a fool," Zachary said. "You're in polka dot tights, a flowered skirt and a plaid shirt. You're the comic relief."

The driver's seat of my car was beginning to feel like an elevator stuck in a cemented skyrise wall between the forty-ninth and fiftieth floor. A bead of sweat crept down the small of my back. "I can't breathe." Letting go of Zachary's hand, I reached for the door handle frantically. "Babe, I'm freaking out. What if I mess up? What if I let the team down?" The door finally opened, filling the car with fresh air. I stepped onto the cement, the clack of my hot pink high heels echoing through the parking garage. "What if the class doesn't think we're funny? What if Professor Emerson hates it?"

Zachary exited the car and came over to wrap me in his arms. "Just breathe. You've rehearsed a million times. The jokes are funny. Seriously, Roxy. I know it's gonna be great because you've put your heart and soul into it." He held me at an arm's distance and smiled at me. "You're gonna steal the show."

I smiled back, the numbing of my fingertips beginning to dissipate. About a week prior, shortly after Zachary and I decided to end our break, I begged him to attend my performance, the thought of him being there the only thing keeping my confidence from plummeting to the earth's core. "But I'm nervous," I whispered.

He pushed a stray hair behind my ear and kissed my nose, not wanting to smear my dark pink lipstick. "It's okay to be nervous. I would be, too. But I know you—and Roxanne Vaughn is no quitter."

I frowned. "Except when it came to Med School."

"That wasn't your passion. This is *literature*—it's just being read out loud. You're doing what you *love*. You should have *fun* doing it."

While he cradled my head under his neck, I took another deep breath. *I can do this. I've been practicing this performance for months.* "I know—I just—I don't want to mess up in front of everyone."

"If you do mess up, play it off. Like I said, you're the fool of the play. People'll believe it's part of the gig."

I looked up at him, rubbing my palms up and down his back. "Thank you, Zachary. I love you so much."

He patted my bottom. "I love you, too. Now, get that cute butt to class. I don't want you to be late."

When the play began, I looked out among my classmates, my anxiety rearing its ugly head, threatening to make me forget every line I had rehearsed. Zachary smiled and gave me a thumbs up, which gave me the confidence to take a deep breath and recite the opening lines without flubbing a single one. And when we gave our final bow, I knew Shakespeare would've been proud with the final product, which gave me a boost of confidence I'd never felt before – at least, not without consuming copious amounts of alcohol. My boyfriend clapped enthusiastically, his crooked teeth and gorgeous green eyes making my heart flutter. It led me to believe that our relationship might stand a chance.

#

ON THANKSGIVING DAY, I found myself sitting in the passenger seat of Zachary's Honda. The morning had been great, Zachary and I having engaged in a passionate make out session in my room after we ate waffles together. It was as if the break truly did help fix the fissures in our relationship. That was until Zachary reached into his pocket and revealed the small golden circle I thought we'd both agreed didn't exist until we were more mature to handle it.

I shook my head and turned my gaze to the white tufts of cotton candy sticking to the sky. "I really hope you're not gonna ask me what I think you're gonna ask me."

He stopped at a red light and grabbed the hand I'd left resting on my thigh. "I'm sorry, but I never told Mom we ended our engagement."

I refused to look at him, afraid I'd scream if I did. He felt no guilt when lying to his family, which I believed meant he had no problem lying to me as well. He still hadn't told his father about the ended engagement either, which forced me to avoid him whenever necessary; this was no easy task when Zachary spent a large majority of time at his father's house because he suddenly disliked the small, illegal room he paid to live in.

"Roxanne, please? I don't want to ruin the holiday with a bunch of questions."

"And I don't feel like lying to your mother," I said. "What if she asks me about a wedding date? Or a dress? What if your grandmother asks me about floral arrangements? You want me to lie to her, too?."

He squeezed my thigh in a failed attempt of reassurance. "I'll be right beside you the entire time. I'll just change the topic to something else and they'll chalk it up to a man being bored by wedding details."

I finally pulled my eyes away from the clouds and looked at him. "Is this *really* a good idea? I feel like wearing a ring when we're not engaged is—I dunno—bad luck or something?"

His puppy dog eyes hurt my heart, making me feel as if I'd just scolded him for piddling on the carpet. He pulled up to his grandfather's house, turned off the ignition and remained silent as the engine clicked. "I swear, I won't leave your side.

178

I'll make sure any and all questions are deflected away from you and us and anything having to do with marriage."

I bit the inside of my cheek. "I don't know."

"Look—Mom adores you. If she finds out that the engagement didn't work out, she's gonna say I messed everything up and be really upset for the rest of the day. I just—I dunno—I don't want to ruin their holiday."

I thought about the words in his love letters, the kisses we shared when the break ended, and the feelings of being cherished warming my chest after he and I made love with one another. Things had been significantly improving, and I didn't want to go back to rock bottom. *If we're really gonna make this work, if we both want to be happy, then we're both gonna have to put forth the effort.* Although still not confident with the idea, I held out my left hand and watched Zachary put the crumb sized diamond on my ring finger. My usual Thanksgiving Day appetite had been replaced by dread, my brain convincing me this was a huge mistake. "You owe me," I sighed.

He leaned over the center consul and kissed me hard, his hands pressing against my cheeks. "I'll give you anything and everything I can. You're the best girlfriend ever. I love you."

I smiled, doing my best to ignore how uncomfortable the ring felt, my skin itching beneath it. "I love you, too."

After walking through the front door, I became surrounded by Zachary's extended family members, each of them grabbing my hand at least a dozen times to gush about the ring and tell me how lucky I am to have Zachary as a fiancé.

At some point, all of the attention became exhausting, and my patience had grown paper thin. *Zachary would be happier if I had a penis*, I wanted to scream. Instead, I bit the inside of my cheek so hard, it bled. *He's just like his father. Guess the apple really doesn't fall far from the tree.*

I would've been able to handle the attention better if Zachary had kept his promise to not leave my side. Once initial greetings with the family were exchanged, Zachary disappeared to play video games with his younger cousin, leaving me to fend for myself amongst this pack of wolves clad in lipstick and costume jewelry, all of whom were hungry for wedding information.

"Oh, Roxanne! I'm so glad you could make it!" a high-pitched voice cooed from behind.

Taking a deep breath, I plastered on a big, fake smile and turned around to face the leader of the wolf pack.

Zachary's mother.

"Hi!" I wheezed, coughing to clear my throat. "Hey there. It's *so good* to see you." I was using my customer service voice, afraid that if I said anything beyond basic pleasantries, she'd see right through my façade.

She opened her thick arms and squeezed me against her plump bosom. "Roxy, Roxy, Roxy," she sang into my ear. "You are looking as *beautiful* as ever. Let me see that *radiant* ring again."

I continued to smile as if I were a Barbie doll and phony teeth were painted onto my plastic face. *Do not cave. Do not tell her the truth. The news should come from her son. Not you.* When she grabbed my hand and squealed, I understood why Zachary had asked me to lie for him. *She's happier than I am about the engagement. She's gonna be heartbroken when Zach finally tells her the truth.* I sighed.

"I am so happy for you! Marriage is such a special thing. And I can't wait for you to become my daughter. I've always wanted one just like you."

The fake smile not only began to hurt my cheeks, but it was hurting my heart as well. I always loved Zachary's mother and her peppy disposition; I hated the thought of upsetting her. She was a kind-hearted and simple woman who did nothing but praise romance and all things love related. It wasn't her fault our engagement was a sham. "Only a matter of time," I managed to lie, now searching for my no-longer-fiancé to save me from the questions I knew were about to ensue.

She pulled me over to the cushioned patio chairs and ushered me to sit in the seat beside hers. "So, how are things going with you two?"

Well, he played grabass with gays on my birthday. He bought me a pita that was completely inedible. We took a break. Got back together because he promised he was gonna try harder and now he's playing video games somewhere even though he promised he wouldn't leave my side. "Things are okay."

Her thin, pink lip-sticked lips turned upside down. "What's wrong?"

I gulped. "Nothing."

"Look, I said things were *okay* in my marriage when I found Zach's father sleeping with another man. I know what *okay* means and it's never a good thing."

I mean—that may not be totally inaccurate. "Seriously, I didn't mean it that way."

She placed her breakfast sausage fingers on my knee. "You can talk to me. About anything."

I shook my head. *Doubtful. You would refuse to believe anything your son has done these last few months.* "Nothing's wrong. We're just—we seem to be on different pages lately. Different books sometimes."

"Is it the videos games? He's been obsessed with them for years. Wouldn't even stand up today to give me a hug because of those damn things."

I chuckled. *I miss when video games were our biggest problem.* "No—not that. He's been complaining a lot about teaching, but he doesn't do anything to solve the problems. Like—it sounds silly—it really does—but he's reading books to avoid completing his lesson plans, and he says his Master Teacher yells at him *all the time*, but he doesn't understand why. It's so obvious to me. He's not trying to be better."

She smirked.

I didn't like how small it made me feel.

"Sweetie, reading is *supposed* to enhance one's intelligence. It's hardly fair to be mad at him for doing something that will improve his mind."

He's not doing it to improve himself. He's doing it to avoid his responsibilities. "I dunno—I guess it's more like he's not listening."

His mother nodded. "I understand how frustrating that can be, but he's a man. They can't multitask when they have something important *really* weighing on their mind."

Like his best friend's penis? "You know, we might just be going separate—"

"He's obviously daydreaming about the wedding!" Her banana hands were now bruising my thigh. "Which, I must admit, I've been wondering about myself."

My mouth went dry. "I know everyone is excited, but we both agreed not to plan anything until after—"

"What about a summer wedding?"

I began to wring my fingers together. "That sounds great, but—"

"A fall wedding? Those colors would be beautiful on you. Oranges, yellows and reds! All of those would go perfectly with your hair."

A bead of sweat formed between my shoulder blades. "Well, you see, my birthday is already in the fall—"

"Have you two started discussing a venue yet? All the good ones get booked quickly."

Before I could try to respond only to get ignored again, one of Zachary's aunts sat across the black, iron table from me, a red solo cup, most likely filled with box wine, in her hand. "Are you two talking about the wedding? I'm sure you've already decided how many bridesmaids are gonna be in your party?"

I shook my head, the urge to scream bubbling in my throat. "I haven't thought about—"

Zachary's grandmother now joined us at the head of the table, her bright pink lipstick accentuating the wrinkles on her lips. "Remember, you must have the same number of groomsmen and bridesmaids. Have you given any thought into the kind of dress you'd like to wear? I can make some appointments at these cute boutiques in L.A. I'm sure you'll want to lose weight before the wedding, so we'll find a local tailor for you."

My ears began to ring. *I don't want to be here. What am I doing? Zach wants me to lie, but he's not even here to help me. This family deserves to know the truth.*

"Oh, Mom, hush," Zachary's mother said. "Roxanne is already thin enough. She should be thinking about bridesmaid dresses. They need to be stunning, without overshadowing the bride, of course."

I'm okay. I'm okay. I'm okay. "Has anyone seen Zach?" I squeaked.

"And you know," Zachary's aunt added, still ignoring me. "The sooner the wedding, the sooner you can give my sister grandbabies. Not that we'd complain about a shotgun wedding, but then you'd have to be sober for the ceremony and that would be *so dull* for you."

The three women continued to talk over one another, their flushed faces and exaggerated hand gestures showing just how excited they were for Zachary to marry me. My chest was hurting at this point, the weight of a thousand invisible bricks threatening to crush my diaphragm, making it difficult for me to breathe. *I can't do this anymore.*

"I need to use the restroom," I said abruptly. I placed my now sweaty palms on the hot, metal armrest. "Excuse me for just one moment."

Shaking and feeling slightly feverish, I quickly walked into the office that was next to the bathroom and stepped in front of the television Zachary was staring at. He tried to look around me, he and his cousin almost knocking heads together.

When he made eye-contact with me, he smiled as if he didn't have a care in the world. "Oh, hi Roxy! Didn't see you come in. How's it going out there?"

It's my personal hell, thank you, Satan. I took a deep breath and turned off the television, doing my best to ignore the displeasure on Zachary's face. When I simply stared at him, remaining mute, Zachary gently placed the controller on the cushion beside him and folded his hands in his lap.

"Okay," he drawled. "You have my attention."

"I'm sorry for having to interrupt your *family bonding time*, but could we speak in private for just a moment?"

"Um—yeah—sure." He glanced at the blank TV screen and then at his cousin. "It really can't wait until later? We're kind of in the middle of an important game and Omar's playing online with us."

My face flushed pink. "Zachary. Bathroom. Now."

I left the office and headed through the hallway without looking over my shoulder to see if he was following. His heavy sighs and heavier footsteps echoed in my ears.

When the door closed behind him, I rested my butt against the sink and crossed my arms. "Do you remember what you said to me in the car?"

He frowned. "When?"

"*When*? When we were sitting out front and you begged me to wear this stupid ring! Right before you deserted me in front of the firing squad so you could play another idiotic video game."

He touched my forehead with the back of his hand. "Roxanne, you're burning up like crazy. Jesus—you're like—dark red. Are you sick?"

"No, I'm not sick," I nearly shouted. "You promised me—*promised*, Zachary— that you wouldn't leave my side because I agreed to wear this *stupid ring* for you. And yet, while your family is hounding me about *wedding details* and *having babies*, you're hiding in the corner playing a video game. It's like I'm flashing back to sophomore year and you're putting those games before our *failing* relationship." With every word I emphasized, I gestured my hands wildly, unable to keep them still.

He sat on the fuzzy toilet seat cover, shoulders slouched. "I wouldn't consider our relationship *failing*. We're just—well—it's a rough patch. Hitting a few road bumps. Getting over some obstacles."

"Zach," I snapped, growing more frustrated. "If you use one more cliché, I'm leaving this house and hitchhiking my way home."

"Why are you blaming this on me? You're the one who wanted to end the engagement!"

"But I'm not the one who wants to *pretend* our relationship is perfect. Face it— things aren't going as planned. I don't want to keep lying."

He ran a hand through his hair. "To my family or to yourself?"

I sat on the edge of the bathtub and rested my elbows on my knees. "Why do you do this? Why do you always assume I want to end things? I'm being honest so we can work through this."

"Roxanne, it's beyond obvious we're not on the same page anymore. You don't want to be engaged, so what's the point of staying together?"

I turned the faucet on just slightly, droplets of water falling from the tub's spout. *I don't want to be alone. And I'm just not ready for marriage – you're my best friend. But marriage is a huge step.* "Just because I'm not ready to be engaged doesn't mean I'll never be ready."

"What's changed since you said yes? How have things gone so wrong between us?"

I should've never accepted the ring. Not when part of my heart still belongs to someone else. I ran my hand under the cool water. *Someone who lives a million miles away and will never have the capacity to truly love me, too.* "You're not the same person I fell in love with."

He stood and looked at himself in the mirror. "Well, neither are you, but people change. It's unavoidable. But when you truly want to be with someone, you keep loving them anyway."

"I'm overwhelmed, Zach. You do nothing but complain about school, about your Master Teacher, your students, your weight, your dad—but you don't do anything to try to fix those problems. I can't take all of your negativity."

"Like you're so positive?" he shouted. "You cry *all the time.* Like—Jesus, Roxanne. Nothing makes you happy anymore. The girl I met in high school was a bundle of energy."

"You broke that girl," I snarled. "You broke her when you decided you wanted to screw everything with legs your freshman year."

Pain flashed in his eyes, but he shook his head as if trying to forget that had ever happened. "Even when you were in Sonoma and we could never see each other, you didn't cry this much."

I just wasn't crying about you. That's the perk about distance – you don't know whether or not I'm happy or sad or cheating on you with the man I still love. "What kind of boyfriend complains about his girlfriend expressing her emotions?"

"Don't throw that bullshit at me. Is that also gonna be your excuse as to why we don't have sex anymore? Because you're *too emotional*?"

I turned the faucet off and shook the water from my hands. "The old Zach would comfort me. The new Zach won't even let me take medication that helps me feel normal because he's too self-obsessed and is only concerned about getting laid."

He rolled his eyes and turned his back on me. "You're the one who's pushing me away. It's like everything I do bothers you, and God forbid you do anything that bothers me."

"You don't even know me anymore!" I stood, resting my hands on the sink. "It's like you don't want to know me anymore. Like—this may not seem a big deal to you—but I'm still upset you don't know what kind of food to order for me. You didn't even get something as easy as a pita right."

"Why can't you let that go?" He grabbed my elbow. "I made a mistake. *A mistake.* And I'll never forget that you hate mushrooms and olives ever again."

"It's not just about that." I grabbed his hand off my elbow and interlaced his fingers with mine. "Zach, you're my best friend in the whole world, but what if we're not cut out to be in a relationship? What if we've changed too much?" I stared into those meadow green eyes, trying not to cry. "What if it's not about how we've changed – but – what if it's about how we've changed in ways that the other can't accept?"

There was a knock at the door. "Are you two okay in there?" Zachary's mother asked. "I know I said I want grandbabies, but maybe *after* the wedding."

"Mom, we'll be right out," Zachary replied, apologizing to me silently.

"Dinner will be ready soon," She added before Zachary and I were alone again.

"Do you think we can get through this dinner before we talk about all this?"

I rubbed my arm and nodded. "Please don't leave me again. I can't deal with their questions on my own."

Zachary kissed me softly—hesitantly. "I won't leave your side ever again. I promise."

#

THIS WAS THE first time Lucy and my mother had seen one another since the broken plate incident, and things weren't exactly going well. The wine glasses had yet to be touched, and that in itself was a bad sign. Vaughn Thanksgivings thrived off of heavy consumption of alcohol. Even Hannah knew something was amiss. Rather than being her bouncy, bubbly self, she sat silently in her purple highchair, rolling peas from one side of the plastic tray to the other. Other than the fact that Lucy was still mad at Mother for their last encounter, I could feel something else wrong—Roger had barely filled his plate, and Lucy hadn't teased me. Not once.

I sliced through a piece of dark turkey meat, wondering how to ease the tension. I didn't enjoy my family's company much, but I hated feeling uncomfortable. "So, Dad," I began. "How's the game going?"

It was playing on the muted television in the kitchen behind me, Mother insisting we have a real conversation during dinnertime because we rarely had the chance to have all of us together. At this point, I was tempted to turn the TV up so it would drown out our lack of conversation.

"Looks like the Cowboys need a new quarterback," he said unenthusiastically. "Romo just doesn't play like he used to."

Although I didn't watch football regularly, I knew enough about it to keep up a semi-decent conversation. But my dad's lack of enthusiasm threw me off—he *hated* the Cowboys. Anything that made them play worse usually put him in a good mood. *Okay, enough is enough. I can't take it.* "Lucy?"

She glanced up from her untouched plate and raised her recently waxed eyebrows.

"Do you mind if we have a chat? Sister to sister."

"Why can't you talk in front of us?" Mother asked, suddenly interested in her wine glass.

Lucy glared at her. "Are you gonna throw another plate on the ground if I leave the room?"

Mother sighed. "I apologized a thousand times. Please don't hold it against me forever."

"It hasn't been that long," Lucy muttered.

I rolled my eyes. *Grow up, you guys.* Hannah continued to play with her peas, mashing them into the plastic tray with her thumb. Roger poured gravy over his mashed potatoes but proceeded to absentmindedly poke at them with his fork. My dad sipped his wine, finally, and stared like a zombie at the television. *I guess it's up to me to save the night.* "You guys, this is getting ridiculous. It's been months since Mom lost her mind. Everyone seriously needs to get over it. There's no reason for all of you to be awkward and mopey. It happened. It's over. Give it a rest."

Lucy glared at me now. "Don't talk about things you know nothing about."

"You're all acting crazy! There's no reason to *still* be upset over the plate situation."

Lucy started to say something, only to be interrupted by my mother, who was then interrupted by my father, who was then interrupted by Roger. They all tried speaking over one another, a cacophony of shouts echoing off the walls. I wanted to cover my ears and run downstairs, wishing they could figure out everything on their own so my mom would stop pretending she cared so much about me and my life.

"I lost a baby, okay?"

Three pairs of surprised eyes stared at my older sister, her husband placing his face in his hands, Hannah finally eating some mashed potatoes off of a small, pink, plastic spoon.

"W—wh—what?" my mom asked. "You mean, last time you were here?"

"I didn't know at the time, but yes." Lucy's eyes turned red, tears welling up along her eyeliner. "I was pregnant. About three months. And—it—it just—"

Roger reached for his wife's hand. "The doctor said this happens sometimes, but that doesn't mean we should stop trying."

"Of course, you shouldn't give up," my mom said, voice high-pitched. "Your father and I had two miscarriages before we had you. And one of them was at five months."

"You never told me that," Lucy said, dabbing at her eyes with her napkin. "Was it hard?"

"Of course, it was!" my dad replied. "It was devastating, but so much has to go right in order for a baby to develop correctly. We wanted to give up at first, but we got through it. And then we had you."

I rolled my eyes. "Why didn't you tell me?" I asked Lucy.

She ignored me. "But what if I don't get pregnant again?"

My mother reached out and held my sister's hand. "You'll get pregnant again. You'll get through this—it'll make you stronger. And it'll make you appreciate Hannah and your future children that much more."

As if on cue, Hannah took a handful of mashed potatoes and began smearing them with the peas on her tray. She giggled and hiccupped, bringing smiles to everyone around the table.

"They grow up so fast," my mom cooed.

Lucy nodded and smiled, but the gesture didn't quite reach her eyes. "Yeah, seriously."

"Look at her hair," my dad said, holding up his wine glass as if his granddaughter was going to cheers him back with her sippy cup full of chocolate milk. "Definitely gets that from my side of the family," he teased.

"Another beautiful blonde this family has been blessed with," my mom added, squeezing Lucy's hand.

I frowned, glancing down at my long, auburn curls. *Wow. Thanks a lot, Mom.*

Roger sipped from his wine and reached his hand beneath the table, patting his wife's thigh. "We truly are blessed, Lucy. We'll try again. Just like the doctor said."

The conversation continued without my presence being acknowledged. Mom and Dad spoke with Lucy and Roger as if they hadn't ignored one another for months. I bit into my candied yams and smiled at Hannah. *It feels so good to be out of the spotlight. I can't wait to excuse myself and hide in my room with Sherlock.* Hannah reached out and offered me a handful of potato-pea mush. I laughed and kissed her pink cheek, ecstatic that things had returned back to normal.

And this normalcy was exactly what I needed to find the strength necessary to figure out what I was going to do about my broken engagement.

Chapter Eleven

WHEN I HAD mentioned to Jasmine and Lacie over dinner and drinks one night that I wanted to throw a party to get to know my coworkers better outside of Sea World, they nearly choked on their margaritas. They suggested it be a themed affair, and after another cocktail, we decided on a Pimps and Hoes costume party. Then once I asked my parents—who were both surprised to discover I had friends outside of Jasmine, Lacie and Luke—if I could use the garage as a venue, they suggested I host the party the weekend they were visiting my sister in Los Angeles so they wouldn't have to deal with any noise complaints or police arriving at the house. However, in an attempt to seem cool and reckless to my peers, I told everyone that my parents had no idea the party was happening, and that there'd be no chance of them coming home early. They didn't need to know that my mom helped me piece together an outfit that was simultaneously tasteful and risqué, or that my dad gave his input on which beers and booze I should provide for my guests.

Jasmine and Lacie showed up two hours early to help with party set up and my makeup, and to begin drinking before anybody else arrived. They took all of the booze, water and soda I had purchased and stocked the outside refrigerator while I filled bowls of various chips, dips, pretzels and candy. The walls were decorated with green table clothes to cover the tools hanging on shelves, large dollar signs were taped to the storage cabinet doors, and furry purple streamers hung from the rafters beneath Christmas decorations that I hadn't seen put out since I was a little girl. Gold, chocolate coins littered all counters and tables, and I bought some glittery, oversized sunglasses that people could use as props in photos.

In order to dress in accordance with the Pimps and Hoes theme, I shook the dust off an old school uniform skirt and borrowed a white button-up from my mother, which she was sure to remind me was what she wore to work when she was pregnant with me. I tied the shirt up beneath my breasts, a black camisole covering my midriff, pulled my curls into high pigtails and slipped my feet into white, thigh-high stockings and some close-toed, black pumps my mother found buried in the back of her closet. Due to my stressful relationship, walking from one side of campus to the other, and waiting tables multiple days a week, I'd *actually* lost some weight, which made me feel somewhat confident when I checked myself out in the mirror. Although still not as slim as my mother or pre-pregnancy sister, my mother did mention that my face looked thinner when she handed me a tube of bright red lipstick. My confidence only soared higher when my best friends pressured me to take two shots of vodka before I even had the chance to complete my eyeshadow.

Although loving this strange confidence, I was still anxious about the party succeeding. It was the second opportunity given for me to spend time with my coworkers outside of Sea World, but it was the first time I'd invited them out to drink with me. I would've been less nervous if I hadn't stupidly agreed to work a shift the next morning. When I initially planned the party, I'd made sure to request the following day off so I could endure my hangover alone and in bed. However, when William, my manager, begged me to work because the first two Dines were completely sold out, I couldn't say no. His kindness and handsome face weakened my resolve and the next thing I knew, I was accepting a shift that began at ten the next morning.

I told Jasmine and Lacie I intended on keeping a steady buzz but needed to drink like a responsible adult so I wouldn't be a mess the next day. Although they both opened their mouths to argue, one glare and quick shake of the head made them stop.

And that had been my non-negotiable plan until Zachary showed up in a shirt that appeared to have shrunk in the dryer, alongside a new friend he had made at Dolphin Point, who was also wearing a tight T-shirt, only, it hugged his muscles in a way that made me want to sign up for a gym membership—yesterday. The friend's name was Scott, and he also helped guests squeeze into wetsuits so that any average Joe could swim with the dolphins. Jasmine and Lacie began to fight over him as if he was a piece of meat and they were two rabid dogs who hadn't eaten in three weeks. I didn't blame them for being unable to control their hormones—when I leaned in to kiss my boyfriend, I felt embarrassed to do so in front of Scott.

He was your stereotypical Southern Californian: a surfer-skateboarder cliché that TV commercials would portray to tourists to get them to the beaches of the West Coast, and spend all of their money in an attempt to look just like him. His freshly cut hair was bleached from ocean water and sun, his tan skin slightly red on his shoulders, and his white, square teeth stood out against his dark lips. His teal green eyes shone bright beneath long eyelashes, but his voice brought his good looks down a notch, the slow, surfer drawl sounding like a surfboard scratching on rocks.

Seeing the two boys standing together made me realize just how much Zachary had let himself go since Halloween. The weight gain still hadn't stopped him from being vain, his belly bulging over his belt buckle beneath a t-shirt I could've sworn fit him only a few weeks ago, his jeans squeezing his legs in a way that made me wonder how his man parts could breathe. While drinking a margarita I made extra strong only moments before, I watched my boyfriend and Scott play Beer Pong against my best friends, hating how disgusting Zachary looked laughing like a troll at some inappropriate joke that involved women and their inability to do anything as well as men did. After taking a large gulp of my drink—only wincing slightly—I made my way to the other side of the garage where three of my coworkers were mingling.

Dominick didn't dress up in theme, opting for a lavender shirt and tight black jeans, instead. Justin, the tall, blonde Casanova at Dine with Shamu, wore blue basketball shorts and a grey t-shirt he knotted up beneath his pectorals to mimic girls who liked to show off a little too much of their midriff. Ricardo wore a purple coat with a green tank top and blue jeans, a fake gold chain dangling from his neck.

I sat on Dominick's lap and wrapped my arms around his neck, careful not to spill my drink, my buzz keeping me on a level that HR would consider grounds for termination.

"Your cheeks are red," I said, pinching his face with my free hand.

He smiled and poked my nose. "Yours are, too."

Justin chuckled. "Dude, Roxy's getting trashed."

I stuck my tongue out. "*Trashed* is such an unappealing description. I prefer *pleasantly intoxicated*."

When I cuddled into Dominick's collar bone, Ricardo patted my thigh. "You, little miss, are white girl wasted."

"Ricky, let's play Pong next."

Dominick nodded, his chin touching the top of my head. "Me and Justin against you two losers."

Ricardo grabbed my hand and pulled me into his lap, my drink sloshing, and sticky liquid spilling over my fingers before splashing against the cement floor. "You two are going down."

I sipped my drink. "You know—why don't we play Flip Cup instead? I'll kick all of your butts at that."

Zachary walked up to the circle, took the cup out of my hand and chugged my drink without asking. "Your friends suck," he said, throwing the cup over his shoulder.

I watched it clatter on the ground, drops of margarita spilling slowly over the rim. "Hey!" I sat up straight, still on Ricardo's lap. "I wasn't done drinking that," I snapped.

"I don't see any reason why you can't make another one." He belched and rubbed his belly.

I tried to fight back my disgust and embarrassment, avoiding the concerned stares of Ricardo, Dominick and Justin. "Where're the girls at?"

"They're busy trying to fuck Scott."

I shrugged, now getting off Ricardo's lap with unsteady legs. "Who cares?" *Clearly, you don't.* "As long as they're having fun. Maybe they'll compromise and share him."

He nodded. "Lucky man."

I glared. "And what is that supposed to mean?"

He sighed. "Of course, you take that the wrong way."

"Oh, *I'm sorry.* Is there a correct way to take that?"

Across the garage, taking note of my raised voice, Jasmine and Lacie pushed Scott away and came to my aid, pulling me toward the speaker playing music on top of the washing machine.

"You okay, Sweetie?" Jasmine asked, her hand resting on my shoulder.

I shook my head. "Zach took my drink."

Lacie gasped. "He's an asshole."

"And he didn't even care I was sitting on some other guy's lap."

"He's probably into that kind of thing," Jasmine joked.

"*And* he made some comment about how lucky Scott would be to get the chance to sleep with two girls at one time."

Jasmine and Lacie glanced at one another.

I crossed my arms. "What?"

"How about we go into the kitchen and make you a new drink?"

I followed the girls into the house, the music disappearing as soon as the garage door shut behind us. However, Lacie and Jasmine didn't lead me into the kitchen. They turned left and headed down the stairs. "Um, guys? The kitchen is over there," I said, gesturing to the right.

They ignored me and continued down the stairs, stopping once they reached my father's liquor cabinet.

"Um, guys?" I tried again. "Do you want to die? Because this is how you die."

Jasmine opened one of the dark, wooden cabinet doors and pulled out a bottle of Don Julio Reposado. "Why don't you take a shot of this and stop being so— you?"

"What's that supposed to mean?"

"It means," Lacie began, taking the bottle from Jasmine. "You're sobering up and need another drink."

I frowned. "I really shouldn't drink my dad's good stuff."

"But you really *should* break up with your sorry excuse of a boyfriend," Jasmine said, grabbing the bottle back.

I sat down on the couch, my legs suddenly too unsteady for me to stand. My coworkers were waiting upstairs to play Beer Pong with me, but I now wished I hadn't thrown the party at all. I wanted to curl up in bed and cry, shutting out the world so I wouldn't have to think about the pros and cons of my relationship with Zachary. "Do you guys *always* have to talk about this? For once in my sorry life, I'd like to enjoy a party without being depressed because of my stupid relationship."

"Then maybe you should stop inviting him to parties." Lacie popped the top off the tequila and pointed to a shot glass, which Jasmine was tall enough to reach. "Because he has a knack for drinking way too much and turning into a total asshole."

Jennifer and Cassandra peeked their heads around the corner of the stairs before glancing at one another and welcoming themselves into the TV room to join us.

"Everyone's wondering where you're at," Cassandra said, sitting on the couch beside me.

"Well, here I am," I said, resting my face on my palm.

Jasmine held up a shot glass of my father's expensive tequila in front of me, the smell making me wince. "Guess that means we gotta head upstairs. Bottoms up, Bitch."

I reached out and grabbed the glass but didn't drink it. "Maybe you can tell everyone upstairs that I'm throwing up so the party's over."

Jennifer sat beside Cassandra, holding her skirt down so it didn't ride up too far. "What's going on? Do you need to talk?"

I cringed. "No. I need someone to take this shot for me."

Lacie shook her head. "No, no, no. This is the good stuff. He can kill us— he can't kill you. You're his daughter. He's obligated to love you."

"Why don't you grab some of the crappy stuff and take a shot with me?"

Cassandra reached into her purse and procured a bottle of Smirnoff. "If you can reach a couple more shot glasses, I can pour."

Jasmine reached for three shot glasses and placed them on the coffee table. We clinked the glasses together, cheersed God knows what and threw back the shots, the girls groaning when they finished. I chuckled and stared at the empty glass in my hand. "Damn, that was fucking smooth."

Cassandra and Jennifer stared at me, mouths agape.

Jasmine and Lacie laughed. "She only says things like that when she's been drinking. You'll get used to it," Lacie said.

Cassandra smiled. "Why don't we do another for good measure?"

Jasmine looked at my father's fancy tequila and then at me. "You wanna risk your dad noticing how much of this has gone missing?"

I briefly thought about the shift I promised William I'd work in the morning, but then thought about Zachary's obnoxious laugh, belly hanging over his pants. "Fuck it." I slurred. "He has to love me, right?" The girls laughed and cheered, bringing a wide smile to my face. "I love you guys," I said loudly, small tears fogging up my eyes. "Like seriously," I continued, turning to face Jennifer and Cassandra. "I'm so glad you're all in my life. Seriously," I repeated. "Sea World is the best thing that's ever happened to me. I've met such wonderful new friends."

Cassandra reached out and grabbed my hand. "Aww—I think the same thing. You're an amazing friend, Roxy."

Jennifer smiled. "We love you, too, Roxy."

I blinked, suddenly finding myself standing in the kitchen of my dormitory sophomore year. Four young women, drunk after a party, pouring their hearts out to one another—the night Amber, Elizabeth, Shannon and I became best friends. I blinked again, bringing myself back to the present, hating how nervous I suddenly felt. *These girls are different. Look at Jasmine and Lacie—they've remained friends with you. Maybe the same thing will happen with Jenny and Cassie—and the boys upstairs. These friendships are real.* I rested my hands on my thighs and stood, not wanting to go down that path, afraid that if I kept thinking about Sonoma, I'd find a way to move back just to see if Lamont and I could actually sustain a relationship with one another. "We should probably head back up. I don't want everyone to think I ditched my own party."

While the rest of the girls herded up the stairs, Jennifer placed her hand on my shoulder, which made me stop. "Are you sure you're okay? You seem a little— off."

I shrugged, swaying side to side on the stairway. "Sometimes the thoughts that run through my mind make me feel like a bad person." I paused and turned to face my friend, her light brown skin looking white beneath her dark, long hair. "I am a bad person."

"No, you're not," Jennifer argued. "Nobody has a pure mind."

"I'm no longer sexually attracted to my fiancé," I blurted. "He's basically a model—and everyone constantly reminds me of how handsome he is—but he's *so gross*."

She frowned, her brown eyes shining with pity, eyebrows furrowed with concern. "Oh, Roxy. I'm so sorry. I didn't know things were that bad. Every relationship has issues—is it just a slump?"

I sat down on the stair and put my face in my hands. "I don't know. Don't slumps end? This thing feels like it has been going on forever."

She sat down beside me and placed a comforting hand on my back. "Well, maybe—I dunno—maybe it's time you make a tough decision?"

"I don't want to break up with him," I admitted. *I can't die alone. At least Zach deals with my anxiety. Nobody else is gonna want to deal with that.* "I love him. I just don't want to have sex with him. Or kiss him. Or be around him." I paused, realizing how terrible that sounded. "But we love each other."

"Roxy," Jennifer said softly. "I'm no relationship expert—far from it—but isn't being in love, like, I dunno – a good thing? Doesn't it mean you want to spend time with that one person, no matter what?"

Jennifer had sworn off men the day her ex-boyfriend broke up with her, impregnated a new girl, and tried to convince Jennifer to get back together with him while he continued to sleep with the baby's mama. Jennifer hated to admit it, but she still loved that boy—and I knew the only thing keeping her out of that toxic relationship was that kid.

The way she spoke of him reminded me of how I spoke of Lamont, so I understood exactly how she was feeling.

Except if Lamont had a child with someone else, I doubt my heart would ever be able to get over it.

Right now, though, full of so much tequila, the last thing I wanted to do was listen to her logic. Luckily, Jasmine shouted down the stairs, telling us to hurry up, so I didn't have to answer her. When we walked into the garage, Lacie handed me a red solo cup with beer in it. Zachary was busy trying to impress Scott with drunken handstands that he didn't even seem to notice I had gone missing.

Dominick, Ricardo and Justin, however, cheered and clapped when I walked up to them, inviting me to join their Beer Pong game immediately. I fell into Justin's open arms and smiled up at his handsome face. His thin cheeks, long nose, dirty blonde hair, brown beard and copper eyes warmed my lower belly.

At first, I wondered if the tequila was making me feel this way. Then, when Justin smiled down at me and winked, I knew it was lack of sexual attention now igniting a sensation between my legs. Just as I was wondering what his pink lips would taste like, Lacie pulled me away and handed me another beer.

"Be careful," Lacie warned. "Zach is still here."

I blinked and shook my head, things beginning to grow a little fuzzy. "Did I do something wrong?"

"Who wants to take a shot?" Jasmine yelled above the music. She turned around, reached for my little lime green iPod, and changed the song to something upbeat and catchy. My friends and coworkers shouted their approval, different bottles of booze being passed around with plastic cups, my skin buzzing with happiness.

I drank because I was sexually attracted to one of my coworkers. I drank because my boyfriend was flirting with Cassandra instead of spending time with me. I drank because I was dancing with my best friends. I drank because I wanted to go back in time to Sonoma State and make the decision not to return to San Diego. The haze helped me forget about my shift I promised William I would work the following morning. The pulsing music made me forget about my toxic relationship. The final shot gave me the chance to forget about my insecurities, so I no longer cared about being myself in front of my coworkers.

I woke up on the couch upstairs in my pajamas, peanut butter smeared on the cushion beside me, breadcrumbs stuck to my lips. I didn't remember saying goodbye to anyone, didn't remember making myself a sandwich, and definitely didn't remember getting myself changed into pajamas.

But as I ran to the bathroom needing to purge my stomach of bad decisions, I remembered that I needed to be at work first thing in the morning and vowed never to drink the night before I was scheduled to work ever again.

#

I PLACED THE noise-cancelling headphones over my ears and began clicking the mouse that looked like it belonged back in 1995. The computer screen was small, plastic dividers placed on the elongated desk that sat eight individuals, the rest of the room filled with small tables that sat one or two people. The lighting was too

196

bright, the computer screen too dull, the headphones making the room too quiet. I took off the headphones, now distracted by the sound of scribbling pencils, crumpled paper, fingertips on the keyboards and mouse keys clicking. I put the headphones back on and tried reading the first line of the first questions of the test but found myself beginning to panic because I could hear ringing in my ears. Frustrated, I adjusted the headphones, keeping one on my left ear, leaving the right ear free.

Picking up my freshly sharpened pencil, I took another stab at the math question staring at me. With only sixty minutes to answer forty questions of different difficulty levels, I wondered if a failed math portion would ruin my chances of getting accepted into the MFA writing program. *Why start this stupid test with math? What couldn't they start with vocabulary? At least let me pretend I'm gonna ace this thing.*

After memorizing something like two hundred flashcards of vocabulary words, practicing potential essay structures and topics, and trying not to burn the book of math sample questions, I truly believed I was beyond prepared for this test. I had no clue we would be forced to leave all of our belongings in assigned lockers in a completely different room or that I would get scolded for attempting to bring in a water bottle. I couldn't believe we were only allotted one bathroom break, which you had to sign out for, and nearly cried when we were told we could use one piece of scratch paper to work out the harder math problems.

The fact that we were being watched through security cameras by three women who resembled professional football linebackers didn't help steady my nerves.

This was the *final* item needed in order to complete my MFA program application. I'd already finished two ten-page stories edited and approved by Professor Palmer, collected my transcripts from Sonoma State, convinced three teachers from SDSU to write letters of recommendation and written a personal statement explaining why I'd be an exceptional candidate for the fiction program. I still believed I was better at writing poetry, but Professor Palmer only agreed to help me if I pursued fiction, and despite the want to throw a temper tantrum, the truth was she knew both of my writing styles. If she believed my fiction was something worth pursuing while my poetry was worth throwing in the trash, then I had no choice but to believe her. The application deadline was in early January, but I wanted it all to be done before Winter Break.

I began to bounce my legs up and down, time ticking away, the questions turning into Chinese symbols on the screen. *Since when did math questions become essay questions? Why do I need to figure out how many oranges fell out of a train going a hundred miles per hour heading straight for a broken bridge? Isn't the broken bridge more important than the oranges at this point?* Everyone else around me was scribbling confidently on their scratch paper and clicking through the test as if they'd been doing math since they developed a heartbeat in the womb. Knowing that I couldn't leave the answers blank, I decided to get out of my head and start answering the questions to the best of my ability.

Before I read the next question, however, I did say a quick prayer to the MFA gods, begging them to disregard my inability to solve math problems and instead focus on what a great writer I'd become if I was accepted into this program.

#

WHEN MY SISTER contacted me because she was going to be in San Diego for the day, it caught me by surprise. Lucy and I weren't particularly close, and since she had mender things with our mother, I'd been enjoying behind the family outcast once again.

I'd been lying in bed on a rare day off of work, school and being required to spend time with my boyfriend, Sherlock purring beside me, the TV playing reruns of *Sex and the City*, when my phone pinged. Lucy and Hannah were going to the Zoo and for some strange reason, she asked me to join them. My initial response was to deny the invitation because my bed felt as comfortable as a cloud in a Disney film and my sister had the tendency to put me down whenever we hung out. Then I realized the last time I'd seen her was on Thanksgiving Day when she announced her miscarriage, and the guilt of not reaching out to her to see if she was okay suddenly made my pillows feel like concrete. I replied that I'd be there in an hour.

Lucy and Hannah met me in front of the Zoo turnstiles, small children in matching t-shirts on field trips crowding the sidewalks. After navigating my way around chaperones applying sunscreen to the children, I bent down and picked my niece up out of her stroller.

"Who's the most *beautiful* niece in the whole wide world?" I cooed, squeezing her in a tight hug before planting a million kisses on her face.

She rewarded me with a series of squeals and giggles.

"You've gotten so big!" I said, putting her back in the stroller, her blonde hair curling at the ends. "Are those *curls*? Maybe I won't be the only misfit in the family."

198

Lucy shook her head, but her smile was warm. "Hair changes. Don't get too excited."

I couldn't believe how much she'd grown since Thanksgiving. She was, by far, the cutest one-and-a-half-year-old in the world. Her green eyes were so bright, they were almost blue, her once pink skin resembled a beautiful shade of peach and her gummy smile had a couple teeth popping through. The Vaughn genetics had taken over, but Hannah did have Roger's pointy nose and prominent cheekbones. My sister, on the other hand, looked worse than I'd ever seen her. She was horribly thin: collar bones sticking out, hip bones peeking through the top of her yoga pants, very little muscle on her arms, and her breasts had shrunk by a cup size. She was wearing zero makeup, her usually well-kept hair was greasy, and her tank top was wrinkled as if it had been sitting at the bottom of a hamper for weeks. For someone who was the carbon copy of my mother, leaving the house looking like a quasi-homeless person was unacceptable.

When I wrapped my arms around Lucy, I felt as if I was holding the ghost of my sister—and for the first time in my life, I was *worried* about her. I hadn't noticed her severe weight loss at Thanksgiving, and to my surprise, I felt *ashamed*. I had been so consumed with my own problems with Zachary, I hadn't paid attention to the baggy sweater and slacks she'd worn to the house. I tried to push down the uneasiness now settling in my belly.

"How about we get some margaritas and let Hannah watch the monkeys?" I suggested, hating how fragile my sister felt.

She frowned. "I really shouldn't. I've done some research and my drinking habits could've contributed to—to—you know—what happened."

I showed my membership card and ID to the Zoo employee standing beside the turnstiles. "You didn't drink when you were pregnant *or* when you were breast feeding. *And* you were basically a low-key alcoholic when you were in college and look how beautiful your daughter is. There're drug addicts who get pregnant *all of the time*, so stay off WebMD because whatever you're reading is a load of crap."

Lucy grabbed a park map out of one of the compartments on Main Street and handed it to me. Another bad sign. Lucy *always* wanted to be in control of the day's schedule. I folded the map, shoved it in my purse, and led my sister to the small cantina that had the best frozen margaritas ever, and offered to buy a drink for her.

"For your information, it wasn't WebMD. I'm a *real* doctor. I have access to *real* medical journals."

At least she's still full of herself. The old Lucy is hiding in there somewhere. "So," I began when we got to the counter. "Do you really not want one? Because I'm not gonna not get you one just because you're being stupid."

She glared. "Did you just use a double negative?"

I placed cash on the counter, along with my ID. "Could we please have two frozen strawberry margaritas?"

"Would you like to add an extra shot for three dollars more?" the pimpled teenager asked from beneath his Zoo issued, blue baseball cap.

I smiled. "Now *that* sounds lovely. Let's do one extra in each."

"Roxanne," my sister hissed. "It's only noon. I have a child."

"Oh *please*," I scoffed. "You've never been one to care about the time. In fact, *you're* the one who taught me it's five-o-clock somewhere when I was *sixteen*."

I thanked the young man for the drinks and handed one to my sister. After a brief pause, Lucy grabbed the cup and placed it in the stroller's cupholder. "Yeah, well, that was before my life went to shit."

Hannah was babbling incoherently in her stroller, hugging the stuffed Eeyore-blanket combination I gave her the day she was born. I bent down and kissed her cheek—noticing the stuffed donkey smelled like the tropical breeze detergent my sister loved most—her giggle warming my heart much like the margarita warmed my stomach.

"Your life isn't bad." I sipped my drink and smacked my lips. "You have a devoted husband, a beautiful house and a healthy daughter. *And* to top it all off, you have me as a sister. Doesn't get much better than that."

She glanced at me, then at her drink. "Well, when you put it that way." She picked up the cup and took a large sip of the margarita, not breaking eye contact.

I pouted. "Being my sister sucks that much, huh?"

We stopped in front of the flamingos, their pink feathers clashing with the murky water in which they stood.

"Only tequila can heal the wounds brought upon by a sister."

I nudged her. "Then I should be an alcoholic by that logic."

Continuing down the path, we found a bench by one of the monkey exhibits. We sat in silence, enjoying the sounds of laughing children, a breeze rustling the leaves, and monkeys grunting at one another. Hannah remained quiet in stroller, her head lolling to the side, ready for her nap.

"Why didn't Mom warn me about this?" Lucy took another sip from her drink and sighed.

"You mean our family's tendency to use alcohol to solve all of our problems?"

She snorted and elbowed me in the ribs. "No, Punk. You know what I'm talking about."

"Maybe she really didn't think it was a big deal since we turned out okay." I paused, sipping my drink. "Although, she may argue that point about me."

Lucy laughed.

I smiled. *I know you're in there somewhere, Lucy.*

"I'm being serious," she continued. "Mom's a gynecologist. After everything she's told me over the years, she decided to omit that miscarriages run in our family."

A small monkey with a long, black tail and a white face began climbing the metal fencing of the enclosure, his human-like paws moving with ease. I leaned forward and rested my elbows on my knees. "You heard what Mom said, though. This happens *all of the time* with her patients and they end up having perfectly healthy, fat babies over and over again. You need to pull yourself out of this rut you've allowed yourself to fall into."

"But what if I can't? If this happens again—I—I don't know if I'll ever be happy again."

I placed my hand on my sister's once-upon-a-time strong thighs and gave her a reassuring squeeze. "Then you'll have to find a way to make yourself happy again. You can't fall apart like this—you have a husband *and* a little girl." After another squeeze, she looked at me. "Lucy, honestly, you look like crap. You should be ashamed."

This time, she threw her head back and laughed, the sound so melodious, it put the singing birds in the Aviary to shame. "You're such an asshole."

"Lucy—on a serious note—you have Hannah. That *gorgeous* little creature napping in that stroller right now is depending on you to take care of her." I glanced up and watched a little boy pointing excitedly at the monkeys, his mother snapping photos on a little, red camera. "If you let this darkness overwhelm you, that little girl of yours doesn't stand a chance."

My sister sniffled and wiped her nose on her arm. "For some reason, this whole—*thing*—has destroyed me. I can't seem to snap myself out of this haze."

After taking another large gulp of my drink, I gave my sister a piece of advice she'd given me one too many times. I smirked at the primate fidgeting with his tail. "Why don't you go home and have monkey sex with your husband?"

She stared at me, her green eyes glistening in the sunlight. "Did you *really* just advise me to have sex?"

I nodded, holding back a smile.

She shook her head and laughed again. "When did you become me?"

I shivered and stood, already beginning to feel a buzz thanks to my lack of breakfast. "Please don't ever say that again or I'm gonna have to grow a mustache, change my name and move out of the country."

When she stood, she hugged me, which caught me by surprise. "Thank you. I needed that. And you were right about the margarita. I needed that, too."

I pushed her away and stuck my tongue out. "Don't get all mushy on me. You're supposed to hate me, remember?"

She grabbed the stroller and began making her way to the next exhibit. "Mom's right about you. Turns out, you're not as bad as we thought."

Chapter Twelve

I WALKED THROUGH my section, handing out small check holders that held after dinner mints on top for each guest sitting at the table. Most of my guests were in line to take a photo with Santa, but I hoped they would remember to leave me a tip before they packed up their belongings to enjoy the other festivities included in the Christmas celebration at Sea World.

The speakers had begun blasting Christmas music the day after Thanksgiving, *Here Comes Santa Clause* now haunting my dreams.

For the entire month of December, Sea World hosted an event called "Breakfast with Santa," which took place at the Dine with Shamu restaurant. So, for an entire month, the trainers put on killer whale interactions while kids and parents ignored the black and white majestic mammals to wait in line and take pictures with Santa Claus, who was probably paid well above the California minimum wage to smile, wave, and *ho ho ho* every other sentence.

The long-term Dine with Shamu workers had warned me about the overwhelming holiday festivities, but I'd brushed them off, assuming they were being overdramatic. After having to sweep up crushed Cheerios, wipe vomit off a table, and wash my hands any time I touched a plate because it was sticky with only God knew what, I understood what they meant.

Breakfast with Santa was no joke, and the seagulls were taking full advantage of it.

The falconers had yet to make their regularly scheduled appearance, so I was walking around my section with a spray bottle full of water to make sure nobody was being attacked by a hungry gull. The seagulls screamed at me as I sprayed them with the aim of John Wayne, my guests laughing as if it was part of the show and not a serious attempt by me to prevent their tables from being ransacked by winged scavengers.

"Thank you for joining us today," I said to the two women watching the whales with so much joy on their faces, I smiled genuinely at them. When they completely ignored me, I sighed and returned to the kitchen to make myself a cup of coffee. Unfortunately, as I was stirring creamer into my mug, one of the older female servers decided that was her chance to hound me about the bird problem.

"Where are those bird boys of yours?" The woman's frizzy, thick, black hair was pulled into a tight ponytail, the wrinkles in her forehead more pronounced by the frown she wore. "Those pigeons are bombarding my tables."

I sipped my coffee, relishing in the instant comfort the scalding hot liquid brought me.

"Seriously," one of the dark-skinned servers said, pulling her braids into a ponytail beneath her Sea World baseball cap. "Why aren't they here? What did you do to upset them?" she asked in her thick, French accent.

"We're not friends," I said, rethinking my decision to find a moment of peace from my guests. "And I don't have their phone numbers. That would be weird."

"It would actually be helpful," another server, older, with short gray hair and round glasses, added. "You could ask why they haven't been showing up lately."

I sipped my coffee again and went to the far end of the kitchen where the runners were delivering food and snacking on leftovers. The last thing I wanted to be accused of was mingling with the falconers—on *or* off the clock. Ever since Zachary accused me of being *too friendly* with them at the Halloween Spooktacular event, I made it a point to keep my distance. Especially from Ronnie. His initially innocent jokes had begun to take a turn for the raunchy and were making me uncomfortable.

Strangely enough, since I'd stopped interacting with them, the falconers stopped showing up to Dine. I chose to believe it was a happy coincidence, having nothing to do with me.

Jennifer walked through the silver door leading to the buffet room and smiled at me, emptying the rest of the fingerling potatoes into the trashcan. "These kids are the worst. They touch *everything*, sneeze on *everything*, and breathe on *everything*. I can't serve snot potatoes. I'd sooner die."

I smiled. "I just had a seven-year-old throw up on one of my tables and the parents told me to clean it up. I get it."

She grimaced. "They're awful. I love kids, but something about this place brings out the worst in everybody."

"And it's only ten." I sipped my coffee again, sighing happily.

"Don't remind me," Jennifer sighed. "How're things with you and Zach?"

Not having told anyone from work about my birthday, the pita and Thanksgiving, I continued to pretend my relationship was great so I wouldn't have to face the Inquisition. Jennifer knew we were having problems, but the last thing I wanted to do was risk having my coworkers overhear. "Let's just say, the situation hasn't changed much. The other night, when we were—um—you know—I was staring at the ceiling and wondering about what my professor thought about the latest writing assignment I turned in."

"Maybe you should avoid intimacy at all costs instead of having to fake it."

I sighed. "If only it were that easy. I don't want him to know how I really feel."

She stepped closer, making sure the runners couldn't hear. "You need to talk to him. You're just gonna make yourself more and more unhappy if you stay quiet."

"Roxy!" Dominick yelled from the area just outside of the silver kitchen doors. "One of your tables left and the seagulls are making a mess!"

"Shoot," I breathed, forgetting about my coffee and my conversation with Jennifer. Grabbing my tray off the server table, I ran outside, only to find two seagulls fighting over a flourless chocolate brownie that was crumbling all over the table. Before I could chase them off with a wave of my tray, the familiar sound of bells made its way up the Dine with Shamu entrance, signaling the appearance of one of the falconers and his hawk.

It wasn't Ronnie and it wasn't his son, Peter—it was the falconer I'd seen during Spooktacular with the square, black glasses and the pronounced part in his hair. The seagulls took off frantically, knocking a small plate to the ground, which broke into pieces once it hit the cement. Frustrated, I threw my round, black tray on the table, bending down to clean up the ceramic fragments.

"Sorry 'bout that, Darlin'. If I coulda been here sooner, I woulda."

I looked behind me and smiled, the falconer's voice melting over my heart like cold butter on a hot skillet. "Oh, it's not your fault these birds are such jerks. All they see is cake. I don't blame them. It's pretty decadent."

He chuckled, his lips parting slightly, deep dimples forming on his cheeks.

I stood and brushed a stray curl behind my ear. "What's so funny?"

"Don't the trainers here teach people not to give animals human emotion?"

I smiled. "You obviously haven't tried the desserts here. In fact, I'd say they actually turn humans into animals."

This time, he laughed, his small, straight, white teeth capturing my attention. "I guess I'll have to try it sometime then, won't I?"

"Try not to break any plates like your seagull friends if you get a chance to, okay?" I walked toward the kitchen, through the double doors and toward the back storage-area where we kept the white bucket reserved specifically for broken glass and ceramic shards. Resting my back against the industrial refrigerator, I took a deep breath and tried to steady my heart rate—this was the first time this particular falconer had spoken to me, and I couldn't believe the way my body was reacting. I breathed again, wiping my sweaty hands on my apron. *He's not even that cute—I mean, compared to Zach. Why am I feeling like this? He's just another falconer. No big deal.*

When I returned outside to finish cleaning my tables, I kept my eyes averted, hating how cute he actually was. He didn't have the handsome and pronounced features that Zachary had, but there was something about his smile that forced me to take another deep breath. *Why'd he talk to me?* I put some glasses on my tray. *And how is it we've never talked before?* I stuffed the cloth napkins in between the glasses. *Okay. I'm not thinking straight.* I then stacked three plates seeping with macaroni and cheese and ketchup. *I need to focus on work. Only work. This isn't gonna help patch things up with Zach.* I could feel his eyes studying me curiously.

"Is there anything I can help you with?" There was a slight twang in his voice, as if a small corner of Alabama had crawled across the country to give Southern California a bear hug.

My lower belly warmed with an anticipation I wasn't expecting—and completely inappropriate to experience in the work place. *Stop it, Roxanne. You want things with Zach to get better, not worse.*

When I didn't respond, he stepped closer. "Every time I come to Dine, I don't see you. Just that once in the stadium. Maybe a dozen times around the café. You have another job?"

He remembers me. Slowly, I looked up at him, continuing to wipe the same spot on the table one hundred times. I seemed to be hypnotized by his round cheeks, brown eyes and small nose. *Why does he remember me?* A hawk was perched on his glove-covered wrist, but for the first time since I encountered the falconers, my attention was captured by the man, not the bird. "I'm usually here Friday through Sunday. I'm in school right now—feels like a full-time job all on its own."

"Makes sense." He took another step closer, ignoring the pigeons landing on the tables on the opposite side of the whale tank. "This is my first Saturday shift alone. Ronnie finally trusts me enough. Don't have him tripping over my heels, for once."

I shifted my gaze to Dominick's section, where a pigeon was pecking a piece of cheesecake, three more joining from the top of the trainer's fish house. Although I knew Dominick would be upset, I didn't care. The falconer's attention left me feeling exhilarated, and I wasn't ready to lose that high. *None of this makes sense.*

He's not flirting. He's not being inappropriate like Ronnie. He hasn't even looked at my boobs this whole time. "Maybe he's hesitant to trust you alone because you're neglecting those pigeons over there," I teased.

"That's because I'm busy." He smirked, his gaze never wavering from my face. "The name's Tony."

I glanced briefly at my nametag before biting the inside of my cheek. *Don't be sarcastic. Be charming. Try not to get too distracted by those dimples. Don't say something stupid.* "My parents named me Roxanne—but uh—um—most people call me Roxy." *So much for not saying something stupid.*

"Well, Roxy, have you ever held a bird of prey before?"

Stacking the small dessert plates from another table, I laughed. "Maybe that's a normal question in your world, but in real life, *uninteresting* people like me don't just go around holding gigantic birds all willy nilly."

The older woman who yelled at me in the kitchen earlier walked past Anthony in a huff, her wavy black hair bouncing in a ponytail between her shoulder blades. "There's pigeons everywhere," she snapped. "Think you could do something about it?"

Anthony smiled. "Sure can't. I'm just here to look pretty." After winking at me, he walked over to Dominick's section, pigeons panicking as he neared.

Not fully understanding why my pulse was racing so quickly, I stacked more plates and silverware on my tray and walked to the kitchen to unload everything. My hands shook so much, a plate nearly slipped from my fingers as I scraped food bits into the trashcan.

"You alright?" Jennifer asked bringing bowls from the buffet room to the dishwasher in order for them to be cleaned before the lunch service. Her black apron had ketchup smeared across the belly and powdered sugar dotted sporadically around her chest.

I smiled and nodded, despite feeling as if I'd consumed five espresso shots. "Yeah, why?" Realizing how defensive that sounded, I cleared my throat. "I think I just need water or something—like—dehydration—or something."

After placing the three bowls on the dirty dish station, Jennifer brushed her hands off on her apron. "Your cheeks are pretty flushed." Although I could tell she was suspicious, after glancing at the teenage dishwasher with acne, she didn't question me further. I knew she was going to ask me about it later. "Just wanted to make sure you don't have a fever or anything."

Needing to do something with my now trembling hands, I filled a glass of water and drank it greedily. *I don't have a fever, but something about that man is making me warm.* I filled a second glass. *Why do I feel like this? He's just another stupid falconer.* I placed the glass into a dirty dish rack and shrugged and Jennifer. "For some reason, I'm terrible at staying hydrated at work."

She raised an eyebrow and stepped closer, lowering her voice so the teenager couldn't hear. "Doesn't help there's a falconer out there you can't seem to stop staring at." She paused and smirked. "And vice versa."

I grabbed my tray and ignored her comment, returning to my section to bus the remainder of the dishes off my tables. *Focus on work. Don't let anyone think you're distracted. Especially Tony.* There was another seagull attempting to swallow half a hot dog. As I approached, he sloppily took off, his panic causing even more plates to crash to the floor. I sighed and squatted, carefully picking up the ceramic shards.

Bells chimed behind me, signaling the return of Anthony and his hawk.

I thought about what Jennifer said and blinked, trying to look casual and not smitten. "Too bad you can't be in two places at once, huh?" I placed the shards on my tray, pulled a moistened rag from the belt loop of my pants and began wiping another table. "You owe this place some new plates."

"I'm here to kill seagulls, not worry about some corporation's dishes," he replied, gently stroking the large bird perched on his wrist. "It's just hard to do what I need to do here because I'm not allowed to kill anything in front of customers—and Dine *always* has someone here. Or there are people staring from the other side of the pool."

"How can you kill *anything* with those guidelines?" I moved to the next table, turning my back to him. "This park has thousands of people here *all the time.*"

He leaned against the metal support beam behind him. "Now, that's the fun part of my job. The challenge of remaining hidden."

I glanced over my shoulder and raised an eyebrow. *How can you stay hidden with that smile? Girls must search for you every minute of every day.* "You must think you're pretty good at it."

"Have you seen me before?"

I would remember those eyes. "Just that one time in Shamu Stadium when you were with Ronnie and the other falconer."

"Then I guess I must be good at it because, like I said before, I've seen your beautiful face about a dozen times."

I looked down at the rag in my hand and smiled, feeling my face flush again. I picked up my tray and moved to the next table. "You mentioned that before, but maybe I didn't see you because I wasn't looking."

He shook his head. "You didn't answer my question."

The four whales swam in circles around their pool, blowing air through the holes on their heads whenever they completed a lap. I finally allowed myself to be consumed by those light brown eyes and swallowed back the butterflies fluttering up my throat. "Well, Tony, I believe I've answered every question you asked me."

Anthony gestured to his hawk with his free hand. "You missed the one about holding my bird."

I tried to ignore the sexual innuendo hidden beneath the innocence of the question. "Oh. I thought my blatant sarcasm made that clear."

He grinned. "Well, would you like to? Hold it?"

I nearly dropped the final tray of glassware I'd collected. "W—wh—what are you saying?"

Stepping closer, he held the bird toward me, the hawk's wings spreading wide for balance, the bell jingling on its anklet. "I think you already know the answer. Go put that tray down and come back." His voice reminded me of banjos, back porches and gumbo. I wanted to sit in a rocking chair and listen to him tell me stories all day.

I took a deep breath and smiled, my cheeks beginning to hurt. "I'll be right back."

When I returned to the kitchen, I placed my tray on the server table and walked to the front counter where my favorite manager, William, was standing at his computer. "Is it okay if I hold the bird really quick? I'll sweep my section right after and be ready for the next Dine."

After having puked in the bushes and begged William to go home the morning after my "Pimps and Hoes" house party, I was afraid to talk to him—especially to ask him a favor. That morning, he gave me a hug and told me it was okay when I broke down in tears and confessed I'd made a huge mistake. In that moment, I'd felt the most embarrassed and ashamed I'd ever been. More ashamed than I'd been when I had sex with Lamont one night and sex with Zachary the next morning. Messing up at work was completely different from messing up my personal life. Messing up at work affected other people—not just myself. William had reassured me and told me it was fine. He forgave me and chuckled, believing the games going on in my head were punishment enough.

Now, William glanced at the clock hanging on the wall, and then at Anthony, who was still standing in my section. "Only if you really hurry up. I don't want the other servers getting pissy—all you servers are bad enough as it is." He smiled and nodded.

I squealed and clapped my hands together, just as excited and anxious as I'd been when I stepped into my very first college-level English class. "Thank you, thank you, thank you!"

Not wanting to waste any time, and also not wanting my other coworkers to judge me for getting special treatment from one of the falconers, I briskly walked back to Anthony, hoping I didn't appear to eager. *So, what? He offered to let you hold the hawk. Don't let him see how excited you are. Play it cool. Pretend this is no big deal. Pretend this isn't the coolest thing to ever happen to you.* I smiled at him, shoulders back, ready to hold the bird with the confidence only a true animal trainer would have.

"You ready?" he asked with that jambalaya voice of his.

I glanced over my shoulder briefly, looking beyond the Shamu pool, half expecting to see Zachary crying behind the glass while I ogled Anthony and his bird. "What's her name?"

He held the large, leather glove next to a railing, urging the bird off his wrist, the bells on her anklets ringing with every move. Anthony held onto a thin, blue rope that attached to the leather anklets above her talons and removed the glove from his left hand with a finesse that led me to believe he'd been handling birds his entire life. "Now, the glove goes on your left hand." I reached out, doing my best to ignore the growing excitement burning in my chest. "Her name is Ruby." He pulled the glove over my wrist and patted my forearm, my skin tingling at his touch.

William watched from his manager perch, but the other servers continued to clean and prepare their sections, oblivious to the once in a lifetime opportunity I was experiencing mere steps away from them. I smiled at Ruby, my upper body remaining slightly tilted to the right, nervous and intimidated by this majestic creature. She ruffled her feathers before looking at me, her black eyes piercing through me like talons. I was mesmerized.

"She's absolutely stunning," I finally managed.

Anthony gently grabbed my free hand and put it on the bird's back, my fingers caressing the soft, dark brown feathers that put the stuffing in my down comforter to shame. "Now *this* is a sight for sore eyes."

Hiding behind my eyelashes, I smiled bashfully at Anthony. A man hadn't made me feel this special since Lamont kissed me in front of everyone at his twentieth birthday party. I could feel my resolve wavering, the desire to flirt back with this man hanging dangerously on the tip of my tongue.

"Wrap it up, Roxanne," William yelled from his desk, tapping his wrist even though he wasn't wearing a watch.

Although disappointed, I didn't want to push my luck. *Well, he's saving me from saying something stupid I might regret later when I'm not being doused in charm.* "Thank you, Tony. This was—this is—beyond words." I hesitantly stroked the hawk's feathers again. "Never in my wildest dreams would I have imagined doing something like this."

Anthony guided my arm down so that Ruby would return to the railing. I blushed when he pulled the glove off, his fingers touching mine. Despite the leather, his touch sent sparks straight up my fingers and into my heart. He winked at me from behind those black, thick-rimmed glasses. "Darlin', I'll let you hold my bird anytime. Just say the word, and I'll do whatever I can to make it happen."

#

JOCELYN PALMER WAS one of the most intimidating women I'd ever met—*especially* because she had one of the friendliest smiles I'd ever seen. It was like she had invited me out for Happy Hour, promising we'd be the best of friends by the end of the night, only to disappear to the bathroom and never return, leaving me to pay for her five margaritas *and* her three shots of the top shelf stuff. She and I were sitting in her office, me trying to keep my feet from tapping nervously, her reading over my latest piece of fiction for her class. Instead of having her students take a test—which she said we'd fail anyway—Professor Palmer thought it was best for each of us to schedule a meeting where she would read our final piece. While sitting in front of each student. Grading everything right then and there.

I had already witnessed a fellow classmate leave the office covered in snot and tears, her paper bleeding red ink.

Nervous was an understatement.

The guidelines the professor created for the assignment were strict and an automatic fail would be granted if the student neglected to follow them. These same guidelines made me cry nightly, each of my stories either too long, too short, too cliché, too unordinary, too cutesie or too dark. Professor Palmer wanted a total of four pages—no more, no less—zero grammatical errors, a strong protagonist, at least three never been seen metaphors, and an underlying message within the story line that only an educated individual could unveil, unload and understand.

In the office, Professor Palmer turned to the last page of my story, her red pen tapping the desk, her hazel eyes scanning the words, her face giving away zero clues for me to figure out whether she loved it or hated it.

Please just like it enough to give me a B in the class. This is the last grade I need to get and I really don't want to ruin my near perfect GPA.

She placed my story on her desk, pushed a blonde curl behind her ear and folded her hands together. "Did you send in your application?"

I nodded mutely.

"Did you use the story we went over?"

I nodded again.

"Tell me, how did you come up with this?" She squared her shoulders against the high back of her chair, her curls spiraling around her red sweater.

I crossed one leg over the other. "Honestly, I was driving home late one night and almost committed accidental murder because two bunnies ran in front of my car out of nowhere."

Professor Palmer chuckled, her large teeth so white, I made a mental note to pick up some Crest Whitening Strips on the way home. "And that turned into a dystopian rabbit society where running in front of a car decides where you rank in this—rabbit communist group?"

"I just like to think that rabbits aren't so stupid, they'll just run out in front of cars because of panic. I thought it would be more fun to imagine that they're doing it to impress the lady bunnies, and to reign supreme in their colony."

She nodded curtly. "Smart. Very clever."

My heart palpitated in a way I'd only felt when my parents complemented me. It happened so rarely, I found myself light headed. "Uh—wh—you—really?"

She learned forward, her red sweater dipping low enough that I could see the lining of her salmon colored, lace bra. "There are a couple things you need to work on, though."

Of course, I thought. *Shouldn't have gotten my hopes up.*

My face must've given away my feelings because she shook her head, uncapped her red pen and circled a couple sentences on each page. With each red circle, my shoulders dropped lower and lower. She turned the paper toward me and pointed at the first circled sentence. "You need to be careful when you personify animals."

When I didn't respond, she slid the paper completely across the desk and placed the pen on top of it. "I want you to reread the story and pay close attention to how you turn the rabbits into humans."

"You want me to reread this—in—in front of you?" I swallowed. "Right now?"

Professor Palmer stared me right in the eyes. "And while reading, I want you to write down different ways to describe what the rabbits are doing without having your readers imagining Bugs Bunny."

Suddenly, the typed words in front of me resembled a million doctors' signatures scribbled together. "Like, *right now*, right now?"

"Would you rather take it home and bring it back tomorrow?"

My heart leapt. "I mean—yes—if that's an option."

She laughed, rolling her sweater sleeves up to her elbows. Her bracelets jingled. "No, it's not an option. I was joking."

I blushed.

"You take everything so seriously. Of course you're going to edit it at home. You *must* find the plot holes and cliché descriptions and *fix* them. The story has potential. Once you've taken the time to thoroughly edit it, you'll bring it back for my creative writing class next semester. You'll then volunteer to have it workshopped before anyone else gets the chance to raise their hands."

Now's probably not the time to tell her I was planning on avoiding her classes at all costs. I folded my hands in my lap and chewed on the inside of my cheek.

"For now, I'm going to give you an A minus."

My jaw fell just enough that Professor Palmer actually laughed at me. "So—you mean—I passed?"

"As amusing as your obvious self-loathing and lack of self-esteem is, you really need to start finding some confidence when it comes to writing."

I was torn—on one hand, I passed the class, but on the other hand, my professor took pleasure in seeing me struggle. I tried to shrug off my discomfort so I could focus on the good news: I passed the class. "It's just—I dunno—it's fiction. I'm better at poetry. Fiction is weird."

"Roxanne, you need to let go of this poetry thing." She picked up a wooden cat off her desk and began fiddling with the plastic whiskers. "Someone has to give you the cold hard truth."

Slumping in my seat, I wondered why I didn't take the A minus and run. "It's not that—"

She held up the wooden cat, stopping me mid-sentence. "You *are* talented, Roxanne. It's obvious you have a wonderful imagination and with the right training and attitude, your writing will go places. But poetry isn't the path you're supposed to follow. I know you love it because that's what 'saved' you from the medical field, but your poems aren't great."

Although there was a desk between us, it felt as though she'd taken her wheelie chair and bashed me across the head with it. My eyes began to water.

"But your stories," she continued as if she didn't just rip the head off my favorite childhood toy, laughing just before lighting it on fire. "Are *beautiful.* You have a way of setting a scene that is extremely captivating. Yes, there are *many* technical things you still have to learn—and we *really* need to delete every cliché from your database—but the skill is there. You just need to follow through with it."

I couldn't find my voice, any and all of her compliments hidden beneath the shards of my broken dreams. *She hates my poetry. But I've tried so hard. If it was so bad, why did anyone pass me? Why did I think I'd actually get to do what I love?*

Professor Palmer placed the wooden figurine back on the desk and began twirling a strand of curls. "Well, looks like we're done here."

Done? How can you say that? You just took my dream and stomped on it.

When I didn't move right away, she turned the cat shaped clock sitting on her desk toward me. "I have *many* other students I need to meet with—so—not to be rude, but leave."

I nodded silently. *Why don't I drop out now?* I slid my backpack over my shoulder, wondering if Professor Palmer enjoyed being compared to Satan.

"Don't stop writing," she added as I walked out of the door. "And do some reading! It'll help aid you as you continue to develop your unique writing style."

I purposely averted any eye contact with the next student waiting to enter hell, not wanting the pale, redheaded boy to see my eyes watering. *Why did I think it would be that easy? That I would be good at something I love?* I glanced down at the red circles and scribbled notes on my short story and wondered if I should just give up on writing all together.

#

THE END OF the world was going to take place on the twenty-first of December because the Mayan calendar had reached the end of a cycle, and word quickly spread that humanity was on its way out. A lot of people actually *did* believe midnight would be the last moment of their existence, but *most* were using it as an excuse to act horrendously out of character because the world was ending anyway.

I was one of the latter.

Bars all along the main stretch of Pacific Beach were having exceptionally cheap drink deals, so Lacie, Jasmine and I decided to participate in the chaos to celebrate the world splitting like a fractured mirror, all of mankind falling to a painful death and burning alive within the earth's molten lava core. I'd already felt like my world had come to an end anyway, my final paper for Jim Harvey's class due the day prior—a paper that had taken me two weeks of crying and forcing myself to watch *Trainspotting* so I could write a decent research paper on how drugs can simultaneously kill your brain and bring out your best artistic abilities.

I was more than ready to drink until the world went black.

Thankfully, Zachary had some stupid video game date with his best friend, Omar, so that meant I could have a guilt-free girls' night without having to text Zachary every few hours pretending to miss him.

Once I finished getting ready, I walked upstairs and found my dad sitting at the bar top, drinking a cup of coffee and watching Family Feud on the television. He looked at me and raised an eyebrow. "Are you wearing *that* out to a bar?"

I sat on the bar stool beside him and frowned. "What's wrong with my outfit?" I asked, gesturing at my high-waisted jeans, red V-neck and black undershirt. "I'm *engaged*. I have no need to impress anyone."

"Nothing is *wrong* with it. Your sister just used to dress differently when she went out at your age."

I smirked. "That's because Lucy was a whore."

My dad snorted into his mug, coffee dripping from his grey and black mustache. "That's *not* what I meant." He paused and pointed at my naked ring finger. "You should probably stop saying you're engaged when that ring isn't even in your possession anymore."

I moved my hands into my lap and shrugged. "Still slips up when I mention him. I know breaking it off was my idea, but it still makes me feel crappy sometimes."

"You can't *force* him to be *the one*. You're still *dating*. Just tell people you're dressed like that because you're in a relationship. You don't have to be engaged to be in love with someone and respect their wishes."

I glared. "You know, most dads would be *thrilled* to see their daughter dressed like this."

He finished the rest of his coffee. "Not saying it's a bad thing, but you're twenty-two. Just don't want you to regret not living your best life."

The doorbell rang, the front door opened, high heels began clacking on the tile and two loud *Hello Vaughn Family* sounded through the living room. Jasmine and Lacie walked up to the bar top, enveloping me in a hug full of breasts nearly falling out of their halter and crop tops.

Jasmine looked me up and down. "You're gonna get too hot in that."

I stood and shrugged. "It's December. You're the ones who're gonna catch a cold."

"At least we'll get free drinks."

I frowned at Lacie. "I work hard. I don't need some pathetic loser buying me a drink."

My dad stood and jingled his keys, abruptly ending the argument that was about to ensue. "Alright, ladies. No need to pre-game. Let's get outta here before the Missus gets out of the tub."

Jasmine flipped her shiny, straight, dark brown hair over her shoulder, her bangs hanging just above her brown eyes. "That woman is my idol."

I glared at Jasmine, wondering how she could forget all of the stories I'd told her about me and my mother. *Yeah. Definitely someone you should aspire to be. Not.* "Because she's taking a bath?"

"No. But because she has the *perfect* schedule. Monday through Friday? Eight to five? A husband who loves her more than anything in the world? Sign me up!"

Lacie nodded. "And because she can take time off *whenever* she wants."

My dad laughed. "That's not true. She's just smart about saving up her vacation time."

"I'm gonna be a gynecologist," Lacie added, ignoring him.

"I think they already pre-gamed," I whispered to my dad, now noticing my friends' flushed cheeks.

"Yeah, right," Jasmine laughed, nudging Lacie. "You're *already* gonna take five years to graduate. You wanna tack on another five?"

Lacie placed her hands on her hips and pouted. "That's not very nice. Psychology is a very admirable major."

"What're you gonna do? Ask the vaginas how that makes them feel?"

Jasmine and I laughed, Lacie shaking her head. "At least I haven't already changed my major fourteen times."

My dad opened the front door and ushered us outside—me in my casual attire, my friends' shorts so short, I could see things my mom saw daily at work. "Instead of arguing about what you're doing with your future, why don't you reflect on the fact that you're spending the end of the world in a bar. What does that say about you?"

I shook my head. "Like you and Mom aren't gonna drown yourselves in three bottles of wine, each."

"Nope. I got Bourbon for the occasion."

Jasmine laughed. "Ending the world drunk is the only way to go about it."

"You don't want to remember your last moments on earth?"

Lacie nodded. "There's a lot of things alcohol has helped me not remember. And I'm better because of it."

My father covered his ears. "No more. Just get in the car." He opened the driver's side door of his BMW SUV and slid onto his leather seat. "I think you're right about the whole pre-gaming thing," he mumbled to me as he started the engine.

The girls giggled in the back seat.

"I think they like to make you feel uncomfortable," I replied.

Twenty minutes and five unsuccessful conversation changes later, my girlfriends and I were walking into a favorite Pacific Beach bar of theirs: Cabo Cantina.

Jasmine and Lacie directed me toward the bar and squeezed us through the crazy crowd trying to take advantage of Cabo Cantina's two-for-one drink special. Jasmine and Lacie were weekly regulars, blacking out every Thursday night because they had become familiar with the bartender, who in turn, would hook them up with extra booze in each of their drinks.

"Hi Dave!" Jasmine shouted flirtatiously at a tall, broad-shouldered man with a shiny, bald head. "Your favorite customers are back!"

The man turned and smiled, a large gap between his front teeth, a dimple on his chin. "Be right over, ladies!" he shouted over the chaos, adding lime wedges to the pint glasses in front of him. "You want the usual?"

Lacie rested her elbows on the bar top, her cleavage peeking out above her top. "Are we *really* that predictable?"

Dave handed off drinks to the group standing in front of him and calmly ignored all of the orders that were being shouted at him. "You're what we in the bar business call *regulars*. Predictable, and the patrons who keep the establishment in business."

Jasmine flipped her silky hair over her shoulder and adjusted her bra straps. "As long as we're helping the economy, I see no reason for us to stop drinking."

I stood next to my friends trying not to judge them for flirting with someone old enough to be my father. I smiled at the man but felt completely invisible when he glanced at me—glanced *through* me, actually.

"We'll each have a Margarita," Lacie said.

Dave nodded and began pouring tequila and sweet and sour mix into a silver shaker, scooping ice into two pint glasses. "Predictable," he teased, winking at my two friends.

I continued to watch as Dave finished making the two drinks that he handed off to Jasmine and Lacie before walking away to help another group of guests. My friends sauntered off to find a table, also oblivious to the fact that I was still standing there, drinkless. *Oh, okay. Guess I don't need a drink.* I studied the bar to make sure I didn't miss something, then looked at my finger to see if my engagement ring had magically appeared. I pouted before joining my friends, who had already begun drinking. "You guys, he completely ignored me."

Jasmine frowned, her big lips covered in crimson lipstick. "You were standing next to us, weren't you?"

Lacie nodded. "I ordered drinks for all of us, didn't I?"

I shrugged. "He looked right through me. We even made eye-contact, but he didn't seem to notice."

Jasmine handed me her margarita. "Dave must've misheard us. I'll go get another one."

"Get us some shots while you're at it," Lacie said before sipping from a big, red, plastic straw.

Jasmine headed back to the bar, pushing through the crowd as if she were a movie star trying to avoid the paparazzi.

I sat beside Lacie, placing Jasmine's original margarita on the table in front of me. "Why did he ignore me? I have money just like everyone else. And I'm a server, so I tip well!"

"You should know better than anyone, then."

"Know what?" I winced after taking a sip of the drink. *If the world doesn't end tonight, this might just kill me.*

"That this whole industry is a game. When you're dressed like a nun, you won't get a chance to score."

I glanced at my clothes before glaring at her. "What's wrong with what I'm wearing?"

She shrugged. "It screams *I'm in a relationship.*"

"But I am!"

Another shrug. "You *really* think bartenders care? They wanna see some titties!"

Annoyed, I took a larger sip of the margarita. I winced again, but my body warmed immediately. "That's stupid. It's freezing outside!"

Lacie laughed. "I'll give you ten bucks if you take your undershirt off. I guarantee the bartender will give you a free drink."

"I refuse to use myself as a piece of meat." After taking another generous sip, I felt my confidence shake through some cobwebs, making its way back into the public. "I have a brain."

"But if it weren't for us, you wouldn't have a drink."

I scowled.

Jasmine brought over another margarita and two shot glasses filled with tequila. She placed one in front of Lacie. "Dave is *so sweet*! He told me these were on the house."

Seriously? Even my own friend forgot about me? I folded my arms over my chest, my confidence returning to its fetal position in the shadows. "Great, thanks."

"Sorry," Jasmine said, not sounding the least bit sorry. "Dave only gave me two before walking away. He's used to it just being me and Lacie—you never come out with us."

Lacie winked at me. "Lose the undershirt. I know what I'm doing. He'll notice you."

I continued to drink my margarita, refusing to believe I needed to disregard my dignity simply to acquire a cocktail. "And I'm telling *you* I'm not gonna do that. I don't want any unnecessary attention. I have a boyfriend."

"Yeah, but you don't have a shot of tequila," Lacie repeated.

The girls laughed as I drank more, my level of self-confidence reaching an all-time low. *I'll show them. I don't need to dress like a slut. I just need to find a better bartender.*

Chapter Thirteen

ONE MORE DOUBLE margarita and shot of tequila later, I was stumbling out of Cabo Cantina, following Jasmine and Lacie as they debated which bar they wanted to go to next. I didn't care where we went, my lack of dinner allowing the alcohol to course through my lower intestines without any obstacles. The beachy night chilled my nose, both girls commenting on how cold they were.

"Don'tcha wish you had on a long sleeve shirt and pants, now?" I teased, pulling at the hem of my shirt, stretching the fabric further down than the V-neck I had over it.

Jasmine rolled her eyes. "Johnny V's is plenty warm. And I'll *actually* get a drink at the bar, unlike you."

I stuck my tongue out at her, hating that both she and Lacie had gotten my other drinks for me at Cabo Cantina because Dave still refused to acknowledge my existence.

"Is that Roxy Vaughn?" A deep male voice caught my attention from somewhere across the street.

I squinted into the night, the streetlights not helping my slightly blurred vision. "Who wants to know?"

An extremely handsome figure emerged from the shadows.

"Justin? Oh my God, hi!" I shouted.

He wrapped me in a hug, his slender, toned runner's body suddenly making me wish I hadn't worn the long-sleeve after all. "Well, well, well. You do have a life outside of school and Dine with Shamu." His surfer-dude drawl was even sexier than I remembered, and we had just worked a shift together a couple days ago. "Didn't you just tell me at work you didn't like coming to PB?"

"I sure did," I replied. "And I still don't. My friends dragged me here to celebrate the world ending."

"Celebrate?" he asked. "I thought most people were upset about it. I like how you shake things up."

I smiled. "I guess I'm actually celebrating the fact that every bar tonight has some sort of buy one get one free drink special."

Justin nudged my side with this elbow. "I don't think you're the same Roxanne I work with."

"Why, hello there," Jasmine said, stepping closer to Justin.

Lacie and Jasmine introduced themselves, their sudden hair twirling and hip twisting indicating that they, too, appreciated his sun-bleached hair, brown beard, angled face and dark brown eyes. I reminded my girlfriends that they had already met Justin at my house party.

Justin glanced at his phone before returning it to the pocket of his black jeans. "Well, if the Mayans are right, we've only got an hour left. Mind if I join in on the celebration?"

Before I could conjure a witty response in my head, Jasmine and Lacie nodded their heads eagerly, gesturing for him to follow them into Johnny V's. "They're handing out shots of vodka for a dollar!" Lacie said excitedly, pulling her ID out of her side boob to show to the bouncer. "I wish it was the end of the world every night!"

I nudged Justin back. "See? Drink specials."

Justin chuckled as he stood closer to me, his red and black flannel grazing my arm. He was always friendly at work—borderline flirty, really—but seeing him out of uniform was different. I felt an attraction to him I didn't feel when we were waiting tables together. Maybe it was the tequila or maybe it was the fact the world was supposed to end, but I suddenly wanted Justin to wrap me in his arms again so I could memorize the feel of his lean muscles.

"Where've you been so far?" he asked, showing his ID to the bouncer as well.

"Just Cabo Cantina," I said, showing the bouncer my ID last.

"Okay, well they have drink specials every night, so I don't think that's an end of the world special."

Once I walked through the doorway, I knew why they were offering such cheap booze. Compared to the last bar, this place was deserted. Only a few patrons sat with one another at the bar top. There were Beer Pong tables with solo cups sitting on them, but nobody was around to play. The music was loud, and the black lighting hurt my eyes, but my bank account was far too small for me to complain. One-dollar shots were ideal.

"How about you?" I asked, wondering just how drunk he was and why he was alone when he found me.

He shook his head. "First bar. Got started at home. Was about to meet some buddies at Tavern when I saw you. I already let them know we'd head over after this."

I liked how he said we—an indication that he wanted to hang out with me, too.

"C'mon losers!" Jasmine shouted over her shoulders. "Let's get some shots and then I gotta pee."

Justin chuckled and placed his palm on the small of my back, leading me toward the bar. I faintly wondered if he knew I was in a relationship, then wondered if he would even care before telling myself to go with the flow. *If Justin buys me a drink, then I'll have proved the girls wrong about this long-sleeved shirt, thing.* I waited to reach for the cash in my back pocket, hoping Justin would offer to pay for my shot.

The female bartender—all breasts, curves and lips—smiled at Justin, her hot pink lipstick washing out her pasty-white skin. "Hey there, good looking. We've got shots for a dollar tonight—end of the world special."

He dropped his hand from my back and placed it on the bar counter. I hated how I felt disappointed and jealous. "Any liquor is free game?"

The bartender nodded and leaned against the side of the bar. It was a miracle her bustier didn't burst. "Technically, just the well vodka, but I can pour *you* something special." When she winked, I felt a breeze from her long, fake eyelashes.

"Why don't you surprise me?" Justin responded, coyly.

I frowned. *The girls are right. Boobs control the universe.* I looked at my friends, who were smirking at me. I grabbed a dollar from my back pocket and handed it to Jasmine. "I already know what you're thinking, so shut up. Could you get me one? I really have to use the restroom. Oh!" I said, remembering Jasmine said she had to go as well. "You wanna come with?"

"I'm gonna get my shot first," she said, readjusting her bra, her eyes scanning Justin's lean muscles.

I sighed. "Be right back."

In the bathroom, I stared at myself in the mirror that hung above the sink. *What's wrong with me?* Instead of wanting to spend the potential last night on earth with my boyfriend, I wanted to get drunk with my girlfriends and get hit on by a coworker. Instead of wearing short shorts or a low-cut dress, I hid my hatred for myself behind baggy jeans and layered shirts. *I just wanna be noticed without being a slut. Is that so much to ask?* Drunk and questioning how ugly I must be, a memory flashed through my mind long enough to make me smile. *Lamont told me he liked the Roxanne in the baggy clothes, not the one who dressed like a hooker just to fit in.*

I pulled out my phone and scrolled to the unsaved number in my text messages, a small part of me wishing our last night on earth would've been spent together. *What're you up to, Stranger?* Before I could change my mind, I pressed send and shoved the phone back into my jean pocket. "Why am I like this?" I asked my reflection, leaning over the sink to get a better view of my eye shadow. "At least my new makeup setting spray is working." I then looked down at my covered-up cleavage and sighed. "Just shake it off, Roxanne. Your slutty friends can order drinks for you." When I turned to exit the restroom, an extremely skinny girl in a *very* form-fitting pink dress stumbled through the door, her legs wobbling like those of a newborn calf. Her black, thin-heeled stilettos made her at least three inches taller than me. Although caught off guard, we smiled at one another. She seemed to look right through me, but I stared at her intently, somehow recognizing her angled, oval face, green eyes and diamond nose piercing.

As I stressed my brain to recall her familiarity, I pushed open the restroom door and almost ran into a man standing in the hallway, his left foot resting on the wall behind him, his ballcap over his eyes, a grey sweatshirt hugging his chubby body.

And then everything came crashing down on me, my Deja-Vu nearly knocking me over.

"Leo? Is that you?"

The man looked at me, made eye contact and smiled, his teeth rimmed with brown, the one tooth missing behind his canine tooth. "Little Miss Roxanne. What're you doing here?"

"Me? What're *you* doing here? Pacific Beach doesn't really seem like your scene."

He gestured his head over toward the bar where there were a bunch of girls in tight dresses similar to the one his girlfriend was wearing, and a couple burly boys in hoodies and sideways hats. "It's not. It's my buddy's birthday and this is where he wanted to go." He looked me up and down, raising an eyebrow. "You look comfortable."

I rolled my eyes. "Look, it's cold outside. Just because I'm at a bar doesn't mean I need to be someone other than me."

He flashed a crooked grin. "I'm gonna assume you've been getting shit about it all night and decided to take it out on me."

My cheeks warmed.

"It's a good look on you."

"What?" I asked, surprised. "What did you say?"

"You look good," he emphasized. "My girl walks around like she strips for a living. It gets me free drinks though, so I'm cool with it."

I shook my head. "I'm invisible wearing this. Not the ideal situation when you're trying to get drunk." I sighed. "Even my dad subtly accused me of being a prude."

He shrugged. "I'd buy you a drink the moment I saw you."

I laughed. "Then maybe you should be my bartender because the others refuse to take my money."

His girlfriend exited the bathroom and wobbled right past us as if we were ghosts. Leonard smirked. "I gotta get over there before the bouncer kicks her out."

"It was great seeing you."

He opened his arms, inviting me in for a hug as if we'd been friends for years.

Although he was a stranger, something about him made me feel...*okay*. I graciously fell into his arms and accepted the embrace.

"Do you have Facebook?"

I pulled away and lifted an eyebrow. "It's 2012. Who doesn't have Facebook?"

"How about you add me, then?"

"I don't have a smart phone."

Leonard laughed. "It's 2012. Who doesn't have a smart phone?"

I playfully smacked his chest. "I'm an old-fashioned kind of gal."

He squeezed my forearm. "Would've never guessed by your outfit." He pulled his phone out from his pocket, clicked the internet icon and logged onto his Facebook page. "Why don't I add you, then?"

I smiled. "Now, we can definitely do that." He handed me the phone, so I typed *Roxanne Vaughn* into the search bar, found my profile and clicked *add friend* before giving the phone back to him. "As soon as I get home, I'll accept it. And it'll be official—we're friends."

He put the phone back in his pocket. "Just don't tell my girlfriend. She'll think I'm cheating."

"Only if you don't tell my boyfriend. He'll think the same exact thing."

We went our separate ways, my step a little bit lighter than when I entered the bathroom. The fluttering in my stomach came as a surprise, but suddenly, I felt pretty again. Once I returned to my girlfriends and my coworker, I found two full shots of vodka placed in front of the empty seat at the table they occupied. Jasmine sat across the table from Justin while Lacie sat in the seat directly next to him. They both were fighting for his attention, Lacie leaning closer and closer to his shoulder, Jasmine's breasts nearly popping out over the table. I took the empty seat, hating that I was too afraid to attempt to ask the bartender for a Coke so I could chase the vodka down.

I gulped, grabbed the first shot and threw it back. Pleasantly surprised, I smiled.

"Do you like it?" Justin asked.

"It's fruity!" I licked my lips. "I was expecting rubbing alcohol."

He grinned. "Well, I remembered you mentioning at work one day that you like fruity drinks, so I got you some super girly shit. Best part was seeing the bartender's face when I told her that's what I wanted for my 'special shot.'"

I stared at him, slowly connecting the dots. "You bought a drink for me? I thought you told her to surprise you?"

Jasmine and Lacie were now talking to one another across the table, seeming to have given up on gaining Justin's approval.

He chuckled. "I mean, *technically*, it was free. The bartender was about to pour me some scotch, but when you walked away, I decided to surprise you, instead."

Blushing, I grabbed the second shot and took it quickly, noticing that it tasted like how nail polish smells. I tried not to gag. "The one you gave me was *way* better."

He stood and walked over to me, extending his hand. "Why don't we get you another then?"

When I grabbed his hand, all of the blood rushed from my head to my fingers, and the electric current passing between us made the hairs on the back of my neck stand straight up. "It won't work. It's like I don't exist. God forbid I don't put my boobs on display."

He laughed, the sound deep and penetrating, my heart now picking up the pace. "Who decided that was the only way to get a drink?"

"Jasmine. Lacie. The bartender at Cabo Cantina. Boobastic over there behind the bar."

"Well, I've gotten drinks and I don't have tits." Justin placed his palm on my lower back again, which steadied me as the mixture of vodka and tequila kicked in. "You're gorgeous, Roxy. People act that way around you because they're nervous to talk to you."

I looked up at his white smile, confused. *Is he flirting with me or am I imagining things?* "Yeah, right. I'm not delusional."

"Well, I don't care what you think." He moved his hand, wrapping his arm around my shoulders, pulling me into his side. "We're gonna get little Miss I Don't Want to Show off My Boobs a drink."

My back jean pocket vibrated, reminding me that I had reached out to Lamont in the bathroom. I tried to ignore it, tried to continue to live in the moment with Justin, but my skin began to itch. *I'll check really quick without him noticing. I just need to see what he said.* When Justin turned to focus on the bartender, I took out my phone only to be overwhelmed with disappointment.

It was Zachary, asking where I was and if I was having a good time with the girls.

"Here you go, Roxy."

Feeling as if I'd been caught looking at pornography, I shoved the phone back into my pocket and smiled shyly at Justin, thanking him for the pretty pink drink he handed me. His long fingers brushed against mine momentarily before he asked the bartender for a double whiskey and Coke. I glanced over my shoulder and caught Leonard looking at me, his wink making me blush. *What is happening right now?* My phone vibrated again, but this time, I didn't care. Justin's dark brown eyes roamed over my face as if he'd never seen something so beautiful. *Who cares about Zach and Lamont? Justin is right here paying attention to me.* Nervous and self-conscious, I slurped my drink a little too quickly, Jasmine and Lacie coming up to join us as I swayed left and right.

"Let's go somewhere else. This place is boring," Lacie said, sounding annoyed.

"How about the beach?" I replied, my tongue rolling against my teeth, my words tumbling incoherently together.

Jasmine nodded. "There're more bars that way, too."

The last thing I could clearly remember was finishing my drink, a little bit of brain freeze, and then leaving Johnny V's with my and Justin's elbows linked together, my face cold from the wind, Justin's surfer dude drawl sending chills up and down my spine as he whispered, "Man, Roxy. I *really* wish you didn't have a boyfriend."

I felt another vibration, thought about Lamont, and hated myself for wishing that exact same thing, knowing that I would never have the courage to make that wish a reality.

#

"ROXANNE! MY FATHER called from his office, which was located next to the television room. "Can you come here, please?"

Although the world didn't end the night before, I was suffering from a hangover that made me wish it had. Zachary was working, so I was blissfully alone. I didn't have to explain why I had such a bad hangover, didn't have to hide the fact I spent most of the night trying not to kiss my coworker, and I didn't have to work at small talk when all I wanted to do was silently watch TV. Sherlock was curled up on my lap purring rhythmically, a sappy Disney movie playing on my father's big-screen TV.

I rolled my eyes. "Why?"

"Do you need to give me attitude? It's not like I asked you to do anything crazy."

"Not yet."

"It's not my fault you're hungover. I even made you a bagel this morning."

I looked down at Sherlock and patted his head. "You don't have to rub it in." I paused. "But thank you. The bagel was delicious."

My dad sighed. "You're gonna regret not listening to me."

Pausing the movie, I placed a newly annoyed Sherlock on the cushion beside me and stood, dragging my feet. "Okay, what's so important?"

Without turning to look at me, he shifted the computer screen in my direction. "What do you think?"

When I glanced at the monitor, I shrieked.

My dad held his finger up to his lips and shushed me. "Be quiet! I haven't told your mother yet. It's supposed to be a surprise."

I eagerly made my way to my dad's desk chair so I could get a better look at the picture. "You're surprising her by picking out a Christmas present for yourself?"

He chuckled and leaned back, interlacing his fingers on his lap. "I guess it's a present for *both* of us."

I smiled, my heart fluttering like the wings of a hummingbird. There, in the picture, was a litter of puppies—black, white, grey, brown and yellow colors swirling together. Their stubby legs and big, round heads blended in with one another, eight puppies attempting to get closer to their very tired looking mother. "When are you gonna get one?"

"Today."

"*What?*" I squealed.

My father placed his hand over my mouth. "Will you *please* get your act together? Your mother is upstairs and you're gonna give away the surprise."

I began bouncing up and down but lowered my voice to a whisper. "Can I come with you? Please?"

He chuckled. "Oh, so *now* Little Miss Don't Bother Me I'm Hungover wants to leave the house?"

I rolled my eyes. "Puppies change everything. What're you gonna tell Mom?"

After exiting the Internet window, he slipped on a brand-new pair of house shoes and shrugged. "I'm gonna tell your mom we're going to lunch. If you want to come, you can't act excited. Your mom'll think it's about food and then I'll have to listen to her explain how a diet works for the hundredth time."

Sherlock entered the office, rubbed against my calves and meowed at me. "I don't get *that* excited about food." I bent over to pick him up and cradled him in my arms like a baby. He began to purr. "*Actually*, I have a gym membership now and I've been eating healthy for about a month. *And* I've lost five pounds. So, *there*."

After holding Ruby, Anthony's hawk, a couple of weeks prior, I'd decided to cut sugar out of my diet and joined the gym on campus to shed some pounds, suddenly caring about my appearance in ways I hadn't cared about since before Zachary and I started dating. Anthony and I hadn't shared any more conversations since that day—with final tests and final papers taking over my life, my work schedule had dwindled down to one day a week—but when I did get the chance to briefly spot him across the Dine with Shamu restaurant, we exchanged smiles that were somehow shy and flirty at the same time. Now, without classes, my availability at work was wide open, so I was scheduled four or five times a week, and the last thing I wanted was to look like a fat cow in my already unflattering uniform.

My dad stood. "*Wow*. Five whole pounds." He rolled his eyes, laughing when I nudged his ribs with my elbow. "I honestly don't care what you talk about— just avoid anything with puppies. And your sister. I'm tired of the fertile versus infertile conversations."

I never told my parents about the secret trip Lucy and I took to the Zoo, not wanting to endure the fifth degree of questioning my mom would've thrown at me.

"You know deep down she's gonna get pregnant again, right? She's just not used to not getting what she wants when she wants it."

He held up his hands. "Don't want to hear it. Get your shoes—and change your shirt, dear God, you're a mess. I'll go get your mother."

After a quick wardrobe check and a fifteen-minute car ride later, we pulled up to a very fancy neighborhood filled with cookie cutter houses and red sports cars.

My mother glared at my father. "This isn't a restaurant."

My father smiled. "I guess not."

"I knew you were up to something. I heard Roxanne scream downstairs."

I'm sorry. Don't hate me, I tried to telepathically tell my father when he shook his head at me through the rear-view mirror.

"Are we looking at puppies?" Mother asked.

My father parked the car, unbuckled his seatbelt and shrugged. "So, what if we are?"

I climbed out of the car and closed the door behind me, suddenly nervous. *Is Mom gonna be okay with this? I mean, how could she say no to those chubby little things?*

"Seriously?" My mother glanced at her reflection in the window, pushing her bangs to the side, puckering her lips and pinching her cheeks. "If I had known we were meeting people, I would've put on lipstick."

I rolled my eyes. "These people want to sell their dogs. I don't think they'll care whether or not you put your lips on."

"And another thing," she added, ignoring me, zipping up her black sweatshirt. "Sweetie, are we ready for another dog? After everything that happened with Molly?"

My dad grabbed my mother's hand and pulled her in for an embrace. "It's been over a year. I think it'll be good for us."

Suddenly embarrassed, I walked ahead of my parents, heading toward an open garage door that had an animal pen set up. "Hurry up, slow pokes! Puppies!"

The breeder waved and welcomed us into her garage, her long, thick brown hair pulled into a high pony-tail, her dark blue eyeshadow and magenta lipstick a little overwhelming on her overly-tanned, wrinkled face. She smiled, a smudge of magenta coating her two front teeth. "Are you the Vaughns?" Her accent was thick—almost Italian—as if she'd spent most of her life in New Jersey.

I nodded and extended my hand. "I'm Roxy."

The breeder appeared confused until my dad introduced himself, then my mother, clarifying that I was their daughter.

"He showed me the photos of the pups on the computer and I just had to tag along," I said, resisting the urge to push past her so I could see the little lumps of puppy cookie dough just waiting for me to eat them up.

"My wife didn't know we were coming," my dad added, entwining his fingers with my mother's before kissing the back of her hand. "I wanted to surprise her with a little bundle of fur for Christmas."

My mom smiled at the breeder, shaking her head. "I'm not entirely sure we're ready for a puppy, but I'm willing to take a look."

The breeder nodded and gestured for us to follow, her brief eyebrow raise and subtle smirk confirming—to me at least—that nobody left her house without purchasing one of her puppies. "The few with the collars are already accounted for. Their owners should be picking them up this week. However, the naked ones are up for grabs."

I tried not to walk too closely behind the breeder, watching her feet to avoid stepping on her heels. When we reached the doggy playpen, I felt every single organ, muscle, tissue and bone of mine melt into a giant puddle. There, playing with one another as if they weren't being watched by complete strangers, was the litter of eight puppies my dad had shown me on the Internet, only they were a little bit bigger and ready to go home with their new owners. "Can we hold them?" I asked, no longer caring about pleasantries or being polite.

The breeder asked me to point out which one we wanted to look at. I turned to ask my dad for silent permission, to which he smiled and nodded, motioning for me to go ahead and pick one out. I examined the litter—focusing on the brown and white faces of those still available. The puppy that really caught my attention was the one snoozing in the corner alone. Unlike the others that had a shiny black coat on their backs, this one had tan patches spotting within the black. His ears were huge and floppy compared to his head, and his stubby legs were nothing but rolls even though he was happily sprawled out.

I swooned. "How about that one?"

The breeder reached over the pen and grabbed the pup, handing him to me as if I'd never held a puppy before. I placed each of my hands beneath the dog's armpits and pulled him in close, his soft fur and wet nose giving me a sense of comfort. I hadn't felt anything like it since I'd held Molly as a puppy.

"That's the last boy," the breeder mentioned. "Since these are of show dog breed, many buyers don't like the imperfections of his coat. He's bigger than the rest, though, so he definitely takes after his father."

I rubbed my cheek against the puppy's head and giggled when he licked my chin. "He's considered big? He weighs, like, five pounds!" When the puppy yawned, I cooed, the cuteness threatening to make me explode.

"He actually weighs eight pounds," the breeder said. "His siblings are four to five pounds."

My dad held out his hands and took the puppy from me, holding one hand behind the puppy's butt and the other under its chest. He looked directly into the puppy's big, black eyes and grunted. "What do you think? You want to come home with us?"

The puppy yipped and squirmed, trying to reach my father's chin with his little, pink tongue.

My mother took the puppy next and curled it against her chest where the puppy promptly rested his head and fell fast asleep.

I knew at that moment no matter how much my mom tried to reason with herself that a puppy was completely out of the question, that little bundle of rolls would be coming home with us tonight.

#

ONCE I PARKED my car in the employee lot, I flipped the visor down and studied my makeup for the hundredth time. My eyeshadow was light brown with a tint of orange glitter, my mascara dark brown, and my bronzer highlighted my high cheekbones. I puckered my lips and applied a bright pink lipstick now matching the bright pink bow tied around my ponytail. I readjusted the bobby-pins in my hair to keep any lose strands from going astray, and I readjusted my breasts to make sure they looked perky in the push-up bra I'd purchased at Victoria's Secret that weekend.

This had become my new routine at work for reasons that made me ashamed of having a boyfriend—a boyfriend that I didn't think about anymore because a new man had taken precedent over my thoughts. I no longer cared about how I looked in front of Zachary, but I cared *tremendously* about how I looked in front of Anthony. Having run into him nearly every shift as he and Peter pushed against the exiting Shamu Show patrons in order to attack the seagulls in the stadium, and having had at least five conversations since he let me hold Ruby, I realized I had developed a crush on him, and I wanted to look effortlessly flawless whenever he saw me.

Which meant I now spent an extra forty-five minutes getting ready for work.

I didn't see him every time I worked, but I never wanted to risk being seen as anything other than beautiful, so every day I was scheduled, I wore a bow that matched my lipstick, had eyebrows that were plucked, and had teeth that were whitened while I took a shower.

Unfortunately, my coworkers had also noticed the change in my appearance. My female coworkers questioned my intentions, asking who I was trying to impress. I convinced them I needed money to compensate because of the holidays and was trying to make more tips during my serving shifts, hoping they didn't realize I still dolled myself up when I was carving meat in the buffet room or washing dishes in the back. My male coworkers, on the other hand, flirted with me subtly: making sexual innuendos whenever the moment allowed, emptying the trash for me when I was given that closing duty, or playfully nudging me as we rolled silverware together.

My boyfriend also noticed my sudden interest in my appearance when I was at lunch one day eating with my coworkers. Still focused on my diet—and the eight pounds I'd lost—I was delving into a salad, trying not to be jealous that my coworkers were devouring the chicken and cheese enchiladas the cafeteria was serving that day. Zachary sat in the empty seat beside me without asking if someone else was sitting there and planted a kiss on my cheek.

My coworkers pretended to not notice how uncomfortable the environment suddenly became, and continued talking about how incredibly hyper the children were at Breakfast with Shamu that morning.

Zachary placed his hand on my leg. "You're all gussied up today. What's the occasion?"

I glanced at him and shrugged. "I always look nice when I'm at work."

"I mean, you're beautiful *all* the time, but you even have glittery bronzer on. You only wear that during special occasions."

Why do you know what bronzer is? I thought back to my birthday and his homosexual behavior. *Stop that, Roxanne. Don't think about it. Not now.* "I'm trying to make some extra money, that's all." The words spilled out easily, having practiced over and over again with my coworkers.

The sound of a bell made my salad toss itself in my stomach. I glanced over my shoulder and spotted a Harris' Hawk perched on the cafeteria roof, its head bobbing up and down, its big, black eyes on the lookout for its next kill. Then, walking through the entrance to the employee area from the park was Anthony, Ronnie and Peter. My breath quickened, the feel of Zachary's hand now weighing down on my thigh as if he were pushing a block of lead against me. *I need to hide. I can't let Anthony see me with Zachary. It would ruin everything.*

I leaned forward and hid my face in my hands, quickly trying to come up with a way out of this situation. My belt buckle dug into my belly, giving me an easy way out. "I'll be right back. I have to use the restroom." Without giving Zachary time to react, I hurried past my seated coworkers and snuck around the corner where our employee lockers were located. It was childish to hide—there was no doubt about that. However, being seen with my boyfriend by the boy I couldn't stop fantasizing about was not something I wished to endure.

I stared at myself in the mirror hanging over the sink and smiled at the pretty reflection staring back at me. I readjusted the bow around my ponytail and took a deep breath, wondering which of the three falconers would be present at the next Dine.

Anthony's dimples flashed through my mind, my face flushing scarlet. I washed my hands and exited the bathroom, seeing the rest of my coworkers heading back to Dine with Shamu via the employee only street. Zachary was standing outside the bathroom, leaning against the wall.

"You alright?" he asked, squinting at me, the sun shining off the cement. "Other than Christmas, I feel like I've barely seen you all break."

The urge to roll my eyes boiled just beneath the surface of my skin. "You and I have both been busy with work. Mom and Dad got the new puppy and I've been helping them with training and such. It's tough when our schedules are completely opposite, you know?"

He sighed. "I know—I just—I miss you. I was hoping we'd both get a day off to do something fun and stress free."

The bells of the bird sounded again. When I looked up, I could've sworn the hawk was staring right at me. Knowing that Anthony, Ronnie and Peter would be looking for it any second, I decided to cut the conversation short and tell Zachary what he wanted to hear. "Why don't we do dinner tonight after work? Just the two of us?"

Zachary smiled, the skin beside his eyes crinkling into small seagull feet. "I would love that."

"Okay, great!" I gave him a quick hug and turned away, needing to catch up to my coworkers. "See you tonight!" I shouted, not bothering to feel guilty about Zachary's frowning face. I lifted my apron just high enough so I wouldn't trip over it, slowing once I reached Cassandra. Only then did I decide to look back.

Zachary was no longer standing there, but a certain round-faced falconer was smiling at me, his Harris' Hawk perched peacefully on his wrist.

#

OMAR AND ZACHARY were sitting at Zachary's father's antique dining room table, their laptops in front of them, their fingers clicking the same three keys on the keyboard repetitively. Although they invited me to join like old times—I'd learned how to play League of Legends while in Sonoma as an attempt to bond with my long-distance boyfriend—I politely declined, telling them I had some writing to do. It wasn't a total lie because I did need to fix the short story Professor Palmer critiqued, but I mainly didn't want to play because I hated Omar and he tended to yell at me every time my character got killed.

Before I actually dug into my story, however, I decided to peruse Facebook because I wanted to let my brain go numb for a little while. My timeline wasn't all that interesting, my "friends" posting selfies with inspirational quotes beneath them, or photo after photo of my coworkers with dolphins or killer whales behind them, the trainers usually allowing those who worked at the nearby restaurants special behind the scenes opportunities for animal interactions.

It made me wonder. *If I became closer to the trainers, maybe they'd let me do some of those cool things, too.* I spoke to some whale trainers more than others because we usually worked the same hours, and we were on a first name basis, so I thought adding them on Facebook wouldn't be weird.

I clicked on Dominick's page, then clicked on his friends list and began scrolling, stopping at the names that stuck out to me. I squinted at the photos beside those names and felt my stomach churn. The first trainer had a profile picture of herself in a Sea World wetsuit with Ruby, the Harris' Hawk, on her wrist. The second trainer had a profile picture of herself in a Sea World wetsuit, also with Ruby on her wrist.

The third, fourth and fifth all had the same.

My infatuation with Anthony burned into a pile of ashes, which promptly blew out of the window and into the wind. *All of this time, I thought I was special. He lets every single female trainer at Sea World hold his bird. Every. Single. One.* I closed my laptop and excused myself from the table, telling Zachary I had to use the restroom. Omar ignored me as I squeezed behind him, our mutual hate for one another not seemingly enough of a reason for Zachary to make us stop hanging out with one another. I walked up the narrow, creaky, wooden staircase and into the tiny bathroom, the uneven doorframe not allowing the door to close all the way. I stared at my reflection in the dusty mirror—pale skin, hazel eyes, dark eyebrows and a note of exhaustion hiding just beneath the surface.

I wanted to cry.

Here I was, again, lusting after some guy who made me feel special for two seconds—a guy who *obviously* used his bird to get into girls' pants—when I should've been lusting after my boyfriend, who really did go out of his way to make me feel special, even if he also did have a knack for driving me crazy.

"Why can't I just be happy with what I have? It's not so bad. Why do I always want something more?"

I turned on the ancient faucet and cupped my hands beneath the trickling stream of water, splashing my face with the small puddle I managed to hold. *Get a grip, Roxanne. Instead of always pointing out your boyfriend's flaws, why don't you focus on his positive qualities?* When I opened the bathroom door, I jumped, Zachary standing there with a silly grin on his face.

"You scared the bajeezus out of me," I said, my palm now resting over my racing heart.

He placed his hands around my lower back and pulled me into his pelvis. "I just wanted to give you a kiss." He frowned. "You seem a little down. I wanted to cheer you up."

I leaned into his lips and felt my shoulders relax, the comfort of him—the comfort of knowing he loved me—easing my anxiety. It was in that moment I realized that if I really wanted this relationship to work, I'd have to start putting some real effort into it and stop coming up with excuses as to why it was destined to fail.

Chapter Fourteen

ONE OF THE things I hated most about working at Sea World was that the theme park was open three hundred and sixty-five days a year. Whether it was one hundred degrees in the shade, or whether lightning was striking right above the park, employees were required to show up for their shift and smile at guests as if it were just an ordinary day. Holidays, in particular, were the busiest days of the year. It was as if everyone outside of the United States decided that Thanksgiving, Christmas and New Year's Day were the perfect days to go to an American theme park, as if our holidays didn't actually exist. Lazy Americans also decided to come to theme parks on holidays because they didn't want to cook or do dishes. They, too, didn't care that they were the reasons servers, just like me, couldn't spend those special days with friends and family of their own.

This year, instead of going out on New Year's Eve and partying like a normal twenty-two-year-old, I was working the last two Dine with Shamu dinners, then going home to take care of Loki and Sherlock. I didn't mind, initially. My parents were going to be in Los Angeles with the Lovelace clan, so I thought Zachary would jump at my invite to drink champagne together and ring in the New Year making love. However, when my boyfriend informed me he was invited to drink at a bar with some buddies from high school, and would rather catch up with them since I had to work until ten anyway, I suddenly *hated* having to work holidays.

I wanted to attend a house party with Jasmine and Lacie just so I could make Zachary feel bad for not wanting to spend the holiday with me, but the girls would be arriving at the house at nine, and I didn't want to show up to a strange house alone.

For some odd reason, though, about thirty minutes into the final Dine of the night, I began to feel nauseous and light headed. I was handing a table two sodas and an iced tea when the world beneath my feet tilted side to side. My panic rose into my throat and I feared I might fall over my own feet. Although I wanted to cry, I smiled at the guests, held my tray between my ribcage and my hand, and asked each table if they needed anything else.

Thankfully, the Shamu interaction had just begun, so everyone was happy with their food and drinks, their eyes transfixed on the white and black whales swimming in the pool.

I walked through the double doors leading to the kitchen and closed my eyes in an attempt to steady myself. *Do not cry in front of your coworkers.*

Dominick placed a gentle hand on my shoulder. "Roxy, are you alright?"

I shook my head and leaned my hip against the server table, my stomach tying itself into tight knots. "I'm not sure what's happening right now. I'm just—I'm super dizzy."

Justin poured me some water from the soda machine and handed it to me. "Have you eaten anything today?"

I sipped the ice-cold water and nodded. "I literally just ate a sandwich and yogurt on break."

Jennifer walked over next, placing her palm on my forearm. "Do you need Ibuprofen or something?"

"I took some Aleve already," I told her. I didn't elaborate, but she nodded her understanding, our conversations about shark week revolving around how horrible our cramps were for the second and third days. She squeezed my forearm, her sympathy radiating through me. Tears began to touch my eyelids, the want to vomit making its way through my body. "I don't know if I can work—can any of you take my tables?" I sniffled and turned away from my coworkers, embarrassed. *Stop crying.* "I think I need to go home."

Dominick and Justin nodded. "We can split the tables. We're not that busy."

Jennifer wrapped me in a bear hug. "Are you sure you'll get home okay?"

I shrugged. "I'm gonna call Zach and see if he can come pick me up." I grabbed my elbows, shivers running over my skin. "Is William gonna hate me?"

Justin chuckled. "We'll talk to him. Just let him know you're sick."

"Are you guys sure?"

Dominick nodded. "You're really pale, Roxy. Please get home safe."

After I grabbed my purse from my locker, I walked over to the management counter and asked William if I could go home because I was feeling sick. As another wave of dizziness washed over me, I grasped onto the edge of the counter, my knuckles turning white. I began to cry.

"Roxy, what's going on?" William grabbed my elbow and pulled me out the side doors that lead to a path where guests were able to enter the splash zone of the Shamu Stadium. It was empty while Dine with Shamu was in session, so I was free from prying and judgmental eyes.

I tried to stop crying, but the sobs now racked my chest, making coherent speech nearly impossible. "I—I—I feel d—d—dizzy and I'm—af—afraid I'm g—g—gonna faint or—throw up—or both."

He gave me a hug and patted my back. "Do you have someone who can drive you to the hospital or something?"

I nodded into his chest. "I'm gonna call my boyfriend."

"Text me later and let me know that you're okay." He frowned. "I'm sorry you're feeling so terrible. We'll make sure your tables are covered."

As I walked to the parking lot, I dialed my boyfriend's number. It was only nine. He wasn't hanging out with his friends until ten, so he should've been at home getting ready. The call went to voicemail. I tried again thinking that maybe he was in the bathroom. Frustrated and feeling more nauseous than before, I opened the front door of my little car and slid into the driver's seat, not sure how I was going to get home. I called Zachary again, still without an answer. *Why isn't he answering?* I continued to cry. *I have to get home.* After taking a deep breath, I reached into my purse and grabbed my water bottle. *Okay. I can do this. I don't have anyone who can help. I have to take care of myself.* I took a generous sip of water and forced myself to breathe. *Remember what Mom and Dad said – don't let your anxiety control you.* Although a panic attack was climbing its way up each vertebra, threatening to take over my sanity, I pushed the symptoms deep inside, convincing myself that I could get home just fine. For fifteen minutes, I repeated *I'm okay, I'm okay, I'm okay*—the usually short drive having morphed into a cross country road trip in my mind.

But I did it—I made it home safely, ignored Loki whining at me from his play pen, crawled into bed fully clothed in my uniform, and listened to Sherlock meow repeatedly from the bedroom doorway. *Why hasn't Zach called me back? I'm scared. Something is wrong with me.* I dialed his phone number for a fourth time, leaving a distressed voicemail when he didn't answer again. My panic intensified, pins and needles running through my fingertips, my stomach feeling as if someone had rammed a knife through me, my head now throbbing behind my eyes. I couldn't stop sobbing, Loki's pleas for love upstairs now making my heart hurt, the guilt of being unable to care for him overwhelming me to the point of breaking.

I ran into my bathroom and fell to my knees in front of the toilet. Dry heaving and shaking, chills began their journey from my forehead to my heels, my skin burning red like an electric stove top. My chest felt heavy, my heart beating so quickly, I wondered if I was experiencing a heart attack. *I'm dying. I'm going to die alone in a bathroom.* I tried swallowing, my mouth dry, throat feeling like it was closing shut. *My cat is gonna eat my face. The dog is gonna pee itself. My heart is gonna to explode. Zach is cheating on me with one of his friends. Why else wouldn't he answer his phone? H's probably sucking Omar's dick.* I inhaled, unable to catch a breath, my lungs refusing to function properly. *He's never there when I need him. I'm all alone. I'm gonna die all alone.*

The sound of my phone vibrating against the tile broke my panicked thoughts, my boyfriend's name flashing across the front screen.

"Zachary," I wheezed. "Where are you?"

He didn't answer, loud laughter and an echo of voices pulsing through the speaker.

"Zach?" I asked again. "Are you there?"

"Hi Roxanne," he slurred. "How's work going?"

I cried even harder, another round of dry heaving suffocating me, my muscles contracting painfully. "Didn't you listen to my voicemail?"

Zachary's friends were talking over me. Instead of listening to me and responding, he spoke to his friends as if we weren't on the phone together.

"Zach? Can you hear me? Can you please come over?" I begged. "I think something is wrong. I'm having a heart attack. I don't want to be alone. *Come over.*"

The phone beeped and fell silent, Zachary hanging up on me.

Not knowing what else to do, and fearing one of my major organs was on the verge of failure, I dialed 9-1-1. My head was spinning, my body simultaneously on fire hot and ice cold, the knots in my stomach tripling in strength, my chest feeling bruised and battered, and the pounding behind my eyes had spread to my ears, my pulse beating like a drum. The dispatcher asked a couple of questions, obviously annoyed by my uncontrollable weeping and loud heaving, before getting my address and informing me that paramedics were on the way.

I texted Zachary to let him know the ambulance was en route and placed my cheek on the tile, the rest of my body covering bathmats in front of the toilet and sink.

My phone vibrated again, and when I answered, my boyfriend's incoherent worry made me feel ten times worse.

What's wrong?

I can't drive. I'm fucked up.

Maybe my friend can drive.

Call Omar. He can get me.

Are you okay?

Wait, I'm with Omar. He said he'll try to sober up to drive me.

Want me to stop by the store and get you a drink?

The more questions he asked, the angrier I grew, hating that he was too drunk to help me when I was dying. Instead of talking, I hung up on Zachary, left my phone in the bathroom and zombied my way up the stairs, just as two well-built and fully bearded firemen rushed through the front door.

Loki barked a couple of times before deciding the group of men—and one butch woman—who were now in the house were not an immediate threat, and wagged his tail while the paramedics sat me down on the couch and hooked me up to some beeping machine. The men fussed over me while the woman battered me with questions that made me feel insignificant, weak and lacking good judgement. They told me my vitals were fine except for my quickened pulse and raised blood pressure, and inquired if I needed to get in the ambulance to go to the hospital. I shook my head, embarrassed that I'd called for help, and silently watched as the first responders picked up their equipment. One of the men stayed behind, needing me to sign a waiver, which confirmed I didn't want, or require, a ride to the hospital.

"Are you on any anxiety medicine?" he asked, much kinder than how the firewoman spoke to me.

I shook my head. "I'd been for a little while but stopped. Didn't think I needed it. I dunno." Although he was a medical professional and was sworn to confidentiality, I didn't mention that Zachary was the reason I stopped taking it and that my emotions had been unpredictable ever since.

The man nodded. "I'd recommend taking it again—consistently. From what you told us, I'd say you just suffered a massive panic attack. They can make you feel like you're dying or having a heart attack. Your nerves can strain your muscles and your brain has the power to play tricks on you."

I handed him the clipboard with the paperwork on it, but avoided eye contact. "I'm sorry I wasted your time. I'm sure there's *actual* patients that need you right now."

He smiled before shoving the clipboard into his satchel. "Honestly, I'm glad it was just a panic attack. I always prepare for the worst on New Year's Eve."

When the man left, I filled Loki's bowl with food and let him out of his pen so he could eat and drink water before taking him out into the backyard to do his business. I picked up the pup, brought him downstairs with me, cuddled on the couch and turned on the television, watching a replay of the countdown that happened in New York earlier. My panic may have subsided, but a constant thud still remained behind my eyes, a slight tingle nipped at my fingertips and the pain in my stomach had only begun to dissipate. I curled my arms around Loki and inhaled his scent, his puppy fur tickling my nose.

With Loki's steady breathing and Sherlock curled up next to my feet, I wound up dozing off, not caring that my phone was still where I left it in the bathroom.

At some point during the early hours of the morning, I woke abruptly, Loki and Sherlock no longer next to me, the television black, my stomach grumbling with hunger, my heart aching for human affection. I didn't want to believe Zachary had completely ignored me and focused instead on drinking with his friends, not caring that I thought I was dying. However, as I wandered through the dark hallway to my bedroom, I knew that he did, in fact, choose drinking cheap whiskey over making sure I was safe and healthy.

It was in that moment that I truly questioned why Zachary and I were in a relationship when it was blatantly clear the love that had once blazed between us had simmered out completely.

#

THE NEXT TWO weeks of winter break flew by with work, sleep, Loki and avoiding my boyfriend keeping me busy. Lacie and Jasmine had joined me for a couple booze-induced movie nights. Luke had dragged me out to lunch in Hillcrest twice so he could brag about his new boyfriend. My parents fought over differing opinions on how to successfully train a Beagle puppy. Most importantly, I started taking Lexapro every night before bed, deciding that Zachary's opinion no longer mattered, *especially* because he was too intoxicated to care about me on New Year's Eve.

He'd shown up when the sun was already in the sky, let himself into my parents' house, and woke me from a nightmare filled slumber. He wreaked of cheap whiskey and mozzarella sticks, and his drunken concern only annoyed me further, his inability to form coherent sentences climbing to the top of the list of reasons why I hated my boyfriend. When he cuddled behind me, his erection digging into my lower back, I wished he'd never shown up, his bear-like snores bringing back the headache that had finally disappeared behind my eyes.

When he left later that afternoon, complaining of a hangover and wanting a shower, I turned off my phone and threw it in my nightstand drawer, knowing without a shadow of a doubt that I wanted nothing to do with him anymore.

A week of different color roses and chocolate bars left on the front porch softened my resolve a bit, but not enough to convince me to answer Zachary's phone calls.

242

I told my parents we were going through a rough patch, intentionally leaving out that my panic had gotten the best of me and I'd called 9-1-1 truly believing I was dying. The last thing I wanted to do was make my parents more embarrassed about the fact that I was their daughter. Even work was hard to get through, my complete mental breakdown making my coworkers act differently around me—as if standing too close to me would set off another crying fit, forcing me to leave work early. I knew I was in a funk when I found myself excited to be sitting in Jocelyn Palmer's classroom again. The other students seemed frightened, their last interaction with her probably including a conversation that crushed their hopes and dreams, much like she did with me.

Three minutes before class was officially scheduled to begin, a man with tan skin, wavy, thick brown hair, and wire-thin reading glasses on the bridge of his pointed nose dropped his backpack on the table at the front of the room and unzipped it. He pulled out three large paperbacks and a notebook before looking up at the students. "Welcome to English whatever number the school assigned this stupid class."

I laughed along with the other students, this man looking quite familiar. I hadn't taken any of his classes, yet, but I remembered seeing him in one of my previous classes for one very brief moment.

"In this class, I will be teaching you how to properly use your writing assignments as tissues because crying is a key component of the course."

Although some of the other students gasped, eyes bulging from their heads, I found a strange sense of comfort in the man's voice, and the slight Mexican accent that danced with some of his words.

"Ezra Castillo," a woman's voice snapped from beyond the classroom doorframe.

The sound of high heels on the tile echoed into the room as the man at the front of the classroom pushed his glasses past his forehead and into his glossy mane. "My oh my, Professor Palmer. Are you aware that you're late to your own class?"

In walked Jocelyn Palmer, blonde curls pulled back into a ponytail, cat earrings dangling from her lobes, a pastel green sweater somehow hugging her curves without the slightest bit of sensuality. The mood in the room shifted to something foreign – something I had never experienced before in Jocelyn Palmer's classroom. It was light and airy—on the verge of flirtatious. It was then I remembered Professor Castillo bursting in on one of my previous classes with

Professor Palmer, and her telling me Professor Castillo was one of the professors I'd be dealing with if I made it into the MFA program.

Jocelyn looked down at her naked wrist. "Looks like it's get out my class o'clock."

Ezra smiled. "I was hoping I could join you on your first day."

Jocelyn pushed past Ezra and his horizontal red and white striped shirt, placed her satchel on the table and pulled out a stack of papers, which she shoved against Ezra's chest. "Then make yourself useful and pass out the syllabi for me."

After returning his glasses to the bridge of his nose, he winked at the professor and began handing out a packet to each student, a total of about twenty-five people in attendance.

Professor Palmer sighed, shook her head and grinned, her dark purple lipstick accentuating her big, white, square teeth. "I recognize some familiar faces, but those of you who are new to my classroom, I'm Jocelyn Palmer. Welcome to Flash Fiction. Unlike every other class you've probably taken up to this point, instead of having every writing assignment *full* of unnecessary *fluff*, every single one of your stories will be *less* than one page."

"Clearly, she didn't get the memo for her own syllabus," Professor Castillo murmured to me as he placed a five paged packet in front of me.

"Ezra," Professor Palmer snapped. "Don't you have a class to teach?"

He smirked. "Not until nine."

"Then why don't you take the next four and half hours to prepare your lecture and let me teach my students the *beauty* of Flash Fiction?"

"I'll see you tonight."

When he left the room, Professor Palmer's cheeks flushed pink, her hazel eyes sparkling like the glitter on her acrylic nails. I smiled down at my desk thinking that if two people who liked to make their students miserable were happily in love, then anything was possible.

#

A FEW WEEKS into the Spring school semester, Zachary asked if I could come to Sea World two hours before my shift because he wanted to give me a surprise. Initially, I ignored the invitation because Zachary and I hadn't seen much of each other since he didn't come to my rescue on New Year's Eve, and I knew his "surprise" would be yet another attempt to earn my forgiveness.

However, curiosity got the best of me in the end, so I agreed to his request. I pulled into the East parking lot of Sea World two hours before my scheduled shift and met Zachary next to the entrance of the Wild Arctic attraction. He was in the

244

blue t-shirt, black basketball shorts and rubber boots that were worn by employees who had to step into the water at some point during their shift. Unfortunately, Sea World made the entire zoological staff wear that uniform—even those that led guests from the check-in room next to the Dolphin Stadium to Dolphin Point so that *real* trainers could help guests into the water to interact with the dolphins. So, Zachary was able to lie to his friends and family about his job because of his uniform even though he *wasn't* a dolphin trainer. I often corrected him when he said he was an assistant trainer, informing everyone within earshot that he was actually a glorified dressing room attendant.

He reached for my hand and pulled me in for a kiss. I turned to the side, giving him my cheek, pointing to my bright red lips. "Don't wanna turn you into a drag queen." *Don't want to kiss you right now, either.*

"You've seen me in eyeliner," he said, fingers intertwined with mine. "You know how good I look in it."

Cringing, I turned away. *The only straight man who looks good in eyeliner is Johnny Depp.* "So," I said, needing to change the subject. "What is this big *surprise* you have planned for me?"

"If I told you, it wouldn't be a surprise."

We walked in silence for a bit, the park already surprisingly crowded for the morning. Although technically it was the "off season" for San Diego, winter was far from cold, so many individuals trying to escape *real* weather conditions were in town for a warmer vacation. Thankfully, it was no longer Christmas time! The CD that repeated the same fifteen songs daily on the speakers had changed to the music that was played at the different animal shows. Zachary stopped at a bench next to the Wild Arctic gift shop, flashing a goofy grin in my direction.

"You gonna buy me a stuffed animal or something?"

He shook his head. "I talked to some of the trainers, pulled some strings and got us into a behind the scenes tour."

Although I wanted to remain mad at him, I couldn't hide my excitement. I bounced up and down, a squeal escaping my lips. "Really?" I wrapped my arms around him and kissed him on the cheek, forgetting about my lipstick. "You're the best! I've always wanted to do this.

He flushed, his grin spreading from ear to ear. He didn't even try to wipe off the lipstick mark I stamped onto his skin. "Well, I know you've been stressed about school already and I thought this might be a good distraction."

You mean a distraction from you being a horrible boyfriend? We met with a small group of people who were also participating in the tour, a young man in a uniform that matched Zachary's informing us all to follow him.

"You know, if I became a trainer, I could do things like this for you more often," Zachary said, nudging my ribs.

You're terrible with animals. I'm not going to encourage you to do something you suck at just so you can take advantage. "Not being able to do stuff like this all of the time is what makes it special."

As we followed the group, Zachary continued to talk in a rushed whisper, informing me he had to get assigned a new Master Teacher because the original one was going to fail him. He admitted he didn't want to teach history anymore, and asked me what I thought about him training for the next swim test, which would give him the chance to pursue his *true passion*—training animals. I bit the inside of my cheek, reminding myself he was just venting because he'd been having such a difficult time with his original master teacher and had hurt feelings because someone didn't like him. *He can't be serious. All he's ever talked about is wanting to be a teacher. Even when I was in high school, he did nothing but brag about how he was gonna be the best history teacher ever once he graduated college. Did I miss something?* Thankfully, I didn't have to say anything because a *real* trainer showed up to lead the group into a back area where a giant walrus was playing around in a large, square enclosure.

His name was Dozer—he was blind, so his eyes looked a bit swollen and strange, but his rambunctious attitude was the *cutest* thing I'd ever seen from a blubbery mammal. Each individual in the group went up to the tall, metal bars and "gave" the walrus a "behavioral command," the trainer actually doing the command beside them. When I walked up for my turn, the trainer had Dozer blow me a kiss with his huge left flipper, and every part of me melted into a puddle beneath my non-slip shoes. *A walrus makes me feel more special than my boyfriend does. That's just sad.*

"How long have you been a trainer?" I asked the man with the long, brown mustache, green eyes and olive colored skin.

He smiled, his yellow teeth crooked much like my boyfriend's. "I've been doing this for four years now, but I was an assistant trainer for three years before and volunteered at a homeless dog shelter for two years before that."

I glanced over my shoulder at Zachary, hoping he was listening. "So, you must've known you wanted to be a trainer when you were a little kid?"

The man nodded and held up a bucket that had a bunch of fish in it. "You ready to feed him?"

I cringed when I grabbed a hold of the slimy little walrus snack and threw it through the bars where Dozer could catch it.

"Now, hold the back of your hand out to him."

Doing what I was told, Dozer pressed his mouth against my skin and gave me a kiss. Chuckling, I clapped my hands together. "This is a romantic walrus."

Zachary joined my side as the group continued forward for the next part of the tour. "Having fun?"

I nodded. "This has been wonderful."

"Wouldn't it be great to be able to do this more often?"

"Zach, I already answered that earlier. It's special because it's something we don't do often." I looked at his green eyes, not trying to hurt his feelings but tired of listening to his arrogance. "These people don't become trainers so they can brag to everyone about being a trainer. They do it because they have a passion for animals, and they've had that passion since they were little."

I could tell my boyfriend was getting upset with me, but I didn't care. I hated how he only wanted to do things to try to impress people or show off to strangers just so he could feel good about himself. "Why is it so hard for you to believe that I have a passion for animals?"

"Because I've *seen* you interact with Sherlock and Loki and you're quite literally the *worst* trainer I've ever seen. You're rough with my cat and now he scratches people. And you *still* haven't learned *not* to touch Loki when you walk into the house because he piddles, and my dad has told you *at least* a million times to pet him outside. If you can't handle a cat and a puppy, how are you supposed to handle an animal that weighs over a thousand pounds?"

We walked into the back area of the polar bear encounter, where we found two majestic creatures cuddling with one another against a cement wall in the back of their extremely well protected cage. It reminded me of one of the cages that had been constructed for the dinosaurs in Jurassic Park. The trainer began speaking about how careful each animal handler must be when dealing with polar bears because while they may appear cuddly and adorable, they wouldn't hesitate to rip a human being apart in a second.

I gestured at the bear. "Did you hear that?"

"Loud and clear."

I sighed. "Why do you want my opinion when you obviously don't want to hear what I have to say?"

He glared at me. "You don't support a damn thing I do."

"Fine. Become a trainer. Get eaten by a bear."

"Fine. I will."

We didn't speak for the rest of the tour, not bothering to say goodbye to one another when I had to run to the other side of the park. I wished at that moment that Zachary would just break up with me so for once, I wouldn't seem like the villain in our relationship.

#

THE WEEK BEFORE Spring Break season was notoriously slow at Sea World, so I was stuck inside of the buffet room, slicing beef for the guests who were smart enough to come to the park *before* the craziest week of the year.

The worst part about being the meat carver was the fact that you had to smile at every guest who walked in, and it was usually the same people over and over again because one person from each table would collect seconds and desserts for their friends and family watching the whales. The best part about being the meat carver was the fact that you could people watch through the windows and open doors, and pretty much get paid for zoning out for an hour.

It also gave me the opportunity to learn more about the killer whales because the trainers' microphones were wired to the speakers throughout the restaurant, and once the patrons were seated at the tables, the buffet was blissfully quiet. I loved the educational portion of the show because I *wanted* to know more—the whales' weight, dorsal fin shape meanings, natural behavior versus trained behaviors, and their differing blowhole noises.

After each table was happily served with their plates piled high, I placed the knife and tongs on the cutting board and leaned my back against the wall, the female trainer's melodic voice lulling me to sleep.

"Roxy," Jennifer said, walking through the entry doors to my right.

I stood up straight and smiled. Although she had become one of my best friends, she was my Food Lead at work, and I respected her as my superior. "What's up?"

"One of the falconers is asking for you."

Confused, I removed my cutting glove, shoved it into my apron pocket and walked outside where I found Anthony, tapping the toe of his shoe as if he was nervous. When he beamed at me, I couldn't help but return the gesture. He and I hadn't talked in a while—in fact, I'd only seen Ronnie as of late—but whenever we

248

did happen to cross one another's paths, we smiled warmly. It still made my heart somersault into my throat, but I usually repressed my crush, reminding myself he was a womanizer because every female trainer had a picture with *his* bird on *her* wrist.

"Hi, Tony," I said casually. "Everything alright?"

He nodded and gestured for me to step closer, glancing around him to see if anybody was standing near us.

I raised an eyebrow and remained silent, enjoying his struggle.

"So, I know you have a boyfriend and I'm engaged, but I think you should give me your number so we could—chat—and, you know—be—be friends."

You're engaged? I wanted to ask. "Are you okay? You seem – antsy," I replied coolly, hoping he couldn't hear how loudly my heart was pounding.

He licked his lips. "I'm just not supposed to be here, but I haven't had a chance to talk to you lately. Didn't want to miss out – again."

I shrugged and nodded, reaching into my pocket for my serving notepad and a pen. "I could always use another friend," I said, scribbling my number on the small paper. "I'm flattered it was so important of you to ask me."

"Don't sound so surprised. I thought we've been getting to know each other pretty well as of late," he said, his smile infectious. "I'll text you later."

"Sounds good." Suddenly nervous and uncomfortable, I gestured behind me. "But I gotta get back in there. The meat won't cut itself."

The bird on his wrist spread her wings in a stretch before shaking her tail feathers. The bells on her anklets jingled, my pulse racing even faster. "Um—yeah. Same. Pinnipeds is under attack. Just wanted to make sure I caught you before the Dine ended."

"Don't be a stranger," I said before I walked back into the buffet room.

Jennifer was waiting for me. "Everything okay?"

I tried to relax my smile, but I couldn't. "Tony just asked for my phone number." I paused, letting his words sink in. Then, I frowned. "He's *engaged.* Did you know that?"

She shook her head. "That's surprising. He's asked Julia for her phone number a couple times now. As far as I know, she's turned him down every time.."

I blinked, doing everything to hide my hurt feelings. Julia was one of the newer employees at Dine with Shamu. She was a knockout—*easily* the prettiest girl at Dine, trainers included. Her skin was tan from the two years she lived in Hawaii. Her hair was shiny, dark brown and wavy in all the right places, light brown highlights radiating in the sun. She was also skinny, swimming almost daily because she wanted to become a dolphin trainer, and she needed to pass a vigorous swim test in order to do so. Although I'd been working out and dieting successfully, her athletic figure, pointy nose, angled chin and high cheekbones pushed my self-esteem right back into the hole it had dared crawl out of.

"I wouldn't dwell on it," Jennifer added, noticing the color drain from my face. "You have a boyfriend. He's engaged. He shouldn't be asking for girls' numbers anyway."

"He said he wanted a friend."

Jennifer looked at me skeptically, her long, dark hair in a side ponytail curling at the ends.

I held up my hands in defeat. "I know how stupid that sounds. I just—I dunno. I thought he liked me. But that can't be true if he's asking Julia for her number."

She sighed. "Remember all of those Facebook photos you showed me? He probably likes anything that has a—" She gestured at her pelvis.

I nodded, still hating how rejected I felt. "I know you're right. I guess I just read into his attention too much."

"I'm sorry, Roxy."

I swallowed and shrugged. "I'll get over it."

When Jennifer returned to the kitchen, I stared through the windows at the killer whales swimming in their pool. Most of the guests were focusing on the dessert table, so they paid no attention to me. My brain agreed with Jennifer, urging me to believe Anthony wanted nothing other than to sleep with every woman here. The proof was all over Facebook, and apparently, with Julia at the hostess stand. But my heart was convinced Anthony didn't randomly ask for my number—he approached me for a reason.

He'd been nervous. He'd sought me out more than once. It couldn't have just been about a booty-call. *I mean seriously. There must be some other legitimate reason why he asked for my number.*

I just wished I knew what that reason was.

#

ANTHONY DIDN'T TEXT me until I was heading home from work that evening. Although my heart hammered with anticipation, Jennifer's words rang through my ears, warning me not to respond. So, I didn't. I figured I could mull over the situation at home and then come to a conclusion on how to handle it.

Even though Anthony was engaged, he was going around asking women for their phone numbers. That led to me believe he was unhappy in his relationship. I knew the feeling, so I didn't find it fair to judge that behavior. He had, yet again, made me feel special, but now it seemed like a farce because he had asked someone prettier than me for her number first. *Is he wanting to stay in his relationship or have a secret fling? Or is he looking for a way out? Or does he actually like me? Or does he really need someone to be a friend of him? And just a friend?* Anthony made me feel alive. A feeling I hadn't experienced with Zachary in over a year. Unlike my boyfriend, who made me feel comfortable like a cushy couch, Anthony was like a glass coffee table—beautiful to admire, but dangerous if you got too close.

This whole thing also made me question the sincerity behind engagements. Why bother promising yourself to "that one special person" when you're bound to go behind their backs to find love with someone else? Even if it was just for one, fleeting moment?

When I arrived at the house, Zachary's car was parked out front. Guilt overwhelmed me. I didn't want to spend time with him. I wanted to text Anthony to uncover his true intentions one question at a time. After I took the keys out of the ignition, Zachary stepped out of his car holding a quart of cookie dough ice cream and a bouquet of tulips. "Surprise!"

Smelling the tulips, my guilt grew to the size of the killer whale tank. *Zach is trying so hard. Why am I not in love anymore? Why can't I just be happy with the way he treats me? He's far from perfect, but so am I. And yet, he still loves me.* "Ice cream? You know I'm on a diet."

We walked into the house, his free hand resting on my hip. "You don't need to diet. You're beautiful all around."

I blushed. *Who cares about a falconer who wants to talk to a million girls even though he's engaged? I have a loyal man who really loves me. The good and the bad.* "That's a lie, but thank you."

Loki, along with his flopping ears, tubby legs and clumsy paws, came tumbling around the corner, his love and energy bringing me a joy that had disappeared when Molly passed away.

"Hello, sweet boy," I cooed, not touching him, knowing that he needed to calm down; otherwise, he'd be standing in a puddle of urine, which I'd have to clean while my father yelled at me.

Zachary, on the other hand, removed his grip from my hip and began reaching out to pet the little, tri-colored ball of happiness. I saw it happen in slow motion, my "no" stuck in my throat. The instant his palm touched the puppy's head, piddle rained down on my mother's freshly mopped tile. And because Loki knew peeing in the house was bad, he ran away, his piddle now creating a trail on my mother's expensive Italian rug.

"God damn it, Zach!" I yelled, throwing the tulips on the ground. "How many times do I have to fucking tell you not to touch the fucking puppy!"

He stared at me with a mixture of surprise, shame and anger. "Why are you yelling at me?"

"Because you know better." I walked through the living room, into the kitchen and called Loki over to put him away in his pen. "And you want to be an animal trainer," I muttered.

"What's wrong?" my dad called from downstairs.

"Nothing!" I replied, not wanting my dad to get mad at Zachary *again.*

"Did he touch the fucking puppy?"

"Zach," I hissed. "Can you *please* stop standing there and *help*? My parents are gonna be pissed if it stains." I walked into the kitchen, grabbed a hand towel out of the drawer and turned on the sink so the water would get hot. Zachary didn't move. My father's footsteps were heavy on the stairs, his frustration mounting with every step he took. "Zach," I hissed again. He stared at me, eyes moistening. *For the love of God.* I walked up to him, grabbed the ice cream out of his hand and slapped the wet towel into his palm. "Can you *please* help?"

My dad made it to the top of the staircase and glanced at Loki cowering in his pen. "You've got to be kidding me."

"It was an accident," I said. "I just got too excited and couldn't wait to pet him."

My dad glared at me, but that didn't compare to the daggers he stared at my boyfriend—who I now believed had turned into stone because he *still* hadn't moved. "Some man you are," he spat. "Letting your girlfriend take the blame for something you do *every time* you step foot in this house." He stormed into the garage, mumbling to himself.

"Zach, *please* clean the carpet before it stains," I begged.

"If I move, the dog'll pee," he whispered.

I rolled my eyes. *Oh, get over yourself. Just don't touch the dog until he calms down.* I shoved him toward the carpet. "Just scrub. The dog is locked up. You caused this—I'm not gonna clean it up for you."

My dad came back into the house with two large towels, stomping over to the puddle by the front door. "How hard is it not to touch the damn dog?" When my father dropped the towels on the ground, Zachary finally found his ability to walk, dropping to his hands and knees to scrub the carpet. "Don't tell your mother," my dad snapped. "I don't want her to freak out."

Nodding, I walked over to the towels now sopping wet with urine and told my dad that I would clean up the mess and throw the towels in the wash. "She's in L.A. with Lucy again, right?"

"Lucy wants fertility testing done, but your mother's trying to convince her not to." He headed into the kitchen and opened the refrigerator, pulling out an iced tea. "You should call Lucy to check on her. She *really* believes she won't have another baby."

I rolled my eyes. "Just because things don't go right when she wants—" I bit my tongue. "I'll give her a call."

Without another word, but sure to glare at my boyfriend one last time, my dad returned downstairs and slammed the office door shut.

I picked up the towels, held them as far away from me as possible and tiptoed to the garage, afraid the urine was going to roll off the cotton and drip on me. When I returned, Zachary was still scrubbing, so I picked up Loki out of his cage, cuddled him against my chest and kissed his nose. "Should I text him back or not?" I whispered.

Loki wagged his tail and began to move his paws excitedly, his tongue covering my chin with puppy kisses. I placed him back in the pen, took my phone out of my back pocket and replied: *So, Tony the Falconer. What do you like to do when you're not playing around with birds?*

#

I SAT ON the foot of my unmade bed, Sherlock sitting beside my bare feet, his tail swishing from side to side. Upstairs, Loki played with my parents, their shoes and his paws resembling a stampede above my head. Earlier, when my father handed me the letter nonchalantly, I figured it was another credit card company pre-approving me for some ungodly interest rate on a card I most certainly didn't need. I almost threw it into the trash without looking at it, but the San Diego State University emblem stopped me in my tracks. Not wanting to draw any attention to myself in front of my parents, I silently walked down the stairs, closed my bedroom door and sat down, staring at my possible future.

"This is it, Sherlock," I said. "This is the letter."

My little black cat meowed and jumped on the bed beside me, now rubbing his head against my knuckles. I took a deep breath and turned the envelope over, staring at the rectangle currently sealing my fate.

253

"What if I didn't get in?"

I closed my eyes and found myself back at Sonoma State, standing in front of the communal mailboxes of my student apartments. At the time, I'd been so conflicted seeing that San Diego State University emblem, knowing at one point, I had wanted to leave Sonoma State forever. However, at the time I was holding that envelope, I wished I hadn't gotten in because I wanted to start a life with my three new girlfriends and a potential relationship with Lamont Carwyn. I remembered opening that letter and wondering if I'd made the right decision, nervous to tell my best friends I was going to be returning to San Diego at the end of the semester. When I opened my eyes again, I ripped open the envelope and began reading the letter inside.

I stopped when I read the first word.

Congratulations.

"Sherlock!" I dropped the paper to the ground and picked up the cat, much like Rafiki does to Simba in *The Lion King*. "I did it! I got in! I actually got in!" Sherlock's eyes widened in fear, his paws reaching out for my face to steady himself. "I'm going to be a writer!" I set him down, grabbed the letter, now letting myself read the entirety of it all. I wanted to run upstairs and tell my parents but knew they wouldn't be excited. I thought maybe I could text Jasmine and Lacie, but worried they'd turn my happiness into an excuse to go out and drink. Instead, I picked up my phone and dialed the number of the one person I knew would be proud of me. The one person who would share my excitement. The one person who had been rooting for me since day one of this journey.

"Zach! Guess what? I got accepted into the MFA program!"

Chapter Fifteen

"CAN YOU PLEASE put your phone away, Ms. Vaughn?" my very bohemian Children's Literature professor asked me mid-way through his lecture about Dr. Seuss. "Or is there some comedian sitting on your lap making you smile like that?"

My head snapped up, my classmates snickering around me. To say I was mortified would be an understatement. I'd always wondered why people couldn't wait until after class to return a text message, my phone never leaving its home in the small pouch of my backpack. Now, I got it. They were obviously having a textual affair with a man who was engaged to another woman. And they were too afraid to wait until they got home to return the text messages because there was the potential to get caught by their current significant other. "S—S—Sorry," I stammered, my cheeks warming uncomfortably.

He continued his lecture, commenting on how Dr. Seuss had some ulterior motives when writing *The Cat in the Hat* because it was actually meant for adults, not children.

Although I had a pen in hand and an open notebook on my desk, I couldn't focus on my professor's borderline rotting teeth. He always smelled like cigarettes and his hair looked as if he'd woken from a nap before rushing to get to class on time. Usually, his lectures kept me entertained, engaged and educated because he was intelligent and charismatic, but tonight, I anxiously bounced my leg beneath the desk, wishing the clock would tick faster.

Anthony and I had been texting non-stop since the night I responded to his introductory text message. Our conversations distracted me from anything associated with my real life: schoolwork, writing short stories, providing great customer service, giving my parents attitude and being a good girlfriend. I avoided text messages from Jasmine and Lacie, locked myself in my room without the television on, and avoided any activities that could possibly take me away from my phone for more than ten seconds.

I was a girl obsessed.

It didn't help that now, when we ran into one another at Sea World, we no longer shied away, instead continuing the conversations that had originated in digital print. And if we couldn't stop to chat, we would beam at each other from afar, giving away the crush both of us obviously had on one another. If anybody caught us, or asked if something was going on between us, we both denied their allegations feverishly.

I hated that I was leaving for Costa Rica for Spring Break. I would only have access to communication on my phone when connected to Wi-Fi via Facebook Messenger because I didn't own an iPhone. I wanted to add Anthony on Facebook but had refrained from hitting the "friend request" button whenever I stalked his profile because I was afraid his fiancé would seek me out and kill me, and I didn't want to face my boyfriend's inquisition.

I was smiling at my lap when my professor caught me because Anthony had just admitted he was bummed he wasn't going to see my face or talk to me for a whole week. *He is going to miss me.* And just like that, I completely forgot about the female trainers holding his hawk, about him asking Julia for her phone number before he asked me for mine, and about his engagement. I had officially fallen *hard* for this guy, and I refused to get up.

#

SPRING BREAK SEASON was historically busy at Sea World, so I was only given permission to take off the seven days that I needed for the family trip to Costa Rica. That meant I was scheduled to work the day before I left, and on that day, I decided to doll myself up as if I was going clubbing downtown because I'd woken up to a text from Anthony asking if he'd be lucky enough to see me at work before I left for my trip.

The entire Breakfast with Shamu, I found myself distracted: forgetting drink orders, running into my coworkers in the kitchen, and having to ask guests to repeat themselves when they asked me questions about the whales or the menu. My ears remained alert for the sound of jingling bells, my eyes remained alert for the blue polo worn by the falconers, and my heart remained alert for the feelings that overwhelmed me whenever Anthony was near.

Dominick and Ricardo noticed something was amiss, cornering me when I poured myself a cup of coffee once I was sure my tables were happily watching the whale interaction.

"What?" I asked, scooting the two to the side so I could grab some creamer from the refrigerator. "Does one of my tables need something? I honestly just asked everyone if they were okay."

Ricardo laughed. "I don't care about them. What's going on with you? I watched you pour iced tea into a mug and you almost gave it to that lady with the blue hair."

I flushed. *Didn't think anyone saw that.* "I—uh—just zoned out. You know—I'm—uh—ready for vacation."

"You can't be *that* excited to go to Costa Rica with your family," Dominick pointed out. "You've made it clear you don't *like* them. And I feel like being trapped in a third world country with them might make you hate them even more."

I sipped my coffee and awkwardly scooted between them, making my way to the rolling cart that stored desserts for the lunch and dinner Dines. The sugar cookies were my weakness. Even though I'd generally been avoiding sweets—I snuck a cookie every once in a while. "Don't you both have work to do?"

Ricardo laughed. "You're eating a cookie. You've sworn off junk food."

"That's not true," I argued, dipping the cookie in my coffee. "Haven't you ever heard of a cheat day?"

Dominick tapped the rim of my mug and shook his head. "Just admit you're all dolled up because you're waiting to see somebody." He paused. "Is Zach coming to Dine?"

"Or are you waiting for someone else?" Ricardo pried.

I snorted, throwing the other half of my cookie in the trash. When they both stared at me, I sipped the coffee again and placed it in the dirty dish rack. "It's nothing. Really. I just had some extra time this morning, so I put makeup on." Although it was obvious they didn't believe me, I grabbed my server tray and pushed through the double doors leading to the guests.

However, I almost crashed straight into Anthony who was birdless and panting. He smiled at me before brushing a hand over his hair, which didn't move because of the hair product in it. I could tell he was trying to control his heavy breathing—resisting the urge to rest his hands on his knees—forcing himself to stand as straight as possible, eyes squinting behind his glasses. "I'm glad I ran into you."

"Almost." I placed my tray between my hip and forearm. "You *almost* ran into me."

"Oh, okay, Smartass," he teased.

I blushed, absent-mindedly playing with the string of my apron. "Where's Ruby?"

"Pete has her somewhere," he replied. "I just had to come over here for a quick minute—the birds recognize me even if I don't have the hawk."

My disappointment returned. "You've got some other bird emergency to run off to already?"

Dominick and Ricardo walked past us, shooting me a glance that said *You're being watched. Get back to work.*

"Actually, I was wondering if I could borrow a pen."

I cocked my head to the side. "You wanna write me a love note or something?" *Stop flirting. He's engaged.*

"If I was gonna do something like that, I wouldn't tell you about it," he flirted back. "And even if I *was*, you'd be *so* blown away by it, you'd fall *in love* with me on the spot."

I think I already might be.

I reached into my apron and grabbed him a green pen. "What do you *really* need it for?"

He shrugged, trying to act indifferent, but his eyes radiated excitement. "Jack Hannah is here, and I want his autograph."

Jack who? "No way? He's here?" I asked feigning excitement. *I'll have to Google Jack Hannah later.*

"Pet Stadium. He's hosting a special show. He's only here today, so I gotta catch him before he leaves."

I looked over at my section, noticing the stacked plates and empty glasses piling up. "Well, you better hurry! I gotta get back to work." We began walking away from one another, but after getting a quick idea, I turned back and shouted his name. He smiled. "I'd like my pen back before the end of the day. Those are precious commodities around here."

He nodded and winked. "I'll bring the love note, too."

Although I knew he was kidding, when I continued toward my tables, I smiled, happy with the situation. *Every employee is required to have a pen on them at all times, and he ran all the way here to see me.* A small voice in my head reminded me that he also needed to check on the bird problem, but I ignored it. *I know he has a crush on me, too. I can feel it.*

Later that evening, I walked out of the Dine with Shamu gate, my shift over, the dinner servers now rushing around to get their guests seated. Anthony had yet to return my pen, but I couldn't wait around for him because Zachary was taking me out to dinner, and I had to finish packing for Costa Rica. I had thought about texting Anthony, but realized that'd be crazy—who *really* cared that much about a pen?

In reality, I did.

I wrote my poetry and fiction by hand, so each pen I owned was used until the ink ran dry.

I was more disappointed he hadn't realized I didn't care so much about the pen, but that it gave me a reason to see him before I left. *Maybe he doesn't have a crush on me.*

Walking up the hill, I pulled my phone out and scrolled through my messages so I could let Zachary know I was heading to my car. Just as I was about to press send, the sound of footsteps and a jingling bell captured my attention.

"After threatening me earlier, I'm surprised you were *actually* gonna leave without your pen." His voice glided through my ears and nested happily on my brain, shadowing any and all thoughts of my boyfriend. He pulled the pen out of his black work shorts and wiggled it between his thumb and forefinger. "And to think I would've wasted my time rushing all the way over here for you."

Ruby stared at me with her big, black eyes.

"Even your bird is judging me."

He smiled, placed the pen back in his pocket and ran his palm over his hawk's feathers. "She must be noticing how pretty you look tonight."

I tried to push my bangs behind my ear, but they were already pulled back with a bobby-pin. *Just talk to him like a normal person. You're not a freshman anymore. You know how to talk to boys now.* "So, did you get your autograph?"

The excitement from earlier still shone behind his glasses, but he shrugged coolly. "I actually got something better—Jack Hannah flew Ruby with me. And Pete recorded it."

My phone vibrated in my hand, my boyfriend probably wondering why I hadn't contacted him yet. I shoved it into my pant pocket, not wanting to get distracted from the man in front of me. "That's awesome! You should show it to me sometime when you get the chance."

"Pete put it on my Facebook. You can see it there."

I smirked. "Are we Facebook friends?"

He raised an eyebrow. "I don't think we are."

"You should fix that."

He grinned. "Find my page when you get home."

I shook my head. "There's only *one* Roxanne Vaughn in the world, so I'm easier to find."

The walkie-talkie attached to Anthony's belt crackled before a feminine voice mentioned something about seagulls at Dine with Shamu. Anthony glanced over his shoulder, almost as if we were being watched. "Gotta get back to it. But before I forget." He reached into his pocket and produced my pen again. "Thanks for letting me borrow it."

I grabbed the pen, trying not to focus on the tingles that shot through my body when our fingers touched. "I appreciate you bringing it back in one piece."

He smiled once more before heading down the hill and into the Dine with Shamu gate. As I continued making my way toward the car, I noticed something stuffed between the pen and its handle. Curious, I took it out and unraveled the brown paper napkin, which could only be found at the kiosks by Pets Rule Stadium. My knees grew weak, my heart now pounding against my chest.

The napkin had "love" scribbled on it, with a messy music note beside it.

"He wrote me a love note," I whispered, smirking at the pun. "A literal love note."

I stared at the napkin the entire walk to my car wondering why I was still pretending. It was flirtatious and exciting, but nothing more could come of this. Anthony had a fiancé and I had a boyfriend. That realization bummed me out more than a failing grade. *Maybe I should start thinking about what I'm doing because this won't end well for anyone. Especially me.*

#

THE PLANE WAS scheduled to leave in three hours, and Loki's butt resembled a broken fire hydrant. I had woken up to my mom and dad yelling at one another, which was not normal for the two love birds, and couldn't fall back asleep because of the foul smell wafting into my bedroom. My father ran by the door with what looked like Loki in his outstretched hands, my mother following suit with what looked like Loki's small kennel, which he slept in every night in my parents' room.

Still confused, I crawled out of bed, rubbing the sleep from my eyes. "Lucy isn't gonna be happy," I said to Sherlock, who was stretching on the foot of my bed. "She's grumpy in the morning as it is."

Turning left, I walked through the small hallway leading to my parents' bedroom, where the rancid smell forced me to pull the neck of my pajama shirt over my nose. "Did something die in here?"

I flipped on the light switch and felt my stomach tighten uncomfortably. All over my mother's lush, expensive carpet was something brownish gray and lumpy. Then I began to worry knowing this horrible mess came from poor little Loki. My mom came bounding down the stairs and into the bedroom with a stack of towels in her hand, a variety of cleaning supplies resting on top.

260

I placed the bottles of cleaner on my mom's dresser and grabbed three towels from her. "Remember how Molly destroyed everything when she was a puppy? And she turned out to be a God send."

"I had to replace the deck because of her. She must've thought she was a beaver."

We smiled together, reminiscing, before another wave of puppy diarrhea smell brought us back to the present.

"We're gonna need a trash bag. Or five."

My mom cringed and threw one of the towels on top of the mess. "Can you wake Zachary and ask him to help? Your dad is outside washing Loki's kennel—and washing off Loki."

Zachary was sleeping in the guest room across from Lucy's old bedroom, next to the nursery that Hannah was staying in. As I made my way upstairs, I heard Hannah crying and Lucy shushing her. Roger was making a pot of coffee, and my boyfriend was nowhere to be seen.

Lucy half-smiled at me. "She hates mornings more than I do."

Her shrieking echoed off the walls and launched deep into my ear canal. "Sweet Jesus. Get that girl a pacifier or something."

Roger turned on the small television that sat in the nook above the microwave and the oven. "You think that's crying? If you're ever gonna have a baby, you're gonna have to develop some strength."

I snorted. "There's a reason I'm on birth control."

Lucy winked at me. "The *one* thing you *actually* listened to me about."

With all of the commotion, I doubted Zachary would still be sleeping. However, when I opened the door and pressed the button on the desk lamp sitting on the nightstand, he was in bed snoring softly. My dad was outside the window while Loki howled nonstop. "How are you *still* asleep?" I stared at him, studying his strong facial features and his open mouth, drool pooling on his pillow. I remembered how happy I used to be when I looked at him like this—how grateful I was to be in a relationship with someone as genuinely kind and as handsome as him. Now, I wondered when I stopped finding his high cheekbones, long nose and defined jaw line attractive. Women and men checked him out all of the time, and while I agreed he was a handsome man, the spark that hit my loins whenever I found someone good looking had disappeared whenever around Zachary, and with the way we'd been disagreeing on everything lately, I doubted it would ever come back.

Anthony flashed through my mind, his crooked smile igniting those sparks I longed to feel again. *I need to break up with Zach, but I don't want to be the bad guy. He's miserable too—why won't he just break up with me?*

"Good morning, Zach," I said, reaching out my hand to rouse him.

He opened his eyes briefly before turning onto his back to stretch. "Good morning, Little Woman." He turned away from me and readjusted his pillow. "Have fun in Costa Rica."

I sat on the bed and rested my hand on his bare shoulder. "We're not leaving yet. There's been a bit of a crisis with the puppy and we need your help."

He glanced over at me without moving. "I didn't pet him, so it's not my fault."

I nudged his shoulder. "We're not blaming you. He's really sick. I think it's something he ate."

"And what's that gotta do with me?"

"Can you not be a jerk?" I rolled my eyes. "My family and I have to leave for the airport soon and we need your help."

He threw off his blanket and sat up. "I'm not being a jerk. Your parents have been treating me like crap lately—*especially* when the dog is around. Why should I help them?"

That's because you don't listen. Mister I Deserve To Be An Animal Trainer. "You may need to take him to the vet when we leave. He's *really* ill, Zach. I'm worried about him. We've gotta figure out what happened."

Zachary pulled a shirt out of his duffel bag and threw it on before tying the string of his pajama pants. "Your parents are gonna blame me. Somehow, someway—it's gonna be my fault."

"Can you *please* grow up? The puppy is leaking from his butt. Do you hear him crying outside? This has *nothing* to do with you, so *stop* making it about yourself."

"Thanks for the *great* wakeup call," he mumbled, slipping his feet into a pair of black sandals.

I bit my tongue. *Let it go. Loki needs you.* "My mom is in her bedroom and needs help cleaning up. I'm gonna help my dad with the puppy. Please don't give her attitude. She's already stressed out enough about the trip."

He stormed out of the room without saying another word.

#

THREE DAYS INTO the family vacation and I was ready to go home. The strange thing was that it wasn't my family driving me crazy. No. My boyfriend back in the states had successfully found any and all ways to ruin what was supposed to be a well deserved, relaxing Spring Break.

It really made zero sense. I was in one of the most beautiful resorts I'd ever seen—my parents were paying for everything from food to booze to clothes to living arrangements—but I was completely miserable.

And my family was over it. They didn't even bother inviting me to join them on their ziplining trip. They instructed me to watch Hannah and bolted the door behind them before I could consider arguing. Thankfully, there was a large television in the casita that Hannah was happy to watch while I pulled an Imperial Lager out of the refrigerator and mulled over my decision to allow Zachary to ruin my vacation.

Day one: he didn't message me back when I informed him I'd arrived at the resort. Costa Rica is only two hours ahead of San Diego. He'd been awake when we left. The flight had taken about six hours. He should've answered immediately. In that entire time he hadn't even bothered to update me on Loki or what the vet had to say about everything. It took him *two hours after* I arrived at the casita to *finally* respond, which I knew meant he was playing a stupid video game and Loki was *not* being monitored.

My family and I entered the open, wood building, large glass windows emitting sunshine on the wooden tables covered in dark, red table cloths. Although I couldn't speak any Spanish, Roger was fluent, able to speak to the resort's staff as if he grew up in South America. The waiter sat us at a table next to one of the large windows, another staff member bringing over a high chair for Hannah. The fans were blowing cool air inside the restaurant, which was a refreshing break from the humidity and heat outside.

First thing I did was order a grande margarita, second thing I did was suggest we split a few appetizers, and the third thing I did was change the subject when my dad asked how Loki was doing. Instead of responding, I asked my sister and Roger how baby number two was coming along. That sparked an emotional conversation between my mom and Lucy, which gave me a chance to enjoy my margarita in peace—I just had to avoid the glare my dad was shooting me from the other side of the table. When I happily dug into my red beans and rice, my dad asked about Loki again. I informed him Zachary had yet to message me, and he threatened to contact my boyfriend himself.

Still connected to the resort's Wi-Fi, I pulled up Skype on my phone, excused myself from the table and called my boyfriend while hiding behind a giant, leafy bush.

Our conversation hadn't been a good one.

He answered rather grumpily, the curtains on the living room windows pulled closed behind him. He assured me that Loki was improving—lesser diarrhea, small amounts of water intake and lots of rest. He didn't take him to the vet because he was a trainer and it was unnecessary to spend money listening to someone tell him what he already knew.

After a stunned silence where Zachary asked if the screen froze, I had to take a deep breath so I wouldn't scream at him. "But you're *not* a trainer," I emphasized, hoping my family couldn't hear. "How could you think this is okay? And more importantly, you're *not* an animal doctor, Zach! It's not up to you to make that decision because he's not your dog. My dad *specifically* told you to take him."

"He's fine," Zachary snapped. "I know more about animals than any of you."

"Oh, do you?" I argued. "Is that why Sherlock runs away from you whenever you come near? Or why Loki pees all over the house *anytime you touch him?*"

He hung up on me, which made me want to throw the phone into the pond surrounded by orange, green, pink and white flowers. Instead, I closed my eyes, wiped the bead of sweat off my forehead, put on my customer service smile and returned to the table so I could lie to my father's face. I told him the dog would be eating a bland diet of chicken and rice after fasting for twenty-four hours. That the vet suspected the bone we'd given him the night before was rotten, therefore causing the stomach issue.

A quick Google search before entering the restaurant had given me that information, which I assumed was the same Google search Zachary had done in the morning instead of taking the puppy to the vet like he was asked.

I then ordered another margarita and wondered what Anthony was doing, wishing I'd known him well enough to ask him to take care of the animals instead. He was a real animal trainer, after all.

Day two: things seemed to be going better. After allowing ourselves to sleep in, my family and I returned to the restaurant to enjoy breakfast and then rang the front desk so we could sign up to milk the cows and partake in an ATV ride along the beach at sunset. My mom volunteered to watch Hannah so she could sit at the pool, have some wine and read a book. Zachary and I were back to messaging one another normally as if we hadn't fought the night before and I was stoked to do a bit of exploring—especially to do things I was usually too afraid to do or couldn't afford to do back in the states.

Milking the cows was strange, but hilarious, the sexual innuendos flowing from Lucy's and Roger's mouths freely—unlike the milk that would only occasionally splash into the pail because all of us were laughing too hard to get it right. My favorite part of that activity was feeding hay to the cows and petting them, their fur thin, but soft. We wandered around the resort, taking pictures of wild birds, lizards and monkeys, my stomach flipping, yet again, when Anthony came to mind. We found a playground that we thought Hannah would enjoy, making a mental note of its location so we could find it tomorrow.

The ATV was difficult at first, mainly because my anxiety vibrated through my body alongside the ATV's motor, but I ground my teeth together, reminding myself I'd eaten and drank plenty of water, so there was no reason to feel faint and shaky. The ride was bumpy through the dry sand, the guide leading us to the compact sand still wet from the earlier high tide. The mist hitting my face was refreshing against the sticky heat, which had made me uncomfortable in the long-sleeve I wore to keep the mosquito bites to a minimum. The reflection of the lowering sun was blinding against the ocean's waves, birds flying over the ocean, dark clouds building in the distance.

The entire ride, I had to remind myself to stay in the moment and get out of my brain because Zachary and Anthony were halfway across the globe doing God-knows-what. It didn't matter *what* they were doing because I was on the vacation of a lifetime and needed to focus on these opportunities that I'd never get to do again.

However, after my father, Roger, Lucy and I took a final photo of us on the beach with an orange and purple skyline, the drama from the states overwhelmed me. The skyline darkened, the clouds now beginning to loom toward us. The tour guide warned us to get moving because it looked like it was going to rain—which was unusual this time of year—so, I tried not to panic, hopped on the ATV and focused on the road in front of me. When we arrived back at the casita, I made the mistake of scrolling through Facebook, only to find Zachary had posted a picture of himself and Omar drinking at a bar. *What is he doing? Loki is sick. He's not supposed to leave the house except to go to work.* I looked out of the window, the clouds even more threatening than before. *He promised he'd watch Loki. Instead, he thought it would be more important to get drunk with his horrible best friend.* A flock of white birds flew across the sky, again making me think about Anthony. *It seems like neither of us is very good at keeping promises.* Even though the smell of an impending storm hung heavily in the moist air, I wandered into the common room and asked Lucy if she'd take a walk with me. Knowing I wasn't one to want to get my hair wet because of how badly it frizzed compared to the rest of my family's straight hair, Lucy agreed, asking me if everything was okay.

I only wanted to mention how upset I was with Zachary for leaving Loki unattended, but wound up telling her every little detail that I'd kept bottled inside since the party in Hillcrest. I cried hard, admitting that coming home for Zachary after I completed my sophomore year was a mistake. That our entire relationship was built on a foundation of secrets and lies. That I had been in love with him at one point, but now, the main thing I felt was fear of losing him simply because I didn't think anyone else could deal with my panic attacks and nervous breakdowns. I admitted that I couldn't remember the last time I wanted to have sex with him, but there was comfort in the way he held me in his arms. The last thing I mentioned was calling the ambulance on New Year's Eve after Zachary refused to help me.

She listened without interruption, but her facial features did give away how she felt about my confessions. She led me into the restaurant and asked the waiter for two Imperial Lagers once we sat down. It had begun to rain, but the restaurant was warm and stuffy, the fans not doing much to ease my panic.

Lucy asked me the million-dollar question: "What's the point of being with someone that makes you miserable more than they make you happy?" When I couldn't muster the strength to respond, she continued. "You're just one little bird in a big ass sky. Maybe it's time for you to get out of your comfortable nest and fly away."

I glanced at the one couple and three other families dining in the restaurant, hoping no one was able to hear our conversation because I was embarrassed at how pathetic I was. Thankfully, the waiter brought us our beers, which gave me the opportunity to really *think* about how I wanted to respond to my sister.

I hadn't been able to give her an answer, instead shifting the conversation to Lucy, and how she looked much more alive than the last time I'd seen her.

Now, day three: I was missing the opportunity to zipline through a Costa Rican Forest because Zachary and I got into another fight about Loki. His diarrhea had returned with a vengeance because Zachary had forgotten to close Loki's kennel, and he dug through the trashcan to find the Jack in the Box leftovers that Zachary and Omar had eaten when they returned stupidly drunk from the bar. I yelled at him, told him he would ever become an animal trainer, and emphasized what a terrible father he was going to be, hanging up before he could respond. At that point, I wanted to go home, afraid that Sherlock wasn't being shown any love or attention. Luckily, I had filled his food and water bowls until they overflowed, hoping it was enough to get through the length of the trip.

Hannah clapped and giggled, my choice of some Spanish soap opera obviously entertaining her toddler brain. I smiled at her and chided myself for letting Zachary get under my skin. "I'm in the middle of paradise, a billion miles away from him, and yet, he *still* knows how to ruin everything."

I watched the beautiful, dark skinned actress on the screen toss her dark, black hair over her shoulder and pout those plump, red lips at the camera before saying something fierce in an accent that made me feel bad for the light skinned man who supposedly loved the woman's sister instead.

"I mean, I'm *actually* getting along with my family and I'm letting his stupidity get to me. Like—why? Why do I do this to myself? I can easily ask Jasmine or Lacie to check on the animals if it's that bad."

I pulled up Facebook on my laptop and began aimlessly scrolling through the news feed, wondering which picture I should post to prove to Zachary that I was having a great time, not thinking about whether or not my animals were going to survive the next two days under his lack of care. That's when an update captured my attention. I pushed the computer away from me, stood and took a lap around the casita. Hannah watched me curiously before I picked her up, resting her against my hip.

"Let's find a distraction," I mumbled, searching through her diaper bag. "Can't have you watching what's on TV right now." I found a stuffed tiger and handed it to her, also doing my best to ignore the spicy scene making me blush. My nerves hummed.

I was taken back to that moment sophomore year when my roommate, Amber, informed me that Lamont had broken up with his hometown girlfriend only a couple weeks after Zachary had asked me to be his girlfriend.

Anthony Wright had gone from engaged to single an hour ago.

Suddenly, everything Zachary had messed up the last couple of days disappeared from memory, and I began to calculate the best time to contact Anthony without seeming over eager. "It seems fate has thrown me another curve ball," I whispered to Hannah, who was bouncing the stuffed tiger up and down, mumbling incoherent sentences and giggling to herself. "What am I gonna do?"

#

LACIE AND JASMINE scooted into the large, corner booth before me, our favorite waiter greeting us before asking if we'd like the usual. Considering I was in the middle of a well-thought out plan that I openly denied to my girlfriends when they called me out on my sketchy behavior, I agreed to the drink because I needed something to drown out the guilt building in my chest.

I returned home from Costa Rica a week prior with a brand-new attitude, sunburned skin, bug bites, and a pile of homework I needed to complete before classes resumed. Zachary wasn't at the house when the taxi van dropped us off, which was a relief. Lucy, Roger and Hannah disappeared into their room to sleep off their jetlag, my mom rifled through a pile of mail sitting on the living room table, my dad took a very thin Loki out onto the deck for some overdue playtime, and I went into my room to cuddle Sherlock, who hadn't stopped meowing since I stepped foot through the front door. I didn't forget to thank Zachary for taking care of the animals, but did promptly turn off my phone after pressing send so I wouldn't be tempted to text Anthony that I was *finally* home. He and I had been Facebook messaging nonstop since his relationship status changed to *single*, but now that we were only a few miles away from one another, our innocent flirting verged on dangerous.

Schoolwork kept me pre-occupied at first—and the best excuse I was able to give Zachary as to why I wasn't answering my phone—but after being home for four days, I had to come face to face with the two emotions I was doing my best to ignore.

The first emotion I had to battle was fear. Zachary finally cornered me in the library, knowing I couldn't escape because I had a paper due the following day. I knew Zachary was behind me before he plopped into the chair beside me, his presence like a ghost dancing on the back of my neck. Although he kissed my cheek, I refused to look at him, my anxiety now making the pen in my fingers shake on top of my notebook.

"Hey," I whispered, not wanting to bother any of the other students sitting at the long table who had also waited until the last minute to finish whatever assignment they were sweating over.

"I know you're really focusing on your school work, but it feels like you've been avoiding me."

After taking a deep breath, I finished the sentence I was working on and turned to face my *biggest* fear. This man no longer made my stomach flip like Hollywood wanted all hopeless romantics to believe it would—he made it churn like how colonial women used to make butter, my anxiety reaching a level my Lexapro couldn't control. I also hated that he had yet to apologize for being such a jerk and attempting to ruin my once in a lifetime vacation. Instead of telling him my true feelings, I cleared my throat to give myself two more seconds to think of a better answer. "I just didn't get enough homework done over break." I flashed a half-smile that I hoped my once-upon-a-time fiancé would see through, but he thought nothing of it, smiling as he shrugged off his backpack. "I just can't afford any distractions," I continued.

He rested his hand on my thigh. "Mind if I join you?"

What part of no distractions don't you understand? "Not at all."

When he removed his hand to reach for his laptop inside his backpack, I breathed a little easier. At least he was going to get his own work done. It would give me the chance to really get my assignment completed. Unfortunately, I struggled to write my paper from that point forward because all I wanted to do was turn to him and inform him we shouldn't be in a relationship anymore.

The second emotion I was forced to face: inappropriate infatuation.

Anthony had showed up to the final Dine with Shamu seating the following day and smiled at me from across the restaurant. I smiled back before disappearing into the kitchen where I fanned myself with my tray. Jennifer noticed my flushed face from the other side of the kitchen and motioned for me to meet her behind the food warmer, which was where we met to hide from everyone else so we wouldn't get in trouble for not working.

"You doing okay?" she asked.

I inhaled, surrounded by the scent of freshly cooked macaroni and cheese, and leaned against the three-compartment sink. "I'm fine. Just dealing with some unwanted feelings."

She frowned. "You and Zach having issues again?"

"Just had an unwanted epiphany when I was in Costa Rica."

The cook was stirring mashed potatoes, the spoon clanking against the tin while the dish machine spat water and sanitizer against the plates caked with leftovers.

"Did it involve Tony?" Jennifer's voice was so soothing that hearing her vocalize what was really eating me alive made me want to tell her everything.

"I'm drawn to him. He makes me feel special. I'm just—I'm full of butterflies whenever I think about him, see him, talk to him."

"I get it," she replied, glancing around the industrial sized warmer to make sure the runners were replenishing the food in the buffet room. "But you need to figure out what's going on with Zach before you start focusing on Tony."

I agreed with her both out loud and in my head, but when Anthony came over and began talking to me while I was wiping down my tables, all logic dove straight into the whale tank. Instead of keeping my distance so I could figure out what to do about my relationship, I invited Anthony out for margaritas on Saturday night.

Now, here I was, sitting in my favorite booth at the local Mexican restaurant, celebrating a girls' night out because I didn't want Zachary to invite himself out with us. Once the waiter dropped off our drinks—a jumbo, blended margarita for me and two mango margaritas for my girlfriends—I lifted my glass to cheers them and their willingness to keep my secrets no matter the circumstance.

"So, when are we meeting this guy?" Jasmine asked, breaking a tortilla chip in half.

"I told him seven. I wanted to give myself time to build confidence before he gets here."

"And how do you plan on doing that in thirty minutes?" Lacie wondered.

I smiled over my glass and took a large gulp, wincing slightly. "Oh boy—he made them *really* strong this time."

Jasmine laughed. "I'm not sure you *really* get confident when you drink. A little less awkward. Maybe."

Dipping a chip into the salsa, I glared at her. "Can you *not* make me overthink things right now? I'm already freaking out enough as it is."

Lacie nudged me. "But getting in your head is *so easy*. You haven't stopped tapping your feet since we sat down."

Sometimes, I hate them. "Should I cancel? I should cancel. There's still time. I'll just text him quick and—"

Jasmine shook her head, her long, black hair swishing over her breasts, and pointed at my drink with her newly manicured, nude colored nails. "Don't worry. Lacie and me are here to stop anything from going too far. If you're uncomfortable, give us a signal and we're out of here."

Lacie chewed a chip and swallowed. Her hazel eyes were full of mischief, her pale skin shining bright against her self-dyed black hair. "*Maybe* we should order a round of shots. You know, to muster up whatever confidence you can find deep down inside."

Jasmine waved down our waiter and ordered the shots, also asking if he could bring us another basket of chips because we had more people joining us.

I drank from my margarita nervously, the waiter returning too quickly with three tequila shots rimmed with salt, limes on the side. "Will this *actually* help? Will it make me worse?"

Lacie smiled and patted my forearm. "Relax, Roxy. I've seen you do some crazy ass things while drinking. Sitting at a family establishment so you can get to know a guy is one of your tamer decisions."

I licked the salt, threw back the Jose Cuervo and sucked on the lime right before my heart beat kicked up a notch. I didn't have to hear a jingling bell to know that he was there—my skin warmed and my lower half squirmed with anticipation. When he walked into the bar portion of the restaurant, he gazed over the other patrons, his dimples coming to life when we made eye contact.

"He's here," I whispered to the girls, now all sorts of giddy and giggly. "He's actually here."

"You thought he was gonna blow you off?" Jasmine asked, exasperated.

I shrugged. "Why wouldn't he?"

Lacie exhaled loudly. "We should've ordered another round of confidence."

"There's not enough tequila in the world to help her out," Jasmine teased.

The people milling through the bar slowed, the clanking and blending behind the counter silenced, and the lights dimmed, all of my senses zeroing in on his slightly flushed, round face. His hair was heavily gelled, per usual, the part standing prominent on the left side of his head. He was dressed in a red and black flannel with a black undershirt, black jeans, and white and blue shoes that were so shiny, I briefly wondered if he stopped at the mall to purchase them right beforehand.

And this handsome man had all his attention on me.

"Oh my God. You two are matching," Lacie said, slapping her palm against her forehead. "Jazz, are you seeing this?"

I scooted out of the booth and stood, my four-inch high red and black plaid heels making me extremely tall, accentuating my legs beneath my black miniskirt.

"I already need another drink," Jasmine said behind her smile.

Anthony wrapped me in a hug, which was the first time we'd actually touched one another on purpose. His body was soft, a small belly touching mine beneath his shirt. I reminded myself to breathe, his scent of Marlboro cigarettes and soap making me light headed. He looked at my heels and laughed. "I thought I was going crazy for a second. I wondered when you got that tall."

I blushed, fidgeted with my curls and sat back in the booth, making polite introductions.

Anthony reached across the table to shake my friends' hands before resting them on his lap. "I hope you ladies don't mind, but I invited a friend."

His fiancé briefly flashed before my eyes, but I blinked her away and focused on Anthony's dark brown beauties. "The more the merrier!" I picked up my margarita and drank as if the drought in California was actually in my mouth, and not destroying the entire state's agricultural business.

"Peter found out we were having drinks and wanted to join. He's not twenty-one yet, though."

Jasmine and Lacie rolled their eyes. "*Great.* You invited a baby."

"Lacie, you're not even twenty-two yet," I said, reminded of how the girls were snobby about going to Matthew's house party because they were newly twenty-one. "I remember not too long ago when I had to sneak some whiskey into your Diet Coke because you weren't old enough to drink."

"Is he cute at least?"

Anthony reached out for a chip and scooped some salsa. I noticed his fingers were wrinkled, as if he were in his fifties and not almost thirty. "Why don't you tell me? I'm not really into guys, so I don't know."

I giggled, the first rounds of tequila beginning to hit me. "He has grey hair! And pretty eyes. It's funny that he's only twenty."

"Well, when you work with this guy, you age quickly." Peter showed up out of nowhere and patted Anthony on the shoulder before scooting into the booth beside Jasmine. "Hello ladies. I'm Pete."

Shortly after that, our waiter returned to get drink orders for the boys, to refill our margaritas and to bring two more baskets of fresh tortilla chips. The night turned a bit blurry after Anthony ordered another round of tequila shots, my second drink emptied and a third placed in front of me. Anthony's hand made its way to my inner thigh at some point, our loud and drunken laughter scaring away some of the other patrons who had been dining with their children, our waiter replenishing more drinks without even asking whether or not we wanted them.

I interlaced my fingers with Anthony's and squeezed, resting my head on his shoulder. When he kissed my temple, I silently asked God to stop time so that I could remain this carefree and happy forever.

Chapter Sixteen

ANTHONY AND I sat in the back seat of his SUV, panting. The windows were fogged over, the air inside the car was moist and sticky, and my confidence had gone from that of an Olympic gold medalist to that of a grasshopper trapped in a bird's nest.

Why does this keep happening? It has to be me. I'm not pretty. I'm fat. I held back the urge to cry. *I'm the only aspect of the situation that's the same. All other variables change. All of the men are different.* I closed my eyes and rested the back of my head against the seat, the small curls on the back of my neck slick with sweat, my brain transporting me back to the first time Lamont and I attempted to have sex. I'd loved him so much, I hadn't cared he couldn't get it up, but I remembered thinking it was my fault, even though he'd promised me it was the fact he felt "guilty" for cheating on his girlfriend back home. *Anthony doesn't have a fiancé anymore. They broke up. He doesn't have a reason to feel guilty. I'm the one who should feel guilty.*

"I hate using condoms. They don't do me any justice." He was talking in a playful, somewhat embarrassed, voice. "I perform better without them, especially after I've been drinking."

"Oh." It was all I could muster.

Anthony reached over and grabbed my hand. "I'm sorry. I had way too much beer, and we took tequila shots. I don't usually do tequila."

I opened my eyes and looked at him, knowing he was trying to make light of the situation, but unable to pull myself out of my head.

He smiled his white, square teeth at me. "Give me, like, ten minutes and we can try again."

I half smiled, my heart deflating like a popped balloon. "You really don't have to."

He furrowed his brows and poked my forehead. "What's going on in there?"

I looked away, focusing on the stars beyond the window, sucking in my stomach as hard as I could. *Don't tell him anything. Guys like confident girls. He can't know how much I hate myself. I don't want him to know the real me.* "Nothing. Just drunk."

When Anthony scooted toward me, his undone belt buckle clinked against his open zipper. "You know how beautiful you are, right?"

To prevent him from seeing how close I was to a margarita meltdown, I smashed my lips against his and grabbed his cheeks with my hands. His lips were the softest I'd ever felt against my own, his tongue was gentle, and his teeth applied just the perfect amount of pressure when he nibbled on my bottom lip. His hands found my breasts beneath my red, long-sleeved shirt, quickly moving down my stomach and under my skirt, moving my thong to the side so he could drive me wild all over again.

Instead of letting him lay me down on the backseat awkwardly like he did the first time, I climbed over him, my knees resting on each side of his thighs. I moved my hips front and back, beginning to feel his soft organ harden. *You can do this, Roxy. Let him know just how sexy you can be. Make him want you. Convince him you know how beautiful you are.* He moaned, grabbing my hips with an urgency that gave me the confidence to continue. I glanced behind him, noticing a bunch of bird poop staining the inside car walls and windows, a green box sitting next to a bird perch, which probably had a bird in it. *Focus, Roxy. Focus.* Although grossed out, I closed my eyes and began to breathe through my mouth, now noticing the stench of feces and something dead lingering inside the car. *I'm sure he didn't think we'd be doing this right now. If he did, he would've cleaned it all out.*

"Can I trust you?" I asked, having adjusted myself so I could look him straight in the eyes, my drunken high taking a backseat to the feelings I knew were developing for a man I hardly knew. I wanted to explore him without any inhibition.

Since he'd been in a long relationship prior to this moment, I knew he was telling the truth when he nodded. "What about you? I don't want you to hurt me." His emotion told me he didn't mean physically. *He's nervous, too. It's not just me. Maybe he's telling the truth.*

"I have feelings for you, Tony. Feelings that make zero sense because I don't know you much. I don't understand it."

He smiled, his eyes penetrating my own. "I'm glad I'm not the only one."

This time, he and I fully connected, our bodies moving in rhythm with one another, everything bare, including our vulnerable hearts. I kissed him tenderly, loving how alive my body felt—it was as if I'd been in a coma for months, finally waking against all odds.

I made love to Anthony, giving him every last inch of my mind, body and soul, so lost in our intoxication that I forgot Zachary Cameron even existed.

#

THE NEXT MORNING, I woke up drenched in sweat, shivering as if I were neck deep in an ice bath, not beneath three blankets in the safety of my own bedroom. Sherlock lay curled against my belly, his motorboat purrs vibrating through my pajama shirt, my heart rate slowing just enough to let me breathe in and out. Not wanting to disturb my snoozing feline, I clenched my jaw and tried to fight the tremors racking through my body. Sherlock stretched and yawned, turning his head just enough to face me. His big, green eyes were nothing but inquisitive, which made me feel even worse.

I wrapped my arms around him and pulled him snuggly into my chest, my eyes burning with tequila-soaked tears as Sherlock's purrs grew louder. "Why do I do this to myself? To Zach? To everyone around me?"

My head felt heavy, my tongue fuzzy, my stomach upside down. Another wave of shivers overwhelmed me, so I sobbed into Sherlock's fur, not wanting to close my eyes for fear of replaying the previous night's events, but unable to keep them open because they were overly swollen from crying and lack of sleep.

"I don't deserve to be loved," I whispered, my heart clenching so tight, my chest hurt as if I'd been punched repeatedly. "Zach doesn't deserve this." Moving Sherlock to the side, I swung my feet off the bed and placed my bare feet on the carpet, waiting a few moments for the room to stop tilting from side to side. "Nobody deserves to be treated like this. I'd be devasted if he was doing the same thing to me."

I slowly made my way into my bathroom, turned on the sink faucet, cupped my hands beneath the cool water and tilted my palms toward my mouth, guzzling down the liquid until the taste of stale lime dissipated. My stomach growled at me, the water sloshing uncomfortably against my nausea, my skin craving hydration despite my want to heave out everything in my body.

"Why can't I have a normal hangover?" I asked my reflection. "Why do I *always* have to overthink what happened? Why can't I just blame what I do on alcohol like everyone else?" *Because you probably would've done the same thing sober*, my conscience reminded me, sending another round of shivers through my core, followed by another round of tears. "I can't do this anymore."

After I opened my bedroom door, I turned to the left and walked through the hallway leading to my parents' room. The small TV sitting on the bench at the foot of my parents' king-sized bed was on the gameshow network, my dad lounging on the grey and blue recliner that lived on his side of the room alongside a tall, silver reading lamp that reminded me of interrogation tools used in old detective movies.

When he looked at me—smeared makeup and snot all over my face—he stood and embraced me silently, rubbing my back while I cried into his chest for five minutes. "You wanna talk or did you just want to ruin the shirt your sister gave me for Christmas?" He held me at arm's length, studying me.

I snorted. "When have I ever wanted to talk about anything?"

He gestured for me to sit on the edge of the bed. "Why don't you tell me about last night? Did you have fun with the girls?"

Too much fun. Instead, I nodded. "I'm hungover."

"You could've fooled me."

I playfully slapped his arm. "Not funny."

We both sat down as he laughed. "Is *that* why you're having a meltdown? Because you feel *yucky*?"

The gameshow ended on the television and had been replaced with the news, the weather lady standing in front of a digital map of San Diego county, boasting about sunny skies and temperatures in the mid-seventies all week. "Maybe part of the reason. Your patronizing me doesn't help." I fiddled with my fingertips, pulling at my cuticles. "I woke up in the middle of a panic attack."

He reached over and squeezed my shoulder. "Maybe call it a father's intuition, but it feels like this has more to do with—I dunno—something *other* than drinking too much."

I had sex with someone who isn't my boyfriend. I have feelings for someone who isn't my boyfriend. My eyes began to water, my heart clenching into a fist again. *I don't love my boyfriend anymore.* "That's partially true."

"It's okay if you don't love Zach anymore."

This time, I brought my hands up to my face and cried into my palms, wiping my nose on the sleeve of my pajama shirt. "If it's okay, why do I feel like this?"

My father stood, walked over to his recliner, grabbed the remote and turned off the television. "Because you don't want to hurt him. He's more than just a boyfriend – I know he's also one of your best friends. But believe me, pretending to still be in love with someone when you're not hurts way worse."

"But what if I regret leaving him? What if we're going through a rut? What if I'm supposed to just be patient and find a way to make it work?"

"You can ask *what if* a million times and your brain will give you a million different answers. But it appears to me that your heart has already made a decision, and the rest of your body is on board—your brain is always going to play games with you when it comes to stuff like this. You have to trust your gut."

I stared at my dad with sad eyes, knowing he was right. "I don't want to break his heart."

My father nodded his understanding before lounging in his recliner. "Zach is a good guy. I like him—despite a couple of things—the way he treats Loki and his clothing decisions to name a few, but that doesn't make him a *bad guy*. You two are in different places right now and realizing that your lives are no longer on the same path doesn't make *you* a bad person, either. Some people grow together, some grow apart. Neither is right or wrong. Maybe, someday, you two will cross paths again and wind up together—if things are meant to be, life has a funny way of making them happen. But right now, you need to do what's best for *you*. And your heart."

I glanced down at the carpet wanting to respond but unable to.

"No matter what decision you make, remember you don't have to go through the bullshit alone," he continued. "Me, your mother and your sister are here to help you." He paused, before turning the TV on again. "Sherlock and Loki love you unconditionally, too. You're never alone, Roxanne." He sighed and turned up the volume. "Now, I'd like to see what happens on The Price is Right. You can either keep crying in your room, or you can be quiet and join me."

At that moment, I couldn't think of anything I'd rather do, so I lay back on my parents' bed and allowed myself to relax so I could finally fall into a comfortable slumber.

#

I TEXTED ZACHARY and asked him to meet me at s local park—a place we frequented the summer before he left for college. He'd asked me why, but I didn't respond, instead turning off my phone and hiding it in my desk drawer.

I hoped to arrive at the park before Zachary, but when I pulled up, there he was, sitting on a bench in a light blue button up and light tan slacks. His eyes were hidden behind his Aviator sunglasses, but his slumped posture and deep frown indicated that he knew something was amiss.

The walk from my car to him was agonizingly long, his crooked smile nearly knocking the breath out of me. When he hugged me, all of the great memories we once shared came to life. It reminded me why we jumped into this relationship in the first place, both of us consumed with our love for one another. When we sat down on the bench, I channeled our most recent memories, all of which had been tainted with animosity, jealousy, frustration and disappointment. *It's time, Roxy. He deserves to know the truth.* I took a deep breath and unfolded the paper that was now dampened with sweat in my palms. *It's time for this to come to an end.* However, before I started reading what I had written, I glanced up at Zachary's French nose, strong jawline, tan skin and high cheekbones, briefly questioning why fate had brought us together a second time, especially if we weren't meant to remain in a relationship for the long run. "You know I'm terrible with speaking about how I feel, so I wrote my thoughts down in my attempt to keep everything clear."

He nodded solemnly, removing his sunglasses, stowing them in the breast pocket of his shirt. The sun reflected in his eyes, those light green meadows taking me back to five years ago, before Zachary went to college, to the days where our first attempt at a relationship was untainted by lies, sex, heartbreak, slander and expectations. "Okay, Little Woman."

I closed my eyes, felt the wind shift and allowed myself a blissful moment of nostalgia before the paper crinkled in my grip. It was time.

So, I read aloud:

As much as I want to say it was love at first sight, we both know that'd be a lie. I remember being so upset my friend gave you my number, but that didn't stop me from meeting you for a cup of coffee before a walk in the park. This park, actually. It was as if I were walking beside a completely different person than the jerk I met at the bonfire. Your quirky jokes, awkward conversations and shy demeanor mirrored my own. That summer, I fell for you quick and hard, worshipping the ground you walked on. How could someone who looked like you want to be with someone who looked like me?

"You know you're beautiful, right?" Zachary interrupted, asking the same question Anthony had asked after our failed attempt at intercourse the night prior.

Instead of responding, I continued to read:

You allowed me to fall in love with you and lead me to believe you loved me, too. But we both know that's not how the story turned out and you left me behind when you started college. In some strange twist of fate, we reconnected—a simple Facebook message years later rekindled the love I promised myself I'd never feel for you again.

I sniffled and looked at Zachary. A glistening sheen ran down the length of his cheek, his hands hanging limp between his thighs.

But I felt it. I allowed it to consume me again. I loved you so much that I moved back to San Diego to prove we deserved this second chance. I loved you so much that I proudly brought you to dinner with my parents. I loved you so much that I accepted a ring to try to prove my love was real—even though accepting it had been a mistake. A mistake I wish I could go back in time and fix. I wish I would've told you the truth about me not being grown up enough to deal with that kind of commitment. But I didn't say anything because I was too afraid of hurting your feelings. Too afraid of losing you. So, I hid my true feelings from you over and over and over again.

The paper blurred, my words swirling together into sentences I could no longer read. I crumpled up the paper, dropped it to the ground and turned to face the man I'd been leading on for far too long.

"Zachary, I don't regret getting into a relationship with you. I don't regret moving back here for you. I'm glad we took this chance. If we didn't, I'd always wonder *what if*. The hardest part about this whole thing is that you've become my best friend, and I'm terrified of losing you. You've been my rock over the years. You've helped me deal with my anxiety and self-doubt, and I'll never be able to thank you enough for that. But I can't do this anymore." I inhaled through my nose, noting the smell of fresh grass, and exhaled through my mouth. "I love you as a person. You have so many great qualities that any woman will admire. You're so handsome, sweet, honest and kind. But I'm not *in love* with you anymore. We always fight. We nit-pick one another. Those butterflies I used to feel around you have been struggling to fly as of late."

"I can change that," he said, voice cracking.

I wish that were true, I thought. *But it's too late.* "Zachary, I'm sorry. I want to stay friends because I care for you, but I can't be in a relationship right now. I have my own stuff to deal with and I don't have the energy to keep fighting for—for—whatever this is."

A stray tear rolled down his high cheekbones and splashed on his pant thigh. "Why do you feel like this all of a sudden? Is there another guy?"

The words danced on my tongue, part of me wanting to come clean about Lamont, Matthew, Justin and Anthony, but I swallowed the truth. The other half of me was too proud to admit that I was such a bad person. "Zach, I've been feeling this way for a while. I just—I thought—I dunno—that the feeling would go away. But it's gotten worse." I paused and thought about last night and how my lips sparked with passion each time Anthony kissed me. "There's no other guy. I promise," I lied, further hating myself. "I just—I need to do me for a while. I need to remember who I am – love me again. I can't love somebody else if I don't love me."

We were both silent for a while, the birds chirping in the trees and small children squealing on the playground.

"So, that's it then?"

I glanced at him, noticing that he refused to look at me. "I'm so sorry, Zach. I hate that I'm doing this to you."

"Then why are you doing it?"

For so many reasons I can't admit. "Because if I don't do it now, I'll just hurt you worse, later on."

He stood, took a deep breath and stared up at the clouds scattered across the sky. "Well, I'm still in love with you."

I started to sob into my hands, now realizing there was no way he wasn't going to resent me. Even without knowing the entire truth, I hurt him. Badly. *"Please promise me you'll still be my best friend."*

After a beat, he shook his head. "I don't know, Roxy. I gotta go."

He walked away before I had the chance to say anything else, before I could stand to give him a hug, before I could lean in for one last kiss. I sat on the bench crying, trying to hide my face from the parents pushing strollers along the sidewalk or the teenagers walking by in cleats and shin guards meeting for soccer practice. I watched Zachary drive away without a single glance in my direction and breathed a little easier, a pressure within my chest finally dissipating after months of vacillating thoughts and feelings.

A small, dark brown chested sparrow landed on the bench's arm and looked at me with curious, black eyes. I smiled and reached out, following its flight path as it flew away from me and into the sky. I thought about what my sister had said when we were in Costa Rica and took this little bird as a sign that I'd made the correct decision.

This little bird was terrified to find out what was hidden in that big, blue sky, but she was more than ready to stretch out her little wings and fly.

Turn the page for a sneak
preview of the third book
in *The Games We Play*
series:

Plenty Of Toxic Fish In The Sea

I TRULY BELIEVED I was falling in love. As the soft pink lips belonging to the man who made my knees weak tickled the sensitive spot beneath my jaw, I wondered if it was truly possible to fall in love with someone who was still technically a stranger.

A stranger who I'd drunkenly hooked up with a few weeks prior.

A stranger I couldn't get off my mind.

A stranger I wanted to share my deepest, darkest secrets with.

Those lips worked their way down to my collarbone igniting a fire between my legs.

A stranger who made me feel things I hadn't experienced since the early phase of my and my ex-fiancé's relationship.

An ex-fiancé who was currently somewhere in the garage attending my graduation party.

"Roxanne!" Dominick – one of my best friends and a fellow server at Dine with Shamu – called as he opened the door leading from the garage to the living room area.

I pushed the owner of the pink lips away, guiltily looking over my shoulder to where my friend stood, looking between me and the man whose cheeks were flushed with pleasure. I had a feeling my cheeks looked the same.

"Zach is leaving," Dominick said, judgment laced in his usually upbeat and friendly voice. "I think he's upset."

I glanced at the man sitting next to me, watching as those pink lips curved into a smirk. "You two aren't a thing anymore," he said in the slight twang that made my heart two-step. "What's he expect?"

Dominick crossed his muscular arms across his broad chest and stared at me. My stomach tightened as shame wrapped its hand around my intestines. That feeling was why I'd decided to stop drinking beer and start drinking tequila forty-five minutes earlier. Because I had made the foolish decision to invite both my ex-fiancé and my current love interest to the same party.

A party celebrating me and my accomplishments. I had obtained my English and Comparative Literature degree in four-years and would be continuing my education in the Master of Fine Arts program at San Diego State University. I hadn't intended on inviting Anthony Wright, the owner of the pink lips that knew how to tease me, but after spending many a night talking on the phone with him instead of sleeping, I realized I wanted him to celebrate with me. I wanted him to meet my friends. I wanted him to kiss me until I couldn't see straight.

Unfortunately, I had already invited Zachary Cameron, my ex-fiancé. Although we were already officially broken up, we were in a weird place as both of us wanted to maintain a friendship but didn't know how to properly navigate those waters.

I stared back at Dominick, racking my inebriated brain for ideas on how to spare Zachary's feelings while indulging in a love affair that would leave my lips swollen for days. "Did he say why he was upset?"

Dominick furrowed his black eyebrows and shook his head. His cheeks were nearing a magenta color and his eyes were glossy, the two telltale signs that Dominick was as drunk as me. "He didn't say specifically, but it's probably because the two of you disappeared and everybody thinks you're in here hooking up."

I looked back at Anthony's tantalizing lips, slowly lifting my gaze to the milk chocolate brown eyes above them. Eyes that absorbed every inch of my face as if he couldn't believe I was really sitting in front of him. "But we're not," I said, unable to stop smiling as I looked back at Dominick. "As you can see, we're both sitting right here. Fully clothed. Not hooking up."

My friend shifted from one foot to another, his fingers itching the skin above his elbow. "You can do whatever you want – it's your party and you deserve to be happy. I just – I've gotten to know you pretty well and I think you'd regret it tomorrow morning if you let Zach leave without saying good-bye."

I blinked and frowned, hating that Dominick was right. If I didn't say anything and proceeded to have tequila-induced sexual relations with Anthony, then my hangover the next morning would be served with a side of a massive panic attack. "I'll be right there."

Dominick nodded curtly and returned to the garage, the heavy wooden door slamming shut behind him. A pair of rough hands grabbed mine before lifting my knuckles to his lips, moisture glistening on my pale skin. He winked at me before placing my palm on his cheek.

I blushed, a combination of lust, guilt, happiness and pity swirling like a riptide inside of me. *Get up and go say good-bye to your ex-fiancé,* I thought. *You know it's the polite thing to do, especially after you're the one who broke his heart.* I smiled at Anthony, loving how warm my hand felt on his face. *Zach has always been there for you. Get your butt of this couch so that he doesn't hate you forever.*

When Anthony let go of my hand, it dropped into his lap. I tried not to notice how close my fingers were to his zipper. "So, you gonna say good-bye to him or what?"

I fiddled with his pants pocket. "Yes, but it'll only take a second. I promise."

Although jealousy danced on the surface of his eyes, he flashed those straight, square teeth at me and winked again. "I don't mind, Darlin'. There's a game of pong calling my name. Find me when you're done."

My heart leapt. The last thing I wanted to do was leave Anthony's warmth to deal with the chill that would be surrounding my ex-fiancé. Our break-up was still raw and the shame I felt because I cheated on him with Anthony constantly lingered in my gut – and that was after I had cheated on Zachary with Lamont Carwyn during the first six months of our relationship. Despite the fact that we ended our relationship only a few weeks prior, Zachary had attended my graduation ceremony and brought me flowers to my party. It wasn't right of me to avoid him because it made me uncomfortable. He was my best friend – my rock. I didn't want to be intimate with him anymore, but I still didn't want to lose him.

Anthony and I both stood, his eyes darting to my mouth. I leaned toward him, my tequila haze pulling me in for another kiss. He placed his hands on my shoulder and shook his head. "Look, I know this whole situation is complicated." He kissed my forehead and licked his lips. "Just don't make me feel like an idiot, okay?" he whispered, his hands falling to his side.

I watched mutely as Anthony left the living room, his black, yellow and white plaid flannel disappearing into the garage.

"Why did I invite both of them?" I mumbled, looking down at the red solo cup sitting on my mother's glass coffee table. *Because you were afraid of celebrating alone*, my brain teased. I picked up the plastic cup, condensation leaving a ring on the glass. *Because I'm an idiot*, the other half of my brain responded, annoyed. I chugged the watered-down tequila mixture, swallowing the semi-tart liquid until only ice cubes remained. "And now, Tony probably thinks I'm not over Zach and Zach probably hates everything about me." After taking a deep breath, I placed the cup back on the table. *Let's get this over with.*

I pushed a curl behind my ear. My parents, sister and brother-in-law were laughing and drinking in the TV room downstairs, their boisterous voices carrying up the stairs, teasing me with their merriment. Although my mom, dad and Lucy refused to verbally tell me how proud they were of me graduating Summa Cum Laude, their smiles and graduation gifts spoke volumes. It was difficult for them to understand why I dropped out of pre-med to pursue the written word, but somewhere along the way, they started to care about my happiness.

And that meant they accepted me – *finally*. The black sheep of the family. The writer.

At the ceremony, where the golden Summa Cum Laude cords hung from my neck down to my navel, I watched my family smile and clap while I accepted my diploma from the head of the English Department.

I smiled at their laughter now, wishing I could avoid having to face Zachary and join them at the game table, sipping expensive tequila, playing poker and bragging about their success. "I can do this," I whispered, heart pounding. "You and Zach are friends. Just go say good-bye to him. There's nothing weird about it unless you make it weird."

After brushing the wrinkles out of my glittery, hot pink dress, I pushed open the heavy door leading to the garage and was welcomed by hip-hop music and my friends chatting with one another. I made quick eye contact with Dominick, who nodded his head subtly toward the street, to where my ex-fiancé was getting ready to leave. I ignored the shouts and cheers of my friends trying to encourage me to take shots with them, promising I would join them shortly.

The chill of the late-night air attacked my bare arms and legs, the sweat under my curly hair feeling like ice water on my neck. Speed walking in my silver, 4-inch-tall high heels, my eyes adjusted to the darkness, moistening from the cold. "Zach," I half-shouted, afraid to wake my snoozing neighbors. "Zach, where are you?"

I heard a door close up ahead and found my ex-fiancé slouched against the driver's side of his beat up, horribly maintained, gold Honda. "What do you want?" he asked.

I took a few more steps toward him and stopped when I was close enough to see the features of his face. My stomach constricted, the margarita I chugged threatening to make an appearance. Only a few years earlier, Zachary and I stood in this same spot, embracing one another because I'd told him I wanted nothing more than to be in a relationship with him.

It was winter break my sophomore year of college. At the time, Zachary was living in San Diego while I was living in Rohnert Park finishing my time at Sonoma State University. I had been smitten with Zachary, urging him to make me his girlfriend despite me being blindly in love with Lamont Carwyn. A man who was in a relationship with another woman.

Rubbing my arms to try to ward off the nighttime breeze, I brought myself back to the present. "Zach –" I bit my lip when he looked into my eyes. "Everyone said you were leaving."

He shrugged, crossing his arms, his muscles flexing against his shirtsleeves. "Would've been nice if you'd noticed that yourself."

Although he was right – I should've noticed without Dominick telling me – my chest swelled with indignation. "I know I'm the host and everything, but it's hard to keep track of every single guest."

He sighed. "Why did you invite me?" The shadows beneath his eyes stretched beyond his high cheekbones, the orange streetlight above his car masking his emotions.

"Because you've been here with me through this whole thing. You've helped me study. You've read my papers. We've pulled all-nighters together in the library. I couldn't have gotten through all of it without you."

He snorted – a mixture of frustration and disbelief. "If you really feel that way, why did you break up with me?"

I swallowed, a diamond sized lump stuck in my throat.

He didn't wait for me to respond. "You used me. Like I'm some baby blanket you can just drag around. You don't love me anymore." He coughed, trying to mask the sadness in his voice. "All you wanted from me was to hold your hand until somebody else came along. Someone you actually want to sleep with."

My mind conjured up images of Anthony and those lips that had been on my neck only moments earlier, but I refused to give Zachary the satisfaction of knowing he was right. I'd been able to keep my affair with Lamont a secret. I wasn't stupid enough to show Zachary my cards now. I bit the inside of my cheek. *He doesn't deserve this. He was far from a perfect boyfriend, but you're the one who hurt him. You've been leading him on because you've been too afraid to let go of his friendship. And you know that's not fair.* "The only person I want to sleep with tonight is myself," I began. "But you're right."

He stared at me, the darkness now masking the surprise in his eyes. "What?"

"I said you're right," I emphasized. "I needed you to hold my hand today. To help me get through the graduation. To ease my anxiety. You've been my rock for three years and I *really* wanted you to be here with me. *For* me." I took a deep breath, wishing another margarita would magically appear in my hands. "It wasn't my intention to use you. You're my best friend. I wanted you here."

He chuckled sadly. His melancholy made my heart ache. "No, Roxanne, Little Woman. Lacie and Jasmine are your best friends. Me? I'm the idiot who thought you'd love me forever. Because I love you."

"Zach, I do – I – I did – I'll always –"

Turning his back to me, Zachary opened his car door and slouched into the driver's seat. "Congratulations, Little Woman. I'm really proud of you."

Without another word, he slammed the door shut and started the engine. In a daze, I backed away slowly, watching as the gold piece of junk disappeared down the street. He had every right to say the things he did; in fact, he should've said worse. But watching him drive away left me feeling hollow.

Yes, I'd been the one to end our engagement. I'd given up on trying to make our relationship work. I'd developed very strong feelings for another man while still trying to maintain a friendship with Zachary. I deserved his hatred.

But I still didn't allow myself to believe that Zachary knew the whole truth. About what had happened with Lamont in the beginning. And about what was happening with Anthony now.

Being called out like that sent remorse flooding through my stomach, an all-too-familiar hurt lingering on the inside of my chest. Despite it all, I wasn't ready to completely let him go. Tears touched the corners of my eyes. *It's better this way. After everything you did to him, you should feel bad. You don't deserve his friendship.* After inhaling and exhaling deeply, I steadied myself and buried my emotions beneath my hot pink lipsticked smile. My party wasn't over, and I didn't want Anthony to know the true impact Zachary's departure had on me. I returned to the garage ready to lose myself to Anthony's lips and a few more tequila shots.

Turns out, I didn't have to worry about Anthony's reaction to my worsened mood because he was too busy high fiving my extremely pink faced sister at the beer pong table. Hannah, my two-year-old niece, was resting comfortably on Lucy's hip, a neon Ping-Pong ball in her itty, bitty little hand.

Cautiously, I approached my two best friends, Jasmine and Lacie, who were cheering on the sidelines. "Did I miss something?" I asked, grabbing the red solo cup out of Lacie's hand.

She watched as I downed her watermelon juice and vodka concoction, her eyes widening with each gulp. "Excuse me, Bitch. That was mine."

I nodded toward Anthony, Lucy and Hannah, who looked like a big, happy family. I handed Lacie the empty cup. Anthony's hand was on Lucy's lower back, probably feeling just how thin she was compared to me. And then I observed as they stood even closer to one another, Lucy's shot bouncing off one cup and into another. "He just kissed my sister on the cheek."

Jasmine frowned and handed me her drink, urging me to finish it. "How did it go with Zach?"

I then watched as Anthony high fived her again, and held her hand a little too long. "Obviously it was a mistake. I just let him make me feel like an insignificant insect so that I could come back to make-out with Tony, and here he is making goo-

goo eyes at my sister." I gulped down the remainder of the drink Jasmine gave me, feeling my body beginning to numb. "A sister, I might add, who looks *nothing* like me."

Lacie shrugged, studying my sister briefly before returning her hazel gaze to me. "You both have the same prominent cheek bones."

Jasmine stepped in front of Lacie and grabbed my forearm. "Don't listen to her. Let's go grab some more drinks." Her palm felt warm against my skin, her thick fingers like small sausages with long acrylic nails attached.

"I think if I keep drinking, I'm going to black out."

Jasmine smirked. "Well, then let's go somewhere else so we can talk about what happened without so many distractions."

"Then we can all black out!" Lacie said, grabbing my free hand, guiding me through the garage, out the side door and onto the deck overlooking the suburban homes below.

"This is supposed to be *my night*. How is Lucy *still* the center of attention? Even with a *baby* on her hip – everyone loves her," I complained. "I'm the one who graduated. I'm the one who put in the hard work. I'm the one who broke up with Zach so that I could hook up with Tony. But Lucy is the one who gets everything."

Lacie flipped her straightened, dark brown hair behind her shoulders. Lacie dyed her hair so often, I'd forgotten that at some point in her life, she'd been a natural blonde. "If you wanted Anthony's attention so bad, maybe you shouldn't have invited your ex-fiancé to the party."

I glared at my friend. "You think I don't already know it was a mistake? I graduated Summa Cum Laude – I'm not an idiot," I snapped. "But as weird as it sounds, I wanted Zach here. He's been one of my best friends for three years. He helped me get through so much crap – I still care about him. I don't know how to just turn off caring about somebody, even if I don't love them anymore."

Jasmine opened the red cooler my dad stocked full of beer and wine spritzers, the ice mostly melted. "I dunno, Roxy. You shoved his face into a pile of shit the moment Tony showed up. That's not something you do to someone you really care about." She pulled out a black and yellow bottle. "You wanted your cake – or however that saying goes. You want Zach because he's safe, but you want Anthony to bone. You've been giving Zach false hope by remaining 'friends' and you know it. Stop trying to hide behind the *I still care about him* crap."

My anger boiled to the surface, the tequila heating my temper. I didn't care that she was right – I'd already thought about those very things. But to hear it from her – a woman who was perpetually single and one of the most selfish human beings on the planet? *This is my party! Why is everyone being such a jerk to me?* "I don't need a lecture from *you* about how to handle relationships," I barked, shoving her just hard enough to make her stumble in her thick, black heels. "You've never had a boyfriend before so don't act all high and mighty. Like you've ever cared about anyone's feelings other than your own."

Jasmine closed the cooler lid with a loud thunk. "Don't take your bullshit out on me because your boy toy would rather fuck your sister than you."

Lacie wedged herself between Jasmine and I, firmly grasping my shoulders, forcing me to look into her eyes. "How about we all chill the fuck out and get those fucking drinks we talked about." She tapped my cheeks gently and smiled. "Fuck those guys! You should be celebrating. You just graduated in four years – with honors! You proved your family wrong. Don't let those assholes ruin this for you. You deserve to be celebrated!"

Although my pride stung from Jasmine's insult, I did feel my chest puff out slightly. *She's right. Tonight is about me! I deserve to celebrate and be happy about my life. At least this part of it.* "I know I said earlier I shouldn't drink anymore," I somewhat slurred, now noticing how heavy my limbs felt. "But I think we should do some shots."

"Did Roxy say *shots*?" Ricardo shouted as he rounded the corner connecting the back patio and the deck. Ricardo was another server at Dine with Shamu. He was a couple of years older than me, was one of the most genuinely kind people on the planet, and he was a handsome Latino man with a smile that earned him more tips than any other server at work. He and I had become great friends after laser tagging together at Dominick's birthday the previous year.

Jasmine and Lacie eagerly ran to his side, grabbed his defined biceps and dragged him toward me. Both girls had been fighting for the attention of my male coworkers to no avail. They didn't know when to give up. *Especially* when they'd been drinking.

"Pretty sure everybody bought me booze as a present," I said, smiling at Ricardo. "Might as well making a dent in it with all of my favorite people."

"I'm totally down," Ricardo replied, his voice echoing into the neighborhood below. "Let's cheers to you!" I blushed and smiled when he wrapped me in a huge bear hug. "I'm seriously so proud of you," he whispered to me. "This is a big accomplishment."

I pulled away from him, feeling tears touch my eyes again. "Thank you, Ricardo. That means a lot."

Jasmine opened the screen door that led to the kitchen and returned outside with a stack of plastic shot glasses and a handle of raspberry vodka. "Ready to top off your college experience with a night you won't be able to remember?"

Suddenly, the deck filled with my friends all clapping and shouting my name, eager to help themselves to some raspberry vodka. I felt a hand rest in the middle of my back and turned to find Anthony smiling at me, his cheeks reddened as if he'd been at the beach all day without wearing any sunscreen. I wanted to push him away, afraid that my coworkers would notice what was happening between the two of us and spread the gossip around Sea World.

I didn't want anybody to even *assume* we had feelings for one another – even though they'd been asking me what was going on between Anthony and I for a few months now. If they *knew* what was happening, the interrogation would get even worse.

My ex-fiancé, Zachary, worked as an assistant dolphin trainer at Dolphin Point, which was only a few feet away from the orca tank attached to the Dine with Shamu restaurant. Anthony's ex-fiancé, Bethany, worked as a land mammal handler at the small enclosures beside the Pier 61 restaurant, which also happened to house the park's primary bakery. The same bakery the Dine with Shamu servers and food runners frequented to pick up the desserts that were served at lunch and dinner.

Sea World was like high school. If word got out that Anthony and I were falling for one another, there was the potential for work to become awkward and uncomfortable. I'd already been through high school once, and it was bad enough then. I didn't want to have to go through the rumors and drama all over again. My friendship with Zachary would dissolve into indifference and Bethany would probably get one of her mini horses to kick me.

Aside from the fear of our secret being revealed, I was also angry with Anthony for flirting so openly with my married sister while she was handling her child. Lucy and I were almost exact opposites: she had shoulder-length blonde, straight hair and I had mid-back-length, auburn curly hair. She had forest green eyes while mine were more hazel-brown. She was thin with big breasts, and I had thick thighs with a curvy bottom. I looked away from him and smiled at my friends who were here to celebrate me and only me.

Jasmine and Lacie must've sensed the shift in my mood because they grabbed my forearms and pulled me in the middle of everyone. They then placed a shot glass in each of my hands and winked. "Did you all get a shot?" Lacie shouted as the rest of my friends passed plastic shot glasses around like a well-managed assembly line.

"I know many of you are new friends with Roxy, but I'm sure you have already gotten a taste for her crazy fucking work ethic."

My friends laughed and whooped, Anthony winking at me, his adorable dimples begging me to kiss them.

"And that's why we're here for her. To celebrate how hard she's worked – and how she managed to be in a relationship, have a job and party with us. Talk about time management skills."

Everybody laughed, my cheeks flushing pink from all of their gazes falling on me. I stared at my shots, trying my best to avoid any eye contact whatsoever.

"So even though I could brag about Roxy for hours," Lacie continued, her voice too loud in my ear. "Let's drink to this beautiful bitch and hope we can all be as smart as her one day."

More cheers and shouts swirled around me as I threw the vodka back, the liquid burning all the way down to my stomach. I followed with the second shot, keeping my eyes closed to focus on not throwing everything back up.

When I opened my eyes, all I could see was the hopeful twinkle in Anthony's gaze – happiness he reserved solely for me. My stomach warmed and my heartbeat picked up its pace, the voices of my peers beginning to fade into a slight buzz. Anthony's lips called out to me, luring me across the deck, my high-heels feeling like clouds beneath my feet. I fell into his chest, resting my cheek against the soft fabric of his flannel, loving how warm and safe I felt with his arms around me.

"Hi Darlin'. You doin' okay?" His voice melted my senses like butter on freshly baked corn bread.

I looked into his milk chocolate eyes and smiled. "I am now."

He leaned in slightly, his nose inches from mine. "Good. Because for a second there, I thought you were mad at me."

The vodka muddled my brain. I remembered being angry with him, but I couldn't pinpoint why. And with Anthony holding me so close to his body, looking at me and only me, I didn't care that I'd been upset earlier. I placed a palm on each of his cheeks and planted a kiss on his lips so forcefully, he took a surprised step back to balance himself.

Gasps and giggles tickled my ears. *Stop*, a voice deep inside warned. *Stop before it's too late and you hurt Zach.* But that voice didn't stand a chance against the Herculean grip of too much mixed alcohol. The world began to grow fuzzy, darkness threatening to consume my vision. Anthony broke off the kiss, his cheeks flushed, a nervous laugh escaping his lips.

I fell into his chest again and woke up in my bed. I blinked, confused, the ceiling above me spinning like a roulette wheel. After taking a deep breath, I looked at my alarm clock and moaned. Somehow, it was four thirteen in the morning and I was in my pajamas. Alone. When the numbers on the alarm clock began to tumble over one another, I bolted out of bed and ran to the toilet, my knees hitting the bathmat in front of the porcelain. *I can't believe I kissed Tony in front of everybody.* My stomach churned, so I placed my forehead on the toilet seat, the cool sensation causing the hairs on my arms to stand up.

Sherlock, the black cat I'd adopted from the Humane Society when I returned to San Diego after my sophomore year in Northern California, followed me into the bathroom. He stretched, his paws reaching far in front of him, his tail sticking straight into the air. *Why? Why did I kiss him? Especially after what Zach said to me.* I sighed. *And why can't I remember what happened after we kissed?* I turned and rested my cheek on the porcelain, looking at Sherlock. He rubbed against my leg and meowed at me. I reached out and pet his back, finding comfort in his soft fur and gentle purring.

"Why am I such an idiot? When will I learn that drinking doesn't ever do me any good?" I started to cry. "Now everybody is gonna know you cheated on Zach. They're gonna know what a horrible person you are." I rubbed my eyes, black mascara smudging my knuckles. "I don't deserve to be loved by anybody. Not one bit."

The bathroom spun before I was forced to heave the mixed alcohol and snacks not settling in my stomach. I may have graduated Summa Cum Laude, but when it came to my life choices – I rested my cheek on the porcelain seat after flushing the contents down the toilet. *I'm an idiot. A big, dumb, drunk idiot.*

#

Acknowledgments

I'd like to thank the individuals that changed my life at Sea World. The friends I met there had been in my life for my most influential years, and although we no longer speak with one another, I find it important to thank them for being in my life. If it weren't for them, for the weird but sincere friendships we formed while serving horrible theme park guests, I truly wouldn't be who I am today. They saved me from a lot of emotional traumas without even knowing it. They didn't judge me when I made poor life decisions, but became the voices of reason I needed, *especially* when I didn't want to hear it. Because of the servers and whale trainers I worked alongside for years, I will forever think of Sea World fondly.

I'd also like thank my boyfriend, Joshua, for continuing to support me through the ups and downs I experience in life, and in my writing. Thank you for understanding my need to disappear and write. Thank you for understanding me when I cry about not being able to write. Thank you for holding my hand while I question whether or not my writing is worth sharing with the world. You are a true partner. I appreciate and love you.

I will always thank my parents, Kim and Rich, for bringing me into this world, for helping me determine wrong from right, and for loving me unconditionally – especially in those moments where I know it was difficult for them to do so. Special shout out to Rich, my dad – the original Uber driver, before the app existed.

Lastly, I'd like to thank my two once upon a time best friends, Kayla and Renee. While we had one of the worst falling outs I've ever experienced, I have to thank them both for being my best friends when I needed people like them in my life. These girls showed me the best and the worst sides of friendship. They taught me the importance of being true to myself, of speaking the truth even if it hurts, and that true friends will be there for you no matter what. Not only when booze is involved or when it is convenient for them. I now know what true friendship is. And although it was one of the hardest lessons I've ever learned in my life, I wouldn't have learned it if it weren't for the two of them.

About The Author

Jacquelyn Phillips is a graduate of San Diego State University, having attended Sonoma State University for the first two years of her undergraduate English Program. She then continued her education in grad school, obtaining her Master of Fine Arts in Fiction writing in 2016 at San Diego State University. She was the editor and co-writer of Amazon Best-Seller, *ORCAstration*, with former killer whale trainer, Rich Phillips. She writes many dark fairy tales and hopes to create a novel out of them one day, but she currently is working on *The Games We Play* series, which she began writing in 2011. The first book of the series, "Cat and Mouse" is available on Amazon and online through Barnes and Noble. She lives in San Diego and believes that such a great city should be put on the map in literature. She currently resides with her boyfriend of eight years, 3 dogs, 2 cats and multitude of birds of prey, making her household a strange one indeed. After 15 years in the restaurant industry, she changed her occupation when COVID took over the world. She now works in the insurance industry, but continues to pursue her dream of becoming the next great author, hoping to inspire those who read her novels to follow their dreams and never be afraid to fall in love.